NIGHT
OF THE
LIGHTBRINGER

PETER TREMAYNE

NIGHT
OF THE
LIGHTBRINGER

HEADLINE

First published in 2017 by
HEADLINE PUBLISHING GROUP

1

Cataloguing in Publication Data is available from the British Library

ISBN 978 1 4722 3869 6

Typeset in Times New Roman PS by Palimpsest Book Production Limited,
Falkirk, Stirlingshire

Printed and bound in Great Britain by
Clays Ltd, St Ives plc

MIX
Paper from
responsible sources
FSC® C104740

HEADLINE PUBLISHING GROUP
An Hachette UK Company
Carmelite House
50 Victoria Embankment
London EC4Y 0DZ

www.headline.co.uk
www.hachette.co.uk

In memory of my 'anam cara'

DOROTHEA CHEESMUR ELLIS
(11 September 1940–30 March 2016)

There was a Door to which I found no Key:
There was a Veil through which I could not see
Some little talk awhile of Me and Thee
There was – and then no more of Thee and Me.

> *Rubáiyát* of Omar Khayyám
> transl. Edward FitzGerald

Quomodo cecidisti de caelo lucifer qui mane oriebaris corruisti in terram qui vulnerabas gentes.

How art thou fallen from heaven O Lucifer, son of the morning! How art thou cut down to the ground, which did weaken the nations!

Isaiah 14-12
Vulgate Latin translation of Jerome 4th century

PRINCIPAL CHARACTERS

Sister Fidelma of Cashel, a *dálaigh* or advocate of the law courts of 7th-century Ireland
Brother Eadulf of Seaxmund's Ham, in the land of the South Folk, her companion

At the Lateran Palace, Rome
The Venerable Gelasius, *Nomenclator* of the Lateran Palace
Brother Pothinus Maturis, *Praecipuus* of the Secret Archive
Brother Lucidus, agent of the *Nomenclator*

At Cashel
Colgú, King of Muman and brother to Fidelma
Dar Luga, *ainbertach* or housekeeper of the royal palace
Fíthel, Chief Brehon of Muman
Alchú, son of Fidelma and Eadulf
Muirgen, nurse to Alchú
Nessan, a shepherd, Muirgen's husband
Spélan, a shepherd
Brother Conchobhar, an apothecary
Rumann, the tavern-keeper
Curnan, a woodsman in charge of the Samhain bonfire
Febal, of the Uí Briúin Seóla of Connacht

Warriors of the Nasc Niadh, or Golden Collar, the King's Bodyguard
Gormán, commander
Aidan, second-in-command
Dego
Enda
Luan

Religious council of Cashel
Brother Mac Raith, steward of the Abbey of Imleach
Brother Sionnach of the Abbey of Corcach Mór
Brother Duibhinn of the Abbey of Ard Mór
Brother Giolla Rua of the Abbey of Ros Ailithir

At the Hill of the Bullock
Brancheó, the raven-caller
Torcán, a woodsman
Éimhin, his wife

At Ráth Cuáin Abbey
Abbot Síoda
Brother Tadhg, *aistreóir* or gatekeeper
Brother Gébennach, *leabhar coimedach* or keeper of books
Sister Fioniúr, the herbalist

At Cnocgorm
Erca, the Druid and hermit

Secondary Named Characters
Della, Gormán's mother
Aibell, Gorman's wife
Abbot Cuán of the Abbey of Imleach
Gelgéis, Princess of Éile

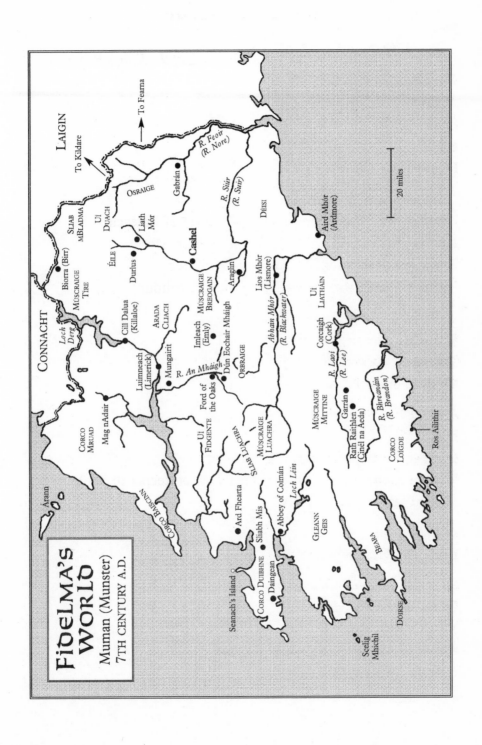

FIDELMA'S WORLD
Muman (Munster)
7TH CENTURY A.D.

LAIGIN

To Fearna

To Kildare

CONNACHT

R. Feoir
(R. Nore)

OSRAIGE

Gabrán

R. Siúir
(R. Suir)

SLIAB
MBLADMA

UÍ
DUACH

Liath
Mór

DÉISI

Biorra (Birr)

MUSCRAIGE
TÍRE

ÉLE

Durlus

Cashel

Airú Mhór
(Ardmore)

20 miles

Cill Dalua
(Killaloe)

ARADA
CLIACH

MÚSCRAIGE
BREOGAIN

Araglin

Lios Mhór
(Lismore)

Loch
Derg

Luimneach
(Limerick)

Mungairit

Imleach
(Emly)

Dún Eochair Mháigh

Abhain Mhór
(R. Blackwater)

UÍ
LIATHÁIN

Mag nAdair

R. An Mháigh

ORBRAIGE

Corcaigh
(Cork)

CORCO
MRUAD

UÍ
FIDGENTE

Ford of
the Oaks

R. Laoi
(R. Lee)

MÚSCRAIGE
MITTINE

Garrán

R. Bhreandín
(R. Brandon)

SLIAB LUACHRA

MÚSCRAIGE
LUACHRA

Rath Raithlen
(Cinél na Aeda)

Arann

Ard Fhearta

Sliabh Mis

Abbey of Colmán

Loch Léin

CORCO
LOIGDE

Ros Ailithir

CORCO BAISCINN

GLEANN
GEIS

Seanach's Island

CORCO DUIBHNE

Daingean

BEARA

DOIRSE

Scelig
Mhichíl

AUThOR'S NOTE

The events in this story follow in chronological sequence from *Penance of the Damned*. The year is AD 671 and it is the end of the month known in Old Irish as *Mí Forba*, the month of completion. This equates with modern October. This was considered the last month of the old Celtic year.

The following month was *Cet Gaimrid*, the 'first of winter', which is, of course, November. The ancient Irish, like their Indo-European cousins, the Hindus, believed that the year started in a period of darkness and eventually wakened into light. So the end of summer was marked by the pagan feast of Samhain (*sam* = summer and *fuin* = end of). It was one of the four great festivals of the Celtic year. The Irish, like all the Celtic peoples, marked the passage of time by nights followed by days – and so their celebrations began during the night.

Samhain was a time when the start of the dark period was marked by the building of bonfires; a festival of light, with attendant rituals, to ward off the dangers that darkness brought. Samhain was also a time of spiritual danger, for it was then that the borders between the natural and supernatural worlds ceased to exist; a time when those who had been wronged could return from the Otherworld to wreak vengeance on the living; a time of primeval chaos.

The early Christians found such pre-Christian beliefs hard to suppress until Pope Gregory I (AD 590–604) instructed that pre-Christian beliefs and sacred sites should be Christianised simply by re-dedicating them to the New Faith instead of attempting to destroy them. The Roman Christians had already begun to hold a special festival for their martyred dead and Pope Boniface IV (AD 608–615), who had consecrated the Pantheon as a new Christian church in honour of these martyrs, had set aside 1 May as All Saints' Day.

However, in AD 834 Pope Sergius II found that most people in Western Europe were not observing this feast day, preferring to observe the more ancient pre-Christian festival of Samhain at the start of winter, in memory of the dead. He therefore transferred the feast day to 1 November, naming it All Souls' Day. As the Anglo-Saxon word for 'saint' was *halig* it also became known as All Hallows' Day in the English-speaking world, and the evening before thereby has become Hallowe'en.

As diluted as the rituals of the modern Hallowe'en have become, it is still remembered as the one night of the year that great spiritual danger threatens the living by the Shades from the Otherworld.

It should be noted that, in spite of Fidelma's earnest hope expressed towards the end of this story that Christian abbots and bishops would not always enjoy secular power as princes, at least three of her own Eóghanacht descendants were King-Bishops of Muman (Munster). These were Fedelmid, son of Crimthainn (*d.* AD 846), Ólchobar, son of Cináeda (*d.* AD 851) and, most famous of all, Cormac, son of Cuilennáin (*d.* AD 908).

CHAPTER ONE

T here were some who said that old Pothinus Maturis had been
one of the officials of the Lateran Palace since the Emperor
Constantine had given it in perpetuity to the Bishop of Rome. That
was obviously not so, because the Emperor's allegiance to the New
Faith and his declaration that it become the Faith of the empire was
three centuries earlier to the very day that Pothinus Maturis entered
service in the Lateran Palace. It had taken him twenty-five years to
attain the position of *Praecipuus* of the *Archivum Secretum* of the
*Sacrosancta Laternensis ecclesia omnium urbis et orbis ecclesiarum
mater et caput* . . . the palace of the Holy Father of the Universal
Church of Christ.

Praecipuus Pothinus was now an elderly man. He was almost a
recluse in the palace for he spoke to none and had made no friends
in all the years that he had worked among the archives. He was a
sober, reflective man, keeping his own counsel and guarding the
archives as if they were the very Gates of Heaven.

Only the most senior officials of the papal palace were allowed
into the archive, which had been constructed behind the old
Basilica. Constantine himself had ordered its construction when
he had the stables of the imperial horse-guard barracks demolished after the guards had not shown sufficient loyalty to their
Emperor. The archives remained secure, set apart from the rest

of the ecclesiastical buildings. The documents contained in the *Archivum Secretum* justified their place there by virtue of their controversial nature. Most had been declared heretical to the accepted theology after such ideas were overturned by one council or another. Many were gospels that were at odds with those texts chosen to constitute the main fabric of the Faith. Damasus I, as Holy Father, had ordered Eusebius Hieronymus Sophronius to translate and compile the chosen texts into a Latin standard which would be the *Biblos*, the sacred foundation for the faithful.

Praecipuus Pothinus was proud of his unique position of trust as keeper of the abandoned contentious works which had been rejected as divisive tools which might further split the factions of Christendom. It was because of this, on one particular day, that an astounding thing happened in the Lateran Palace. Those who knew *Praecipuus* Pothinus by sight could not believe the evidence of their own eyes. The elderly man was witnessed almost running through the corridors of the palace towards the office of the *Nomenclator*, the chief secretary to His Holiness. The awkward slap of his sandals on the shiny marble floortiles resounded along the corridors and made people stop to stare in awe and concern.

He finally reached his destination – a forbidding oak door. Apparently forgetting all sense of protocol, he did not pause to knock but grasped the brass handle and burst into the room beyond. Only then did he halt before the man seated at the desk in front of him. *Praecipuus* Pothinus' shoulders were heaving at the exertion of running; his breath coming in short staccato rasps.

The man at the desk glanced up, startled at the arrival. Even seated, it was obvious that he was tall, with tufts of black hair emerging from under his skullcap. His swarthy skin spoke of one who spent time in the sun of Rome and not just in the darkened interiors of the ecclesiastic buildings. His prominent, aquiline nose would have graced any Roman patrician, especially with the addition of a mouth twisted into a permanent sneer, the thin lips darkened as if artificially coloured. The hooded eyes seemed to carry no place for compassion. Even if the features did not declare his position of authority, the jewels set into the ornate silver cross that hung round his neck, the scarlet *tunica* of office, the *udones,* white stockings, and *campagi,* black slippers, protruding from under the desk, all proclaimed it.

It took a few seconds for him to recover from his surprise and for *Praecipuus* Pothinus to regain sufficient breath.

'Gone, Venerable Gelasius!' Pothinus gasped. 'It's gone!'

The *Nomenclator* sat back and regarded the other man coldly.

'Gather yourself, Pothinus. Gather yourself and then tell me carefully and explicitly . . . what has gone that you bring yourself unannounced before me in such an unseemly fashion?'

Praecipuus Pothinus sucked in a few more breaths until he was confident that he could express himself clearly.

'The *Sefer Ya'akov,*' he finally managed. 'It has gone from the archive.'

The Venerable Gelasius frowned. 'I am no scholar of the Hebrews, Pothinus. What has gone missing?'

'The *Biblos Iakobos.*' The man translated to the Greek before adding, 'It has gone and—'

The Venerable Gelasius held up a thin, almost delicate hand and glanced around him as if seeking any potential eavesdroppers. 'We would not want any heretical expression to be overheard by the wrong ears.'

Pothinus waved a hand as if it was of no consequence.

'The point is that during the night, someone forced an entrance to the archive, got in and stole it. When I came to the archive this morning, I could see an open window and knew that it had been closed when I left. So I began to check the manuscripts and the archives. It did not take me long to see that the section of works in Hebrew and Aramaic had been tampered with. I immediately checked each one against my index and found that the *Biblos Iakobos* was missing. Of all the books in the archive, that one is the most dangerous to the Faith. What shall we do?' He began to wring his hands.

'What shall *we* do, *Praecipuus* Pothinus?' the Venerable Gelasius asked icily. 'For the factions of heretics who deny the divine birth, that book would be of tremendous support in advancing their cause. It is already hard to suppress all the works that refer to Iakobos as the brother of . . .' He halted and shrugged. 'If I recall correctly, this work was purportedly written by Iakobos, or Iacomus as we call him, before he met his death at the hands of the Sanhedrin. The Nazarenes, whom Iacomus led, are still in existence, claiming they are merely part of the Jewish Faith and that Jesus was just a Rabbi.'

'But what *are* we to do?' *Praecipuus* Pothinus' voice was almost a wail.

'You have not spoken of this to anyone?' the *Nomenclator* demanded.

'Not to report the loss of the book. I did question one of the *custodes*, Licinius.' The *custodes* were the military guards of the Lateran Palace. 'He was on duty last night outside the archives. I simply asked him if he knew whether there had been any suspicious or untoward activity around the building during the night.'

'Are you sure you did not tell him about the loss of the book?' Venerable Gelasius insisted.

'I did not. However, the *custodes* told me that he had encountered two pilgrims, the worse for our good Italian wine, outside the building. He remonstrated with them on their indecorous behaviour and they eventually left for their hostel.'

'You speak as though they were foreigners.'

'They were. Licinius said they were barbarians. He identified them as coming from that western island that gives the Holy Father such problems with the date of the Paschal ceremony, with rites and ritual and even the way religious should dress. They refuse to accept the changes to these matters that the councils of Rome have declared as the more accurate and appropriate. You know – those strange, wild people who prefer their own interpretations of the Faith to the wisdom that Rome can offer them.'

'You mean the Five Kingdoms of Éire?' The Venerable Gelasius almost smiled in recollection. 'I learned much about that country from a woman who was a lawyer of that peculiar race.'

Praecipuus Pothinus looked shocked. 'A woman? A lawyer?'

'She had a good deductive mind,' admitted the *Nomenclator* thoughtfully.

'Well, if those barbarians were involved in the theft then they have already fled Rome,' declared the *Praecipuus*.

'How do you know that?' the Venerable Gelasius asked sharply.

'*Custodes* Licinius told me that he had asked these barbarians where they were staying. Their leader told Licinius that they had been celebrating their last night in Rome before beginning the journey back to their godforsaken island.'

Venerable Gelasius shook his head reprovingly at him. 'No island on this earth is godforsaken, Pothinus. Did this *custodes* obtain the names of these barbarians?'

'He tried, but they had strange, foreign names which he did not understand so took no note of. They merely admitted that they were from this western island and the *custodes* observed that they were not as abstemious as are most pilgrims to our city.'

'So you believe that they have probably already left Rome?'

'I would say so. What makes me suspicious is that the *custodes* observed that the leader carried a book satchel. It is an odd thing to carry when one is out celebrating.'

Venerable Gelasius frowned thoughtfully for a few moments, drumming his fingers on his desk top.

'Tell no one of this loss until I give you leave. We must not admit it publicly, especially not about so dangerous a document. The contents and the name of its author could destroy all that we have built over the years and call Christendom.'

'What shall I do then?' the *Praecipuus* asked weakly.

'Forget the entire matter. You may leave it to me to deal with. The loss of the book and this conversation never happened. If you have indexed the book, expunge it. It does not exist. It has never existed.'

The Venerable Gelasius sat for a while in silence after *Praecipuus* Pothinus had left. It was only a dry cough from the doorway of the adjoining chamber that made him swing around in his chair.

A tall young man, handsome and with a permanent expression of amusement on his features, stood almost lounging in the doorway.

'You heard all that?' asked the *Nomenclator.*

'I did.'

'Well, Brother Lucidus, it seems your warning that there might be an attempt on certain manuscripts in our archives was correct, although I did not suspect that it would happen so soon. But it is logical, I suppose. If ever a manuscript could do harm to the theological decisions of the councils over the last centuries, it is that one. It seems that the *custodes* have identified your countrymen as the suspects. Do you know who these men are?'

'That I do not. I only heard a rumour yesterday that a plan was afoot to remove a Nazarene item from the archives, which is why I have come to see you this morning. The trouble is that the streets of Rome are thronging with pilgrims from the western islands.'

'We must find these thieves!'

The young man chuckled sourly. 'You and your poor *Praecipuus* cannot even admit that the book existed, let alone that it has been stolen. All your guard saw was two of my countrymen being a little drunk and raucous outside the library building.'

'We must find out who they are and whether they have taken the book,' pressed the *Nomenclator*.

'Pothinus was astute in observing that it is not often that a pilgrim, celebrating in the fashion that the *custodes* reported, would be carrying a *tiag luibhair,* a book satchel, as we call them. I think it

6

is safe to say that they were responsible – and that the missing book was in the satchel.'

'From what Pothinus says, they could now be on their way to one of our seaports to start their journey back to your homeland. We must retrieve that book, because in the wrong hands it could fuel a movement that might overturn the Faith throughout the whole of Christendom.'

'You have said so before – and I know it. Unfortunately, it will be hard to track them down among the teeming hordes of pilgrims who come and go from this city, even though we know the land whence they came.'

The Venerable Gelasius began drumming his fingers on his desk again. 'Already, your island is of great concern to Rome; our advocates make slow progress against the differences of Faith that stand between us. We may have won the debates at the councils in Streonshalh and in Autun, but we have not yet won the hearts and minds of your people. Most of them stick rigidly to their insular traditions – except for the abbot of a place called Ard Macha. He has declared that he will accept the authority of Rome, but only if we recognise him as the Chief Bishop of the entire island.'

Brother Lucidus grimaced. 'There are many difficulties with that claim – namely, that there are numerous other claimants. The Abbot of Imleach, for instance, who is declared Chief Bishop in the south of the island, has similar claim – and half the island supports it. There are several others. The Blessed Fiacc's Abbey of Sléibhte, for example, claims to be the oldest abbey in the island. Several other abbeys have put forward good arguments for their claims to be the primacy of the Faith in my country.'

'Well, that is not my concern at this moment. The task of trying to bring the various churches in your island under the control of Rome is one that can wait. The fact is, this ancient text could do that cause irreparable damage. It must be recovered.'

7

Brother Lucidus smiled thinly. 'So you continually point out. However, I shall have to be the one to retrieve it for you.'

'How do you intend to accomplish it?'

'I shall track down these two Irish pilgrims and identify them. If they have already left for the Five Kingdoms with the book, I shall follow and get it back – or I shall destroy it.'

'You sound very confident,' the Venerable Gelasius observed, 'but can you accomplish that much? First you will have to discover who the thieves are. What if you cannot do so? And how will you find the ancient text? Surely, there are many hiding places in your island.'

'If the thieves *are* taking the book back to my country for the purpose of spreading the heresy it contains, then there are only a few places to which it could be taken. I have a very good friend, a great scholar, Brother Sionnach of the Abbey of Corcach Mór. His knowledge and contacts cover the Five Kingdoms. The island is not so big that I shall be unable to track it down. Indeed, the news of the acquisition of such a book to one or other abbey will be signalled throughout the island like a blazing beacon. The fraternity of scholars will hear of it almost immediately.'

'Do you know of Fidelma of Cashel?' the *Nomenclator* suddenly asked. 'She was the woman lawyer of your country that I mentioned to *Praecipuus* Pothinus a moment ago.'

The young man drawled, 'Who, in the Five Kingdoms, has not heard of Fidelma of Cashel or of her companion, the Saxon Brother Eadulf? I have certainly heard of her but never met her.'

'She might be of some help to you in your mission to recover the book. I will send her a message by one of the monks departing for that kingdom tomorrow, as I don't wish to delay you now. I will say nothing of your task, apart from the fact that a book has been stolen and that you are authorised by me to retrieve it. Should you need her assistance, I shall tell her that you will identify yourself as Lucidus and give my name as your authority.'

'I will contact her only if necessary,' replied Brother Lucidus confidently. 'And I shall not be using the name Lucidus after I reach the Five Kingdoms. I will use my native name while I am there. But, if I need the help of Fidelma or anyone else, I will use Lucidus and its meaning as a password. I am sure, however, that I can accomplish this mission without involving her.'

'Then the sooner you depart, the sooner this may be accomplished, Brother Lucidus. May God go with you.'

The young man inclined his head towards the *Nomenclator* and said with a cynical smile, 'Amen to that, Venerable Gelasius. But this is a task, I believe, that I can accomplish alone, without even His help – or that of Fidelma of Cashel.'

CHAPTER TWO

'Can we look at the bonfire, *athair*?'

Little Alchú's voice was full of excitement as he pointed across the town square to a massive unlit pyre of logs and branches that rose, almost dominating the buildings that surrounded it. Eadulf regarded his young son with tolerant amusement.

'What is there to see, little hound? At the moment, it is just a pile of old wood. It is tomorrow that it will be set alight and then it will be more interesting.'

Aidan, the young warrior of the bodyguard of the Golden Collar, who had been designated as their companion for the ritual morning ride, gave an indignant snort.

'The symbolism of that bonfire makes it more than just a pile of old wood, friend Eadulf,' he protested.

The three of them had just ridden down from the fortress gates of Cashel, the palace of Colgú, King of Muman, the most south-westerly and largest of the Five Kingdoms of Éire. They had halted their horses on the edge of the town square. Usually, Fidelma preferred to accompany her young son on the regular morning ride, but when she was busy with matters that fell to her lot as legal adviser to her brother, the King, it was Eadulf who escorted the child – but always with a member of the King's bodyguard. It was not forgotten that the boy had once been abducted when he was a baby by the evil Uaman, lord of the passes of Sliabh Mis.

'One bonfire is the same as another,' Eadulf responded, but a close observer might have detected some apprehension behind his light-hearted dismissal. He knew well what the symbolism of the bonfire was and what it meant to the townsfolk who, for some days now, had been bringing in logs and branches from the surrounding woodlands.

Aidan, who did not observe his uneasiness, shook his head in reproof. 'You have been long enough in this kingdom, my friend, to know that there is a special time approaching.'

'I know all about the festival of Samhain,' Eadulf said.

'So you must know that this is the time of darkness,' the young warrior went on. 'That is why the fires of Samhain are so special. When lit, they express our hope that we may survive the threatening shadows of the night and be reborn into light. Remember that tomorrow night, at the festival of Samhain, dark forces will surround us. There will be much evil abroad and all that is malevolent and vengeful will stalk the land.'

Eadulf tried to restrain himself from nervously rebuking his companion for prattling on. Eadulf himself had been raised in the pre-Christian culture of his own people. In his village of Seaxmund's Ham, in the land of the South Folk of the East Angles, there was a similar festival called the Modraniht, or 'Night of the Earth Mother'. After this came the month of Blótmonath, the time of the sacrifices to the gods and goddesses in order to protect folk from the supernatural entities that inhabited the gloomy woods and desolate places, intent on wreaking harm, and vengeance. He suppressed a shiver. Christian missionaries had begun to convert the Kingdom of the East Angles to the New Faith and as a youth Eadulf had eagerly accepted their teaching. But the old ways and beliefs, beliefs practised from the time beyond time, did not vanish so quickly. There were still times when he found himself believing in the old ways; ways that the New Faith had not been able to suppress and therefore had tried to absorb. Even the great Roman Pope, Gregorius Anicius, had told his missionaries to stop destroying pre-Christian shrines and temples and simply re-dedicate them in the name of the New Faith. Therefore, many old practices and beliefs took on the mantle of the new religion.

'Can't we go and see the bonfire, *athair*?' His son's almost plaintive wail came again, interrupting his thoughts.

Eadulf hesitated. 'We'll ride by it,' he conceded with a sigh. 'I promised your mother that we would call at Della's to pick up some jars of honey.' He added this as an unnecessary attempt at self-justification for the concession of allowing his son to cross by the wood pyre.

They proceeded at a walking pace across the open ground towards the large but as yet unfinished bonfire. Although it was well after dawn, the town square was mostly deserted. Many people had already departed to their work or left to attend to the various daily tasks that kept the township thriving. Since the day when Conall Corc became King of Muman, and had ordered his fortress to be built on the great limestone rock, rising over sixty metres above the plains and visible for considerable distances, the small township that had arisen in its shadows had prospered and grown rich. It was now the heart of the Eóganacht territory.

The few trees at the centre of the township were still in the process of changing from their summer hue, like the dome-shaped ash tree with its distinctive leaves, which thrived in the lime-rich soil. The square looked curiously bare now that the many wild flowers that had previously formed bright patches of colour had disappeared for the winter months. The sound of the distant ring of metal on metal broke the silence as a blacksmith plied his art. In the pauses they could hear the persistent 'chee-ip' call of sparrows nesting under the eaves of nearby buildings, making sure of their place of warmth for the time to come. The nearest building was the tavern of Rumann with its adjacent brewery. The large, good-natured figure of Rumann himself had just appeared at the door, preparing for the day's business. The tavern-keeper saw them and raised his hand in greeting.

Young Alchú had halted his pony, in spite of Eadulf's instruction that they were not going to stop by the bonfire. He was leaning across his horse's neck, staring at something among the wood.

'There's a bundle of rags in there, *athair*.' The boy pointed. 'What's that for?'

Before Eadulf could reply, Aidan exclaimed, 'That's a sure way to ruin a good bonfire! Rags just create smoke and will do nothing to aid a good blaze.'

Leading his horse alongside the boy's pony, he gazed to where Alchú had indicated, muttering, 'What kind of idiot would shove rags into the base of a bonfire . . .?' His voice died away and Eadulf, who had been riding slightly ahead, pulled rein and glanced back in annoyance at the delay, failing to see the warrior's expression of shock.

'Friend Eadulf,' Aidan said quietly, 'would you mind taking young Alchú across to Rumann and asking him to keep an eye on him for a moment or two, and then come back here?'

Eadulf was surprised at the request, but quickly becoming aware that something was wrong, he did not argue but turned to his son, saying, 'Come with me, little hound. We'll get Rumann there to give you some cold apple juice.'

A quick-witted lad, Alchú could sense the tension in the air. 'Why can't I stay and see what has been found here?' he asked.

'I am not sure anything has been found,' Eadulf replied firmly. 'It is just that we want to see why someone has put old rags among the wood, which will surely ruin it. Now, come along. We won't be but a moment or two.'

Reluctantly, the boy followed his father across to where the tavern-keeper, seeing their approach, came forward to greet them.

'A good day to you, Brother Eadulf. I see you and your son are in good health. Is the lady Fidelma well?'

'She is well indeed, Rumann,' Eadulf assured him. 'We noticed someone has pushed some old rags into the pile of wood for the Samhain fire. That is not good for the coming blaze. Aidan and I mean to deal with it before riding on, and I would be obliged if you could give young Alchú a drink and keep an eye on him while we do so.'

'Certainly,' the man replied, adding, 'rags? But that is a ridiculous thing to do! Children playing games, perhaps? Even an idiot would not seek to ruin the sacred fires of Samhain on the night before they are to be lit. Curnan will not be pleased.'

'Curnan?' Eadulf frowned.

'He's a woodsman from the western woods beyond the town. He is in charge of the fire this year and will be upset to learn that it has been tampered with. Anyway, I'll keep your boy here while you help Aidan. I shall tell Curnan all about it when he comes to finish building the bonfire.'

Having given instructions to Alchú, Eadulf returned to Aidan who by now had dismounted and was poking agitatedly into the stack of wood and logs. Eadulf left his horse alongside Aidan's and joined the warrior.

'What is all the fuss about?' he asked. 'Surely we can remove a bundle of rags without such drama.'

Aidan grimaced. 'More drama will come, friend Eadulf. Those rags cover the body of a man.'

'What?' Eadulf stared at the warrior for a moment before slowly turning to look where Aidan had begun removing some branches.

A pale arm had been uncovered, stiff and protruding from the pile.

The two men did not exchange another word but fell to the task of removing as many branches as they could from what was obviously a corpse. While they were doing this, they had to be careful not to dislodge the entire structure of the huge bonfire. Before long, they were able to drag the body by the shoulders from its temporary tomb and away from the remaining pile without it collapsing. That done, they stood, breathing heavily from their exertions and staring down at the corpse.

The dead man was dressed in the brown homespun of a religious robe. His slightly emaciated features were crowned by a rough-cut tonsure . . . the tonsure of the Blessed John rather than the distinguishing Roman cut of Peter, thus denoting that he followed the churches of the Five Kingdoms. The man had been approaching the end of the middle period of his life; his features were weather-beaten and ill nourished. To Eadulf's mind, the fellow hardly had the appearance of a religious – but that was a personal opinion. Just then, Eadulf caught an aroma on the air and sniffed. There was an overpowering smell of . . . what was it? He recognised it from his studies of the healing herbs. The Greeks called it *nardus* but to the Romans it was *lavandarius*, for they used it to bathe with. The body positively reeked of it.

Eadulf was about to look away when he realised that there was something strangely familiar about the man. He had definitely seen him before . . . but after some long moments of searching his memory, he could not place when or where.

'Do you recognise him?' he finally asked Aidan.

'I was about to ask you the same question,' replied the warrior. 'I think that I have seen him somewhere before, but cannot be certain of it.'

Eadulf knelt beside the corpse and started to make an examination of the man's wounds.

'He cannot have been dead long,' he muttered, testing the stiffness of the man's arms. 'There is much blood and some of it not completely dry.'

'Did he kill himself?' asked Aidan. 'Even I can see that his throat has been cut.'

Eadulf could not help but smile at the young warrior's question, despite the grim circumstances. 'A man does not kill himself and then contrive to place his body in the bottom of a bonfire so that it will be consumed,' he replied.

'So he was murdered?'

Eadulf pursed his lips thoughtfully. 'True, the throat has been cut . . . and savagely, too. However, you will also observe the tears in the robe, here.' He drew back the robe so that the torn and bloody skin was visible. 'There is one knife wound straight into the heart.'

Aidan exhaled softly. 'A religious, murdered here? It just doesn't seem possible. Who would do this – and why?'

'You are asking questions that I cannot answer, my friend.' Eadulf pulled away the cowl of the robe from around the neck of the corpse and gently moved the head to one side. 'He has also sustained a heavy blow on the back of the neck which, judging by the wound, would have been enough in itself to kill him.'

Aidan's face suddenly drained of colour. His lips worked silently for a moment or two but no sounds came. He gazed from the corpse to Eadulf's face and then back to the corpse. Finally, he was able to articulate slowly: 'You have been living among us long enough to know what this signifies.'

But Eadulf was not entirely sure what the young man meant and so countered: 'What does it signify?'

'Why . . . it is the threefold death!' blurted out Aidan. There was fear in his tone. 'God protect us! This is a ritual killing.'

Eadulf's mouth tightened. 'A ritual killing? But what purpose does it serve?'

Aidan pointed to the bonfire. 'Tomorrow night is the feast of Samhain. Christians tolerate it but its origin was old before the Druids. What else would this mean but the fulfilment of some ancient rite?'

Eadulf rose slowly and dusted himself down. 'What I *know*, my friend, is never to draw conclusions without gathering the facts.'

He glanced towards Rumann's tavern. 'I want you to stand guard here over the body. News of its discovery will soon spread, but for the moment I need you to ensure that this area is kept clear and no one is to touch the body.'

'What do you intend to do?'

'I am going to take Alchú back to the fortress and report the matter. The Chief Brehon Fíthel will have to be informed. I will return with him so that an investigation can be started at once.'

'I am bored!'

Colgú, King of Cashel, looked up from his chair of office and gazed at his red-haired sister with a somewhat tired smile.

'So you have said . . . several times this morning,' he sighed but not without some exaggeration.

Fidelma of Cashel was annoyed. 'I am not expecting sympathy, I just want something to do,' she snapped. 'Something to occupy my mind.'

'I wasn't going to offer you sympathy,' her brother replied dryly.

'Well, at least you could have sent me on the mission to sort out whatever problem has arisen among the Arada Cliach instead of sending Fíthel. I am told a message came last evening and that Fíthel set off early this morning. It must have been important.'

'Fíthel is the Chief Brehon of this kingdom, Fidelma,' her brother reminded her, 'and it is therefore appropriate that he undertake the request from our cousin Prince Gilcach.'

Fidelma knew Gilcach ruled a prosperous part of the kingdom; prosperous because of the presence of silver mines in its territory. One of the mountains was so abundant in the metal ore that it was called Sliabh an Airgid, the Silver Mountain.

'What's Gilcach's problem?' she demanded.

'It seems that he has been losing shipments of smelted silver during the summer months.'

'Losing?'

'The smelted ore is taken by wagons to boats on the River Siúr, the great river. It is eventually transported down to Port Lairge for foreign trade. Some of these shipments have been disappearing recently.'

'What – entire boats? Doesn't he send warriors to guard the wealth?'

'Not entire boats,' corrected her brother. 'It's the sacks of mined silver that are carried off. The boats have been boarded and attacked by half a dozen thieves armed with crossbows.'

'That's not a weapon of choice among our people,' pointed out Fidelma.

'They are effective, nonetheless. Anyone who resists is dead or badly injured.'

'Surely it is not beyond the capability of Prince Gilcach to track down such a small band of robbers. Where do these attacks take place?'

'Just north of Gabhailín, at the fork of the two rivers.'

'That's not very far from here.'

'After the first two attacks, Gilcach placed warriors on the boats – but then the thieves failed to appear. When it was thought they had given up, the warriors were withdrawn, but then the boats were attacked again. It was as if the thieves were keeping a close eye out for opportunities, or else were receiving inside information.'

'So why has Fíthel gone north to Gilcach's fortress at Béal Atha Gabhann? He won't find an answer there. If the boats are being ambushed just north of the fork of the two rivers, surely it is around there that he needs to look.'

'He has to start his investigation somewhere,' her brother said. 'He felt that he should see if he could find the person supplying the information about which boats carried the silver and were the easiest to attack and rob. He thinks the informant probably has a direct connection with the mines themselves.'

Fidelma tossed her red hair back with an impatient motion of her head.

'I could have dealt with this,' she told Colgú. 'I've solved a matter for Gilcach before and I know the silver mines. It would have been a good opportunity to visit that area again.'

'I am surely allowed to conduct the affairs of the kingdom as I see fit?' The reply was softly made but with a certain edge which indicated that her brother shared the same fiery nature as his sister.

'Well, there must be something else that I can do. I dislike it when my mind grows idle for want of some challenge or a riddle to resolve. Which reminds me,' she paused and frowned, 'three strange religious arrived here at different times yesterday. It seems they were all expected. What are they about?'

Her brother sighed. 'A request from the new Abbot of Imleach, Abbot Cuán, exercising his role as Chief Bishop. It is some religious council about the discipline of smaller communities. The religious are scholars representing some of the teaching abbeys of the kingdom. Ard Mór, Ros Ailithir and Corcach Mór.'

'Why aren't Imleach or Mungairit represented if Abbot Cuán has called them together to discuss such matters? It seems odd to exclude two of the leading teaching abbeys in the kingdom,' Fidelma observed.

'Abbot Cuán is sending his steward here as his representative and he should be here soon.'

'Also, why choose Cashel as the place in which to discuss their theology?' frowned Fidelma. 'Surely it would be more appropriate to have a discussion on such matters in Imleach itself.'

'Abbot Cuán seemed worried about the allegiances of some of the community in his abbey,' Colgú explained. 'He wanted the scholars to meet somewhere away from any undue influence.'

Fidelma thought for a moment and then shrugged. 'I suppose I can understand that. Abbot Cuán has only just taken over following the murder of our dear friend Abbot Ségdae . . .'

'A mystery you solved and thereby saved several lives,' her brother intervened approvingly.

Fidelma made a dismissive gesture with her hand. 'The point is, I know Abbot Cuán, and if he has concerns about his community, then his fears must be real.' She paused and then asked: 'Do you know what matters of discipline are involved?'

Colgú became irritated. 'If you must interrogate me, Fidelma . . .'

'It is in my nature to do so,' she replied calmly.

'Abbot Cuán suspects more than indiscipline among his community. He thinks there might be some plot to revolutionise the Faith as it has been taught to us. Now, no more. Surely there is something else that you can find to occupy your mind apart from the comings and goings of the religious? I thought you might want to spend more time with your son and your husband Eadulf. Don't you ever relax?'

Fidelma sighed, realising that her brother's will was just as strong as her own. She raised her arms and let them fall in a resigned gesture by her sides.

'When I relax, my mind withers. What is there offered to me? A dispute about fences between two farmers, the loss of some fleeces ready to be spun for a weaver's loom and a claim of infidelity. Give me some real mystery to unravel, some conundrum that needs an explanation – that is what I crave.'

Colgú was exasperated. 'I thought that you would welcome having some free time after you came back from the Uí Fidgente fortress. I know Eadulf dislikes those long journeys he has to undertake on horseback with you.'

It was well known that Eadulf was no horseman and only climbed into the saddle reluctantly when there was no other method of transportation available.

Fidelma was immediately on the defensive. 'Eadulf is more used to horses now. He takes his duties as a father conscientiously and goes riding almost each day with young Alchú. He enjoys it.'

Colgú caught the clatter of horses in the courtyard outside. He rose and went to the window. 'Well, he seems to have arrived back earlier than usual this morning,' he commented.

'That can't be right.' Fidelma joined her brother to look down into the courtyard. 'He only left with Alchú and Aidan a short while ago.'

A few moments later, after a slight commotion in the corridor outside the King's chamber, the door swung open and Dar Luga, the *ainbertach* or housekeeper to the palace, announced Brother Eadulf.

'Has anything happened to Alchú?' was Fidelma's first anxious question on seeing her husband's flustered features as he entered.

Eadulf quickly reassured her. 'The boy is quite safe. I've brought him back with me. He is with Muirgen.' He turned to Colgú. 'One of the guards has told me that Brehon Fíthel has already left Cashel. What a pity. I came back to see him.'

Colgú exchanged a swift glance of surprise with his sister. 'You have heard correctly, Eadulf. The Brehon has already left. Why?'

Eadulf took a moment to gather his wits before he explained, 'The matter that has brought me back to the fortress is a death.' He sighed. 'You know the big bonfire the townsfolk are building in the square below?'

'Of course,' replied Fidelma. 'It is the Samhain fire. What is the matter?'

'We were riding by it and Alchú thought he saw a bundle of rags shoved into the base of it. We stopped and Aidan examined them, and well . . . the rags turned out to be the body of man – a religieux – and he had been murdered.'

'What? Did our son see this body?' Fidelma asked sharply.

'No. I had given him into Rumann's care so that he should not see while we extracted the body,' Eadulf told her.

'How did you know this man had been murdered?' Colgú asked. 'And who was he?'

'I don't know who he was,' Eadulf admitted. 'I have a feeling I have seen him somewhere before, but cannot be certain. I've left Aidan guarding the body. As for how he was murdered, you will know the symbolism of it and understand the cause for our concern. He had been stabbed in the heart, his throat was cut and his skull smashed in. Any one of those wounds would have been fatal.'

There was a moment of shocked silence.

'Are you sure?' Fidelma's voice was a whisper. Then she pulled herself together. 'Of course you are sure. I am sorry.'

Colgú spoke softly, almost to himself. 'I have heard stories about the ritual threefold death, but only from the storytellers – and, of course, there are rumours of such happenings among those areas in the dark mountain gorges where the New Faith has not been accepted. What does this mean?'

'It means that there is a mystery to be resolved,' Fidelma replied grimly, yet not without a certain relish. 'You say that you think you have seen this religieux before?'

'His features did seem familiar; even Aidan felt that he knew him. But neither of us could recall where we'd seen him before, nor could we identify him.'

'How did you know he was a religieux?'

'The man was in the religious robes and wore the tonsure of the Blessed John.'

Colgú had resumed his seat and was staring moodily into the log fire. His tone was troubled as he said, 'This news is not good, especially at this time of year.'

'I will take charge of this matter in the absence of Brehon Fíthel,' Fidelma announced, as if someone would challenge her.

'You have your wish, Fidelma,' Colgú said bitterly. 'You were complaining of boredom a moment ago. Hopefully this matter can be cleared up before the Samhain feast. I am expecting many of the local princes and religious leaders to join us. The Princess Gelgéis of Éile is coming and . . .' His voice trailed off as he contemplated his guests' reactions to this news.

Fidelma's expression was not sympathetic. 'Disquiet at this news will not just be confined to your guests, brother. The townsfolk

22

below will be alarmed that the body was found in their Samhain bonfire.' She then recalled that Colgú, as a boy, was always deeply disturbed by tales of Samhain ghosts and vengeful spirits. Was that what was bothering him? She smiled kindly, promising, 'Don't worry, brother. I will sort out this matter.'

Fidelma first made sure that Alchú had been transferred to the safe care of his nurse, Muirgen, and checked that the young boy had suffered no ill effects from the discovery of the body. Muirgen had become an essential part of their household since the recovery of the child after his abduction some time before. She was a middle-aged woman of ample proportions with greying, untidy hair. Her weathered skin showed that she was more used to the open air than the enclosures of the palace. Alchú called her by the familiar form *muimme* rather than the formal *mathair* which he used to address Fidelma. It was a custom of the language that Eadulf had never become used to. The intimate forms such as 'Mummy' and 'Daddy' were reserved for foster-parents while the formal 'Mother' and 'Father' were reserved for blood parents.

Fidelma and Eadulf decided to walk the short distance from the main gates of the fortress down to the town square. The warrior, Dego, whose life Eadulf had saved by amputating his right arm, stood on duty at the gates. By natural dexterity and dogged practice, the warrior had become as good a fighter with the use of his left arm as ever he had been when he had two good limbs.

'What's this I hear about a body in the Samhain bonfire?' he greeted them as they paused at the gate.

Fidelma frowned in annoyance. 'Has the word spread so quickly?' she asked.

Dego shrugged. 'With merchants and townfolk crossing the square and coming to the fortress, you would not expect such news to be kept a secret for long, would you? The story is that there are some who are fanatics for the Old Faith and who do not wish Samhain to be sullied by the New Faith.'

'Is that what folk are saying?' Eadulf said with interest.

'The merchants who came here just now think that it is some Druidical protest at the Christian use of the Samhain bonfire,' Dego confirmed. 'News of the murder is widely known. Are you investigating this matter, lady?'

'I am,' she replied, 'unless, of course, everyone has already made up their mind about why the man was killed and who did it, so making the task of a simple *dálaigh* superfluous.' There was no missing the sarcasm in her voice as she went on. 'The same sources who are so free with their information did not reveal the identity of this religieux, did they?'

Dego blinked uncomfortably. 'They did not, lady,' he muttered.

'Then at least they have left me one task to fulfil.'

Eadulf followed as she stalked on through the gates and headed down towards the township below.

'You were a bit harsh on poor Dego,' ventured Eadulf after they had gone a short distance. 'He was only repeating what people were saying.'

'That in itself is dangerous.' Fidelma was sharp. 'The prudent keep their tongues silent, for such whispers can lead to the birth of evil intent.'

There was a small group of townsfolk gathered at the bonfire when they reached it. However, Aidan had covered the body with some sacking that Rumann had brought him and was vainly trying to keep people back from the site. They moved away nervously as Fidelma strode up with Eadulf close behind. After greeting Aidan with a quick nod, she turned and stared disdainfully round at the townsfolk. She saw Rumann's broad face among them.

'Are there no chores to be done in your tavern or in your brewery, Rumann, that you can waste time here to gawp at a body?' she challenged him. 'And you, Gabhann, your smithy fires will soon be out if you stand gawking here. Are there no horses to be shoed, no bridles to be fixed or other metalwork to be repaired?' She then addressed some of the women. 'I see baskets of clothing on the banks of the stream yonder, but no one is engaged in washing them. Will they wash themselves? There is nothing for you here. We have all seen dead bodies before. It is time to get back to your duties. If there is news to tell you, then I shall let you know soon enough.'

There was a soft muttering, a few resentful remarks, but the group began to disperse and move off in various directions.

Fidelma waited a moment and then turned to Aidan. 'They haven't interfered with anything?'

The warrior shook his head. 'I asked Rumann to bring the sackcloth, as I felt the body should be covered. Then, I suppose, there were whispers of the news and several people began to arrive but I told them not to approach too close. And there were some merchants passing up to the fortress who stopped to ask questions.'

'And with the few answers that they were given, I hear that they have already resolved the whole mystery,' she replied dryly.

Aidan's expression was one of bewilderment. Eadulf explained what Dego had said.

'I told the merchants nothing about the threefold death,' the young warrior protested. 'Rumann must have mentioned it to them. He saw that the body was clad in the robes of a religieux when he brought me the sackcloth to cover it with.'

'A pity,' was all Fidelma replied before indicating that he should remove the sacking so that she could examine the body.

To their surprise, she actually knelt on the grass by the side of the corpse and stared long and hard at the man's face. Then she sniffed cautiously. Eadulf saw the gesture.

'He seems to have been bathing in lavender,' he offered. Fidelma did not reply but reached forward, turning the dead man's head this way and that as if to confirm the style of his tonsure before indicating to Eadulf that he should help to show her the wounds. Having closely examined the three mortal blows that he had mentioned, she

25

then turned her attention to the robes, rubbing the material between her fingers as if to judge its quality before removing a simple carved wooden cross which hung around the man's neck on a leather thong. This she put into the *marsupium* that hung from her *criss* or belt. Then she gave sigh and rose to her feet, looking from the corpse back to the unlit bonfire from which it had been dragged.

'He is as you found him among the branches of the bonfire, Aidan?' she asked. 'There was nothing else with him save what he has on him now?'

The warrior gave a nod of confirmation. 'I had a look because it is odd that a religieux doesn't have a belt or cord as a means of fixing his robe. I searched the bonfire thoroughly.' The latter words were slightly raised in protest because Fidelma had walked to the stacked wood and peered in herself.

'Do not worry,' she said, over her shoulder. 'It is in the nature of a *dálaigh* to observe for themselves so that they might see all at first hand.' Then she turned back, and said, 'I would have been surprised if I had found anything else.'

'I don't understand,' Eadulf said.

Fidelma returned to the corpse and knelt down again, motioning them both to follow her example.

'Observe the body,' she invited. 'Tell me what you see.'

It fell to Eadulf to do so.

'Rough, weatherbeaten skin. A man more used to being in the open in all sorts of weather than in the dark cloisters of some community. The hands are callused and used to hard work. Ah . . .'

'What else do you see?' prompted Fidelma.

'I see marks on the wrists and,' Eadulf moved swiftly to the feet and came back again, 'also on the ankles. The poor devil has been tied up and very recently. The burn marks of where the ropes cut into his wrists and ankles are unmistakable.'

'Perhaps he was abducted from his community for this vile sacrifice,' offered Aidan. 'A victim of someone who maintains the evil pagan practices associated with this time of the year. A member of the religious would be a natural target, being one who is considered to have overthrown the Old Faith.'

Fidelma waited a moment or two before prompting them again: 'Nothing else? Eadulf has mentioned the texture of the man's skin – as if he had spent all his time in the countryside. Does that suggest anything?'

'Nothing in particular. Most of the self-sustaining religious communities have brethren who work the land. Not all religious are scribes and copyists or into booklearning,' Aidan pointed out.

Fidelma smiled in approval. 'Anything else?' she asked.

'The man has shaved himself badly, at least the last time he shaved,' Eadulf noted.

'A good point,' Fidelma agreed. 'And from the unevenness of the stubble and the tufts that are left, this man had a thick beard before he shaved it off.'

'So do a lot of members of the religious in this kingdom,' Aidan said. 'He wears the tonsure of the Blessed John, not that of a Roman religieux – so that indicates he was from one of the local churches or abbeys.'

Fidelma tutted. 'He only recently shaved off his beard,' she corrected him. 'And in making that point, Aidan, you have missed the most important point of all.'

Aidan exchanged a puzzled look with Eadulf but saw no enlightenment on his face.

'What have we missed?' Eadulf asked.

'You have said that the man's beard was badly shaved?'

'I did.'

'Now look at the cut of his tonsure.'

Eadulf bent forward. 'You mean that it is also badly cut? The shaving has not been done by a steady hand. There are several deep cuts and scratches, some stubble left and even a few tufts of hair.'

'You do not remark on the paleness of the skin where the tonsure has been cut? It is soft and almost baby-like in texture against the dark weathering of the man's face.'

'You mean that he has only recently become a religieux,' Aidan suggested eagerly, 'and so that is why the tonsure is newly cut? Well, that might help us track him down the more quickly.'

Fidelma had a faint smile on her lips as she shook her head. 'It could also mean something entirely different,' she said.

'I don't understand,' Aidan confessed.

Fidelma gazed thoughtfully at the face of the corpse. 'Tell me, Aidan,' she said, 'how closely did Rumann look upon the face of this man?'

The warrior was puzzled by the question. 'Not that closely, as I remember. I shouted across to him to bring sacking to shield the body when I saw people becoming interested and moving across the square. When he did so, I took the sacking from him and laid it over the body. So he did not see the face.'

'Are you sure?'

'I am. Why?'

'Is that important?' Eadulf added.

'I am sure that Rumann would have recognised the man even without his beard,' she replied firmly. 'You both said that the corpse looked familiar?'

'Yes,' conceded Aidan. 'But then I find a lot of people do.'

Eadulf bent to gaze down at the features of the man again. 'I do feel that I have seen him before,' he repeated.

'Cast your mind back to last winter, Eadulf. Remember the attempt on my brother's life? And remember how we found Aibell, who is now Gormán's wife, and had to seek confirmation of her story of how she came to Cashel?'

'I do remember that.'

'Do you also recall how we questioned a shepherd who kept a flock on the far side of the Road of Rocks to the west of the township?'

Eadulf was frowning. 'The shepherd who confirmed that he had seen that traitorous merchant, Ordan, giving a lift to Aibell on his cart from the Ford of the Ass? I can't recall much about the shepherd; he was not an important witness.'

'All witnesses are important,' Fidelma rebuked sternly. 'Now look at the face of the corpse again. Do you recognise him now?'

Eadulf peered closer. 'It is a year ago,' he protested. 'I cannot be certain. He wears a tonsure and the robes of the religious.'

'I told you that the tonsure was recently and badly cut,' replied Fidelma patiently. 'The body that is lying there is that of the shepherd we questioned, one who, as I recall, often drank in Rumann's tavern. He is certainly no religieux. As you originally said, Eadulf, the man has been murdered. But why would anyone want to murder a shepherd with this pagan ritual, try to disguise him as a religieux and then hide the body in a bonfire? There is something very wrong here; something that smacks of evil.'

CHAPTER THREE

E adulf stared at Fidelma in surprise. He knew that his wife was
not beyond giving way to dramatic moments when presenting
cases before the Dál, the courts of the Brehons, but, as he recalled,
she had never done it just for his benefit.

She was saying to Aidan: 'Go and fetch Rumann. Don't mention
anything to him about the identity of the corpse. I merely want him to
come here and independently confirm what my memory has told me.'

Aidan trotted off to the tavern and returned shortly afterwards
with the innkeeper, who was told to look on the face of the corpse.

Rumann's astonishment showed immediately on his features but
he did not speak at once. He examined the dead man's features
carefully, peering at him from different angles before he gave a sigh
and said, 'Even without his beard, lady, I would recognise Spelán,
the shepherd. I don't understand. He was no religieux – the fellow
was in my tavern drinking only a week ago.'

'You have no doubt that this is Spelán?' pressed Fidelma.

'No doubt at all,' affirmed the bewildered man. 'If the truth was
known, he was often in my tavern during the summer and usually
getting drunk. Why is he wearing a tonsure?'

'If my memory serves me well, this man Spelán had a flock of
sheep to the west of the township?' Fidelma asked Rumann, ignoring
the question.

'That's so,' the tavern-keeper confirmed. 'I think he had a flock on the slopes of the Cnoc Bológ. But how on earth did he come to be wearing that robe and to have a tonsure? I would describe him in many ways but never as one interested in religion. Not at all.'

'Tell me what you know about him,' invited Fidelma.

'I know precious little,' conceded the tavern-keeper. 'Like most shepherds, he was tight mouthed. And it was only recently, during these summer months, that he came to my tavern more frequently to drink. I think his flock must have been bringing him a good return as he was never without funds. He met other shepherds but didn't seem to be particularly interested in matters relating to sheep. But then, I never heard him discussing religion either.'

'Where did he live, did you say?'

'I was told he kept his flock in the hills to the south-west, exactly as you recall, lady; well to the west beyond the Road of Rocks.'

'You said the place was called Cnoc Bológ?'

Rumann rubbed the back of his neck reflectively. 'That's it. The Hill of the Bullock – yes, I am sure that was the name of the place. But there was one person with whom he usually spoke a word or two when he was in the tavern, and he should be able to confirm that.'

'What is the name of that person?'

'The husband of your nurse.'

'Nessan?' Eadulf queried.

'Yes, Nessan, who looks after King Colgú's flock,' confirmed Rumann.

Fidelma suddenly remembered that it had been Nessan, the husband of Alchú's nurse, Muirgen, who had identified Spelán a year ago when she was trying to trace the shepherd as a witness.

'But you also talked to him?' Eadulf said to Rumann. 'You surely know most of the people in this vicinity.'

Rumann shrugged. 'In the township – yes, I know most people. But this man came from the countryside. He was, as I have said, not given to gossip. I recall that he had a bad lambing season earlier in the year. Yet during the summer his visits to the tavern were more frequent, not less – and as I mentioned before, he did not lack funds for ale.'

'Are you sure that he never talked about religious matters?'

'Never in my hearing. He was not the kind of man that you asked for details of his life.'

'Can you tell me nothing then, of Spélan's family, of his wife, of his home or his background?'

'Nothing at all. He kept quiet when it came to his background, family or other connections . . . although, come to think of it, I realised that he was not originally from these parts.'

'What makes you say that?'

Rumann raised a shoulder and let it fall. 'He spoke with the accent of the north-western lands. I once heard that he had married a local woman who originally owned the sheep flock, and it was her flock he looked after.'

'I thought you said that you didn't know about his wife?' Fidelma did her best to control her exasperation.

'I do not,' returned the tavern-keeper. 'He hardly ever mentioned her. I don't think anyone even knew where his cabin was. Often he would consume so much liquor that I feared he would have no hope of finding his way home, but he never let anyone accompany him or tell them where his home was.'

'So he was a drunkard?' Eadulf was disapproving.

'He drank to excess by my reckoning, but without losing control.'

'So, without knowing anything of the man's background, you have told us several important facts,' Fidelma concluded. 'He was a shepherd named Spelán. He probably came from a north-west territory. He married a local woman who lived at the Hill of the Bullock, so you think. You thought his flock was not doing well back during the lambing season yet despite that, he recently had more than enough coin in his pocket. He came to town and drank frequently and to excess in your tavern. He occasionally talked with other shepherds, most notably with Nessan. Now, is there anything else you don't know about him?'

Rumann did not catch her irony as he shook his head, saying, 'I know nothing more about the man, lady. Truly, I am sorry.'

Fidelma glanced around the square. It would not be long before the curious townsfolk would be filtering back in large numbers to discover what had happened.

'Rumann, I want you and Aidan to take the body into the shelter of your tavern for the time being. I presume you can place it in an outhouse?' Before he could object, she went on: 'I will arrange for it to be removed to the fortress as soon as possible.' She glanced apologetically at Eadulf. 'I would like old Brother Conchobhar to make a further examination of the corpse.' Then she turned back to the tavern-keeper. 'I want your solemn oath, Rumann, that you will discuss none of this with anyone; say nothing about who this man was. Do you understand?'

'My lips are sealed, lady,' the tavern-keeper promised almost indignantly.

'That is good and should be no hardship.' Fidelma knew that Rumann liked to gossip. Then she added to Aidan: 'When you have helped Rumann with the body, I want you to join us at the stables of the fortress. I will need you to accompany us to Cnoc Bológ, to this Hill of the Bullock.'

They watched as Aidan and Rumann lifted the body, still covered by the sackcloth, and started to carry it towards the tavern. Fidelma signalled to Eadulf and they began to make their way back up the steep track towards the gates of the fortress.

'What now?' he asked breathlessly.

'As I said, I'll send men to bring the body into Brother Conchobhar's apothecary away from curious eyes and comments. I shall also seek out Nessan to see if he can add anything else to what Rumann has told us. We will need to make a trip to Cnoc Bológ to find the man's wife and discover more about this shepherd.'

Eadulf's expression showed some reluctance. 'I know there are hills in that direction but no one ever seems to venture into them. Gormán once told me it was an area of bleak hills and forests all the way to the great river and on no main track at all. We don't want to venture anywhere that is inaccessible and get stuck there. Don't forget that tomorrow evening will be the feast of Samhain.'

Fidelma's eyes twinkled at the anxiety in his tone. 'True, those hills are infrequently visited, but they are not at the ends of the earth.' She glanced at the sky. 'Providing we can find Nessan shortly, we could be on our way and reach there before the sun is even near its zenith.'

'Nessan will be with your brother's flock in the northern fields,' pointed out Eadulf as they resumed their climb towards the gates of the fortress.

'Not so,' replied Fidelma. 'I was speaking to Muirgen this morning and her husband is due to see my brother this morning to go over some accounting of the condition of the sheep flock now it is the end of summer.'

'Condition? I thought the King's flocks were fairly strong.'

'So they are. The ewes started early breeding several months ago. So they could be lambing as early as Dubh Luacrán, the month of the dark days. It is Nessan's task to report on their condition and prospects.'

They paused at the gate and requested Dego to inform a couple of his warriors to make ready to accompany Brother Conchobhar, the chief apothecary of the palace, to Rumann's tavern. Fidelma placed her full confidence in the old man's unerring eye and knowledge. A friend of her father, Fáilbhe Flann, Conchobhar had been one of the most trustworthy mentors in the lives of her brother and herself when they were children.

Stopping only to instruct the stable master to prepare their horses, the couple crossed the courtyard by the chapel and went over to Brother Conchobhar's apothecary.

The elderly man was at his door and his eyes lit up when he saw them approaching. Then he saw the expression on Fidelma's face, and his smile died.

'Is there something the matter?' he asked immediately.

'I need your expertise, old friend.' Quickly explaining the situation, Fidelma told him that two warriors would accompany him down to Rumann's tavern to bring back the body. He was to examine it and prepare it for burial, for it was the ancient custom to bury or cremate bodies as quickly as possible, usually at midnight on the day following the death.

Brother Conchobhar shook his head slowly to express his bewilderment.

'You say that he is a shepherd but dressed as a Brother of the Faith? Who do I notify of the death and burial? Should this not be reported to a priest so that all ritual observances can be made at the funeral? I presume, in the absence of Brehon Fíthel, you will take all legal responsibility?'

Fidelma hesitated a moment. 'He was not a religieux,' she finally told him. 'The trouble is that at this time we know nothing of the man except that he is, or was, married and possibly dwelling in the south-west hills at Cnoc Bológ. We mean to ride there immediately and discover what we can. If I am able to do so, I will inform his wife and bring back what I have learned.'

'Cnoc Bológ? Then you might well be back before nightfall. The funeral will now have to be the day after tomorrow, as no funeral can take place on the night of Samhain,' Brother Conchobhar added by way of explanation.

'As to any legal responsibility, that is mine,' Fidelma assured him.

'It shall be done as you wish,' he assented.

They turned away in search of Muirgen the nurse, who told them that her husband was still making his report to the King. Fidelma immediately led the way to her brother's council chamber, waving aside the warrior who stood guard outside and who raised a half-hearted protest that the King was engaged in business. Inside the chamber Colgú raised his head with an angry look at being disturbed while Nessan, his shepherd, turned awkwardly and rose on seeing who had caused the interruption.

'I need to ask some urgent questions of Nessan, brother,' Fidelma explained. 'We must leave for Cnoc Bológ at once, otherwise I would not have intruded.'

Colgú did not proceed to chide her, aware that his sister would not interrupt like this unless it was important. 'I presume it has to do with the body of the religieux that Eadulf found?' he said.

'A religieux, who is not a religieux,' she confirmed quietly.

Nessan stared at her, eyes wide. 'But what has this to do with me, lady?'

'I will explain. I am told that you used to drink with a shepherd called Spelán in Rumann's tavern.'

The man inclined his head in agreement. 'I did not see him that often, lady. Certainly during these past summer months he would come to the tavern and drink his fill, and more, but liquor did not make him loquacious. He was not an easy man to talk to. I would often find him sitting alone over his ale. I sometimes took pity on his isolation.'

'What can you tell me about him?'

'Not a great deal. He had a flock near a place called the Hill of the Bullock, just as you said. It was his wife's flock, for I gathered he had come to these parts as a penniless itinerant. I can't vouch for it, lady, but I think he was of the class of *sen-cleithe*, who had fled from his clan territory without rights or capability to sustain him. He would have remained an itinerant had he not married.' The shepherd snorted. 'He did not seem to know a great deal about sheep.'

'Marriage would not have altered his status,' reflected Fidelma. 'In law he would simply be deemed as working for his wife. Who was she? What is her name?'

Nessan shook his head. 'He never said.'

'He never mentioned her name? Not once in passing?'

'Not in my hearing. I always thought that it was odd, that he dwelled over at Cnoc Bológ. It is a long way to walk for a drink at Rumann's tavern and an even longer way to walk back when the drink is upon you.'

'That is a point well made, Nessan. Did you ever get any impression of where he came from originally?'

'He talked once about the Sliabh Eibhlinn mountains.'

'It is a long range, over forty kilometres from one end to the other, with many impassable areas,' explained Fidelma, seeing that Eadulf did not recognise the name. 'It is not a particularly good place. If he was of the *sen-cleithe* class, then he certainly did not have the legal right to leave his clan territory without the permission of his chieftain or without redeeming himself in the eyes of the clan. Do you have any idea at all of how long he had been absent from his home territory?'

'No, lady.'

'When did you last see him?'

'Over a week ago, I think. He was drinking in the tavern as usual.'

'How did he seem to you, that last time you saw him? That is, compared to his usual manner.'

'No different to any other time. I was always surprised by the fact that he never had any trouble paying for his drinks. Four months ago, he was always worried about money.'

'Why was that? Do you know?'

'Earlier this year I gathered he had lost several sheep. Maybe it was because of *cuili biasta*, the fly infestation. I seemed to recall that he had once allowed them to wander in the marshes below the hills where he grazed them. That is where you would pick up the disease. That was careless – and no good shepherd would abandon his sheep to wander freely near marshland.'

'So you did not think that he was a good shepherd?'

'I will probably do him injustice, but no. He did not even know about the merits of finding good grazing land, such as the patches of the *seamair dhearg*.'

'The what?' Eadulf had not heard the term before.

'Red clover. They have just ceased to flower now it is the end of summer. When the rams are among the ewes it is well known that the red clover helps the ewes conceive and ensures a good lambing season.'

'So both you and Rumann seem to be of the opinion that he was a shepherd only because of his wife's flock?'

'So it seemed to me,' agreed Nessan. 'Anyway, he never mentioned sheep after the start of summer.'

'He gave no reason?'

Nessan thought a moment before answering. 'Never. But as I said, he seemed to have no problems about paying for his ale. He even paid for others when he was shamed into doing so . . . though that did not happen very often. He was by nature a mean man.'

Fidelma was disappointed. 'Apart from these impressions, you learned nothing more about him?'

Nessan thought deeply before giving a sigh. 'I cannot think of anything else. Oh . . . there is one thing though. He once said he was going to set up home in the Comeraigh mountains.'

'But those mountains are to the south of here. I thought you said he came from the north?'

'I can only say what I remember, lady,' Nessan replied.

'Thank you, Nessan.' Fidelma turned to Colgú. 'I will interrupt no longer, brother.'

The King was frowning as if trying to solve a puzzle.

'I don't understand, sister. Are you saying that the religieux in the bonfire was this shepherd?'

'The body found dressed in the robes of a religieux was the

shepherd called Spelán,' she confirmed. 'We are now on our way to Cnoc Bológ to find out more.'

It appealed to her sense of the dramatic to quit the room at that moment, leaving her brother with a baffled expression on his features.

Outside, Eadulf shook his head in disapproval. 'You should not irritate your brother as you do. After all, he is the King.'

Fidelma gave her husband one of her rare mischievous grins. 'But he is still my brother, just the same.'

'Anyway,' Eadulf dismissed the subject, 'we did not learn much from Nessan. This shepherd Spelán seems an odd sort.'

'On the contrary, I thought we learned quite a lot about him. Obviously, we will find out even more from his wife.'

'I was thinking,' Eadulf mused, 'if he never spoke of sheep, of his flock, after the start of summer, perhaps he sold them? That would explain why he suddenly had funds.'

'Just because he was married, if the flock was his wife's, it does not mean to say that he had rights over it or over any of her property. From what Nessan told us, Spelán's marriage was one of a woman with a man who contributed nothing to their joint wealth. The marriage is specified in law as *lánamnus fir thathigtheo* and, even more specific, Spelán was from another clan area. Therefore, if a man is from another *tuath* or clan and has brought no property into the marriage, the wife retains all the rights to the property and, even if she is dead, that property remains with her kin unless a contract has been agreed allowing some payment to the husband. It would seem, on the surface, until we verify the situation, that Spelán's flock would not have been his to sell. So either the new wealth came from his wife or somewhere else.'

She walked on along the passage towards the main doors of the King's quarters and failed to notice the troubled look on Eadulf's face.

It had struck him that he was exactly in Spelán's position in terms of marriage to Fidelma. He remembered how he had talked over the matter with old Brother Conchobhar on the eve of his marriage. He had struggled to come to terms with the fact that he was marrying a princess of the Eóghanacht; sister of Colgú, fifty-ninth generation descendant of Eibhear Fionn, son of Milidh, who brought the Children of the Gael to the island of the goddesses Éire, Banba and Fodla; a princess whose brother was lord of Deas Muman, Tuad Muman, Oir Muman and Iar Muman, King of All Muman. He unconsciously found himself reciting the titles to himself before coming to the root of his troubled thought . . . who was *he*?

Eadulf of Seaxmund's Ham, in the land of the South Folk of the kingdom of East Anglia. True, he was an hereditary *gerefa* or law-giver of his people, but he was no noble; only a wandering religieux without wealth and a stranger in a strange land. He shivered, for he had often found himself wondering what would happen to him if, and God forbid it, anything happened to Fidelma. He was welcomed and accepted by Colgú, even being accorded an honour price to reflect his rank as Fidelma's husband and father to her son. Others of the Eóghanacht princes and clerics also accepted him, with only the clerics designating him 'Brother' Eadulf because of his religious calling. But to most, he had become 'friend Eadulf'. He knew Fidelma would rebuke him if he voiced these concerns to her. But there were times when his secret fears and his knowledge of the ancient laws of this land came foremost in his thoughts. He could easily become an itinerant without position or land if . . .

He realised Fidelma was waiting for him at the door.

'What is it?' she asked. 'Have you thought of something?'

'Not exactly.' His mind raced for a moment, not wishing to reveal the truth. 'I can't help thinking that the fact the body was put into the base of the Samhain bonfire might be significant.'

'Other than to get rid of it? Surely that was as good a reason as any?'

'Maybe not,' Eadulf replied determinedly. 'If he was from this Hill of the Bullock, why bring the body all the way into the town square and risk discovery? The killers would then have had to lay the body down while they spent time making a hole in the wood-pile. If that was not done with some care and patience, it might have led to the whole bonfire collapsing, people hearing the noise and rushing out to see what was amiss. The space they made to put the body in wasn't quite big enough, was it? So maybe they wanted the body to be found?'

Fidelma pondered this new idea for a moment before saying approvingly: 'Now that is good logic, Eadulf.'

He pointed across the courtyard towards the gates. 'Look – there's Aidan returning. He seems excited about something.'

It was true. The young warrior had burst into the courtyard as if in a great hurry. Catching sight of Fidelma and Eadulf, he ignored a surprised Dego, on guard at the gates, and hastened towards them.

'What now . . .?' began Eadulf, but the young man did not wait.

'A stranger. A stranger arrived in the town square while we were in Rumann's tavern,' he said breathlessly. 'It was a woman. She demanded to see Spelán's body. Spoke of him by name. Neither Rumann nor I could prevent it. The woman stood a moment, staring down at the corpse, refused to answer my questions but walked back to the woodpile and stood there muttering to herself. Do you think it is the killer returned?'

Fidelma said patiently, 'Now if you had killed someone and hidden them in the wood pyre, would you really return the next morning, in broad daylight, to announce the fact? Calm yourself and tell us about this stranger anyway. You have left so many details out. Think carefully and describe this person.'

But Aidan was not to be calmed. 'It's a woman,' he repeated. 'A strange woman.'

'Do you mean that she is a stranger, or that there is something strange in her behaviour or appearance?'

'Both.'

'Did you ask her who she was and how she knew Spelán or had heard of his death? Was she Spelán's wife?'

'I don't think so. As I said, she would not speak to me. There was something sinister about her. I felt, if anyone questioned her more vigorously, then it should be with the authority of a *dálaigh*.'

'Did you hear what she was muttering when she stood at the Samhain bonfire?'

'I followed her to try to get some answers. I heard her say that Spelán's death would not be the only one. That he would be avenged. Finally, she turned to me and spoke clearly. She had noticed my golden torc and realised that I was of the Nasc Niadh. Then she said that she would come again to remind people that the Rock on which the Eóghanacht had built their capital was a portal to the Otherworld and that Samhain is tomorrow. She cursed all who dwelled under the shadow of Cashel and said that they would be made to regret the death of Spelán. Tomorrow, she said, Donn would come to claim his vengeance.'

Fidelma's eyes widened. 'What then?'

'No more, lady. With that she turned and strode off and I could think of no reason to prevent her.'

'I would have thought both her actions and her words would be sufficient grounds to apprehend her,' Eadulf pointed out in disapproval. 'It seems that this woman wants to put fear in the people about Spelán's death and Samhain.'

'I maintain, as I always have, there is no speculation without information. And I am afraid, Aidan, you have brought us little information about this stranger. I agree with Eadulf that you should have detained her and brought her to me. You should have sought her name or at least whence she came.'

Aidan looked indignant. 'Oh, but I did. As she strode away, I called after her, to demand who she was, to threaten the Eóghanacht.'

'Did she actually give her name and where she came from?'

'She said that she came from Tech Duinn.'

Fidelma's reaction was a slight step backward and then she started to laugh. Aidan stared at her with an expression of surprise. Eadulf was trying to remember where and what he had heard about Tech Duinn and finally asked.

'It is the House of Donn,' Fidelma replied, still chuckling, 'the place where the dead assemble. It is said to be an island to the south-west; the gathering place of the dead, presided over by the ancient god of the dead, Donn. From there, Donn transports them on their journey to the Otherworld.'

Aidan was trying to control his growing consternation as he was reminded what the name meant.

'I see nothing of humour in the fact, lady,' he protested.

Fidelma immediately recovered her composure. 'Come, Aidan. Do you expect me to take seriously anyone who claims that they have come from the Otherworld? Did she look like some ephemeral spirit when you spoke with her?'

Aidan did not look reassured. 'I told you she was a strange woman. She was not young nor, I would say, handsome. Her features were so sharp that she looked as if she had hardly any flesh to cover the bones. The skin so white, the eyes so dark and piercing . . .' He halted when he noticed the smile spreading on Fidelma's features again.

'I can only repeat what I saw,' he added in a hurt tone.

'I don't doubt your observation,' Fidelma said kindly. 'It is only your sense of humour that I think is missing.'

'But consider it, lady,' Aidan countered. 'The threefold death, the ritual of the ancient religion. Now this stranger arrives with curses on this place and claims to be from the House of Donn.'

'Well, if that is what the woman claimed,' Eadulf put in, his tone revealing nothing of the dread that he secretly felt, 'then her intention was to get herself noticed. I would say that she has succeeded.'

'She has succeeded very well,' Fidelma added, 'cleverly timing her visit to make her claims when the feast of Samhain starts tomorrow night – and with all the ancient beliefs about what could happen that night.'

CHAPTER FOUR

B y the time they returned to the town square, no longer on foot
but on horseback, the place was thronged with people. Several
men were rebuilding the damaged pile of logs and stacking more.
They were being directed by a burly, red-faced fellow, whose instructions to his helpers showed his impatience. Some merchants had
now set up their daily stalls with goods they had brought in from
the surrounding farms, including cuts of meat and fresh fish. For
Cashel, the ordinary trading day had started, perhaps a little late
but there was no sign now that anything had been amiss. Fidelma
was busily scanning the crowd.

'There is no sign of your ghostly woman from the House of
Donn,' she remarked lightly to Aidan, who rode behind them.

Aidan ignored her gibe. He had also been searching among the
groups milling about. In fact, he had called out to one or two people
that he recognised and asked if they had seen a female stranger but
received only negative answers.

They made their way across the square towards the growing pile
of logs. The muscular, red-faced man paused in supervising the
others and raised his hand in salutation.

'A bad business this, lady,' he greeted her in a low voice, as she
halted before him. 'I am Curnan, the woodsman whose task was to
prepare the Samhain bonfire this year.'

'I see that you are working hard to repair the damage,' she commented, indicating the woodpile.

'There was not much to repair,' admitted the man. 'Whoever put the body into the pile knew how to adjust the lower branches so that it did not cause the rest to collapse.'

Fidelma regarded him thoughtfully. The man appeared to support what Eadulf had already observed. 'You mean some care was given to hiding the body?' she asked for clarification. 'It was not just pushed into the pile?'

Curnan rubbed a hand across his sweating brow. 'Lady, there is an art to building bonfires. You could dislodge everything if you did not know what you were doing. Remove a centre strut and the entire pile would come crashing down. That is why it has become the tradition of woodsmen such as me to build the Samhain bonfires here in Cashel for generation after generation.'

'But,' Aidan intervened, 'from what we have been told, the deed was done during the night. How could that be, if things were so delicately balanced and liable to topple if the wrong piece of wood was touched?'

'Doesn't that just prove what I said?' countered Curnan. 'Whoever did this was knowledgeable about fires and how to build them. Any idea who it was and why? Tomorrow night is Samhain and I would not like to find other bodies hidden in this pile before then.'

Fidelma replied honestly, 'At the moment, Curnan, I have little information to give.' She hesitated. 'You work in the western forests, don't you?'

Curnan nodded slowly. 'I work in the forests between here and the great river.'

'Did you know the murdered man?' was her next question.

'I am told it was Spelán. I would have thought most people who drank at Rumann's tavern knew him by sight.'

'Can you tell me anything about the man?'

'Ah, apart from his drinking? He once ran a flock of sheep on the Hill of the Bullock, or did until the start of the summer. Few people liked him so there is not much to tell. He was secretive and discouraged questions.'

'I heard that he was married?'

'That is so.' Curnan scowled. 'She was a member of my own *tuath,* the Sítae. Our clan dwells on those hills and in the forests. Her name was Caoimhe.'

'Was?' Fidelma caught the past tense.

'She died of a fever earlier this year, so I was told.'

'So she's dead?' Fidelma hid her disappointment. 'I am sorry. Did Spelán take over the flock?'

Curnan shrugged. 'I don't think so. I haven't seen sheep on the Hill of the Bullock in many months. He would never speak to me anyway.'

'Why not?'

'We were not friends!' The emphatic pronunciation caused Fidelma to decide not to pursue the matter at that time.

'No matter then.' She raised a hand in thanks before turning and leading the way across the square to where Rumann was standing surveying the crowds with an expression of satisfaction. Obviously he was appraising the business possibilities, for after the people had made their purchases from the merchants, they would make straight for his tavern, seeking a thirst-quenching drink before starting for home. Some merchants might even decide to stay overnight in his establishment. Rumann acknowledged Fidelma as she dismounted in front of him.

'Brother Conchobhar and a couple of warriors have taken the body up to the palace, lady,' he informed her, glancing around to make sure they were not overheard. 'Just in time too. It would not have done much good for trade here if it became known there was a body lying about.'

'I am sure it would not have been Spelán's wish to disrupt your trade,' Fidelma replied dryly.

Rumann flushed. 'I did not mean . . .'

Fidelma made an impatient gesture of her hand. 'I understand that a strange woman came and demanded to see the corpse before it was collected by Brother Conchobhar.'

'Yes. A strange woman, indeed. I have never seen her before nor do I wish to see her again. She was a tall person, clad all in black. I'm no coward, but her appearance filled me with alarm.'

'Alarm? In what way?'

'Her manner of dress, the black feather cloak . . .'

Fidelma cast a disappointed glance at Aidan. 'A black *feather* cloak?' she asked with emphasis.

'Yes. She wore a cloak that was made entirely from interlaid black feathers, like those of the crows or ravens. I gathered from Aidan there that she went to the bonfire and uttered some curses against Cashel.'

'You did not hear these curses?'

'I remained here but Aidan followed her across the square trying to learn her name and where she came from.'

'I gather no one knows where she has gone or what her business was in Cashel?' Fidelma reflected. 'A pity, as we would have liked to have a word with her before we proceed to Cnoc Bológ. Never mind, she will probably be staying somewhere nearby for the festival.' She paused and added: 'I suppose you have mentioned the circumstances of Spelán's death to several people?'

The sheepish look on Rumann's face confirmed that he had done so.

'I was wondering how this woman knew that it was Spelán who had been killed, and how she came to you to demand to see the body by name?'

'I swear, lady, I do not know.' Rumann looked positively fearful as he understood the point that Fidelma was making. 'I had never seen the woman before.'

Fidelma stared at him a moment before she inclined her head.

'My thanks, Rumann, for your help.' With a gesture to her companions, she remounted and led the way around the corner of the tavern along the main track towards the western end of the township.

News of the find at the bonfire seemed to have spread throughout the township. Many of the inhabitants stood at the doors of their houses, some with heads bent together, talking in low, worried voices. They glanced up almost furtively as the three rode down the street. Some acknowledged their passing, but without the carefree greetings that they usually reserved for Fidelma. She was well liked by the people of the township. Eadulf looked round and saw that, the moment they had passed, heads were bent once again in muttered conversation. The apprehensive mood of the townsfolk was all too clear to see.

At the western edge of Cashel lay the home of Fidelma's friend Della, the mother of Gormán, the commander of the Nasc Niadh, the elite bodyguard of her brother Colgú. It was not exactly a farmstead but Della kept a small paddock with horses, and some outhouses with a few animals; she also specialised in bees and the production of honey. One of Eadulf's tasks that morning had been to collect some containers of honey for Fidelma; as they approached, he was reminded that it was a task that still needed to be accomplished. Gormán's young wife, Aibell, had already seen their approach and came to the gate to greet them accompanied by a dog. Della always kept, by tradition, as a guard dog, a *leth-choin*, a cross between a wolfhound and a terrier. The animal had recognised Fidelma and Eadulf and decided that barking a warning was superfluous; it stood merely wagging its tail in silent greeting.

'Have you come to collect the honey?' Aibell asked with a smile, about to pull open the gate. Fidelma stayed her with an upraised hand.

'Not this time. We are passing by, not stopping, so I won't come in.' She swung down from her horse, however, but stood at the gate holding its reins. Eadulf and Aidan remained mounted.

The girl frowned. 'You all look so serious,' she said. 'Is something wrong?'

At that moment, Della appeared from her porch and hastened down to the gate. Fidelma had once successfully defended her from a false accusation of murder, and the two of them had been good friends ever since. Della was a woman of short stature and over forty years of age now, but time had not disguised the fact that she had once been a real beauty – and even now, she was handsome, and still with a golden sheen in her hair. She had overheard Aibell's remark and she, too, caught their worried expressions.

'Has something happened?' she asked.

'Nothing to concern yourself with,' replied Fidelma. 'News travels fast hereabouts, so doubtless you will soon learn that a body was found stuffed into the base of the Samhain bonfire they are building in the town square.'

Della looked shocked. 'We had not heard,' she replied. 'Whose body is it?'

'A shepherd named Spelán.'

Della's reaction was unexpected. 'I know the man,' she said, to their astonishment. 'He lives up beyond Cnoc Bológ.' She pointed towards the south-westerly hills.

'How do you know him, Della?'

The woman gave a deprecating sniff. 'Perhaps "know" is the wrong word. A few times I have found him, the worse for drink, sleeping in my hedge – no doubt coming back from Rumann's tavern and incapable of making his way home. Was it the drink finished him off?' Then she paused, recalling what Fidelma had said. 'Did you say "stuffed into the base" of the woodpile? So did he climb in to sleep it off and died there?'

But Fidelma was shaking her head. 'He was hidden there deliberately, by someone else, and his death had nothing to do with drink, Della. He was murdered. That is why we are on our way to the Hill of the Bullock to discover more about his background. Do you know anything about him?'

Della sighed. 'That he lived on the hill and kept a flock of sheep there was about all I knew. I was told that he did not mix much with people here. I don't think he was particularly successful as a shepherd – I doubt he made much money out of it.'

'Why do you say that?'

'The state of his clothes, for example.'

Eadulf leaned forward from his saddle with an interested expression. 'What could you tell by the state of his clothes?'

'Oh, they were practically rags, full of holes and tears, and never an attempt to mend them. He obviously did not have a good woman to sew for him.'

'But we are told that he had a wife,' Eadulf informed her.

Della raised an eyebrow. 'If that is so, then she contributed little in taking care of his appearance.'

'Perhaps he could not afford decent clothes because he spent most of his earnings on drink?' mused Aidan.

'Quite possibly. The fact was, he never changed his clothes nor washed them – or his person – so far as I could discern, for the smell of him was vile. He was not a nice person, and one I avoided if at all possible.'

'Smell?' Eadulf frowned, remembering. 'Did he ever douse himself with fragrances to disguise the stale odours? Something like lavender, for example.'

Della stared at Eadulf, wondering if this were some kind of a joke – but then saw that he was serious. 'How would a creature like that afford such a luxury?' she asked reasonably. 'Thankfully, I hardly found myself in close proximity to him. He stank as if he had wallowed in a pig-pen. What makes you ask about lavender? That is something few people around here can afford.'

Fidelma cast a warning glance at Eadulf. Usually she kept no secrets from her old friend Della, but these were early days in their investigation and she did not like being diverted from her guiding principle that there should be no speculation without information.

'It was just an aroma that came to mind,' Eadulf said contritely.

'Do you know much about Cnoc Bológ, Della?' Fidelma asked then. 'Frankly, I have never been due west of the Road of Rocks. There are easier highways to the great river and to Ara's Well, or even more south-west.'

'Although it is only a short ride from here, it is an isolated area and sparsely populated.'

'I am told it is the territory of the clan Sítae.'

'To call them a clan is to pay them a compliment. They are more like a small group of families. I've only been up there a few times, myself. It is a lonely place. The hills are bare and stony and the forests in the valleys are dark, cold places. I recall that part of the hill has a circle of standing stones on it, from which you have a good view of the entire area.'

'What made you go there then?' Fidelma was curious.

'It was when I was a young girl,' Della explained. 'Once you cross the main summit of the Hill of the Bullock, immediately south-west is another rocky summit on which stands Ráth Cuáin. It is a religious community.'

Eadulf was mystified. 'A religious community? I thought a *ráth* signified a fortress?'

'You are not wrong, Eadulf,' confirmed Della. 'It is usually a fortified residence of a chieftain or a larger fortress.'

'So now it is a small religious community,' Fidelma commented. 'I have never been there even though it is so near.'

'It used to be the residence of the chieftain of the Sítae,' Della revealed. 'As I remember, it still looks very much like a fortress. The approach from the south is difficult as there are small cliffs. I was told that it was built above a complex of caves. When the New Faith was sweeping the land, a woman called Gobnait came to the area. She had joined the Abbey of the Blessed Finnbarr of Corcach

Mór, learned the gift of healing and was famous for her production of honey. She eventually became Abbess of Baile Bhúirne in the land of the Cenél Lóegairi. One of the stories told was that a brigand was robbing her church and she sent her swarm of bees after him to exact retribution. They stung him to death.'

'That doesn't sound like a nice thing to do,' Fidelma said. 'I have seen what happens when a swarm descends on a young child or an animal.'

'Nevertheless, her church was never robbed again,' Della pointed out with a touch of black humour.

'But Baile Bhúirne is far to the west from here,' Eadulf said, trying to follow the story. 'I thought you said she founded this abbey at Ráth Cuáin?'

'So it is claimed,' replied Della. 'Apparently she persuaded the chieftain of the Sítae to turn his fortress into an abbey. Well, there are plenty of stories that are not necessarily true.'

'So this place, Ráth Cuáin, is now a small religious community?' Eadulf strove for clarification.

When Della confirmed it, Fidelma said, 'Strange . . . I do not recall poor Ségdae, when he was alive and Abbot of Imleach, ever mentioning the place. Yet Ráth Cuáin would be in his jurisdiction and he was so particular about keeping in touch with all the churches and communities in the kingdom.'

Della shrugged. 'I really can't say. I only went there when I was young to learn about the art of keeping bees, but I found that they no longer kept up the tradition of Gobnait. That was many years ago.'

'It is odd that we seem to have had no communication at all with the place even though it is such a short journey from here. I can't even recall my brother ever inviting the chieftain of the Sítae to any council or meeting at Cashel.'

'As I said, it is a rough, unfriendly countryside. The hills are not high but there are plenty of rocks and marshlands to the south-west, as well as the great forests that surround the hills. The River Siúr forms the western border. It's no wonder traders built roads that circumnavigate the area rather than go through it.'

'It sounds an inhospitable area. All the same, I am surprised that we have had no contact with the place,' Aidan agreed with Fidelma.

'Have you really never been there?' queried Della. 'I would have thought that members of the King's bodyguard would have known every hill, wood and track around the palace . . . especially when a chieftain's fortress stands so close to Cashel.'

'But you said it was now an abbey,' Aidan reminded her. 'I've never heard of this Ráth Cuáin before. I can't remember any of the warriors of the Golden Collar ever talking about it.'

Fidelma was baffled that so few people were really knowledgeable about the area.

'We must make ourselves acquainted with the territory of the Sítae,' she announced firmly.

'It sounds from what Della says that there are few tracks or paths to follow. Perhaps we might need someone to be a guide?' Eadulf suggested.

'Surely you underestimate Aidan's abilities? Being a warrior of the Golden Collar, he ought to be able to track through the twelve mountains of Na Comeraigh with a blindfold on.' Della smiled.

It was just her mischievous humour but Aidan flushed. 'Indeed. Have no concern. A warrior of the Golden Collar is guide enough through any territory,' he declared. Then he added an afterthought: 'Although, I mean . . . it is best to know something of a country in which one has never been.'

'Well, we won't get there by thinking about it.' Fidelma remounted her horse and glanced down at Della and Aibell. 'Try not to speak about this more than is necessary, my friends, although thanks to Rumann's loose tongue, there is plenty of gossip spreading through the town already.'

'We will keep it to ourselves,' promised Della. 'How long do you expect to be gone?'

'Long enough to pick up some information about Spelán and try to find out who might have done this to him – and why.'

'Don't forget I promised you that jar of honey which Eadulf was going to collect this morning.'

'We'll collect it on our return,' Eadulf assured her.

The trio turned their horses towards the track that was known as the Road of Rocks. It led up a small hill through a large woodland bordering the fringe of the great southern Plain of Femen which crossed to the high mountains called the Sléibhte an Comeraigh, of which Sliabh na mBan – the Mountain of Women – dominated. It was a vast area of pastoral and agricultural wealth which contributed to the affluence and power of the Eóghanacht Kings of Cashel. But it was also a place associated with the legends and origins of the people; here, every hillock, rock or forest was said to be associated with heroes and gods, heroines and goddesses – some good, some evil; a place of dark, primordial origins.

Eadulf had learned much of the lore of the Plain of Femen; of its underground caves that were entrances to the Otherworld. The hills here were the homes of the Everlasting Ones, such as Bodh the Red, divine son of the great god the Dagda, whose curse turned people into demons that flew through the air in search of sacrifice. And it was here that the legendary warrior, Fionn Mac Cumhaill, commander of the Fianna, the High King's bodyguard, fell under an enchantment caused by the Otherworld folk. Eadulf shivered slightly and was glad that their route would take them away from the sites of spirits and demons. Of course he had crossed the plain many times before with Fidelma, for that way lay the Fields of Honey, Cluain Meala, and on to the great Abbey of Lios Mór where they had had so many adventures. But today, at this dark time of year, with the nearness of Samhain, and aware of its equivalent in his own culture, the events that were unfolding made him feel that he would sooner not chance putting his faith to the test.

He found himself pulling a face, an expression of his guilt that he could even think that the old ways had validity compared to the new teachings that had come from the east in the form of the New Faith. He had logically rejected the old ways but the emotional acceptance was something else. He had been brought up accepting the gods and goddesses of his people: Hretha, god of the earth; Tiw, god of war; Thunor, god of thunder; and the most feared, Woden, with his two wolves and mighty horse with eight legs. Eadulf could recite their names even now, and knew the names of the spirits and demons under their command who laid traps for the unwary. Fidelma's people had also worshipped similar beings – so why should he feel guilty that some part of his mind could still believe in their existence and their capacity for evil?

He glanced furtively around but neither Fidelma nor Aidan seemed to have noticed the expressions that chased one another across his face.

The autumnal day had turned out bright. There were few clouds in the sky but the temperature was not warm, and now and then a cold breeze promised to turn into an icy wind later. They came to a division of the track. Eadulf knew that the left-hand path led through the woods towards Ráth na Drinne, the Place of Contentions, where there was a tavern run by Ferloga and his wife; this was a frequent resting place when they had passed on to Lios Mór or Cluain Meala. But now Fidelma was turning to lead the way towards the right, to the south-west, with the track steepening ahead of them.

They emerged through the trees on the northern side of a series of small hills and found themselves in countryside of open rocky land interspersed with brambles and thorns. There did not appear to be a suitable track through it. A small path was the only available route, and it forced their horses to go in single file. Here and there were deep gullies which they came upon so suddenly that, had their horses not been so sure footed, they would have stumbled into them and could have easily broken a leg.

'If Spelán was the drunk that he was reputed to be,' called Aidan from the rear of their procession, 'then it is a wonder he survived so long, coming this way after a night's drinking in Rumann's tavern.'

'Don't you have an old saying that the gods look after fools and drunks?' Eadulf asked, before realising he had used the plural 'gods' instead of the singular. But no one had noticed.

'He must have taken a lot of looking after, to be able to negotiate these paths in the dark,' Aidan grunted. 'Anyway, I cannot see any good ground for grazing sheep in this area except . . .'

His voice suddenly trailed off and Eadulf glanced round to see what was amiss. The warrior was staring at something further up the hill above them.

'What is it?' asked Eadulf.

'I thought I saw a figure up there – something black. It was moving behind the rocks on the ridge.'

Eadulf peered up. 'Well, there is nothing there that I can see. Maybe it was some animal, a wolf or something.'

Aidan grimaced. 'It was no wolf, friend Eadulf. It was a human figure standing watching us. When I saw them they must have ducked down behind a rock or the ridge. There is nothing up there now.'

Fidelma had halted and looked back enquiringly at them.

'Are you saying that someone is spying on us?' she asked.

Aidan shrugged. 'I saw what I saw, lady. There was a dark figure up there and now it has vanished.'

'I didn't see anything,' Eadulf admitted, as her eyes turned to him.

Fidelma sighed. 'Then it can be of no importance. People are naturally inquisitive if they see strangers in their territory. The sooner we press on, the sooner we can find the shepherd's cabin and see what we can discover. Then we can get back to Cashel before dark, for the days are short.'

She nudged her grey-white pony, Aonbharr – the 'supreme one' – forward and the animal responded immediately to her touch. Once more they moved off across the hillside, trying to find an easy path to ascend to the higher levels over the hill. However, Aidan continued to cast an occasional glance upwards. The northern slopes had given way to more pleasant stretches of a soft green sward, for the grassland here was clearly well attended by animal life. It seemed ideal for sheep, and even without the grazing flocks the sight that met their eyes was of small groups of rabbits and hares, who paused at their approach. Some scampered off while others, bolder, waited to ascertain if they were friend or foe. The sides of the hill at this point were precipitous, and it was only when they were moving over the shoulder of the hillside that they found that it was as rocky on the southern slopes with isolated trees and patches of thorn bushes as it had been when they began moving into the hills.

'That is more like shepherd's country,' observed Eadulf. 'But I can see why Della said that the approach was unfriendly. Would Spelán's cabin be situated on these rocky southern slopes?'

Fidelma did not answer for the moment. She had raised a hand to shield her eyes and was squinting across the broad shoulder of the hill to a rise some distance away.

'Those must be the standing stones that we were told of,' she said, indicating some dark shapes on the horizon, made silhouettes by the light sky behind.

'So that is the Hill of the Bullock,' Eadulf replied. 'Though on the slopes I can't see any cabins that might accommodate shepherds or herdsmen of any type.'

They moved on in silence for a while but Fidelma halted again to take stock of the terrain.

'Where to now, lady?' prompted Aidan.

'I suppose we must make for the standing stones for, if Della is correct, that will give us a point of advantage overlooking the northern and the southern slopes. Then we can see if there are signs of a shepherd's cabin nearby.'

'I don't see an alterative,' agreed Aidan, 'but the hillside is very deceptive. There appear to be many nooks and crevices in which an entire cabin could be hidden if constructed with cunning to take advantage of the areas providing natural wind-breaks. Let's hope we can . . .'

He suddenly stopped, staring up at the slopes above them. This time both Fidelma and Eadulf swung quickly round and peered in the same direction – but saw nothing. Aidan was scowling in frustration as he surveyed the empty hill.

'Just for a moment . . .' he said between clenched teeth. 'Just for a moment there, I thought I saw . . .'

'The dark shadow?' enquired Fidelma softly.

'I swear, lady, I saw the black figure of a human being again. You see that rock formation, near where those bushes are? The figure was right there – but as soon as I looked up, it vanished.'

Eadulf tried to conceal his nervousness by making light of the matter. 'If this is what happens to a warrior of the Golden Collar on this path in broad daylight, then I can't imagine what a drunken shepherd would be seeing on his way home at night.'

No one laughed. It was not really funny.

Fidelma appeared to be taking the matter more seriously than before. She knew perfectly well that Aidan was not given to fears and imagination. He was a trained warrior of her brother's élite guard. If he said he saw something – then he saw something. But who or what did he see?

'No use delaying,' she decided. 'Half a *cadar* of the day has been used up already, so we only have a full *cadar* before sunset is upon us. Let us move on again.'

To Eadulf, the way time was measured in Fidelma's world was very difficult to comprehend. The day was divided into four quarters, each one called a *cadar*. Because of the time between sunrise and sunset, the late autumn day consisted of only one and a half *cadar* of full daylight. But surely a full *cadar* would be time enough to achieve what they had set out to do? The sun was nowhere near its zenith. They could see its pale orb high up against a sky so colour-less that even the white clouds provided the darker hue.

The track now broadened and began a gentle swing to their left around the shoulder of the hill; as it did so, a new vista opened up. Fidelma realised that the hill was shaped almost like a horseshoe, with the standing stones on the far curve at a point where the hill descended gently north to the valley below, whereas the southern slopes continued to be precipitous and rocky.

They had arrived at a small, flat area where a waterfall-like brook was spilling down the hill, trickling across their stony path. It was not this that caused them to halt – the flow of water was too slight to cause a blockage to their path. It was the tall figure clad in black and seated on a boulder to one side, slightly above the pathway. The figure was a woman with long, black hair which shone even in the pale light of the autumn day. Around her was an ankle-length black cloak which fluttered in the breeze as if it had a life of its own. It, too, was of a dark sheen and it took Eadulf a moment to realise that the entire cloak was made out of ravens' feathers, all elaborately sewn in layers, one line over another. The blackness of the clothing the woman wore was reflected even in the eyes that bore into them: dark, and penetrating – but in themselves impenetrable. The face was pale, the bones almost protruding as the flesh stretched tight around them. It took the little group some moments before they realised that this apparition was actually smiling at them. It was not a smile of welcome but a mysterious smile of amusement.

When the woman finally spoke, the cadences were clear but with a softly menacing, almost musical quality to them.

'So, Fidelma of Cashel, daughter of the Eóghanachta, are we then well met?'

Behind her, Fidelma could hear Aidan, almost choking in his reaction.

'It's her!' he finally blurted out. 'That's the woman who claimed to be from Tech Duinn!'

CHAPTER FIVE

Fidelma studied the extraordinary woman for a moment or two. Apart from her strange appearance there was nothing supernatural about her, although she seemed to have exerted an intimidating effect on the young Aidan – and even Eadulf was looking a bit spooked. This, Fidelma realised, was an antagonist who should not be allowed to have the upper hand. The woman had made the first move, thereby seeking dominance. Fidelma, a good *fidchell* player, whose favourite board game was 'wooden wisdom', knew that she should make a counter move, to show that she was not overawed.

'Who are you, who appear to know my name?' she asked.

The dark-haired woman's smile broadened a little. 'Who would not know the name of the *dálaigh* whose reputation has spread through all the Five Kingdoms?'

'I am sure there are many.' Fidelma was not to be flattered. 'So you are . . .?'

'My name is Brancheó.'

'That means "raven mist". An interesting name. Where are you from?'

The woman chuckled, a sound without amusement in it. 'I am sure that young warrior,' she indicated Aidan, 'must have told you that. I am Brancheó of Tech Duinn.'

'A curious place to claim acquaintance with,' Fidelma commented dryly. 'The House of Donn, the old god of death.'

'The House of the Gatherer of Souls,' corrected the woman. 'Do gods or goddesses ever get old? Nevertheless, that is the name of my house.'

'Ah, just your house? Which is where?'

'I suppose it depends on what you want to believe.'

Fidelma examined the dark, deep-set eyes of the woman, searching carefully, for in spite of the smile on her lips, she could find no humour in the eyes, only a strange intensity of expression.

Aidan could restrain himself no longer.

'You've been following us,' he said accusingly.

'Have I?' Brancheó turned her black eyes upon him.

'You were seen a couple of times on the high ground above, seeming to keep parallel with our path,' Eadulf put in, feeling he should contribute to the exchange.

'So because of that fact you have deduced that I was following you? Could it not be that it was you who were following me?'

'That's ridiculous! We are on the way to . . .' Aidan began, and then stopped when he saw the look of disapproval from Fidelma.

'You were on your way to find the cabin of the shepherd whose body was discovered this morning,' the woman said, completing his sentence.

'How . . .?' Aidan blustered.

'You are well informed, Brancheó,' Fidelma interrupted.

'Do people not say that news travels fast, especially when there is an ale-keeper nearby?' Brancheó riposted, without answering the implied question.

'So, did Rumann give you this information?' demanded Eadulf.

Fidelma cast a withering glance in his direction and this time there seemed a genuine amusement on Brancheó's features.

'News of Spelán's death spread as quickly as the ravens can fly,' she remarked. 'As you well know, I went to Rumann and asked to see the body of Spelán.'

'How did you know of his death before you went to Rumann?' countered Fidelma. 'What was the shepherd to you?'

'It is given to my kind to know many things,' the woman replied.

'Your kind?'

'Those who have remained loyal to the Old Faith,' the woman responded imperturbably.

'You *were* following us!' snapped Aidan, before Fidelma could frame another question.

'I was following a track on the upper slope.'

'A route that you must have known well, in that it has allowed you to overtake us,' he returned.

'I am the raven-caller,' the woman said again, sneering at the angry young warrior. 'Perhaps I asked their help to speed me here?'

'Mind how you reply to these questions.' Aidan was losing his temper. 'You are speaking to a *dálaigh.*'

'Is that so? Just now I thought I was speaking to a frightened young warrior who does not know the paths and tracks that are adjacent to the very palace of the King whose life he is supposed to guard with his own. I believe the King would be well advised to place no reliance on such a youth, who has not troubled himself to become familiar with every inch of the territory that surrounds his King in order to protect him.'

Aidan flushed, his mouth tightening. Fidelma raised a hand to pacify him before turning to the strange woman.

'Brancheó, you will now address a *dálaigh,'* she said firmly. 'You are telling us that your journey along the pathway, which is parallel to the route we have taken, is in no way connected with our own?'

'I can only assure you that my journey does not have the same objective or purpose as your journey, *dálaigh,*' affirmed the woman, still in the same mocking tone.

'I shall accept that as the truth, for it will be easily demonstrated. Let me ask you this: you did know Spelán, didn't you?'

'Your assumption is correct.'

Fidelma paused, waiting for an amplification of the response and when it was not forthcoming, she said: 'So you went into Cashel to ascertain if the news of his death was correct?'

'That you already know, since you have been informed that I went to see his body at Rumann's tavern.'

'Let me remind you again, I am a *dálaigh*. Why did you utter a curse at the Samhain bonfire?'

'I will accept your role of *dálaigh* in that suspicion is a necessary adjunct to your profession. My answer is that I am Branchéo, the *fiachaire*; Branchéo, the raven-caller. I am the nemesis who will avenge Spelán's murder. On the feast of Samhain, certain people will stand exposed to the vengeance of the Otherworld.' There was a new note in the woman's voice: cold, malignant.

Fidelma's eyes narrowed. 'Are you making a threat, Branchéo?' she said sharply.

The woman's features relaxed back into a cynical smile.

'No threat, Fidelma of Cashel, descendant of Óengus son of Nad Fraoich, who accepted the New Faith on the very Rock on which his ancestors once worshipped in the old ways.'

'No threat?' The words came tumbling from Eadulf. 'A man has been ritually slaughtered just before the Samhain feast and you arrive claiming . . . claiming . . .' Words failed him. 'You claim that this is nothing to do with you although at the same time you claim to follow the old beliefs of your people.'

She turned her dark eyes on him with an almost sorrowful expression.

'Ease yourself, Eadulf, sometime *gerefa* of Seaxmund's Ham. In your true heart you know the old gods and goddesses well, for were you not led from their path when you were a youth? They are still with you and that is why you endeavour to exclude their truth as you labour under this New Faith.'

Eadulf was shocked into silence, suppressing a shiver of apprehension as he wondered how could this woman know so much?

Brancheó turned to Fidelma. 'Spelán's death *will* be avenged – and sooner rather than later.' She stood up. 'I will say this to you now, Fidelma, daughter of Failbhe Flann, sister of Colgú: Cashel was once the gateway to the Otherworld – if you doubt it, ask your mentor, old Conchobhar. On the eve of Samhain, the gate will once more stand ajar, the portal will be opened and the ancient deities will return to punish those who reject and ignore them. More importantly, those who slaughtered Spelán and tried to blame it on the Old Faith will be met with the wrath of those ancient deities that they have insulted. The Eóghanacht already have blood on their hands and the crime of betraying the old gods.'

Fidelma forced herself to laugh but she did not doubt the icy sincerity in the woman's voice.

'You are threatening us, in spite of your denial, Brancheó. To my mind, as a *dálaigh*, it sounds as though you are playing with the act of *tomaithem*, of issuing threats and intimidation by trying to conjure fear in those you threaten, which is in itself, the crime of *ómun*. Whether you have means to make the threats a reality or are just boasting, be careful that those threats are not turned against you.'

Brancheó was unfazed; she continued to maintain her mocking composure.

'Threats? I utter no threats. I have told you that I am a raven-caller – I merely make prognostications by the flight of the ravens. I have seen them circling above Cashel. I can only interpret what that portends.'

'I am perfectly aware that the raven is the symbol of the goddess of death and battles, Brancheó,' replied Fidelma firmly. 'I say that your words can be interpreted in no other way.'

'You are free to interpret what I say as you please. The responsibility of how you perceive things is your own, not mine. And now I will leave you to continue your journey as I have to continue mine.' With these words, Brancheó spun around and began to climb a steep path up the side of the hill, away from the track that they were following.

For a while the three of them sat unmoving, watching her agile form move rapidly upwards until she reached the brow of the hill and disappeared beyond it. Then Eadulf let out a slow, soft whistle.

'What manner of creature is that?'

Fidelma glanced at him and grinned. 'Certainly it is not one from the Otherworld.'

'She claimed to be a raven-caller, lady,' muttered Aidan.

'There are still some that have not embraced the New Faith. That you know well, Aidan. But she is harmless.'

'Harmless?'

'Did you not notice that she was talking about punishing those who murdered Spelán, making them pay for their crime? That means that she must have had some emotional tie with him which would have created the need to strike back. As for the vengeance of the old gods, she is not going to unleash the hordes of the Otherworld on us. We must deal with the entities in this world – and that threat is usually manmade.'

'What was that she said, about asking old Conchobhar?' Eadulf remembered.

'She claimed that Cashel was a portal to the Otherworld. I have not heard that before – I will ask him. Now, we have wasted too much time indulging in Brancheó's raven-calling fantasy, so I suggest we move on and see if we can find Spélan's cabin.'

'Even so,' Eadulf murmured, 'I wonder how she knew about me?'

'Dear Eadulf,' Fidelma smiled, 'you are as well known around Cashel as I am – or haven't you realised that?'

'That's true, friend Eadulf,' Aidan confirmed. 'When people speak of the lady Fidelma, they associate your name with hers – and thus it is known that you are from this place Seaxmund's Ham and that you were an hereditary lawgiver of your people. It would be easy for Brancheó to have picked up such information.'

Eadulf was not convinced but Fidelma was already moving off along the track and so he tagged reluctantly along.

'Aren't you worried about her going around freely?' he demanded.

'Why so? For what purpose should she be confined?' Fidelma replied.

'Because of her threats,' Eadulf said. 'She claims to be of the Old Faith and Spelán suffered the threefold death and . . .'

Fidelma silenced him with a glance. 'Her threats were open to interpretation even if I called them a breach of law. She merely claimed to interpret the circling of ravens; it was not about threatening specific individuals. She is more to be pitied than feared. But she obviously did have some kind of a connection with Spelán. I think we should wait for a more appropriate moment, when we are armed with more knowledge, to revisit our conversation with her.'

'Fair enough,' Eadulf agreed. 'If she is involved with something sinister, then leaving her to her own devices at this stage will allow her to have a false sense of security. I suppose there is something to the saying "Let the wicked fall into their own nets" – as a Psalm of David has it.'

They rode on in silence, and although Aidan was constantly twisting round in his saddle to ensure there was no sign of the woman following them, nothing interrupted them as they trotted under the brow of the hill, came to a rise and saw the circle of standing stones. In fact, now they were close, Fidelma saw that it was more an ellipse than a circle, some nine metres at its widest point. There were nine stones, some of which had toppled, either through soil erosion or by the efforts of man. In the centre was a stone of some dark quartz, which looked like an altar. It was a barren place, and now a cold wind had arisen and was whipping at them and whispering harshly across the rocky fingers.

Fidelma dismounted and the two men followed her example. While Aidan held the patient horses, Fidelma strode into the centre of the ancient stone monument and climbed onto the quartz altar.

'What are you doing?' demanded Eadulf in some concern. The stone circle was a sacred place; it must surely have been built to venerate the old deities and should either be shunned or treated with more respect. Coming in the wake of the threefold death of the murdered shepherd and then the appearance of the woman, Brancheó, he felt rattled and vulnerable.

Fidelma was standing peering round the countryside from her vantage-point.

'I am trying to see if there is any building resembling a shepherd's cabin or, indeed, any other building in the vicinity,' she answered impatiently.

'Be careful. That's probably an ancient pagan altar that you are standing on.'

'Doubtless,' she replied grimly. 'Strange, that this site is so close to Cashel and I did not know of it. I know more about distant places than this. I wonder why it was constructed in such an isolated area?'

'In that may lie the reason,' Eadulf said nervously. 'These circles are best constructed away from the sight of ordinary folk.'

Fidelma smiled. 'Sometimes, Eadulf, you make the most enlightening points.'

He regarded her with suspicion but she was not being sarcastic. She acknowledged that isolation was sometimes necessary in the pursuit of worshipping the old gods and goddesses. Anyway, she had completed her survey of the surrounding countryside and was focusing on one particular area.

'Can you see the shepherd's cabin?' he asked.

'I cannot,' she said slowly, 'but I can see the dark outlines of the top of what must be Ráth Cuáin, the abbey, on the next hill.'

Eadulf had also been examining the countryside around them. 'There is one thing that has been puzzling me,' he said.

'Which is?'

'If this was the area where Spelán allegedly grazed his flock of sheep, I wonder why we have seen no sign of them? Even if they have been taken to another pasture, there are no snatches of wool on the gorse and thorns, and no droppings scattered around.'

'I was wondering if you had noticed that,' was all Fidelma said, turning to survey the countryside again.

Eadulf felt disappointed when she made no further comment. It would not be the first time that Fidelma had disappeared into her own thoughts and speculations and failed to share them with him. But then she suddenly gave a sharp inward breath.

'I think I can see where it must be!' she exclaimed.

'The cabin?'

'Yes. It's quite a way down the slope towards the valley forest. Come up and I'll show you.'

Reluctantly, Eadulf clambered on to the sacred stone altar and followed the line of her outstretched hand.

'See? There is a small copse which would be the ideal place for a cabin to be built. It is sheltered from the winds, and it looks as if there is a stream running through it as well. For want of anything else more promising in the surrounding country, we shall try there.'

The place she pointed out was some distance down the hill, well below the gloomy silhouette of the Abbey of Ráth Cuáin. Eadulf could see a small area of dark evergreens that still had the appearance of summer in spite of the imminence of autumn.

'Yet there are no sheep around there either,' he noted, 'nor any sign of smoke from a fire to indicate habitation. As it is overlooked by the building that you say must be the abbey, perhaps we should go there first to make our inquiries?'

'No, let us find the cabin first,' Fidelma decided. She jumped down from the stone and hastened back to where Aidan was holding the horses.

'Come on, Eadulf,' she called impatiently.

But Eadulf remained on the top of the flat rock, his eyes screwed up in an attempt to improve his vision.

'Someone's going towards it,' he called back, when he was sure his eyes had not deceived him. 'They are climbing up from the valley towards that copse.'

'Is it Brancheó?' Fidelma asked, swinging back up to him.

'No, it's a man . . . ah, even from this distance I can see he's a woodsman by the clothes he wears and the axe he carries. I can see a wagon further down the hill, abandoned on a lower path.'

'From what direction is he coming?'

'From the forest in the valley below,' repeated Eadulf. 'I thought you said this was an isolated spot? What with that strange woman and now a woodcutter . . .'

The oncoming figure was ascending the hill at great speed but clearly with some physical exertion.

'That's interesting. He does seem to be heading towards the copse,' Fidelma agreed. Then she suddenly exclaimed, 'It's Curnan!'

'The woodsman responsible for the bonfire in Cashel?' asked Eadulf in surprise. 'We left him in Cashel. How did he get here?'

'That is what we shall go and find out,' Fidelma replied, turning to mount her horse.

By the time Eadulf had left the stone circle and reached his cob, Fidelma was already riding down the precipitous southern slope with all the skill she had as a horsewoman. Thankfully, there was another, less challenging zig-zag track down the hill, and Aidan had waited behind to help Eadulf in case he came into difficulty. Now he was beginning to catch up with her.

'I see a track below the hill, lady,' called Aidan. 'That must be another easier track from Cashel. He has a mule and a cart, so he must have driven here and left it to climb up to the copse on foot.'

The woodsman had been ascending the incline with his head down, a stout axe slung across his shoulders. So he did not see or hear them until they were almost on top of him.

'Greetings again, Curnan!' Fidelma called loudly.

The woodsman stopped dead and peered upwards, his eyes wide

in surprise as he saw the three riders. He stopped his ascent and stood waiting for them to approach.

'You've chosen a hard climb, my friend,' Fidelma said by way of greeting. 'What are you after – not more wood for your bonfire?'

Curnan seemed to recover himself.

'True, it's a difficult way if you have a cart and an ass, lady,' he replied, as they halted before him and dismounted.

'There is an easier track for horses and carts further over there,' Fidelma said. Her eye had missed little when examining the area from the ancient stone circle. 'Why didn't you bring your cart up that way?'

'Because it leads to the abbey and one can be observed from its walls.'

'Why would you want to avoid being seen from the abbey? In fact, what are you doing here, Curnan? I thought you had to finish preparing the great Samhain fire for tomorrow night.'

'This is the territory of the Sítae, lady. My territory, lady – I told you so before. I was born in those same woods below here. The great fire needs logs and that is why I am out and about with my cart.'

Fidelma smiled sceptically. 'I can understand you collecting wood from the forest below, but up on these bare stretches of hill there is not much to be gathered, especially by a man who has left his cart below.'

Curnan looked uncertain for a moment and then he shrugged. 'I was just . . . just scouring the hillside to see what I could see.'

'There's not much *to* see – apart from that little copse along the path here. The few trees there look like evergreens, so they wouldn't be any use for the bonfire, even if you could cut them down and get them single-handedly to your cart down there.'

This time, Curnan was at a loss for words.

'I don't suppose that copse disguises the location of Spelán's cabin?' Fidelma pressed. 'Is that why you didn't want to be observed from the abbey, approaching it with your cart and mule?'

'Spelán's cabin?' Curnan echoed stupidly, and only succeeded in sounding guilty.

'You told me that you grew up here. Spelán is dead – and you also told me that Caoimhe, his wife, is dead.'

'Then why would I be going there?' blustered the woodsman.

Fidelma gave a thoughtful sigh. 'Oh, there might be many reasons. Perhaps you wanted something from the cabin?'

'Why would I want anything from the cabin? I was not a friend of Spelán.'

'But you knew his wife, Caoimhe, didn't you?'

'Yes – but as I told you, Caoimhe died before the summer months,' the man almost snarled.

'So perhaps you came to look at what might be salvaged if the place was empty?'

'That is not true!' the man said heatedly.

'I am sorry if I have misconstrued your presence here, Curnan,' Fidelma said in a pleasant tone. 'But you must admit that your explanation is hard to believe.'

'It is the only one I have,' he returned sourly.

'How well did you really know Caoimhe and Spelán?' Her voice became stern.

'As told you, I was raised in the woods below. When Spélan came to the territory he managed to ingratiate himself with Caoimhe. She was a local girl and he took to herding her sheep. I would see him from time to time, especially when he went to Cashel to get drunk. I had no reason to like him but none to kill him. Caoimhe possessed little, but she did have sheep. That was good enough for Spelán.' Curnan cleared his throat before admitting, 'All right, I did come here to see what I could scavenge before the news spread and others came.'

'Then it is fortunate that we met you before you reached his cabin, Curnan,' Fidelma said coldly. 'Had you scavenged anything, as you said was your intent, then you might have been facing serious charges of theft. I suggest that you return to your cart and be on your way. Your duty is to the bonfire in Cashel.'

Curnan hesitated, as if he would argue, but he caught the fiery glint in Fidelma's eye and turned to begin to make his way back down the hill towards his cart and ass.

Aidan was about to say something but Fidelma shook her head at him.

'Leave him. We can question him later after we have gained a better knowledge of this Spelán, his wife Caoimhe, and his habits.'

'Then we had best continue to examine Spelán's cabin before night catches up with us,' Eadulf agreed, glancing up at the sky.

'You are right, Eadulf,' she said briefly. 'At least we now know that the cabin is in that copse. Let us hope that we will find some answers to this mystery.'

Aidan did not look happy at allowing Curnan to depart unhindered but he remounted his horse and moved off, insisting on leading the way.

It must have been the angle of the hill and the way the path twisted because Eadulf, looking back up the hill, now saw the abbey building perched on the summit towering above them. It rose, as forbidding as a fortress. The building bore not the slightest resemblance to an abbey. As he stared up, he realised how uneven the slopes of the hill were as, when they moved further south, he saw little areas that were like stretches of cliff.

He called Fidelma's attention to it.

'Well, we were told that Ráth Cuáin was originally the fortress of the local chieftain,' she replied. 'It certainly looks as if it is still more fortress than abbey.'

'It is strange that we could not see it from the vantage point we had from the east,' Aidan said.

'It is to do with the geography of the hills,' Fidelma explained. 'A good way to keep it hidden until you are almost on top of it. Curnan must have known the geography well, to be able to keep out of sight.

Also, that position protects it from any incursion from the great river. Well, it is not our concern now. Let's find out about this cabin.'

'Speaking of curiosities, I have said it before and will repeat myself now: I find it strange that there are still no signs of a sheep flock,' Eadulf said.

They were now entering the small grove, where the evergreens produced both shelter and darkness.

'Look!' Aidan pointed. 'You were right, lady. There *is* a cabin among the trees.'

'But no sign of smoke or animals in the vicinity,' Eadulf said.

'Which is to be expected, if both occupants are dead,' Fidelma replied.

They reined in their horses and examined the surroundings. Everything was quiet except for the soft gurgling of a small brook easing its way across the pebbles as it meandered down the hill, and the chatter of birds among the trees. They could also hear the soughing of a chill wind fluttering through the branches, picking up the few remaining autumnal leaves, sending them spinning this way and that way, eventually to the ground.

'This is too quiet, lady,' Aidan said apprehensively. 'I have a bad feeling about it.'

'If this is where Spelán and his wife dwelled, then it is certainly deserted now, and I would have said it has been so for some time,' Eadulf said.

'Let us dismount,' Fidelma ordered. 'Aidan, you stay here with the horses. Eadulf and I will go into the cabin to see if it is deserted.'

Immediately Aidan began to protest but she quickly waved him to silence, so he slid from his mount, taking the proffered reins from her and Eadulf.

The cabin did not lie far among the shelter of the trees. What surprised Eadulf was the fact that it was constructed mainly of stone. He had expected to find a typical wooden logger's construction. It was a squat affair, covered with a heavy rotting thatch that should have been repaired many seasons before. Indeed, the entire appearance of the place was one of neglect and abandonment; it was dirty and unloved. There were a few rusty tools lying around the place. There was but one aperture that served as a window; a single board, usually closed to shut out the chill of the night, hung lopsidedly from a loose hinge. They noticed that the once stout wooden door, now decaying with the inclement weather, was standing ajar.

As they approached more closely, Eadulf suddenly pointed. Lying partway across the threshold was the carcass of a dog.

'That's been freshly killed,' he declared.

Fidelma agreed that he was right. Although the blood was dry there was no sign yet of the animal decomposing nor that any scavengers had, as yet, begun to mutilate it. Fidelma estimated that it had probably lain there for no more than a day or two. Had it been there longer then it would have attracted the attention of wolves or foxes or even the crows or ravens in search of an easy meal.

'I presume this was Spelán's sheepdog,' Fidelma said grimly.

'Do you think that whoever killed him and his dog made off with the flock of sheep? Is that why we have seen nothing of them?' Eadulf asked.

Fidelma was looking grave. 'I am now more concerned with finding out more about Spelán and the wife who is reported to be dead. We will search inside the cabin.'

Before Eadulf could protest or bid her be wary, she had pushed open the door and stepped over the slaughtered animal.

chapter six

The stench that met them as they entered was so strong that it caused Fidelma to catch her breath and cough. There was little light in the place but enough for Eadulf to notice a candle lying on a side table. A small box lay obligingly nearby and proved to be ready with flint and steel, constituting the *tenlach-teined* or kindling gear as the tinder box was called. Eadulf set to work but he was no expert and, after a few moments, Fidelma took it from his hands and quickly achieved a spark, causing the small cluster of dried leaves and tinder to catch and from that she was able to light the candle.

The couple turned to survey the interior of the cabin. Its shadowy interior revealed little out of the ordinary except that it was barely furnished. There was only one room with a hearth at one end where dusty cooking pots and a spit seemed long abandoned. A wooden bed was at the other end of the room, along with a rotting chest. A shepherd's crook was balanced against one wall. It, too, looked long abandoned.

Fidelma stood in one spot, holding the candle high and turning in a full circle, her eyes searching into every corner.

Eadulf was shaking his head sadly. 'Well, if this was Spelán's cabin, there is certainly no trace of a woman having lived here,' he said. 'At least, not recently. That would confirm that his wife has been dead some time.'

'You are right, Eadulf. It is as if this place was used by an old homeless itinerant who has long since abandoned any pretence to domesticity.'

'Wasn't that more or less what he was, according to Della – or what he became? Spelán doesn't sound like someone who had any admirable qualities of any sort.'

'Bran
cheó indicated that she knew him – but in what way? If she came here on a regular basis, she certainly didn't help him to put the place to rights.'

'True. I suppose we can be certain that this was Spelán's cabin?'

'There is no reason to doubt it,' Fidelma confirmed. 'I'll even go so far as to say that he was killed here before the body was taken to the bonfire in Cashel.'

At this Eadulf pulled a wry expression. 'That is going too far, surely?'

For an answer, Fidelma pointed to the wooden bed. 'I'll take you even further. He was tied to that bed – and it was there that his hair was cut into a tonsure and his head was shaven, in order to give him the appearance of a religieux.'

'What?' Eadulf gulped – and then he noticed the strands of hair that lay on the bed and beside it.

'You will also see the dark stains of blood. They are not old. If you bend closely to the wood you will smell an odour.'

Eadulf sniffed. 'The aroma of lavender – but it is very faint.'

'I believe that he was killed yesterday and taken overnight to Cashel to be discovered this morning.'

Eadulf glanced at her. 'So it was deliberate. You are definitely sure now that it was not just to hide the body?'

'If his killers – for I believe more than one person was involved – wanted him hidden then they had plenty of time and many places to do it round here, rather than transport him all the way to the town square. You yourself have said that the aperture into which he was placed was carefully made – but not so carefully closed. This was deliberate. I am positive they wanted the body to be discovered.'

'But . . .'

She held up a hand. 'Please don't say "why?". That is for us to discover.'

'How can you be sure that he was tied to the bed?'

'That's easy enough. Remember the rope-burn marks on the wrists and ankles? See where ropes have rubbed against the sides of the wooden boards, and the discoloration there speaks of bloodstains.'

'So how would you reconstruct what was done?'

'How was his death carried out?' Fidelma glanced around before turning back to him. 'I think the first blow was to the back of his head, to knock him out. Because of the condition of the wrists and ankles and the shaving of the head, I think he was struck unconscious first. He was then brought in here and tied to the bed. It was then that he regained consciousness and struggled. You saw the burn marks on his wrist and ankles where he fought against the bonds. The killer then gave him a rough tonsure. After that, the second and fatal blow was struck on the head. He was untied and dressed in the religious robes before the brutal ritual was completed: he was stabbed through the heart and his throat was cut.'

'So that is why there was so little effusion of blood.' Eadulf was thoughtful. 'He was already dead when the throat was cut.'

'Just so.'

'But surely the dog might have done something to protect its master? Did they kill it and leave it out there?'

'Most likely the dog was shut out when the attack happened, and when the killers opened the door to leave, the dog tried to enter and was slain. That would explain why the dog is partly lying inside the door and its skull is smashed.

'If the second blow on the back of Spelán's head was what killed him, and everything else was done to him afterwards, that raises a point. The door was shut and the dog was outside. It could mean that the killers were known to Spelán, who invited them in and shut the dog out himself. Then, as he turned his back, he was struck down from behind.'

'A good point. Spelán certainly had to have his back to whoever struck that first blow. His killers were most certainly known to him, and trusted. The shepherd can have had no suspicion of what they intended to do.'

Eadulf was silent for a moment or so. Then he said, rather bleakly, 'It also brings up another conclusion.'

Fidelma smiled thinly. 'Which is?'

'That we would have to rule Curnan out of this affair.'

'Because?'

'Because Curnan would not have volunteered information about the expertise in which the aperture in the bonfire was created and thus drawn attention to himself as an expert woodsman. Why would he take the body all the way into Cashel? Also, would all this ritual of the threefold death have entered a woodsman's mind?'

'Not entirely conclusive, Eadulf. He may have done it and wanted the body to be found. I think it is too early to rule the woodsman out until we have more information.'

Eadulf gestured round the empty cabin. 'That seems to be our difficulty. I see no way of gathering any information here. True, we have found where Spelán was killed and in what manner. We have also learned that he probably ingratiated himself with this local woman, Caoimhe, and hence became a shepherd. I suppose we need to find out more about her. It is not beyond belief that there was some family grudge against him. We know that he drank heavily during the summer and no one really liked him. But why kill the fellow? Why was it done in some old pagan ritual of execution and why was he dressed as a religieux? As you say, by placing the body in Cashel, the killers must have known he would eventually be identified.'

'There are many questions, Eadulf,' Fidelma agreed. 'And those are the questions to which we must begin to seek answers.'

'But where do we start?'

'We have started already. As you said, we have found the cabin where he was murdered, and now we must find someone who knew his wife and her background. We know her name was Caoimhe and that she was of this local clan, the Sítae. We can question Curnan again – but I would like to hear more from other members of this clan.'

'So we continue by seeking the nearest habitation to this place and attempting to find someone who knew Spelán's wife, her family or other information,' summed up Eadulf.

'Exactly.' Fidelma blew out the candle and went to the door, stepping over the carcass of the dog.

'Shouldn't we do something about . . .?' Eadulf indicated the animal with a thrust of his jaw.

'Best let nature take care of the disposal in its own way,' Fidelma called over her shoulder, hastening along the path.

Aidan was standing holding the reins of their horses. 'You have been some time. What news?'

'That was where Spelán was killed,' Eadulf told him. 'There was little else there but a shepherd's crook and a dead sheepdog.'

Aidan looked disappointed. 'Then we have had a journey for nothing.'

Fidelma shook her head. 'For nothing? We are still investigating, Aidan. We are now going to seek information about Spelán's wife.'

'And where do we start with that?' asked Aidan, echoing what Eadulf had previously asked in the cabin.

'Find the nearest habitation.'

'What about asking at the abbey?' Aidan motioned up the hill with his free hand.

'I'd prefer talking to someone unconnected with the abbey first,' Fidelma replied. 'There is a track along the side of the copse leading down towards the forest. It looks as though it has been used, albeit infrequently. We'll follow it, as tracks always lead to dwelling places.'

Eadulf was examining the sky and Fidelma saw his expression.

'Don't worry,' she smiled. 'There is still enough daylight left to us before we have to turn for home.'

'But we are spending a lot of time on this search when we thought it would be quick and easy. What if we can't get back before night-fall?' he protested.

'Then we will have to make do the best we can. The fact that tomorrow is the night of Samhain should not curtail our search. We have this shepherd killed in a manner that is associated with the old pagan beliefs and we have a woman naming herself "raven-caller", pronouncing an ancient curse on Cashel and seeking revenge for his death. Already people are frightened. You could see it in their eyes as we rode through Cashel this morning.'

'Are you saying that all this was merely meant to scare the people?' Eadulf asked.

'I am saying that it would be good if we had some explanation before tomorrow's bonfire and feasting.'

They mounted their horses and, with Fidelma on Aonbharr confidently leading, they left the little wooded area and trotted down the hill. The track eventually came to the edge of a great stretch of forest which Fidelma knew was bordered by the mighty River Siúr. North of the swathe of woodland was the main track that she had always used to cross at the Ford of the Ass and thence travel on to Ara's Well, and beyond to the great Abbey of Imleach where the Blessed Ailbe had first brought the word of the New Faith to the kingdom of Muman. The forest she had often skirted around and did not know well, but she felt sure that there should be at least some isolated habitations among the trees.

In fact, the first indication that people lived hereabouts was from the distant sound of wood being chopped.

Aidan halted, head to one side, listening.

'The sound is coming from over that way, lady,' he called, pointing.

'Very well, let's see who is making it,' she said.

Aidan took the lead, and they soon found themselves following a small path, just wide enough for one horse at a time. They proceeded in line. The sound of the axe cutting into wood became louder and louder until they emerged into a large clearing among the tall oaks of the forest.

A wooden cabin dominated one side of the clearing; before it was an open fire, over which a cauldron hung. A plump, fair-haired woman was stirring something in it and steam was gently rising, sending an aroma of stewing rabbit and vegetables across the clearing to arouse their hunger. There were some outhouses and pens for animals, from which came the satisfied grunting of pigs, a protesting bleat of a goat and clucking of hens. On the other side of the clearing, a tall, muscular man, stripped to the waist, was working with a will, his torso sweating as he swung his axe against wood that he seemed intent on splitting into logs for the fire. A tall wolfhound was rising to its feet with a soft growl as it detected the newcomers. The woman looked up and saw them.

'Torcán!' she called in warning.

The man halted in his action and stood feet apart, the axe balanced in both hands diagonally across his chest. His dark hair was streaked with grey and his skin, under the gleam of sweat, was weatherbeaten. In many ways he was the image of Curnan, albeit with more resolutely set and handsome features. He barked a quick order to the hound and the beast re-seated itself but remained vigilant, watching the newcomers intently as if waiting for the next order.

'Welcome, strangers – if you come in peace,' the man called with a not unpleasant, melodious tone.

Fidelma eased her horse forward a few paces. 'Why would we not come in peace?' she replied with a frown.

'I see a man who is a professional warrior with you.'

'Would you fear a warrior?'

'It depends on his intention. We often see the warriors hired by our chieftain who come to demand the tributes due to him. I say, a curse on all warriors!'

'Warriors *hired* by your chieftain?' Fidelma caught the inflection on the word. 'Are you of the clan Sítae and doesn't your chieftain have a right to call on the clan to serve him as warriors when the need arises?'

'Yes, I am of the Sítae. Why do you ask?' The man was suspicious, regarding them with narrowed eyes and the axe still held ready across his chest.

'I presume that I am in the territory of that clan,' Fidelma responded. She noticed that the woman was standing upright at the cooking cauldron, her body tense. 'Know that I am Fidelma of Cashel. I am a *dálaigh* and you need fear no injustice from me. My companion bears the symbol of the Nasc Niadh, the Golden Collar, and is bodyguard to my brother, Colgú, the King. My other companion is my husband, Eadulf.'

At this the tall man put down his axe while the plump woman now came bustling forward.

'Lady, forgive us. The name of Fidelma is well known for truth and justice, as is her husband, Eadulf the Saxon.'

Eadulf gave a soft groan. 'The Angle,' he corrected quietly, almost to himself.

'Welcome, lady, welcome.' The tall man's features were creased in a friendly smile. 'Get you down and let us offer you such poor hospitality as we can.'

Fidelma swung down from her horse with an answering smile.

'And you are?' she asked.

'I am Torcán, a woodsman in this forest. And this is my wife Éimhín. Éimhín, fetch us beakers of cider, so that these good folk may quench the thirst that is surely upon them from their journey.'

The woodsman waved them across to logs that provided seats by the cabin, near the fire. When they had sat and taken their first sips of cider, according to the ritual of hospitality, only then did Fidelma broach the subject of their search.

'You made an interesting choice of words just now,' she began. 'You said that your chieftain hired warriors.'

'That is so. They are mercenaries.' The word he used was *deorad*, which meant outsiders from other clans or territories.

'Your chieftain must surely have his own clansmen to serve him. Why does he have to bring in outsiders?' Fidelma was surprised. 'He must seek consent from the clan council for doing so?'

Torcán's bitter smile answered her question. She decided to leave the subject for a while. For a few moments she chatted lightly about the quality of the cider before she turned to her main purpose and spoke more seriously.

'I suppose you know most of the people who dwell hereabouts, Torcán?'

The tall man gestured to his cabin. 'I was born in this cabin, as was my father before me and my father's father. There is little I do not know of the folk who live around here. My wife was also born and bred on the banks of the great river not far from here. We are both of the clan Sítae.'

Fidelma was examining his features as he spoke and the thought came to her. 'Are you related to Curnan, who is also a woodsman?'

Torcán pulled a wry face. 'What has he been up to? He is my younger brother.'

'I thought there was a resemblance. I hope he has not been up to anything. Have you seen him recently?'

'Not since he was given the task of building the big bonfire in Cashel township. We are not close. He has his own cabin in the forest but nearer to Cashel. One of my sons is working with him, clearing and cutting back the road to the Ford of the Ass.'

'Tell me, do you know the shepherd called Spelán?'

At once a frown crossed the pleasant features of the woodsman and Fidelma saw that his wife, Éimhín, also looked unhappy.

'Would to God I could deny knowledge of him, lady,' the woodsman said grimly. 'I swear that he was a scion of the Fómorii, so bent and evil is his outlook on life.'

Fidelma glanced at Eadulf, but she knew that he would understand the reference to the undersea dwellers who were regarded in the ancient legends of her people as misshapen creatures who epitomised evil.

'You obviously do not like the man,' she observed.

'I avoid him and I have told my wife and my sons to do the same. What is it that a daughter of Cashel seeks with that spawn of . . .' The woodsman halted, seeing his wife's look of disapproval.

'Spelán is dead,' explained Fidelma bluntly.

Torcán did not appear surprised. 'I suppose it was the drink that carried him off? And not before time either.'

'No. He was murdered. The body was found in Cashel . . . it was hidden within the very bonfire that your brother Curnan had built.'

There was no disguising the shock of both Torcán and his wife.

'You are not telling us that Curnan killed him?' Torcán finally asked hoarsely.

'Is there any reason why he would do so?'

'Everyone has quarrelled with Spelán at one time or another. He was that sort of person. Vain, drunk and argumentative. There were even rumours that he was a thief.'

Éimhin was troubled. 'You will find out sooner or later, lady, that Curnan once felt he had prospects with the woman who became Spelán's wife.'

'But Curnan would not strike him unless it was in self-defence – and Spelán was ever a coward who would never dare to physically provoke another man. His level of violence was in abusing his poor wife.'

'His wife, Caoimhe?' Fidelma asked at once. 'We are told she died. Do you know how?'

'Caoimhe died of a fever during the month of the brindled cow,' Éimhín said sadly.

'Nearly eight months ago?' asked Eadulf, translating the term *laethanta na riabhaiche.*

'Perhaps we should start with what you can tell us about Spelán,' Fidelma invited.

'Little enough is known.' Torcán gave what appeared to be the standard answer to the question. 'He was not of our clan, you see. He arrived here two years ago, perhaps a little less. There were whispers that he had fled his own clan territory because he'd done some wrong.'

'Spelán was supposed to be a shepherd from the northern mountains,' Éimhin added. 'Or so he claimed when he came here.'

'You doubted it?' Eadulf asked, picking up the inflection in her voice.

'When we first encountered him,' Torcán answered for them both, 'I noted that his hands were not those of a shepherd but of someone who had worked in quarries with stone or metal. You can tell a lot by a person's hands.'

'The flock of sheep that he herded therefore belonged to Caoimhe, his wife?'

'I know nothing of legal things, lady. The rumour is that when Caoimhe died he sold the entire flock to the abbey at Ráth Cuáin. At least, those travelling across the hillside during the summer saw no sign of the sheep grazing on their usual pasture. He must have received some payment for the flock, for my brother told me that he had spent a great deal in the tavern in Cashel over the past few weeks.'

'But the flock would not have been his to sell,' pointed out Fidelma. 'If he was a stranger from another clan, even a marriage does not automatically imply ownership of goods belonging to a wife unless some agreement is made with the wife's kin. Who were they, do you know?'

Torcán and Éimhín exchanged a quick glance. 'She had no immediate kin,' Éimhín said. 'I counted her a friend before Spelán arrived here.'

'Then you will be able to help me with what I need to know,' pressed Fidelma. 'Can you describe her?'

The plump woman inclined her head thoughtfully. 'She was a moody sort of person and did not mix well with local people.'

'But you indicated that Curnan had prospects of marriage with her at one time?'

Torcán frowned in annoyance. 'That was a long time ago and nothing came of it,' he said quickly. 'The fact is, she was not interested in him.'

'But she fell for this stranger, Spelán. That must have made your brother bitter?'

'My brother is not the kind of man to harbour bitterness,' protested Torcán. 'Nor was she the sort who would have made a suitable wife for a woodsman. She was too frail.'

Fidelma turned to Éimhín. 'Anything else?'

'There is little to tell,' replied Éimhín hurriedly, perhaps regretting that she had incurred the disapproval of her husband. 'She was the daughter of Boirche. He is now dead, of course. He was a *bóchaill*, a keeper of cows, along the great river banks.'

'Cows? Not sheep?' interrupted Eadulf.

'A *bóchaill*, not an *aedhaire*, a shepherd,' said the woman. 'He was a man of substance but the family were wiped out by the terrible Yellow Plague some years ago. Only his daughter, Caoimhe, survived. She had no immediate kin and so the chieftain of our clan stepped forward to administrate what was left for her.'

'What was the social status of Caoimhe's father?' Fidelma asked.

'A *saerchéile* – a free man of the clan,' Torcán replied proudly. 'As am I.'

'And the chieftain being . . .?' queried Eadulf.

'At that time? It was Tanaide.'

'And where is Tanaide's dwelling?'

'He is now many years dead,' Torcán said. 'Our chieftains are also the Abbots of Ráth Cuáin. The chieftain is now his son, Abbot Síoda.'

Fidelma was surprised. 'So the current abbot, Abbot Síoda, is also your chieftain?'

'That is so.'

'It is strange that I have never heard of him and know little about this abbey and its community, yet both are so close to Cashel,' Fidelma mused and not for the first time.

'Ráth Cuáin has always been the fortress of our chieftains, even after it became an abbey. I remember the stories of how my grandfather's father was said to have helped repair it and cut the timbers for it,' replied Torcán.

'And what manner of man is this abbot who is your chieftain?' Fidelma asked. 'You mentioned that he sends mercenary warriors to collect tribute from you.'

'I have never seen him. Even when I take a cartload of wood up to the abbey gates, the only person I see is the *aistreóir*, the gatekeeper, Brother Tadhg. Tadhg is a surly, taciturn man. If Abbot Síoda is anything like the gatekeeper, then I do not wish to know him. Oh, I have sometimes seen the new herbalist, Sister Fioniúr, when I deliver logs to the abbey. At least she is pleasant and friendly. Usually, it is the chieftain's warriors who come demanding tribute.'

'You appear to be resentful?'

Torcán shrugged. 'Abbot Síoda expects the tributes and homage due to him. That is his right. But in return he does not take on the responsibilities and duties that are the mark of such an office.'

'Why haven't you made representations to the Chief Brehon if you believe he is not fulfilling the duties of a chieftain according to the law? Cashel is less than a morning's ride away – indeed, within a comfortable day's walking distance if you have no horse. Your brother Curnan appears to be in the township frequently. You could bring complaints before the King's Brehon there.'

'And what would they do? Síoda, as I say, is not only chieftain but Abbot of Ráth Cuáin. He claims the protection of the Faith as well as of his mercenary warriors. The abbey is like a fortress.'

Fidelma regarded the woodsman seriously for a moment. 'Do you mean to say that these mercenaries are permanently quartered in the abbey?' she asked incredulously.

'Abbey or fortress, it is the same thing. He has a score of riders, professional warriors. They live in the abbey and ride out to collect tribute for him. They serve Síoda alone, and have no commitment to local people.'

'I see. It seems we will have to have a word with Abbot Síoda on two accounts,' Fidelma said. 'Firstly, about Caoimhe and Spelán. Secondly, about his conduct as chieftain of the Sítae. As chieftain he has the right to maintain a band of warriors, nor is it unusual for a chieftain to employ mercenaries. Yet, as you say, Torcán, with rights come obligations of office.'

But Torcán was shaking his head. 'Lady, I think you will find it hard even to see him. He went on a pilgrimage to Rome during the summer. We hear he has returned, but apparently has now incarcerated himself behind the high walls of the abbey; invisible to us all. When he wants his presence felt among the clan, he just sends out his warriors.'

'It sounds more like a fortress under siege than a house of religion,' muttered Eadulf.

'That is exactly what it is,' agreed Éimhin. 'Many of the brethren and sisters there are not local folk either. Remember that strange religieux who came wandering through here a few days ago?' Éimhín turned to her husband. 'I didn't like him. He was demanding and rude.'

Fidelma addressed her. 'Was he from this Abbey of Ráth Cuáin?'

Torcán addressed. 'No, he was from some Abbey in the south

and on his way to Cashel. But I was sure he came from the direction of our abbey, although he claimed that he had missed the main track. I don't suppose he meant to be rude; it was just because he was in a dishevelled state.'

'Having to spend a night or two in the open is no excuse for discourtesy, especially from one who claims to be a scholar of the Faith,' Éimhín said in a brittle tone.

'He told you he was a scholar?'

'Not exactly.'

'What made you think that he was?' queried Fidelma with interest.

'Because he carried one of those *taig liubhair*, you know – a leather book satchel. Only scholars walk around with books. He asked Torcán here the best route to Cashel.'

Fidelma realised that the wanderer had probably been one of those scholars her brother had mentioned, who had come to attend the small council in Cashel.

'I just want to clarify some matters relating to Caoimhe,' Eadulf said to Éimhin, returning to the subject of their inquiry. 'You say her father and his family were wiped out by the Yellow Plague, leaving only the chieftain to administer things for her.'

'That is so. The land she grazed her flock on was under the control of the abbey, of course.'

'So what was her portion of the property?'

'Precious little. Síoda, as chieftain, claimed it all.'

'How did Spelán come to marry her? You say that she had absolutely no family to support her.'

'After the devastation of the Yellow Plague, and being left without kin, I would say Caoimhe was very vulnerable to anyone who showed her kindness. She needed help with her flock and Curnan was no shepherd but a woodsman. At that time Spelán came wandering through this territory. He saw his opportunity and somehow persuaded Caoimhe to take him as her partner . . .'

Torcán carried on: 'He was an unscrupulous man who saw her

situation and decided to grab what he could. I tell it as I see it, lady. I did not like the man.'

'No one did, lady,' Éimhín added. 'We all came to believe that he was a *deorid cóid* . . . an exile of cup and pillow.'

'A man on the run, wanted for crimes,' Fidelma explained when Eadulf seemed puzzled by the meaning of the colloquial term. Then she turned back to the couple. 'What made you think that?'

'It was the way he kept himself to himself, never mixed with or befriended those in this community. He even walked over the hills into Cashel whenever he felt the urge to get drunk, which was often, rather than risk letting something slip to local people when drink might make him let down his guard.'

'You said that he persuaded Caoimhe to take him as her partner. Does that imply that they were not married?'

'I could not vouch for it. Of course, in the early stage they could have simply declared the trial of a year and a day . . .'

Eadulf stirred uneasily for he knew the custom and it was precisely what he and Fidelma had done.

'I saw Caoimhe rarely after Spelán moved in with her,' Éimhin said. 'When I did, I asked her why there had been no celebration locally and she told me that they had been married in the abbey – but I think she lied.' Éimhín looked sad. 'I saw Spelán drunk; I saw Caoimhe with bruises and working harder than she should. I think she was intimidated by him.'

'So Spelán either married or became partner with Caoimhe and ran the flock on the slopes of these hills. They lived always in the cabin there?'

'In the little copse,' Éimhin nodded. 'Caoimhe ceased to mix with her former friends and neighbours.'

'Are you sure that Caoimhe never complained?'

'My wife has told you,' Torcán said. 'Those who did see her noticed that she was unhappy. I believe it was when she realised that Spelán was over-indulgent in drink. Yet she continued to provide him with the means to indulge, and so the flock gradually diminished through lack of care.'

'Separation and divorce are allowed in our laws,' Fidelma said in a flat tone. She was tired of those who entered marriage without knowing the matrimonial laws. 'There are seven causes for separation. For example, did he denigrate her to people around here, did he strike her, or indeed, if she did not receive what she desired from her husband, all such things may rightfully be given as grounds for separation or divorce. Similarly, there are the same number of reasons for immediate divorce. Why didn't she rid herself of the man if he was proving such a disappointment and making her morose and isolated in this manner?'

'I say again,' Éimhin intervened, 'I am sure he bullied her to the point of making her afraid of him.'

'So that was why she stayed.'

'Who knows what was in her mind! She was not a young woman and had never been married before, having stayed at home to look after her father when he was widowed. She only had his example to guide her in dealings with men.'

'Did Spelán ever express any religious thoughts?' Eadulf suddenly asked. 'Any views either of the Faith or, indeed, of the old ways and beliefs.'

Éimhín and Torcán stared at him curiously.

'Spelán?' Torcán snorted. 'His only faith was in the juice of the barley. That's a strange question to ask, Brother Eadulf.'

'I doubt that he had any interest in such matters, Brother Eadulf,' Éimhin said more respectfully. 'Spelán had no faith save in what he could lay his hands on.'

'In that case, you have given us a sad picture of a couple with no friends,' Fidelma observed. 'A stranger, without means or profession, who arrived in this territory and probably tricked a decent woman into taking him in because she desperately needed a bit of kindness and support.'

'A fair assessment,' Torcán nodded. 'But with the addition that he was a drunk who, by all accounts, beat his wife, exploited her by stealing what few possessions she had, and was not beyond engaging in anything illegal to make money.'

Fidelma regarded him with interest. 'In what way? Was it robbery?'

Torcán chuckled dryly. 'I can believe many things about him, but Spelán had no appetite for anything that might lead him to confrontation. As I said before, the man was a coward. He was more likely to be a sneak thief – the sort to steal a sheep in the dead of night when no one was about.'

Éimhín suddenly rose, pointing to the sky through the entwined branches of the surrounding trees. 'It is well beyond the sun's zenith, so we are approaching the third *cadar* of the day. We would take it as an honour if you would accept our hospitality. Our meal is frugal, a stew of rabbit and the vegetables offered by the forest.'

Eadulf had followed the woman's pointing hand, and now stared upwards through the forest canopy. Even if it had not obscured the sky, he knew the dark clouds of late autumn made it almost impossible to see the sun's position.

Torcán saw his confusion and chuckled. 'When you are born and live within the great forests, my friend, you have an instinctive communion with nature and the elements. You know the position of the sun, the moon and the great stars without having to actually see them. You know by the shadows, the soft winds, the rising or lowering of temperature. That is essential to our way of life.'

'My companions and I will be delighted to join you,' Fidelma acknowledged to the waiting woman.

When Éimhín and her husband had moved off to make preparations, Eadulf turned to say: 'I know these rules of hospitality,' he spoke softly, so as not to offend their hosts, 'but may I remind you that the day grows old. By the time we have eaten and taken our leave, there will just be enough time to get back to Cashel, let alone carry on with our investigation. I thought that we were to go to this Abbey of Ráth Cuáin?'

'You are right, Eadulf,' she replied solemnly. 'However, these kind folk are the only ones who have so far been able to give us good information. We may need their help and goodwill again. We will not insult their hospitality, so let us visit Ráth Cuáin tomorrow. After we have seen the abbot, there will still be time to resolve the matter before the Samhain feast. When we leave here, we shall return to Cashel.'

CHAPTER SEVEN

The sky was darkening and there was a chill in the air as they rode up to the gates of Colgú's fortress. The reassuring figure of Gormán, commander of the King's bodyguard, stood by the gates, waiting to welcome them.

'Brother Conchobhar wanted to see you as soon as you came back, lady,' he announced as the three travellers swung off their horses and the stable lads came forward to take them.

'Thank you, Gormán,' Fidelma said. 'We may as well go to him immediately.'

She and Eadulf passed across the courtyard and went around the side of the chapel to Brother Conchobhar's apothecary. As always, they found themselves halting a moment on the threshold before entering, in order to adjust to the pungent aromas of the herbs and spices that assailed their nostrils in the first tiny room. It was here the old man mixed and sold his potions. Beyond were the living quarters, then a storeroom and the area where the old apothecary examined corpses – if there were questions to be answered about uncertain causes of death – before the bodies were washed and dressed for burial.

'So you have returned with more questions about the burial of the murdered man?' Brother Conchobhar's querulous voice came from the back room. 'I told you . . .' Then he entered, recognised them and smiled apologetically.

'Who were you expecting, to sound so irritated?' Fidelma greeted him. 'Not us, surely?'

Brother Conchobhar shook his head. 'One of the members of that silly little council of scholars has been in here asking questions about the body you discovered. He was demanding that it be handed to the religious and ritually purged of all pagan contamination so that it could be interred in the proper place and not affront the souls of the righteous.'

Fidelma's eyes widened. 'Who was he?'

'Someone from Ros Ailithir, I think.' Brother Conchobhar sniffed in disgust. 'I am not familiar with him. However, from my brief encounter I have learned that he is an impatient man with a foul temper.'

'A fanatic to be avoided then,' Fidelma sighed. 'But what was it that you wanted to see us about?'

'I have been examining the corpse. Most things are obvious and I am sure friend Eadulf will have alerted you to them . . . so far as it goes.'

'What do you mean – so far as it goes?' Eadulf frowned.

'We know that the body was *not* that of a religieux. The head had been shaven and a robe put on the fellow just to make it seem so. A clumsy disguise.'

Fidelma told him: 'We have spent the day finding out who he was, and we have discovered how and where he was killed.'

'So you are aware that the man was still alive when he was tied hand and foot?' queried Brother Cochobhar. 'The binding marks on the wrist and ankles told me that he struggled, and the fashion of the binding revealed that he was tied face downwards.'

'Face downwards?' This fact surprised Fidelma as she could not think how the apothecary could have discerned this new fact.

'When I removed his robe to examine the body, I found that something had been carved on his skin whilst he was still alive. It could only be done when the body was face downwards. Would you like to see it?'

Fidelma and Eadulf allowed themselves to be led to the chamber where the corpse of Spelán lay on a long trestle table, covered with a linen shroud. Brother Conchobhar removed it and then, asking Eadulf to help, he turned the body over on its face to expose the back. Marks had been incised on the soft flesh of the buttocks, no doubt with the point of a sharp knife or *graif* – a metal stylus used for writing on wax tablets. Fidelma regarded the marks with some surprise. It was Eadulf who made the first attempt at recognition.

'That looks like the Chi-Rho symbol of the New Faith,' he said, for the Greek letters, looking like X and P, when placed on one another, stood for the first letters of the Greek name 'Christos'.

Brother Conchobhar shook his head in disagreement. 'Almost, friend Eadulf. But this symbol goes back further than the use of the Chi-Rho. It is what we call a staurograme. Similar to the Chi-Rho, it is composed of two Greek letters – the P is superimposed on the T. The latter is *tau* and P is *rho*. Ephrem of Syria once explained it to his followers, saying that it signified the term Tau-Rho: "the Cross saves". It was used in the early years, when followers of the New Faith needed a secret sign to identify themselves.'

'Why would anyone carve such a thing on a shepherd's buttocks and then kill him?' Eadulf asked, horrified.

Brother Conchobhar came back at him with: 'Why would anyone seize a shepherd, mutilate him, disguise him as a religieux and then kill him with the pagan ritual of the threefold death?'

'There is always a reason why people do things,' Fidelma replied. 'Our task is to find that reason. You said that this mutilation of the flesh was done when he was alive?'

'I believe so. However, he lived only a short while afterwards. Also, there were two blows on the back of the head. One would have stunned him. I think that was struck first to incapacitate him in order to tie him up. After that he was tortured, because the carving of the symbol must have been agony to endure. Was it sadism or used as a means to extract information? Then came the harder blow on the back of the head which smashed the skull: he would have perished instantly. He was probably untied, turned over on his back before his throat was cut and then he was stabbed through the heart.'

'A horrible end for anyone.' Eadulf took a deep breath as he contemplated the full magnitude of what the shepherd must have suffered. It was not something to inflict even on a bully and a drunkard.

'Death is always horrible, in no matter what form it comes,' agreed Brother Conchobhar.

'Is there anything else you can tell us?' asked Fidelma.

This time Brother Conchobhar did allow himself a wry grin. 'What more do you want, lady?'

'I don't suppose you can supply us with the name of the culprit?'

The old man rubbed his chin thoughtfully. 'Had the symbolism been different . . . had it not pointed to some aberration of the New Faith, I might have supplied a suspect rather than an answer.'

'What do you mean?' Eadulf didn't understand.

'I am told there is a mysterious woman in the township who curses Cashel and the Eóghanacht.'

'Ah, that we know,' he said. 'She says her name is Brancheó and gives her home as Tech Duin. We saw her on the Hill of the Bullock.'

'She claims to be a raven-caller,' mused the old man.

'We thought her harmless enough,' Fidelma commented. 'Something of a fanatic for the old beliefs, but I would not have deemed her capable of this man's murder. Besides, she talks of seeking vengeance on his behalf. Why do that if she was involved in his killing?'

'Fanatics, whatever their fanaticism, are never harmless. I would keep a watch on this raven-caller.'

'Why are you so concerned about her, other than her belief in the old religion?' Fidelma asked.

'I spoke to one or two people from the town,' Brother Conchobhar said. 'They reported what this woman was shouting.'

'Well, we know she was free in giving us the benefit of her curse – a curse against those who killed Spelán and, for good measure, against all the Eóghanacht who embraced the New Faith. Surely, no one will take her words seriously.'

'It needs only one person to take it seriously, lady, one person to gossip and start a major panic in the township,' pointed out the old man. 'Don't forget, people still believe in Samhain.'

'She reminded us that on the night of the Samhain feast, the gods and goddesses would return to this world to exact vengeance on those who had wronged them; vengeance on the Eóghanacht who had defiled the ancient sacred Rock and allowed those of the New Faith to desecrate it. If she knew Spelán, I can understand why she would want her gods to take their revenge on those who had killed him, but why on the Eóghanacht? I think the woman is just confused.'

'I understand what you say,' replied the old apothecary, looking worried, 'but it is the wider threat that gives the townsfolk cause for concern.'

Fidelma was smiling. 'There is nothing in those words I have not heard before.' A memory had come back to her of what the woman, Branchoó, had said to her on the Hill of the Bullock. She spoke it aloud. 'What was this about Cashel being a portal to the Otherworld?'

Brother Conchobhar was surprised. 'So you have heard this story? I thought it had long been neglected since the coming of the New Faith,' he said.

'I have never heard that Cashel was a portal to the Otherworld, so why fear it?'

But the old man did not appear to share Fidelma's amusement. His expression grew more serious.

'You do not know the story?' he asked softly.

'I do not, so please enlighten us.'

'Before this great rock was named the "fortress of the kings" it was called Sidh-druimm, "the ridge of the Otherworld people". It was the old gods and goddesses who led Conall mac Lugaidh, son of the Prince of Muscraige, to this very spot in ancient times and told him to make it his capital. They prophesied that, if he did so, he would found a dynasty, the Eóghanacht, who would rule the kingdom of Muman for a thousand years. It was many generations after that when his descendant, Óengus, converted to the New Faith and drove out the priests of the Old Faith from this rock.'

There was a silence in the small apothecary for a moment or two. Then Fidelma gave a tight smile.

'That was two centuries ago,' she reminded them. 'If the prophecy was that the Eóghanacht would rule here for a thousand years, then we, and the people, have nothing to fear.'

'I am not sure that I understand you, lady,' Brother Conchobhar frowned.

'Easy enough. If the ancient deities prophesied that the Eóghanacht dynasty will last a thousand years here, then they are hardly likely to destroy their own prophesy.'

'Except that was when your ancestors followed the Old Faith and not the New Faith,' Eadulf could not help pointing out.

'If the old gods could not see the rise of the New Faith and the conversion of Óengus to it, then they could not have been good prophets,' Fidelma said dismissively. 'Anyway, we have followed the New Faith for two centuries without coming to any harm from the old gods.'

As they left the apothecary, Aidan came hurrying across the courtyard to intercept them.

'Lady, your brother is receiving the Princess Gelgéis of Éile and left orders not to be disturbed.'

Fidelma was hoping that her brother would one day take a wife and, of all the women she had seen him with, she had found Gelgéis of Éile the most suitable. They had become friends ever since they had repelled an invasion of the kingdom, launched through Éile, during the previous year. Fidelma looked forward to seeing the girl and was also happy to learn that Gelgéis had arrived to spend the Samhain feast with Colgú.

'Is there a problem? Are you worried about disturbing him?' she asked Aidan.

'Indeed, lady. Since we arrived back, I have had to take command of the guard. A man has arrived at the gate – alone and without escort – claiming to be of the Uí Briúin Seóla of Connacht. He requests hospitality and behaves as if he is a person of rank. I am not sure what to do.'

'His name?'

'Febal, lady.'

'Aren't the Uí Briúin Seóla connected with the ruling house of Connacht?' Eadulf asked.

'Not directly, but they are very close to the ruling family,' Fidelma conceded after a thought. 'But I see the point Aidan's making. If this Febal is of the Uí Briúin Seóla then he might well be a prince. In that case tradition would say he should be received and offered hospitality in the King's quarters and not placed in the ordinary guest-house.'

Aidan cleared his throat and said, 'It is not just that, lady; he also asked if I knew a certain religieux who had come here and who might be looking for the Abbey of Ráth Cuáin.'

'He mentioned Ráth Cuáin?' Fidelma was surprised but hid it. 'What name did he ask for, Aidan?'

'Sorry, lady, the name escapes me.'

'Where is this noble now?'

'I made the excuse that the King was not to be disturbed but that he would be received and attended to as courtesy demanded as soon as possible. In the meantime I would find someone to welcome him. I have left him resting in the Hall of Warriors.'

'Then we will go to greet this traveller,' Fidelma decided. 'I will inform my brother afterwards. I am intrigued by the fact that today of all days, someone is asking after this remote Abbey of Ráth Cuáin when I did not really know of its existence before. I am not a great believer in coincidence.'

When they entered the Hall of Heroes, the name given to the quarters of the warriors of the Golden Collar in the fortress, a sturdy man, dressed in good quality clothing, rose to greet them. It was clear that he had refreshed himself after his journey. He was young and fit and looked like a warrior. Fidelma noticed that he wore no simple tunic but rather an elaborate one trimmed with badger's fur, and she could see that his shirt was of silk and his trousers, like his tunic, were made of soft deerskin. He had a silver chain around his neck and his cloak was fastened with a brooch of highly polished metal inlaid with coloured enamel, depicting what appeared to be the outline of a boat. He had a full head of sandy-brown, curly hair. His features were sharp boned, with a freckled countenance. On the whole, he was quite handsome. And yet . . . she could not quite place it, but there seemed something calculating, even cruel about his features; perhaps it was the line of his mouth.

The young man glanced from one to another of them obviously waiting for them to introduce themselves. Fidelma decided not to stand on ceremony and wait for Aidan to perform the introductions as custom dictated.

'I am Fidelma of Cashel,' she announced.

The only reaction on the newcomer's face was that his smile increased. It was as if he already knew who she was – and that fact made her uneasy.

'I am a stranger in this kingdom. So forgive my lack of protocol, lady. My respects and greetings to you. And who is your . . . companion?'

There was a hesitation before he uttered the word 'companion'.

'I am Eadulf of Seaxmund's Ham in the country of the South Folk,' began Eadulf.

'And you too are a stranger by the sound of your accent. Let me guess . . . a Saxon?' interrupted the young man.

'An Angle,' Eadulf responded irritably.

The young man was still smiling. 'Close enough, eh? There are plenty of Saxon religious studying in the Five Kingdoms these days.'

'Eadulf of Seaxmund's Ham is my husband,' Fidelma announced coldly.

The visitor gave a courteous half-bow, almost a mockery of a greeting.

'Forgive me for neglecting to announce myself, lady. My name is Febal. I am from the Meadow of Peace, Cluain Fois, the college community of the Blessed Iarlaithe mac Loga.' He added patronisingly: 'It is in the land of the Uí Briúin Seóla in the kingdom of Connacht.'

'Then you are a long way from home, Febal of Cluain Fois,' Fidelma observed. 'You wear clothing that I would say is unusual for one who comes from Cluain Fois, for even I have heard of the college of the Blessed Iarlaithe. I thought that the college he set up was limited to those of the religious.'

Febal did not seem annoyed by the implied question. 'Your knowledge is as great as your keen eye on my poor garments, lady.'

'And no religieux would use fragrance to chase odours from his clothes,' Eadulf noted in disapproval, catching a waft of aroma.

'It is the fashion with many now,' replied the young man. 'This is but a pleasant odour that keeps me content in my travels. I am no religieux, as you observe. I instruct in the art of poetry there. I am an *éces*.'

Eadulf had not heard the term before. 'An *éces*? You mean that you are a bard?'

A fleeting expression of irritation passed over the young man's face but was gone almost immediately. Fidelma intervened quickly. 'Under the law, a bard is one without lawful learning but his own intellect. He is considered a mere rhymer, making verses of inferior poetry,' she explained. 'An *éces,* like a *file,* is understood to mean one who is much more – a poet and a philosopher, for example.'

Febal's smile returned and he nodded in agreement. 'I once had fifteen pupils and was entitled to go on *cuairt;* that is the visitation through the country to chieftains and kings who are expected to provide hospitality in return for our entertaining them with our poems.'

Fidelma was examining the young man curiously.

'Yet I am told that you arrived here alone. You travel without any pupils or followers and far from the college in which you say you were an *éces.* Furthermore, I hear you are asking about the Abbey of Ráth Cuáin.'

'That is so, lady. However, it is not the abbey that my question is concerned with but a religieux who I think might be trying to find Ráth Cuáin. Or, perhaps, has recently joined it.'

'Forgive my curiosity, Febal. Can you tell me more?'

'It is a story long in the telling but I will make it short.' The young man hesitated, but then seeing the determined looks on all their faces he continued: 'As a matter of fact, I am looking for a religieux who I am sure has a connection with Ráth Cuáin. To be honest, I only know of him.'

'Why don't you inquire at the abbey itself?'

'I would, but Samhain intervenes and there was gossip in the town that you have a religious council meeting here to discuss Ráth Cuáin. I thought this person I seek might even be part of that council. This is why I have come here.'

'You heard about the council of scholars from gossip in the town?' Fidelma was surprised and perhaps her disbelief showed.

'It was from the tavern-keeper,' the young poet affirmed.

'Who else?' Eadulf muttered.

'Who is this person that you seek?' Fidelma asked, becoming impatient.

'He goes by the name Brother Fursaintid.'

'It is a name unfamiliar to me. And why do you seek him?' Fidelma added.

'It is a matter of retribution.'

Eadulf looked shocked. 'Retribution?'

Fidelma was regarding the man closely. 'What retribution do you seek?'

Again the man hesitated only a moment before saying: 'He has offended my family.'

'In what manner was your family offended?'

'He forced a lady of my clan to go with him and act as his wife.'

Fidelma's eyes widened a little. 'Are you saying that the man you are seeking is a member of the Uí Briúin Seola?'

'What I said was that he abducted a female of my clan,' the young man enunciated clearly.

Fidelma realised she was dealing with someone who used language precisely.

'So he was not from the land of the Uí Briúin Seóla. Where does this Brother Fursaintid come from, and why do you seek him here, in this kingdom?'

'He was a traveller in our territory when he seduced the woman and dishonoured her and her family.' The young man's tone was curiously calm and cold.

'You say that he abducted this woman. Did he take her against her will or was it a voluntary abduction, which can sometimes happen and is provided for under law?' Often an elopement was considered as 'voluntary abduction'.

'She was taken against her will,' the young man said with gritted teeth. 'She died in childbirth with his child and it did not survive long.'

'Surely the *dálaigh,* or Brehon of your people, would be better fitted to search for this man in the circumstances you describe?'

'I am related to the victim, who was my sister Blathin. So I come to claim the right of *dígal* . . . of blood vengeance on him who has dishonoured my family.'

'As an intelligent young man, you surely know the futility of vengeance?' Eadulf felt moved to rebuke him. 'Vengeance is merely a confession of pain.'

'Our law book the *Crith Gabhlach* says that vengeance can be pursued even across the borders of kingdoms and the territory of clans,' returned the young man. 'So I do claim it.'

'How long ago did this happen?'

'Some years ago.'

There was a silence and then Fidelma sighed. 'You are clearly a man of rank. You say you are a poet and scholar at a respected college. You tell us that your sister was made pregnant and died in childbirth within your clan territory – but how was that possible? Was not a search made immediately for this man?'

'For months there was a search but Fursaintid hid himself well. He finally abandoned Blathin on an island in Loch Oirsean, which borders our territory, where he had kept her imprisoned during that time.'

'An island in a lake should have been no problem to search,' Eadulf commented. 'Surely he could have been traced easily?'

The young man cast him a pitying glance. 'You clearly do not know Loch Oirsean, which has as many islands in it as there are days of the year, and many of them are thick with woods.'

'So he disappeared from the land of the Uí Briúin Seóla? And this was a few years ago, you say?'

'It was. Inquiries were made but to no avail. There were rumours, of course. One was that he had gone to Rome. Now we hear that he has returned and that he might be seeking a sanctuary at Ráth Cuáin.'

'Why there, of all places?' Eadulf asked.

'Because it is isolated,' Febal replied. 'The churl has doubtless chosen it because he believes no one would find him there.'

Fidelma regarded the young man claiming blood vengeance. He stood upright, a man in absolute control of his emotions.

'You have waited a long time before deciding to track him down,' she said slowly. 'This is within the custom of our people, but Febal, vengeance is not a solution to pain.'

'I will answer that when I have tasted it,' declared the young man. 'Now, am I offered the hospitality of this place – or shall I proceed on my way?'

'You are offered our hospitality as is law and custom,' replied Fidelma at once. 'But you come with such a story that you must indulge our curiosity. Is that not so? I would like to know how you found out about Ráth Cuáin – who told you that this Fursaintid had gone there?'

For a moment it seemed that Febal was about to refuse to reply – and then he shrugged.

'A merchant from the township of Tuam an Dá Ghualainn, which is in my clan's territory, was passing through Cashel during the summer months. He was staying in the tavern there when he over-heard a drunken shepherd speaking with the tavern-keeper. He listened to the conversation and realised that this man was speaking about Fursaintid – not by name, of course, but by his description of him. This same merchant pretended to question the shepherd about the price of sheep and managed to ask a few questions.'

'This drunken shepherd . . . his name was not Spelán, by chance?' Eadulf asked.

'I am not sure. The merchant returned to bring this news to my uncle. As I had inherited the task of seeking blood vengeance, I am here now to find Brother Fursaintid and fulfil the vow my family have taken. I will let no *dálaigh* stop me, for I have the right as proclaimed in the *Críth Gabhlach*.' Febal ended by thrusting out his jaw challengingly to Fidelma. 'Perhaps I should seek this shep-herd or ride on to Ráth Cuáin.'

'Spelán is dead,' she said flatly.

Febal stared at her, his head to one side as if he had not heard properly. When he did not answer Fidelma continued: 'The shepherd was found early this morning. He had suffered what in the old days was called "the three deaths".

'I don't understand. Was he executed?'

'He was murdered,' Eadulf said.

'Well, I did not kill him,' the young man protested. 'I regret to hear of his death, if only for the information he could have given me. But I did not know him, nor did I bear him a grudge. In fact, I should be thankful to him in that he unwittingly revealed where Fursaintid was in hiding.'

'You have sought hospitality here and it is granted. In the time that you are with us, I hope that logic and good sense will convince you to abandon your plan,' Fidelma said softly. 'I would ask you to remain here until I have finished my investigation into the murder of the shepherd.'

The young man began to object but Fidelma spoke over him in a firm voice: 'Until I am satisfied, I speak as a *dálaigh*. You will remain with us albeit you will be received in honour as a noble of your people and a guest of my brother, the King.'

'I trust you appreciate who the Uí Briúin Seóla are and the rights of nobles?' the young man said tightly.

'I am acquainted with the *Crith Gablach*.' Fidelma smiled faintly when referring to the laws relating to the rights. 'Moreover, I know the *fir flathemon* – the King's justice.'

Febal shook his head in disbelief. 'So I am under suspicion of the death of a shepherd because I came to take the life of a rapist? Suspicion requires a denial by oath – the law states *dligid doig dlithach*. I did not kill him and so I may swear, even as the *Cáin Domnaig* says: I swear *ó cath anma* – for the battle of my soul.'

Fidelma regarded him seriously. 'That is a warrior's oath. You appear to have come armed with law for the purpose of your vengeance, teacher of poetry.'

'It was felt necessary, pursuing my quest in a strange kingdom. In Connacht, the law is deemed the principal concern.'

'As it is here,' Fidelma responded in annoyance. 'You may swear your oath as you wish, Febal, yet it does not put you above suspicion. Many oath swearers have been known to commit *éthech* or perjury.'

'You will not accept my oath?'

'Oath or not, you will stay with us while we carry out our investigation,' Fidelma repeated. 'I will send another person to you who is qualified in law; they will hear and record your oath, and you may choose your witness to it.'

'The oath was only to put your mind at ease that I was not involved,' Febal explained, suddenly submitting to the circumstances. 'I am prepared to be your . . . your brother's guest. However, if I find that news of my arrival is sent to Ráth Cuáin and that this Brother Fursaintid thereby escapes justice, then you may expect this matter to be pursued by the King of Connacht.'

'Then it is agreed.' Fidelma dismissed the matter as if the young man had made no threat at all. 'Aidan will accompany you to Dar Luga, the *ainberrtach* of the King's household and keeper of the guest-house. She will accommodate you and arrange an audience with King Colgú as soon as it is possible.'

Aidan, a witness to the conversation and who took the threat of force seriously, could not resist the temptation of saying: 'Remember, lest you have other ideas, that this palace is guarded by warriors of the Nasc Niadh, the warriors of the Golden Collar, who do not wear their weapons as mere ornaments.'

'Neither do the Gamanride, the bodyguard to the Kings of Connacht,' retorted the young man.

Fidelma had been turning away, but now she swung back. 'What is meant by that remark? You speak of the Gamanride.'

'I was not always simply a poet,' Febal said. 'As you have rightly observed, I have rank among my people. I will brook no threats to my person.'

'So you claim you are a member of the Gamanride?' Fidelma

asked sharply. 'Yet you arrive without sword and weaponry, claiming to be an *éces*.'

The young man laughed without humour. 'One does not exclude the other. Anyway, a true warrior,' he glanced disdainfully at Aidan who now had his hand hovering over his weapon, 'does not rely on weapons to accomplish his purpose. In that manner I shall give Brother Fursaintid a chance to defend himself when he and I meet up. What I once was, is irrelevant. I am now merely a poet.'

'You will be treated with all due deference and will, to all outward signs, be a guest in my brother's hostel and presented to the King as protocol dictates,' Fidelma replied with emphasis. 'But remember that you will be confined within the walls of this palace until I say otherwise.'

Febal smiled tightly. 'I hope that will not take long, lady.'

Outside the guest chambers, Eadulf was filled with questions.

'Aren't the Gamanride the élite bodyguards to the kings of Connacht?' he asked. Receiving a nod, he went on: 'I can't quite see this man as the killer of a poor shepherd – and in such a gruesome manner.'

'Perhaps not,' Fidelma replied. 'It is just that I do not like coincidences.'

She led the way into her brother's council chamber. Colgú was alone, seated before the fire, wearing a moody expression and nibbling on an apple.

'You have just missed Princess Gelgéis,' he greeted his sister. 'She has retired to her rooms to bathe before the evening fasting.'

Fidelma was glad the princess was absent because she needed to bring her brother fully into the picture before he received Febal. However, his mood worsened as she recounted the events of the day.

'I don't like it, sister.'

'No more do I,' Eadulf found himself intervening. 'The young man turns up here on the morning after this Spelán is murdered, claims he is in pursuit of someone Spelán knew and declares that his purpose is blood vengeance. I have to say, I agree with Fidelma. There is something about this man Febal that I don't trust.'

'Well, until we are sure, I suppose I am to treat him as courtesy and hospitality dictates?' the King asked.

'For the time being and within the confines of the palace,' Fidelma nodded.

Her brother sighed deeply. 'Unfortunately, the news of the killing has spread like a fire throughout the town. Everyone now talks about the curse of the old gods. Tell me more about this woman, this raven-caller. After all, it appears that I have been personally singled out for the vengeance of the old gods.'

'You should not take such curses to heart,' Fidelma admonished. 'What king or chieftain has not been cursed simply because of his position?' However, she was well aware that her brother had a weakness for taking auguries and superstitions to heart, although he tried his best not to show it.

'A curse once unleashed into the air can never be retrieved,' Colgú said heavily.

'At the moment, we are considering the death of Spelán,' Eadulf reminded them. 'The woman curses only those who killed him.'

Colgú was obviously still brooding on the ancient curse.

'Are you telling me that there are no real suspects in this matter? We have until tomorrow night before the Samhain feast, and the township people are terrified. It does not matter whether this shepherd was a religieux or not . . . they see his ritual threefold death as having all the hallmarks of a sacrifice to the gods and goddesses. We have enough fanatics, both as adherents of the New Faith and extremists of the Old Faith, to create a dangerous situation in this kingdom. We have been Christian little more than two centuries. The Faith is held only tenuously in some places and the flames which could be ignited to drive out these new ways might quickly consume us.'

'I would have thought that the Faith, brought to us by the Blessed Ailbe, Declan, Ciarán and Abbán, was safe enough,' said Fidelma.

'Safe? Why, it is not even safe from our fellow Christians!' Colgú observed bitterly. Seeing Eadulf's frown he added: 'The Abbot and Bishop of Ard Magh in the northern kingdom are trying to claim jurisdiction over all the churches in the Five Kingdoms. They claim their authority from Rome, saying that there was no Christianity in the Five Kingdoms before Patrick brought the Faith from Rome and set up his first church there.'

'Well,' grimaced Fidelma, 'we know just how weak that argument is. Even in their own accounts, it is written that Celestine of Campania, the Bishop of Rome, sent a Bishop Palladius to the Irish believers in Christ a year or more before Patrick. So we know there were Christians here before, and our own records show that Ailbe, Declan, Ciarán and Abbán all taught in our own kingdom before Patrick arrived in the north.'

Colgú's mouth tightened. 'This is not the right time for an historical argument, Fidelma. If you must debate, then an old acquaintance of yours arrived this afternoon from the Abbey of Imleach. Argue with him if you wish.'

Fidelma raised an interrogative brow.

'Brother Mac Raith, the new *rechtaire*, the steward of Imleach.' Colgú supplied the answer to the implied question.

'Of course! He has come to take part in this curious council about heresies of the Faith.'

'You'll probably see him later,' agreed her brother. 'But let us return to the main point. It is bad enough that this woman – this raven-caller . . .'

'Brancheó,' supplied Eadulf patiently.

'That this woman is going about spreading alarm and despondency.'

'Do we know that she is doing exactly that?' Fidelma demanded.

'The very fact of the manner of her dress is enough. It is the same as trying to ignore a man's beliefs if he comes into the town dressed as an abbot. No – I am alarmed enough.'

'But one can dress as one wishes. No crime in that. Has she made real threats or anything approximating a real threat other than superstitious curses? Eadulf and I thought she was rather a sad woman, out of touch with reality.'

'Threats? What about this curse – is that not a threat?'

Fidelma sighed. 'I don't see it as being so – unless one believes in such things.'

Colgú's jaw tightened. He knew that his sister understood his weakness and tried to defend himself. 'I am not interested in intellectual exchanges, Fidelma. I want the culprit or culprits involved in the death of the shepherd or whoever he was. I want all the gossip about gods and goblins and so on put out of people's minds. There is enough to contend with in this kingdom without stoking the fires of religious fear and hatred.'

'We can only report progress when we have some developments, brother,' Fidelma said, rising from her chair.

'And when will you have "some developments"?' her brother asked pointedly.

'Soon, I hope,' Fidelma replied, ignoring her brother's challenge. 'I am now going to pay my respects to Brother Mac Raith and find out what this council is all about.'

Colgú's shoulders dropped in an expression of resignation. 'I'll be glad when this Samhain is over,' he said to himself, and was unable to suppress a shiver.

chapter eight

They left Colgú in his uncharacteristic low mood and crossed the main courtyard, turning towards the back of the chapel and the small courtyard there. Brother Conchobhar had his apothecary opposite the entrance to the quarters for accommodating visiting clerics. They were approaching the entrance when the sturdy figure of a religieux came hurrying out, so quickly that he knocked into Eadulf, who staggered and would have fallen had he not been able to reach out and steady himself against the wall. It was hard to identify the man in the dusk, for the lantern hanging in the court-yards was scarcely bright enough to illuminate him. The religieux did not stop to apologise but, to their surprise, hastened on with a muttered curse and vanished into the gloom beyond.

'Who was that?' Eadulf demanded, rubbing his bruised arm which had come into contact with the stone wall.

'I've no idea,' Fidelma replied. 'Certainly he was not a member of the chapel here. It must be one of the visiting religieux but a rude fellow by any account.'

The couple were moving towards the door again when it opened and another figure emerged. It was that of a man about average height, thin and dressed in the robes of a religieux. This time the figure halted as the lantern caught his features.

'Brother Mac Raith!' Eadulf was the first to recognise him.

The young steward of the Abbey of Imleach peered into the darkness and his sharp features broke into a smile that changed his whole face. They could just about distinguish his straw-coloured hair, but not his deepset blue eyes, which they knew from the past. His features loomed pale, the skin taut as if indicating that the young man did not eat well. Brother Mac Raith had been a highly regarded illustrator and cartographer before he became the steward or *rechtaire* at the great Abbey of Imleach.

'We are well met, lady. I was looking for you but was told you were absent from the palace,' he announced after he had greeted them both. He began to fumble in the leather satchel at his belt.

'You were looking for me? That is strange. I was about to say that I was looking for you.' Fidelma was amused.

'Indeed? Well, my task is easy. A member of the brethren at Imleach has recently returned from a pilgrimage to the Holy City. One of the items that he brought back was a message for you from a member of the household of the Bishop of Rome. Someone called Gelasius.'

Fidelma was surprised. 'The Venerable Gelasius? The *Nomenclator* of the Bishop of Rome's household?'

Brother Mac Raith shrugged. 'I have no knowledge of his position, lady, although I believe he is a senior member at the Holy Father's Lateran Palace.' He succeeded in extracting a piece of square-shaped sewn leather and handing it to her. She took it and moved to stand underneath the lantern, turning the item over in her hands with curiosity. She realised she would need a knife or scissors before she could open it and read the message, so she put it safely away in her *marsupium*.

'You remember the Venerable Gelasius, Eadulf?' she asked, turning to him. 'When Wighard, the Archbishop designate of Canterbury, was murdered in the Lateran Palace, he was grateful for our assistance in resolving the crime.'

As Eadulf recalled, Fidelma had done far more than just assist in identifying the murderer, but he merely nodded.

'So now,' Fidelma turned back to Brother Mac Raith, 'let me tell you why I was seeking you, Brother.'

'By all means.'

'I was wondering what the purpose was of this council that you and your comrades are holding here?'

Brother Mac Raith's expression indicated a degree of resignation. 'I am afraid Abbot Cuán has appointed me to be his chief spokesman on a delicate mission. We are to discuss a matter of theology as there seems to be one community which pays little respect to the jurisdiction of the Abbey of Imleach and Chief Bishop of the kingdom.'

Fidelma smiled wryly. 'I could name you a dozen such communities that are not noted for respecting Imleach,' she responded. 'It is in the nature of our people to be independent and not feel they have to obey rules made by others. There are enough arguments among those professing the New Faith to ever be in common accord on everything. Why, there are even enough interpretations of the Faith to make each community entirely different from its neighbours.'

Brother Mac Raith replied sorrowfully, 'That is true. In fact, that is precisely why we are here. Each abbey in a clan territory becomes a law unto itself. But there are limitations beyond which the Chief Bishop of each of the Five Kingdoms should not allow individual communities to trespass. As well you know, Abbot Cuán has only recently become Chief Bishop and . . .' He paused, embarrassed, for without the efforts of Fidelma and Eadulf in resolving the mystery of the murder of Ségdae, the previous abbot, Cuán would not have succeeded to the office. 'Well,' he went on, 'when he started to read the reports of the theological activities of a particular community that had been submitted to Abbot Ségdae before his death, Abbot Cuán could not understand them.'

'Why not?'

'Because he felt that this particular community should have been suppressed many years ago when the first reports came to light about its teaching.'

'Suppressed?' Eadulf was astonished. 'That is a bit extreme, isn't it? As Fidelma says, there are plenty of communities who worship the New Faith in different ways. Trying to impose one set of beliefs on all members of the New Faith has been the purpose of many different councils over the years.'

'And as a result, such decisions created further confusion about interpreting what beliefs we should have,' Fidelma complained.

'What you say is true,' Brother Mac Raith sighed. 'We have indeed seen the rise and fall of many ideas adopted as the principles of the Faith that have since been declared heresies by other councils. Arianism, Docetism, Nestorianism, Sabellianism . . .'

'We know them well enough,' Fidelma intervened swiftly, in case the steward was prepared to enumerate every type of movement within the New Faith that had been condemned by subsequent councils.

'So why should one more or less heresy matter?' Eadulf wanted to know.

'That such a community as this one exists within the jurisdiction of Imleach cannot really be tolerated.'

'Why not? Rome condemns Pelagianism as a heresy but it is central to all the churches of the Five Kingdoms and thereby tolerated here.'

'That is different. This is the worst heresy of all,' declared Brother Mac Raith in a surprisingly forceful tone. 'This is why we have sought advice from the leading theologians of the Abbeys of Ard Mór, Ros Ailithir and Corcach Mór, to meet here and discuss how the Chief Bishop of Muman should respond to such heresy.'

'All our major teaching abbeys?' asked Fidelma, recalling the point she had made earlier to her brother. 'Except that one, I notice, is missing.'

Brother Mac Raith smiled knowingly. 'You are referring to our old antagonists at the Abbey of Mungairit? Indeed. They have been deliberately excluded because they made a dalliance with this particular heresy some years ago, and I am informed that they have kept several copies of texts relating to it. In fact, it was one of our scholars from Ros Ailithir who recommended that we should not invite a representative from there. He informed us that the abbey we are concerned with has been discussing the heresy with Mungairit recently.'

'Your informant seems to have good intelligence,' remarked Eadulf.

'Brother Giolla Rua? He apparently has a sister in the religious who has recently been involved in such matters. In view of that, we thought it wiser not to ask a delegate from Mungairit to debate on this heresy.'

'Which is?' enquired Eadulf. 'You have not told us what this heresy is as yet.'

'It is called Psilanthropism.'

Eadulf exchanged a glance with Fidelma who shook her head slightly, indicating that she had never heard of the movement before.

'I am not sure what that means,' Eadulf confessed, although he had acquired some knowledge of Greek.

'You should study Greek more diligently, Brother,' reproved the steward. 'It was the language in which the New Faith as we know it first emerged. *Psilós* means "mere" or "plain" and *ánthropós* means "humanity" – so this heresy declares that Jesus was a "plain" or "ordinary man".'

'When did this idea originate?'

'It is said to go back to the very foundation of the New Faith among the Hebrews in Judea. Some of them still follow the idea that Jesus was just a prophet and teacher. That concept was accepted by a Theodotus of Byzantium some four centuries ago.'

'Wasn't Theodotus a Greek theologian?' Fidelma asked.

'Most of the early founders of the New Faith were Greek,

converted by Paul of Tarsus who declared that the teachings of Christ were no longer part of the Hebrew Faith. In fact, it was these Greeks who first used the word Christos, from their word meaning "the anointed one". Paul of Tarsus had been Hebrew by religion, Greek by culture and a citizen of Rome; thus did the New Faith emerge from the three cultures. But to many, in those early years, Jesus had been just an ordinary man, a teacher among his people, who was virtuous and just. He was held in such esteem that the people, out of courtesy, call him *a* Son of God, not *the* Son of God. You see the difference?' Brother Mac Raith suddenly coughed nervously. 'I do not subscribe to this, but merely explain to show you what this Psilanthropism teaching is about.'

'We understand,' Eadulf replied solemnly. 'What happened to this Theodotus?'

'He was denounced for his heresy and excommunicated by Pope Victor a full century after his death.'

'Denounced and excommunicated after his death?' Fidelma challenged. 'But not condemned during his life?'

Brother Mac Raith nodded quickly.

'So how long did his teaching, this Psilanthropism, last?' Eadulf asked.

'It still exists,' Brother Mac Raith told him. 'That is the very point. The leader of the movement was Paul of Samosto, a Bishop of Antioch. He added new ideas to this philosophy. He propounded a further claim that not only was Jesus a good man but that he should be regarded in the minds of the people as a man-god. Paul of Samosto further taught that God was just a single being and not a Trinity. It was widely thought that these teachings were eventually merged into the heretical movement of Arianism.'

'You say there is still a community here, which should be answerable to the orthodoxy of the Abbot of Imleach as Chief Bishop of the kingdom, where this curious theology has continued?' Fidelma asked slowly.

'Indeed, there is. Once we have deliberated the facts, I am ordered to confront their abbot and demand that, if he and his community persist in maintaining this heresy, they must consent to appear at a full council where these matters may be argued in front of all the bishops and scholars of this kingdom.'

'Tell me, Brother,' Fidelma queried, 'what is the name of this heretical community that continues this heresy?'

Brother Mac Raith actually smiled briefly. 'The irony of it, lady, is that it bears the same name as Abbot Cuán of Imleach. That could be the goad that impels him to sort out the issue. The place is called Ráth Cuáin.'

Fidelma and Eadulf sat before the crackling log fire in their own apartment, gazing at the dancing flames and listening to the occasional hiss of steam rising from an odd piece of wet timber. Muirgen, the nurse, had taken little Alchú to his bed long ago. So Fidelma and Eadulf had eaten and were resting thoughtfully before the fire. It was Eadulf who finally broke the silence that had fallen between them. He shifted in his chair, stretching a little.

'Do you still think we have anything to learn from this Abbey of Ráth Cuáin?' he asked unexpectedly. 'It sounds a curious place, preaching heresy. Then this strange poet warrior, Febal, with his story about pursuing a rapist there. It all seems pretty odd to me. I doubt that visiting the abbey will lead us to a resolution of how Spelán came to be murdered in such a grotesque ritual fashion or why.'

'Perhaps you are right,' Fidelma sighed, 'but Brehon Morann taught that there will always be a weak link in any chain of events, that opens a path to knowledge. So we must examine every possible link to find the weak one.'

Brehon Morann had been Fidelma's mentor when she had attended his law school near Tara.

'Let us hope he is right then,' Eadulf said. 'So far as I can see, this is a mystery and likely to remain one.'

Fidelma regarded him with disapproval. 'We have faced and resolved greater mysteries,' she reminded him. 'And we will also deal with this one.'

Eadulf saw her determined expression with misgiving.

'So we are to go to Ráth Cuáin tomorrow in order to pursue this matter?'

'Indeed we will. We'll take Aidan again to assist us. I have asked him to have the horses ready after first light.'

'What about this council? Won't Brother Mac Raith feel that we are interfering with his discussions about whatever it is they teach as theology there?'

'Psilanthropism is the word you are looking for, Eadulf,' Fidelma reminded him. 'His mission is nothing to do with us. Anyway, he and his council of scholars will probably take months of argument to discuss whatever they have to before they notify Ráth Cuáin. We can ignore the council and the arguments about heresy. That is a separate issue to the murder of Spelán.'

'It is strange that this community should bear the same name as the Chief Bishop with whom they are in theological conflict,' mused Eadulf.

'Not so strange. Cuán is a relatively common name in this kingdom. But I would certainly like to be a witness to the arguments between the two sides when they meet and see how Abbot Síoda justifies his philosophies. They are entirely new to me. However, for the time being, we have more important matters to pursue.'

'More important than the interpretations of the Faith?' Eadulf asked in a tone of mild rebuke, for he himself still adhered to the rituals and practices of the Roman Church, although he found himself growing attracted again to the teachings of the churches of the Five Kingdoms, to which he had originally been converted as a youth.

'Yes,' Fidelma replied. 'To me, law and justice are more important than which ideas one should adopt with regard to religion.'

Eadulf bit back a retort, saying merely, 'Even if this Abbot Síoda and his community are willing to speak to us, what do we do if they cannot provide any further information?'

'Then we shall have closed that path and have to think where else to turn.'

'What about this strange fellow, Febal? We should question him more.'

'I agree. There is something about his story that doesn't ring true. But we must be careful. If he is a prince of the Uí Brúin Seóla and his people learn that we are holding him here – against his will, as a suspect – it could lead to conflict between Muman and Connacht.'

'Then surely we should let him go?'

'Not yet,' she replied with a shake of her head. 'I wish to question him again.' She then stood up, smothering a yawn. 'An early night might be a good idea. We need to make the most of tomorrow's daylight.'

'Wait a moment,' protested Eadulf. 'You have not read the message that Brother Mac Raith brought you from old Gelasius in Rome.'

'I forgot all about it!' Fidelma declared in surprise. She turned and found her *marsupium* on the table, took the square of sewn leather from it and held it in her hands for a few moments, staring at it, twisting it around as if trying to understand what was inside.

'You won't know what is in it unless you open it,' Eadulf pointed out.

Fidelma pursed her lips thoughtfully. 'It is not often one gets a message from Rome. And it is some years since we last saw the Venerable Gelasius.'

'So are you going to find out what he says?'

Without another word, she found a small knife on the table and proceeded to cut the strings that bound the leather square together. Inside was a piece of papyrus. She read the spidery characters twice before Eadulf pressed her again for information.

'It is in Latin,' she began.

'Naturally.' Eadulf was impatient.

'It merely says that if a young man introduces himself to me as Brother Lucidus, then I should afford him assistance in a matter of great concern. Gelasius says he would forever be in my debt. It goes on that Brother Lucidus has Gelasius' full confidence and approval in fulfilling the task of tracing a book missing from the Secret Archives of the Lateran Palace which, it is suspected, may have been brought to this island. Gelasius adds that if it gets into the wrong hands, then the peace of Christendom might be destroyed.'

She paused and remained looking at the papyrus.

'Well?' prompted Eadulf.

'There is no more,' she said, handing it to him. 'That is all he says.'

Eadulf also read it through. 'I don't understand. Do we know anyone called Lucidus?'

Fidelma gave a shake of her head. 'If the person contacts us, presumably we will know more. But this is all the message says.'

'Destroy the peace of Christendom?' Eadulf echoed the words. 'It is a little over-dramatic, surely, and not in the usual style of the Venerable Gelasius. Is there any peace at the moment with all the arguing factions? How could a book make things any worse than they are already? The only way we will ever achieve peace in Christendom is through a miracle, the greatest miracle of all.'

Dawn came over the eastern hills in a slash of red, orange and gold. Eadulf looked at the coming light with a groan.

'*Et mane hodie tempestas rutilat enim triste caelum,*' he muttered.

'What?' Fidelma asked, not catching the words of his quotation.

'I was just echoing the Gospel of Matthew,' Eadulf explained. '"There will be a storm today for the sky is red and threatening".'

Fidelma looked past him to the sky above the hills. 'Red sky in the morning does usually portend bad weather,' she admitted, 'but not always, Eadulf. We will still ride to Ráth Cuáin.'

Eadulf was rather offended. 'I was not trying to avoid it,' he blustered.

She chuckled. 'I know you too well, husband.'

There was a sudden thunderous knock at their chamber door and Gormán burst in without waiting. He was followed by the outraged figure of Muirgen, who stood wringing her hands apologetically, visibly upset by the guard commander's effrontery at barging into the private chambers of the King's sister.

'Lady, you are wanted in the chapel immediately,' Gormán declared breathlessly.

Fidelma and Eadulf stared at him in surprise.

'Am I?' Fidelma examined his anxiety-creased expression for a moment. 'By whom?'

'A *dálaigh* is needed, lady. One of those religious scholars has attacked his colleague.'

There was a bark of laughter from Eadulf.

'What was I saying last night?' he grinned. They turned to stare at him uncomprehendingly. 'The peace of Christendom? Tell me – what peace!'

Fidelma turned back to the warrior. 'Are you saying there has been a physical assault? You don't mean there was a verbal attack made during some debate?'

'A physical assault, which has resulted in blood,' Gormán confirmed.

In the courtyard they met Aidan, who had been coming to tell them that their horses were ready; they had to explain why they were being delayed. When they entered the chapel, Brother Conchobhar came forward to greet them wearing a rueful smile. Fidelma noticed that the warriors Enda and Dego were there, apparently keeping two groups apart. On one side was an angry-looking

Brother Mac Raith with another religieux, who was holding a hand to a bloodstained cheek, while facing them were two more brethren. One was a young man whose features were twisted in rage. He was being restrained by his companion.

'I am afraid our scholars have declared for a rather forceful manner of debating,' Brother Conchobhar explained in amusement.

The companion of Brother Mac Raith took his hand away from his injured cheek and pointed an accusing finger at the young, belligerent religieux.

'He punched me,' he announced thickly. 'I have lost a tooth.'

Fidelma approached and looked at the man. 'And you are . . .?'

'I am Brother Giolla Rua of Ros Ailithir,' he replied stiffly.

She turned to the young man whom he had accused. 'And you?'

The man thrust out his jaw, making him seem even more aggressive. 'Who are you to question me, woman?' he said rudely.

There was a gasp from the warriors. Gormán stepped forward and thrust his face into that of the religieux, who was of the same height and muscular build.

'This is the lady Fidelma of Cashel, sister to the King and a *dálaigh* who will judge your conduct,' he snapped.

The young man hesitated. A curious light of recognition came into his eyes – and then was gone before she had quite registered it. He dropped his head a fraction and then muttered: 'I am Brother Sionnach of Corcach Mór.'

Fidelma turned to the only man who had not been identified, but as soon as her eyes fell on him he bowed politely and said, 'I am Brother Duibhinn of Ard Mór, lady.'

'Very well. So what was the cause of this quarrel?' She addressed Brother Sionnach.

The young man's mouth tightened. 'It was a scholastic argument.'

Fidelma grimaced in disapproval. 'Usually one argues about

scholastic matters by exchanging facts and opinions. A fist is hardly relevant and does nothing to prove a point.'

'The argument became heated, lady,' he declared.

She gestured to Brother Giolla Rua. 'What do you say?'

'It was, indeed, a matter of scholarship, lady – and I was right,' Brother Sionnach added swiftly before the other man could speak.

'I refused to listen. In retaliation, this hooligan knocked out one of my teeth!' snarled Brother Giolla Rua.

Fidelma stepped forward between them.

'Enough of this. This is an argument for your council. But what has happened here must first be dealt with. Brother Conchobhar, as an apothecary, have you ascertained that this man has received a blow to the face which knocked out one of his teeth?'

'That is correct. As well as dislodging a tooth, the blow, as you will see, bruised his cheek,' confirmed the elderly apothecary.

Fidelma turned to Brother Sionnach. 'Do you admit that you delivered that blow?'

The young scholar shrugged carelessly and then said with a sneer at his adversary: 'Of course.'

Fidelma said icily, 'Under the *Bretha Déin Chécht* this is an assault. It is a physical injury and compensation is immediately due to the victim. Although I am entitled to it, I shall forgo my share of the fine as judge in the matter. However, there are six classes of tooth injury and the penalties vary according to the social status of the victim. Is it agreed I give the judgement?'

Both men looked uncertain for a moment and then, seeing the frown gathering on Fidelma's forehead, they nodded almost in unison.

'What is your honour price, Brother Giolla Rua?'

'I am an Óg Aire,' declared the man proudly. It was a technical term showing that he was not quite an *ollamh* or professor but would be considered the equal of most scholars skilled in decisions concerning his calling.

'We are all of the rank of Óg Aire,' Brother Sionnach pointed out.

'Then the blow is struck between equals? Very well. In this case I shall make a minimal award. As a fine, it will be two *screpalls*. Do you agree, Brother Sionnach?'

The young man said indifferently, 'I agree to the fine but shall not accept the argument that he puts forth. That is heresy.'

'No one is asking you to accept the argument causing disagreement. However, you must accept your responsibility for not debating the argument in a scholastic manner and inflicting unjust injury. If you debate further, make sure that you use only words as your weapon. In fact,' she gave a nod to Gormán, 'I suggest that you place one of your warriors in the chapel to ensure that no further violence occurs. Is it agreed?'

Everyone seemed to shuffle like naughty children before a parent and mumbled agreement.

Outside the chapel Aidan, who had remained as witness to the event, grinned at Eadulf. 'Are all councils of the religious like that?'

'Some have been even worse,' Eadulf replied, thinking of the debates he had seen at Streonshalh and Autun.

'Did you say the horses are ready?' Fidelma cut in, annoyed that she had been sidetracked with such childish bickering.

'We can depart at any time,' Aidan confirmed, but then added, 'You have probably already seen the prospects for the day – they do not look good.'

'We, too, can see the redness of the sky and know its symbolism,' she replied solemnly. 'However, symbolism is not always right. It might not rain at all.'

The rain started to come down in heavy splatters as they were crossing the Hill of the Bullock. Clouds had literally raced in across the eastern hills so that the early stretch of red sky had vanished, leaving the darkening clouds scudding close to the ground in their westward advance. If the truth were known, Fidelma had noticed the noisy, protective circling of birds above their nests in the tall trees as they passed through the woodlands. She recognised the rooks at once, not only by their cries but by their glossy black plumage, which distinguished them from their more fearsome cousins the carrion crows and ravens. It was a sure sign of rain when the rooks behaved in such a fashion.

But the rain held off as the little group emerged from the trees and onto the open hillside. Fidelma had hoped the threat would not materialise even after they stopped to check their path and her eye caught the swelling stems of the lesser trefoil – another sure indica- tion of rain. They had pressed on. Then Eadulf, glancing across his shoulder, pointed to the hammer-headed clouds behind – and even before he could speak there came the reverberating rumble of distant thunder and then the rain started, swiftly increasing in intensity. The heavy woollen cloaks which they had put on were some protec- tion, but not entirely. Icy winds blew from the east and eventually the rain was sheeting against their backs – which was slightly better than riding into the face of it. However, it was no good continuing in this manner and, since they were near the cabin which they had examined on the previous day, Fidelma suggested they might return there until the rain eased off.

Aidan led the horses to the more sheltered side of the stone cabin. Thankfully, some scavenger, perhaps a wolf, had dragged away the carcass of the dog they had left abandoned. Inside, Fidelma and Eadulf set up a wooden bench and one solitary remaining chair so that they could make themselves comfortable. But the cabin was chilly and dank from its long disuse. Aidan, coming in, cast a professional eye around before contemplating the blackened, cold hearth. By the side of it he had spotted a pile of straw and kindling, and there were some logs that had been kept dry. Without asking permission from Fidelma, who was busy rubbing her arms to restore some warmth from the cold rain, he took the small pile of kindling and put it in the hearth.

Every warrior who was accepted into the élite company of the Golden Collar carried with them the means of kindling fire in a small girdle pocket, so that the result was often called *teine creasa* or 'fire of the girdle'. Each warrior had flint, steel and tinder which was also called *tenlach-tein*, fire of the hand. Usually the warriors preferred the kindling to be dried leaves of coltsfoot, so much so that the plant became known as *sponc* after the ignited tinder. Aidan proved no exception to the reputation of the warriors in being able to light a fire quickly and it was not long before a blazing log fire was making the travellers feel more comfortable. Soon they were able to remove their heavy woollen cloaks and relax in the warmth that the fire generated.

Eadulf couldn't help asking: 'So what now? We may have to be here a while.'

Fidelma pursed her lips in annoyance. 'We will remain here until the rain clears.'

Aidan was wandering about the interior, investigating it with interest, holding a candle, which he had lit as an aid to his observation.

'So this is where you believe that Spelán was killed?' he asked. He had waited outside on the previous day while Fidelma and Eadulf had examined the cabin. It had been up to Eadulf to tell him about their discovery.

'It would seem so,' Fidelma replied.

Aidan was peering at the wooden bed which she had identified as the place where the shepherd had been tied down and ritually killed. Aidan shook his head in distaste and turned away – before something made him pause. Holding the candle stub, he bent to pick up an object from the floor.

'It looks as if a bird has managed to get in here,' he said.

'Why is that?' asked Eadulf.

Aidan held the item up to the light. 'A feather. Looks like a crow's feather. This is the sort of place they'd get into, scavengers every one.'

A peculiar look formed on Eadulf's face. 'Are you sure that is not a raven's feather?' he asked.

CHAPTER NINE

Fidelma looked up quickly after Eadulf had asked the question. 'Are you suggesting that Brancheó has been in here?' she asked.

'That feather was not here yesterday,' Eadulf replied. 'She could have watched and waited until we had left. She wears a cloak of raven feathers. It would be easy to lose one.'

Fidelma held out her hand to Aidan and he dutifully placed the feather in her palm. She examined it carefully. Then she put it into the *marsupium* on her belt.

'There is a puncture mark in the spine of the feather as if a needle and thread had passed through,' she disclosed. 'I'll keep it to see if I can identify it.'

'I said there was something sinister about that woman,' muttered Aidan.

'That is what she wants people to think,' replied Fidelma. 'I still have no opinion, except that she has a link to Spelán.'

Aidan shrugged and returned to his examination of the far end of the cabin. To Fidelma and Eadulf's surprise, he suddenly seemed to concentrate on the wall. He held the flickering candle stub higher and took a step closer so that only a hand's width separated his face from the stone of the cabin wall. Giving a soft grunt, he ran his hand over the surface.

Fidelma watched him critically. 'Whatever are you doing?' she said crossly. 'We searched the cabin thoroughly yesterday.'

Aidan did not reply for the moment but had his hand on a small block of stone that seemed unevenly set in the wall. Pushing it from side to side, he soon had it coming loose.

'Sorry, lady. It is my experience that loose stones of this sort are where people hide things in wall cavities; things that are of value to them. Ah . . .'

While he spoke, he had tossed the stone on the floor and inserted his hand into the cavity. A moment passed and he withdrew something.

'A piece of vellum with some writing!' he exclaimed, holding it up in the candlelight.

Fidelma and Eadulf exchanged a startled look. Such an item in a poor shepherd's cabin was unusual, to say the least. However, there might be many explanations.

Meanwhile Aidan had turned and held out the piece of vellum towards them. 'It is written in some strange language of which I have no understanding. Anyway, I think I felt something else in the recess.'

He turned back and thrust his hand in again. When he pulled the object out and found it was simply a small piece of rock, no bigger than a small pebble, he threw it on the bed.

Fidelma was examining the vellum and asked Aidan to bring the candle nearer. He did so and Eadulf peered over her shoulder and immediately declared: 'The letters on that side are Greek. It seems the vellum is cut from something and the text is but a fragment. I can't remember it.'

Fidelma turned the scrap over and there were some numerals in a column on the other side.

'Greek words and a column of numerals on vellum in a shepherd's cabin . . .' Eadulf mused. 'That's unusual.'

'To say the least,' Fidelma agreed thoughtfully. She took the fragment to the solitary window in the cabin and held it up.

'The text seems to be quite old, and appears to be formed in a different hand and with different ink than the numerals. I will have to ask Brother Conchobhar for his opinion, but I doubt whether it is relevant to our inquiry.'

'Maybe the shepherd or his wife picked it up, thinking to use it to help light the fire,' suggested Eadulf, and then realised he had said a stupid thing. Vellum was no good for that purpose; it might smoulder but would not burn well.

'You forget that we know little about Caoimhe. She had a connection with the community at Ráth Cuáin which is the very reason why we are going there. It might be that she obtained it there.' Fidelma turned to Aidan. 'Your eyes are sharper than ours, Aidan. Continue looking around.' Then she hesitated. 'What else did you say you just found in the recess?'

Aidan pointed to the bed where he had tossed the object. 'It's just that hard pebble, lady.'

She bent over and picked it up. 'It is a bit jagged and heavy for just a pebble. It's not round at all. Give me your knife, Aidan.'

She took the warrior's heavy knife and moved back to the window, proceeding to scrape at the tiny object. Then, to their surprise, she went to the bucket of stale water and began to use it to wash the dirt away. Finally, she held up the tiny object, now bright and shiny.

Aidan was the first to react. 'Isn't that silver? How would a poor shepherd come by a piece of silver?'

Fidelma carefully placed it in her *marsupium* along with the vellum.

'There are several questions to be answered. Although that piece of silver would not make him exceedingly rich, it is unusual that a shepherd has possession of it. You have done well, Aidan. Your eyes were definitely better than ours.'

Nothing else was found, however, and the three travellers settled down to wait for the weather to improve. Slowly the deluge began to ease and finally cease altogether. The dark thunderclouds passed on with the rain, leaving long rolls of white clouds with faint blue sky seen between them.

'It is time to move on,' Fidelma announced. 'The weather is clearing and we should be able to reach the Abbey of Ráth Cuáin in the dry.'

As they breasted the hill and caught sight of the full extent of Ráth Cuáin, they halted their horses simultaneously as if at some unspoken order. It was their surprise at the impregnable ramparts of the abbey that had caused them to rein in. They had seen the place from a distance and knew it had been a fortress before an abbey – but they had expected to see the usual wooden walls and collection of huts and, perhaps, a stone-built chapel. But this was a fortress of stone; a fortress with watch-towers and a large sturdy wooden gate. The walls were high, the height of three tall men standing on each other's shoulders. It certainly had the appearance of a military habitation rather than a religious one.

'How could this have existed here less than half a day's ride to Cashel without our knowing of it?' breathed Fidelma.

Aidan was equally amazed.

'Truthfully I do not know, lady. As you are aware, the main roads from Cashel bypass this area, and it has become so secluded that it is rare that anyone comes this way. Of course, we have heard of the existence of a religious community but not of this imposing structure. I do not know what to say.'

'Well, I can say that my brother will not be well pleased to learn that such a fortress has been allowed to exist so close to his capital without even the knowledge of the commander of the warriors of the Golden Collar,' she observed dryly.

'But it is called a religious community,' protested Aidan. 'Surely it is the Abbot of Imleach, the Chief Bishop of Muman, who should have reported it to the King?'

'It is a matter that goes beyond who should have told what to whom,' Fidelma pointed out. 'Colgú should have been aware of it.'

Eadulf could understand her concern, especially as there had been several conflicts in Muman since he had lived in the kingdom, and attempts to overthrow the influence of Cashel.

'There is also the fact that Abbot Ségdae is dead and the new Abbot, Abbot Cuán, has discovered that this is an heretical community, according to the council now meeting in Cashel,' he added. 'It does seem curious that no one has whispered a word about this fortress to the King's guards. No wonder it is called a Ráth.'

'Well, our primary purpose is to make inquiries about Spelán and his wife Caoimhe. That won't be achieved by just sitting here looking at this so-called abbey,' Fidelma declared. 'Come, let us find out the true nature of this community.'

There were no sounds to indicate that their approach had been seen as they rode up to the tall, imposing oak doors. They were closed yet there seemed no watchman or gatekeeper. No one shouted a challenge. The great gates remained closed and a brooding silence hung over the impenetrable walls of stone. It was almost oppressively quiet. Eadulf could not even hear the cry of birds around the place. He shivered, trying to persuade himself that he had too much imagination.

It was then his eye caught a carving on one of the great doors.

'Fidelma . . .' he whispered almost fearfully.

'I have seen it,' she said coolly without turning her head.

Carved on the wooden door was an old Christian symbol. They had no difficult in recognising it as the 'Tau-Rho', which Brother Conchobhar had shown them carved onto the buttocks of the murdered shepherd.

'This does not augur well,' Eadulf muttered.

'It augurs nothing at all,' replied Fidelma in a tight voice. 'Perhaps this is the symbol of the heretics that Brother Mac Raith told us about.'

At a nod from Fidelma, Aidan nudged his mount forward to

where a bell-rope hung. He pulled on it, sending out a surprisingly unmusical peal.

There was no answer as the echoes died away.

He repeated the exercise, this time with much more vigour. Some moments passed before a hollow voice came from the wall above. A pale face was peering down at them. They looked up to where the upper half of a dark figure could be seen, his features more or less obscured by a dark hood that was part of a black religious robe.

'What do you seek here, strangers?' came the harsh tones.

'We are no strangers in this territory,' Aidan snapped, irritated by the manner of their greeting. 'It should be obvious what we require if you are the gatekeeper. We seek entry.'

'As far as I am aware, warrior,' replied the uncompromising tone, 'you are strangers at this gate. This is the community of Ráth Cuáin. We admit no strangers unless we know whence they come and their purpose.'

Aidan abruptly pulled aside his cloak and touched a hand to his golden torc.

'Do you observe that?' he shouted up. 'If you recognise it, you will know what it means and know that I speak on behalf of the bodyguard of the King in whose territory your community lives; lives by his permission, will and protection.'

'Not so, warrior,' replied the figure, apparently unimpressed. 'We are here by the permission, will and protection of our Faith and we answer to no other entity but the one true God.'

'You are answerable to the King and to his Chief Bishop,' Aidan shouted back. 'Have a care lest you earn the King's wrath!'

Fidelma frowned with displeasure at the young warrior's conduct, although she realised that he was more adept at military exchanges than diplomacy with members of the religious.

'We fear no wrath other than it is from God!' the figure had replied from the parapet of the wall. 'The King and his Chief Bishop have no rights over us. So begone.'

Fidelma now eased forward and stared up at the man who seemed to be turning away.

'Wait! I am Fidelma of Cashel, sister to Colgú, King of Muman. I speak as a *dálaigh*. I would dispute in law that you are not bound in recognition of the Chief Bishop of Muman and therefore his acceptance of the authority of the King. There are many texts I could quote to you, if you are knowledgeable of the law of this land, which sets out the rights and obligations of abbots and bishops to obey. They are under the jurisdiction of the judges of this land. So if you do not recognise the authority of the Chief Bishop or the King, perhaps you will recognise the authority of the laws of this land. Just as the King himself is answerable to the law, so is an unjust judge or a "stumbling bishop" – one who leads a community unmindful of his legal obligations.'

'I am no lawyer,' the figure replied curtly, 'but merely the *aist-reóir,* the gatekeeper, of this community.'

'Then, gatekeeper, I suggest you go to find someone who will contend with me on law to see whether you are flouting it by refusing me entry to speak with your abbot, Abbot Síoda.'

As the man hesitated, Fidelma added firmly: 'I presume this community does have someone knowledgeable of the law? It is a requirement that all such communities should have someone who has even glimmerings of knowledge in these matters.'

There was another pause and then the man simply said, 'I shall return.' Then he disappeared from the ramparts.

Eadulf said sourly, 'I thought we would have trouble as soon as I saw the nature of this place.'

'We may yet be surprised,' Fidelma replied quietly.

The gatekeeper suddenly reappeared on the parapet.

'What is it that you wish to see the Abbot Síoda about?' he demanded.

Fidelma took a deep intake of breath which she exhaled in a long, loud fashion for effect to show her frustration.

'Tell Abbot Síoda that I wish to see him about his neglect of his duty of care to two members of the clan Sítae over whom he has guardianship, not only by virtue of his being abbot, but by being chieftain of this clan.'

The *aistreóir* did not reply for a moment. Fidelma felt it a shame that she could not observe his features from the distance between them. Then he disappeared once more. They were made to wait again before there was a noise of bars being withdrawn from the wooden gates and they were suddenly face to face with the gate-keeper. Although he was not as old as they had first thought, his features were aged by their sallow tinge and by their gauntness. His lips were thin; he had a slit for a mouth. The eyes were dark – and it was as if he had no pupils. There was a distinct lack of humanity about the man as he stood regarding them with an expression of hostility.

'I am instructed that Abbot Síoda will see you, Fidelma of Cashel, but your companions will remain here.'

'You cannot leave them outside in this intemperate weather,' Fidelma protested, for it had started to rain again; a light sprinkling but with the ominous thundery threat of increasing in strength.

The gatekeeper put his head on one side as if considering the matter. Then he shrugged. 'They may enter the courtyard and shelter in the stable. The abbot will see only you, Fidelma of Cashel.'

Fidelma gave her companions an apologetic shrug and they entered through the forbidding gates into what had all the hallmarks of a military courtyard. Apart from the gatekeeper, the only other person in sight was a burly smith, stoking a charcoal fire on one side of this square. Next to him were the open doors of a stable in which they saw several horses. The surprise, apart from the fact that it was not usual to find religious communities with accom-modation for horses, was the quality of the beasts themselves. Fidelma's practised eye saw that these were well-bred animals of the type that warriors might use. Then she recalled how Torcán had mentioned the fact that Abbot Síoda, as chieftain of his clan as well, employed mercenaries.

They dismounted in the courtyard while the *aistreóir* closed and barred the gates behind them. Fidelma handed the reins of her horse to Eadulf and whispered in his own language: 'Find out what you can from the smith about this place. Observe and learn as much as possible.' She did not speak his tongue very well but hoped the word *geahsian* conveyed the idea of finding out, discovering and learning. Eadulf smiled and nodded as he caught the idea.

The gatekeeper rejoined them and pointed to the stable entrance.

'You will take shelter there,' he ordered Eadulf and Aidan in peremptory fashion before turning to Fidelma and gesturing for her to follow him through a smaller gate. This led from the entrance courtyard to another enclosed courtyard and then through an arch, along a short passage into yet another tiny courtyard. At the end of this was a stone building with a flight of steps leading up to a wooden door. Fidelma tried to work out the length of time between the gatekeeper's disappearances from the wall to come here to check whether the abbot would see her. He must surely have run in both directions to do so.

The gatekeeper now paused before the door at the top of the stairway and knocked loudly. A voice called and he opened the door to announce in a reverential tone: 'The *dálaigh* from Cashel.' He stood aside and motioned her forward.

She walked into a room which was large, with a high ceiling. She immediately felt that she was entering a library. Had the weather been more clement, the many windows would have allowed a bright southern light to illuminate it. They would encompass the traverse of the sun from east to west. With the stormclouds and rain, the light had to be helped by a series of tall tallow candles placed at strategic points in the room. For a moment Fidelma caught her breath – for the room was permeated with a fragrance as if emanating from incense burners. It was the scent of lavender. Then she realised that her first impression was correct and that the room did indeed appear to serve as a *techscreptra* or *scriptorium*, for there were racks with book satchels, *tiag luibhair*, along one side. It was obvious that the community had many books hung in their leather pouches. There was a desk and chair on which writing materials were placed, such as pens, the horn called *adicín* that was used to contain ink, and pieces of vellum and parchment as well as the wax tablets for making notes called *taibhli filidh* or 'tablets of the poets'. The wax could be softened and smoothed after use so the tablets could be used time and again.

There was an impatient dry cough and Fidelma reluctantly drew her attention away from the section of the room that was the library and found a man seated at a desk on the far side of the room. From what she had been told, she had expected Abbot Síoda to be some thin-faced fanatic, much like the gatekeeper. Instead, a young man sat behind the desk, examining her with an amused expression; he had blue eyes, auburn hair and fair skin with ruddy features – yet with no tonsure to mark his calling. Over his black-dyed robes hung a silver chain with a pendant worked in the form of the Tau-Rho symbol, which she was coming to recognise easily.

He made no effort to rise nor did he gesture for her to be seated.

'I am told that you are a *dálaigh* and need to speak to me on a matter of law,' he said in a modulated tone.

She moved forward – and as she did so, she saw his eyes drop to a leather-bound book on the desk before him. His quick move, covering it with some loose papyrus on which he had been making notes, was done so skilfully that it would have taken a less observant person than Fidelma not to notice the embellishments on the polished covering. Her time in Rome had alerted her to the seal of Vitalian, the Bishop of Rome, and her knowledge of Latin was such that the words, though quickly concealed, were easily recognised. *Non videbunt: habere occultum*. None shall see: keep secret.

'I am Fidelma of Cashel.' Fidelma introduced herself in a confident tone, recovering from the moment as if nothing had happened. 'My brother is Colgú, King of Muman, whom I advise regarding legal matters. I am told you are called Síoda and are the Abbot of this community?'

The corner of the young man's mouth twitched, whether in humour or irritation it was hard to discern, but she did not allow him time to respond.

'I apologise for the delay in greeting you,' she began. 'I was momentarily impressed by your library.' She indicated the books behind her. 'As I find you seated here, do I presume that you also undertake the task of being the keeper of the books?'

'I am Abbot Síoda,' the young man confirmed. 'We do have an eminent keeper of our books in Brother Gébennach, who has recently joined us. A knowledgeable man and much travelled, collecting materials for this library. We have been fortunate that he has decided to join us here. However, you say that you are adviser to the King of Muman on legal matters. But I thought that the Chief Brehon of the kingdom was one called Fíthel?'

'I did not claim to be Chief Brehon. How could I, when I am but a *dálaigh*? As I say, I advise my brother, the King.'

'I live a secluded life here, Fidelma of Cashel, so you will forgive me when I point out that I do not have sufficient knowledge in law to engage in any meaningful discussion.'

'If that is so, then let our conversation be brief,' she replied solemnly. Then, glancing nearby, she took a chair and seated herself. 'It seems strange that one as youthful as yourself is both Abbot and chieftain of your clan.'

The young man shrugged. 'Strange, but not unknown. The Sítae are only a small clan. We do not number enough to be noticed by anyone, nor do we bother anyone. I was raised in this community by my father, who was Abbot before me. The abbey is devoted primarily to inward contemplation and research into the origins of our Faith. Hence this library. I have only been outside this kingdom once, and that was recently with Brother Tadhg, on a pilgrimage to Rome.'

'Brother Tadhg?'

'My gatekeeper who is, perhaps, overly zealous in his protection of my desire for isolation.'

'We share the experience of visiting that city of Rome for I was there several years ago.'

'My visit was more recent, as I say. Frankly, I was disappointed in what I found there. But that is not what you have come to ask questions about.'

Fidelma raised a shoulder imperceptibly and let it fall. 'Just forgive my curiosity. Is this place a *conhospitae,* a mixed house? Was your mother a member of this community?'

'There are several woman devotees here, and their children, like me, are all raised in the service of our Faith. My mother was one such who came to our community from an adjacent clan. She died six years ago during the devastation of the Yellow Plague. We lost many of our community at that time. Anyway, I am told that you have demanded to speak to me on the authority of your office in law. Why?'

'Brother Tadhg was inclined to ignore this authority,' Fidelma told the Abbot. 'I therefore had to enforce my office to demand entrance.'

For the first time, the young abbot almost gave way to a broad grin. 'Brother Tadhg is a proud man and conscious of his position as gatekeeper and therefore steward of the abbey. He takes his role of protecting my isolation most seriously.'

'However, he has much to learn of the rights and duties of members of this kingdom and association with the governance of it,' Fidelma countered. 'But I understand that he has seen the error of his ways and informed you that I need to discuss certain matters with you.'

Abbot Síoda appeared uncomfortable for a moment. 'Our scribes do teach that the law is to be respected. *Ius est ars boni et aequi.*'

Fidelma smiled. 'Those devoted to justice would subscribe to that – that law is the art of the good and just.'

'On that premise, why is it that you wished to see me? I am still at a loss and you have yet to explain.'

'Let me clarify a few things first, so that I know exactly to whom I am speaking. I am told that your community follow a particular branch of the New Faith?'

The young abbot sat back and gazed at her thoughtfully.

'I thought this was about law?' he said.

'So it is. I just want to know how you stand in relationship to it and to the Chief Bishop of the kingdom.'

Abbot Síoda laughed. 'We have no relationship with the Chief Bishop of this kingdom nor do we wish to have one. He would destroy us as his predecessors tried to do. To him we are simply heretics. To us, it is he who is the heretic.'

'Would it not be a means of resolving your differences to meet with the Chief Bishop's representatives and discuss such matters? You would thus preserve the peace of the kingdom.'

'Is that the purpose of your coming?' There was a sudden suspicion in the young man's tone now.

'It was not,' declared Fidelma. 'However, there is a council of religious scholars meeting at Cashel. They intend to come to Ráth Cuáin to discuss and resolve the differences that you have about the essential tenets of the Faith. The scholars are being led by Brother Mac Raith, the *rechtaire* of Imleach.'

'We are not that isolated that we do not know of these scholars,' the abbot replied. 'Brother Sionnach from Corcach Mór, Brother Duibhinn of Ard Mór and Brother Giolla Rua of Ros Ailithir. Their arguments are already well known. I can only wait until these scholars approach me and endeavour to put their arguments. They will find it hard to ignore the evidence that will greet them.'

'I would be more inclined to pre-empt matters and seek a resolution with the Abbot of Imleach,' advised Fidelma.

'How can I resolve such matters when I know the Abbey of Imleach has already wandered from the path of the True Faith,' Abbot Síoda said sourly.

'I would not know who is right or wrong,' Fidelma admitted. 'All I know is that talking surely leads to a means of resolution. Brother Mac Raith tells me that you are what he calls *Psilosanthropos*. Explain how that branch of the New Faith would make you so unreceptive to discussion about the matter?'

'*Are* we unreceptive?' snapped the young man. 'We have stood forward in debate several times and been howled down an equal number of times by those who have made themselves rich by claiming to be followers of their own particular interpretation of the Faith. They do not want to hear our arguments. They do not want to hear our evidence. They shut themselves away from the truth. Truly it is said that the wise have open ears and a closed mouth but the foolish have closed ears and an open mouth.'

'It is a good observation – if one is completely certain that one is not doing the same as they are being accused of,' Fidelma said. 'Remember the ancient saying among the Latins – *asinus asellum culpat?*'

Abbot Síoda's mouth twisted with anger. 'If we are to talk about an ass finding fault with a donkey, Fidelma of Cashel, let me observe that debating with most of the abbots of Imleach on this matter is, as Horace, said, *narrare fabellam surdo asello* – like telling a story to a deaf donkey. I doubt whether the new Abbot and Chief Bishop is any different.'

Fidelma responded only by saying, 'The trouble, Abbot Síoda, is that the donkey gets impatient when it hears nothing.'

'I thought you said that this matter has nothing to do with that which brought you here?' The abbot gave her an unfriendly look. 'I have much other business to attend to, so I desire you to come to the point of your visit.'

'I was merely clarifying your philosophy.'

144

'Then I can only say that we follow the oldest branch of the new revelation from the East which was held by many for three hundred years before the Roman Emperor Constantine called the great council at Nicaea, which asserted rules for the New Faith. Many of the original concepts of the Faith were cast aside. But we, here, maintain that we are of the *true* Faith, believing in a man who was a just and good prophet of the God. Now do you see why we have no common ground with the Chief Bishop of Muman? He means to destroy our community. Perhaps now, lady, you will finally tell me the purpose of your coming here?'

Fidelma paused for a moment, holding the other's eyes in her gaze. Then she said softly: 'The purpose of my coming, Abbot Síoda, is to discuss murder.'

CHAPTER TEN

'Murder?' Abbot Síoda's eyes narrowed for a moment, then his face relaxed and he smiled grimly. 'Ah, you mean the death of the shepherd, Spelán. Oh yes – the news of the body being found on the Samhain fire in Cashel was brought to us by a merchant yesterday. What has it to do with this abbey?'

'Did your informant also tell you that, freshly engraved on the buttocks of the corpse was the symbol of your faith, the Tau-Rho? It was done while he was still alive and must have caused him considerable pain. That was why I was so interested in hearing your version of the Faith that you practise.'

The young abbot's jaw dropped. He struggled to say something and then he finally found and articulated the words.

'Are you accusing some member of this community of his death?'

'I do not know enough to accuse anyone as yet,' Fidelma assured him. 'However, I trust you now appreciate the reason why I have come to see you.'

Abbot Síoda sat silently for a while, head bowed slightly as if examining the desk before him.

'You accept that you are lord of this *tuath,* the Sítae, those who dwell in these hills, and that the people of the *tuath* pay tribute to you as their chieftain, not just as their abbot. Is that correct?'

'I don't deny it. I am the fifth generation of the lords of Ráth

Cuáin who became abbots. Cuán was lord when the Blessed Gobnait consecrated what had been his fortress as a religious house. But she moved on and there came into this land a wise and learned man from the East. His name was Apollinarius and he began to teach us the true path. That is the Faith we now hold. When he perished, it was Cuán son of Cuán who became abbot of the community and so, in accordance with our law, the most worthy son has replaced his father as chieftain and as abbot ever since.'

'So it is to you as chieftain that I want to speak. Do you know of a woman of the *tuath* named Caoimhe?'

'Spelán's woman? She is dead,' he said flatly, confirming what Fidelma already knew.

'When did she die?'

'I am told that she died before the summer months.'

'Who reported her death to you?'

'Spelán, the shepherd, reported it himself. To be completely accurate, he came and spoke to Sister Fioniúr and she reported it to me. I and Brother Tadhg had already left on the pilgrimage to Rome. So we did not hear of it until our return.'

'Sister Fioniúr? Someone mentioned her to me. Who is she?'

'Our herbalist; more an apothecary.'

'Why would Spelán report to her particularly?'

'She looks after the health of our community. I believe Caoimhe sold herbs to her so Spelán would have known her. Also, I had appointed her as my *tánaiste*, taking charge of the abbey in my absence.'

'She is a local woman?'

'She had only joined us in the darkest part of the year in the month of Dubh Luacran. She came from the Abbey of Corcach Mór. An excellent apothecary and very attentive to detail. Moreover, a convert to our beliefs.'

'Can I see this Sister Fioniúr?'

'She is busy – and I am spending more time than I should on this matter,' answered the abbot impatiently.

'It is important. A *dálaigh* does not like to take evidence *sgeal sheoil,*' Fidelma insisted, using the term for hearsay. 'It would be easier for me to obtain the facts at first hand.'

With bad grace, Abbot Síoda reached forward and rang a hand bell. When the thin-faced gatekeeper, who had obviously been standing outside, opened the door, the abbot said: 'Ask Sister Fioniúr to attend me . . . at once.'

There was a chill silence between them as they waited. However, it was not long before there was a tap on the door and a woman entered. Sister Fioniúr came as a surprise to Fidelma. The heart-shaped face was attractive rather than beautiful due to a certain hard set of the mouth and thin lips. The dark eyes appeared to contain a hidden fire that sparked as she examined Fidelma, as if she was contemplating some hidden thoughts.

The abbot made a perfunctory introduction, explaining what he had told Fidelma, to which the young woman simply nodded in agreement.

'You are aware that Spelán, sometime shepherd here, has been murdered?' Fidelma began.

Once more the young woman nodded without saying anything.

'So he came to tell you of his wife's death at the start of summer?'

'He reported that Caoimhe had died from a fever.' Sister Fioniúr frowned as if puzzled by the question. 'She was not his wife, only a partner. He came here to ask permission to sell her flock of sheep, hoping to claim ownership by marriage. But he was not of this *tuath.* As I say, Caoimhe and Spelán were not officially married – just partners under the year and one day rule. Neither had she kin to counter-claim against him. Her family were carried off by the Yellow Plague that devastated so many in this land. I reported Spélan's request to the *leabhar coimedach*, the keeper of books, who knew some law; he wisely took the decision to declare that the sheep were now the property of the abbey. This was confirmed by Abbot Síoda when he returned from Rome.'

'May I see this keeper of books?'

The abbot intervened with a shake of his head. 'He died during the late summer. You may take it that what Sister Fioniúr says is the truth of what he advised.'

Fidelma turned back to the herbalist. 'Tell me what you can about the shepherd.'

Sister Fioniúr shrugged. 'He was a vainglorious little man. I met his woman a few times when she came to the abbey to sell herbs to me. She would often have bruises which she claimed were caused by accidents. I suspected otherwise. She also confessed that he was without religion. He was not of the local clan, the Sítae. I believe that he was a man without morals who came searching for someone to support him because he had no money and was too lazy to earn any through his own efforts.'

'Did you not report your suspicions about his abuses to anyone?'

The herbalist made a negative shrug and Fidelma did not feel it would advance things to pursue the matter.

'So the abbey did not buy the sheep from him?' she pressed.

'Of course not,' the other woman said. 'They were not his to sell. As I say, the keeper of books confirmed the decision. In fact, I was told that the sheep were not Caoimhe's either.'

'Explain,' Fidelma instructed.

The abbot intervened again. 'When Caoimhe's family were wiped out by the Yellow Plague six or seven years ago, she was left with neither land nor other property. The land her family used for their small crop and a herd of cows was granted them by my father as lord of the territory. So, as is the law, it reverted to my father. When Caoimhe presented herself to him and pled her case that she had been left alone without family or support, he followed the law and allowed her to remain in her cabin, use the land and gave her a small flock to tend for her subsistence for as long as she lived. Her tribute to this community for this was one ram and one pregnant ewe to be paid in the spring of each year.'

'Why did Spelán think that the flock was his to sell?'

'He was, by all accounts, an ignorant man,' Sister Fioniúr pointed out. 'I observed that Caoimhe was not a young woman. She was past childbearing age, alone in a cabin, with land and a flock of sheep. Spelán thought he could use her to his advantage and as for her, she seemed willing enough to put up with his abuse.'

'So you can confirm that he had no means of sustaining himself?'

Abbot Síoda answered for her. 'He was reported to be a landless itinerant. He had no claim on any property.'

'And you can confirm that Caoimhe was not married to him?'

'Certainly by none of the ten legal forms of marriage according to our laws,' concurred the abbot.

'With your permission and that of the lady Fidelma,' Sister Fioniúr interrupted, smiling politely at them all, 'I have much work to attend to. May I withdraw now?'

'Only one more point,' Fidelma replied, staying her. 'How would Spelán have come into some wealth during this summer?'

'It's the first that I have heard of the shepherd having any money,' Abbot Síoda declared emphatically, glancing at the herbalist.

'He was living in Caoimhe's cabin, frankly in disgusting conditions,' Sister Fioniúr said with a slight shudder. 'I have never heard he had any assets.'

'Nevertheless, he was able to go to Rumann's tavern in Cashel and purchase drinks for himself on many occasions.'

The abbot shrugged. 'Then I have no idea nor any interest in how he came by his resources, for there was nothing that he could take from that wretched cabin. Not long ago, I sent one of the members of the abbey – in fact, it was the new keeper of books, Brother Gébennach – to assess the state of the place as I will require it for another shepherd. I was told that the cabin was almost derelict, although Spelán was still there. He was warned that he had to leave by the time of the Samhain feast.'

'The merchant who informed you that Spelán was murdered would not have known that the murder took place in his cabin two nights ago,' Fidelma remarked quietly, watching for the effect.

The abbot looked shocked while Sister Fioniúr's features lost even more colour.

'How can anyone tell such a thing?' The herbalist was bewildered. 'The body was found in Cashel, lady.'

'Yes – how are you so sure that he was killed in his cabin, not in Cashel?' Abbot Síoda asked angrily. 'Do you think it was our way of ensuring he left the cabin – by carving our sacred symbol on him and carrying out the killing with pagan rites? That is wicked nonsense!'

'Well, someone ensured that he left the cabin – and this world,' Fidelma replied tersely.

'Then what about the crone Spelán hired to curse the abbey in the manner of the Old Faith when he could not extract what he claimed was Caoimhe's land or property from us?' Sister Fioniúr asked.

The abbot's lips suddenly formed a silent whistle. 'But there you have it! The crone found he had no means to pay and so took her retribution on him!'

Fidelma frowned slightly. 'Are you saying that he actually hired a woman to curse the abbey?'

'He did,' confirmed the herbalist. 'She threatened the abbey, saying that we would be destroyed by the time of the feast of Samhain. The woman came to the gates of the abbey and started to perform her ritual. I had the stable lads chase her away. I told the abbot about it when he returned.'

'Did you know who this crone, as you call her, was?'

'She was a strange woman in a raven-feather cloak,' replied Sister Fioniúr. 'That is all I know.'

'It all happened while I was away,' said the Abbot, 'and was reported to me after my return. The woman has not been back since she was chased from the gates of the abbey.'

'Find the woman and you have found the killer,' declared Sister Fioniúr.

There was a silence for a few moments and then the abbot turned to the herbalist. 'There is no need to trouble you longer, Sister, and keep you from your work.'

The young herbalist nodded quickly to the abbot and Fidelma and then withdrew.

Fidelma remained seated in thoughtful repose for a moment. Then she said: 'You mentioned that your new keeper of books was sent to tell Spelán to quit the cabin.'

'Brother Gébennach, who has recently joined the abbey,' agreed the abbot. 'He went to the cabin and saw Spelán, who also showed him the grave of Caoimhe behind the cabin. And now . . .'

The abbot leaned forward, seized the small hand-bell on his desk and shook it rapidly. A moment later the emaciated-looking Brother Tadhg appeared. Fidelma rose and addressed the gatekeeper.

'You have heard that the one-time shepherd, Spelán, was found murdered. Did you know that the Tau-Rho symbol was engraved on his buttocks, presumably as some part of a ritual at the time of his death?'

'I did not.' Brother Tadhg's features remained expressionless. 'Has the *dálaigh* come here to accuse us?' The question seemed to be put to the abbot. 'Anyone would know that the Tau-Rho symbol was widely used among the early members of the Faith.'

'But dropped in favour of the Cho-Rho symbol,' Fidelma pointed out. 'Therefore, few people use or know the Tau-Rho symbol these days.'

'We have many enemies who know our symbol,' Brother Tadhg argued. 'Plenty of our fellow so-called Christians would like to destroy us, especially those at the Abbey of Imleach. Such enemies of our Faith could easily have made the mark to denigrate and implicate us.'

'While accepting that point, I have to say that I came here only seeking information and not to accuse this community,' Fidelma said softly. 'I am simply after the truth. But there is little here for me to pursue.' She suddenly smiled at the abbot and inclined her head. 'If Brother Tadhg will lead me back to the courtyard, my companions and I will take our leave. Abbot Síoda, I thank you for your enlightenment and your help.'

The young man acknowledged her thanks with a frown, uncertain whether she was being sarcastic or not.

Fidelma was following the gatekeeper to the door, when she halted abruptly and turned, breathing deeply. 'You seem to appreciate the strong aroma of lavender. It permeates the air here.'

'I regret if this scent is not to your liking,' replied the abbot, irritated, as if he saw her broaching a new subject as an excuse to delay her departure.

'On the contrary,' Fidelma smiled, 'I am much pleased by it but wish I could find someone to distil the essence this well for me. Is it something that you have distilled yourself?'

The young man shook his head. 'My talent does not lie with such arts of wizardry. Yet I do confess that it is distilled here in the abbey.'

'And is it produced to sell?'

'It is an essence our herbalist mixes for this community alone. She produces it among her other cures and protections from the many evils with which we are beset.' He went on. 'We were exceedingly fortunate when she came here, having heard that we follow the philosophies of *Psiloanthropism*. In the time that she has been with us, she was been invaluable to the community and that is why I have appointed her my deputy.'

Brother Tadhg grunted. 'I must remind the abbot that I disapprove of her permitting ivy to grow and spread from the hedges of her herb garden so that it creeps up the kitchen walls. I have warned her several times that it weakens the walls and soon I will have to get it cut away if it is allowed to continue its growth. It is destructive.'

'But she is doubtless a good herbalist – and isn't ivy used to deaden the pain of corns according to the ancient remedies?' Fidelma observed brightly.

Brother Tadhg made no reply but simply held open the door and, taking the hint, Fidelma left with a final incline of her head in the direction of Abbot Síoda.

In the courtyard stable, she found Eadulf and Aidan anxiously waiting for her.

'You've been gone a long time,' complained Eadulf. 'We were wondering whether to come and look for you.'

'No need for concern.' She frowned a warning to him not to start asking questions in front of the gatekeeper. 'The abbot and Brother Tadhg here have been most co-operative in answering the questions that I needed to put to them. Now we can return to Cashel.'

Aidan led the horses out of the stable and they made their formal appreciation and farewells to the gatekeeper. Brother Tadhg seemed torn between relief and suspicion as he replied as courtesy dictated. The heavy, forbidding gates of Ráth Cuáin closed behind them with a dull vibration.

It was not until they had ridden some way off that Eadulf could restrain himself no longer.

'What happened?' he demanded.

Fidelma explained as they continued to ride down the hill.

'But it does not seem to tell us much, apart from giving us more suspicions,' Eadulf objected.

'It might not present us with a quick solution but there are two matters that have occurred which I think are worthy of investigation. Firstly, I would like to check that Spelán's woman is truly buried by the cabin.'

Eadulf grimaced in distaste. 'Do you think Spelán killed his woman for her sheep? He would surely not have been so stupid. Yet if he did, who then killed Spelán? Did Abbot Síoda execute him as revenge, when he learned what had happened? Hence the sign of his community carved on Spelán's body?'

Fidelma shook her head. 'You are forgetting the second matter. Brancheó. I don't doubt that this was the crone that Spelán persuaded to curse the abbey. We must find her.'

Fidelma fell silent and she glanced at the sky. Seeing her do this, Aidan said: 'We have enough daylight left and the rains have softened the earth for digging if you want to check for the body of Caoimhe at the cabin. Surely there will be a spade there?'

Fidelma did not respond immediately. They were out of sight of Ráth Cuáin now, and so she swung her horse back around the lower slopes of the hill towards the south-west, in the direction of the cabin. They had only been a short time on the track when Aidan called softly again. 'Do you see that patch of woodland ahead? I suggest that when we get among the cover of the trees, we halt and conceal ourselves by the track.'

Fidelma's attitude did not change apart from a slight tension in her body. When Eadulf began to turn towards the young warrior, Aidan warned him: 'Don't look round, friend Eadulf. We are being followed.'

'Who is it?' Eadulf hissed. 'It is not that woman, Brancheó, again?'

'It is a man,' responded Aidan. 'He is riding an ass but keeps a discreet distance behind us. I think he has been following us ever since we left the abbey.'

'Then we shall find out why he is following,' Fidelma declared. 'Well observed, Aidan. We shall do as you say.'

The wooded area was not large and the cover sparse but they hid themselves as best they could from the track. It was not long before their shadow came in sight. He was, indeed, riding on a tired-looking ambling ass. He seemed not to guide the beast but let it follow the path at will. He was a young religieux in black robes and a symbol hung on a silver chain around his neck. In spite of his clothing, he had the build of a warrior, with head held erect and shoulders straight, and his eyes moved quickly from side to side as if searching for hidden dangers. He was handsome, which showed because the hood of his robe was not raised, with well-formed, sun-bronzed features and dark hair. Although he wore a look of gravity as became his calling, there was something about the eyes and the creases at the corner of his mouth that showed a lively sense of humour.

Aidan was the first to break cover, causing the man on the ass to pull up sharply, one hand reaching automatically to his belt as if it expected to find a sword hilt there. At the last moment the action changed as if he was reassuring himself his purse was in place.

'Who are you, my friend?' he demanded, recovering from his surprise. His voice was deep and somnolent as though every phrase was measured for a song.

'Better it is to know who you are, my friend,' Aidan responded. 'Better to know who you are and why you have been following us. Perhaps you should dismount.'

By now Fidelma and Eadulf had emerged to join Aidan. The newcomer looked from one to another of them in surprise but did not seem intimidated.

'I was following no one,' he protested, as he swung down from his ass and faced them.

'So it is just coincidence that your path has followed our own from Ráth Cuáin, even when we left the main track for Cashel and turned back to go to a certain cabin?' There was a challenge in Aidan's voice.

The young religieux thrust out his chin defensively.

'I do not care what path you take. Because I shall be passing the cabin, which had been occupied by the shepherd Spelán, Abbot Síoda asked me to stop by and check on it,' he told them.

'For what purpose, exactly?' Fidelma wanted to know.

'I was informed that the shepherd who dwelled there is dead, so could I ensure that all was right within it so that the abbot might dispose of it.'

'We were told that it had already been examined and the shepherd had been ordered to vacate it.'

'True. I was asked to perform that task some weeks ago. It was one of my first jobs when I joined the abbey. Spelán showed me the place where he had buried Caoimhe. I blessed the grave, as it seemed no one had done so. And then I gave him due notice to vacate as the abbot had asked. Today, since I was due to ride past the cabin, he asked me to make sure that all was still in order there as the shepherd had been found dead. Also, I must inspect the grave.'

'Why should the cabin be disturbed?'

'The abbot told me that he had been informed that the man, Spelán, had been killed there.'

'I see. And where are you off to?'

'Do you have the right to question me in this fashion?' protested the young religieux.

'I am a *dálaigh,*' she replied curtly. 'I am Fidelma of Cashel.'

He considered this for a moment. 'You have just seen the abbot,' he said. 'Now I understand. Very well, if you must know, I am going no great distance – just to Ara's Well across the great river. I am meeting a fellow keeper of books from the Abbey of Mungairit. We have agreed to exchange some books.' He gestured to the leather satchel that hung from his saddle as if inviting them to check on the veracity of his statement.

'A keeper of books?' Fidelma frowned slightly. 'Then your name is Brother Gébennach.'

'It is.'

'Your name implies that your family were captive at one time,' observed Fidelma, momentarily giving in to her favourite hobby.

'So you have an interest in the meaning of names?' The young man smiled. 'In this case you have been deceived by the similar-sounding root of the word.'

'Then I conclude that your name derives from the root *gébech*. Does that mean you work at illuminating manuscripts at the abbey?'

'I am not an illuminator but the *leabhar coimedach* – the keeper of books,' replied the other with a certain amount of pride. 'I illuminate knowledge.'

'You are surely youthful to be a librarian.'

'I have had six years of study and have attained the degree of *Cli*.'

'A degree in the secular schools, I suppose, and not the ecclesiastical ones,' mused Fidelma, for the degree of *cli* was not obtainable in the latter.

'Just as your degree is from Brehon Morann's law school,' replied Brother Gébennach almost belligerently.

Fidelma's eyes widened a fraction. 'You seem to know something about me, but a moment ago you were asking if I had authority to question you?'

'At that time you had not introduced yourself. It is hard not to have heard of you, lady. Even in Rome your name is mentioned.'

Fidelma ignored the flattering remark but regarded the young man with interest. 'So you have been to Rome?'

'I have recently returned from the Holy City, as have several brethren in the abbey.'

'You also only recently joined the abbey, I believe. Were you in Rome with Abbot Síoda, who I understand was recently on a pilgrimage there?'

'I joined the abbey after my return from Rome. I did not know Abbot Síoda or Brother Tadhg before.'

'Why did you go to Rome?'

'Surely it is the wish of most members who enter into the service of the Faith to set out on a pilgrimage to Rome. Either to go to Rome or, as did the Blessed Helene, the mother of Constantine, to make the journey to Jerusalem itself. Alas, I have never been to Jerusalem but the abbey has a copy of the *Itinerarum Burdigalense* which was written two centuries ago, recounting the stages of the pilgrimage to Jerusalem.'

Fidelma smiled at what she saw as the young man's sudden enthusiasm. She decided to move the conversation on, to a subject closer to her interest. 'I presume that you work in the library chamber? I saw Abbot Síoda there.'

'Abbot Síoda likes to receive visitors there so that they might be impressed with our library, for it contains many ancient books. Usually I work there alone.'

'I would have thought that students would be constantly encouraged to come to the abbey library to make use of such an important collection of books.'

Brother Gébennach smiled briefly. 'Only students who are not enemies of the abbey's theology, lady. Visitors who come to study the truth of its beliefs are always welcome.'

'So that truth is found among the books that you hold in the library?'

'Exactly so, lady.'

'Well, it is fortuitous that we have met up because I have some questions for you, keeper of books.'

The young librarian frowned. 'I thought I was already answering your questions, lady.'

'For which I am grateful,' she replied. 'But I have a few more questions, that is all.'

'Which are?'

'You doubtless know Sister Fioniúr at Ráth Cuáin?'

For a moment Brother Gébennach seemed taken aback; it was obvious that he was not expecting the question. 'That is so. A woman of youth and attraction. She is a herbalist and something of an apothecary, for she has overall charge of the health of our community as well as running the herb gardens. Her one fault is that she is very fastidious, both in her own appearance and in her expectation of others'.'

'I presume that she often leaves the abbey to go searching for her herbs?'

To her surprise Brother Gébennach shook his head.

'Then how can she be the herbalist without gathering the herbs?'

'Others search for the herbs and flowers she wants. Some of the local people bring such items to her. She plants and grows them in the garden.'

'I was interested because she seems to have a fondness for distilling the flowers of lavender and making a powerful oil for the incense burners in the *techscreptra*. I noticed it when I met with Abbot Síoda.'

The keeper of books told her, 'I am responsible for that. You see, I work with the pungent smell of inks, leather, vellum and parchments in stuffy rooms, and often long for the fresh, open smell of the fields, flowers and woodland. I noticed lavender was favoured by Sister Fioniúr and so I asked if she could make a distillation for the *techscreptra*.'

'Who brings her the lavender that she distils so excellently for you? Does she trade for it or grow it herself?'

'She does not grow it, lady. It is not native to this climate. I hear it is imported from the east. She has a contact at the Abbey of Ros Ailithir. As you may know, they trade with Gaul. They send the plants to her.'

'The abbot assured me that the lavender distillation is not exchanged with anyone outside the abbey.'

'That is correct. The distillation is made solely by her,' the librarian declared with pride. 'Its supply is limited and the perfume is used only in the *techscreptra*.'

'It is a very particular distillation.' Fidelma sighed. 'I would find it most memorable.'

Eadulf suddenly leaned forward, having realised why Fidelma was asking the questions about lavender. 'You say that you visited Spelán in his cabin. You would not have taken a container of this lavender oil with you and somehow left it behind?'

The bewilderment on the face of Brother Gébennach was genuine. 'What a curious question. Was such a container found there? I don't understand.'

'If I ever wanted to see Sister Fioniúr, is there any way I could do so?' Fidelma asked, ignoring the exchange. 'I mean, without the abbot or the gatekeeper knowing? I would like to purchase some of that fragrance.'

Brother Gébennach grinned. 'It would be difficult to get by Brother Tadhg. He has eyes like a hawk.'

'Then how does Sister Fioniúr barter with those who come to trade herbs and flowers with her? Does the gatekeeper have to give his approval each time?'

'At the back of the abbey, almost where it balances on those small rocky cliff areas, is the herb garden. While it is part of the abbey it is outside the abbey walls and surrounded by a low wooden wall and hedges. The main kitchen and refectory leads out into it. That is where the herbs and fresh fruit and vegetables are grown for the consumption of the community. There is a gate where Sister Fioniúr conducts business with merchants at her own discretion. Local folk know this and often come to barter goods with her.'

'So I might be able to converse with her there?'

'It would be forbidden unless you have legitimate business. Why would you do so? Just because you like this distillation of lavender? I tell you that she doesn't manage to get enough for our own purposes, let alone a surplus to pass on to other people. She won't part with any to you, I can assure you.'

'I admit, I would like to know more about that distillation of lavender.' Fidelma sighed as if disappointed.

Brother Gébennach raised a shoulder slightly and let it fall, expressing the fact that the situation was beyond his power to resolve.

Fidelma decided it was time to call a halt to her inquiries in case the young librarian began to suspect what she was really seeking. Also, she was aware that during this long exchange in the copse, both Aidan and Eadulf were growing restless.

'It might be coming on to rain again,' Aidan warned. He had been watching the dark clouds gathering again.

'Then let us continue on to the cabin,' Fidelma decided. 'It is not that far away and we need to complete our business there. Brother Gébennach, I am sorry if you have been held up unduly.'

The young librarian said politely, 'As we are travelling in the same direction and doubtless for the same purpose – that is, to examine the cabin – it is of no matter, lady.'

'In that case, ride alongside me and tell me more about your interpretation of the Faith. I presume your belief is why you joined the Abbey of Ráth Cuáin. I would like to understand more about it, although the abbot tried to explain it to me. Why is it so much at odds with the rest of Christendom that it is called a heresy? For example, the meaning of the symbol around your neck . . .?'

They all remounted and the young librarian moved his ass alongside Fidelma's pony. As they began to proceed on down the hill, he revealed himself to be an enthusiastic and committed scholar. Fidelma hardly had time to insert a question or two here and there. Brother Gébennach touched the silver symbol he wore on a chain around his neck. She had recognised it at once.

'This is the Tau-Rho. It is the symbol of our Faith – which we call Psiloanthropism.'

'I am told that it denies that Jesus was Divine?'

'That is true. There are many Christians who agree with us,' replied

the young man. 'We believe that the tales of divinity were just alle-
gories to impress people. The basis of our belief is that a Hebrew
named Yeshua, the man whose name through Greek and Latin becomes
Jesus, preached a new interpretation of the Hebrew Faith. It was Paul
of Tarsus who, rejected by the Jewish followers of the movement,
like Simon Bar-Jonah, decided to open up the movement to the
Gentiles, those outside the original Hebrew faith. So the Gentiles
needed to be persuaded to join the New Faith. Look at the gods and
heroes in all the various cultures that we have encountered – there
is always some miraculous happening at their birth so that people
can identify the founders of the belief as being above the ordinary.
Many Romans worshipped Mithras, who was similarly born of a
virgin. So Jesus was also made into a man-god.'

'But it is essential to the Faith to accept the divinity of Jesus.
To say otherwise . . .' began Fidelma.

'Is heresy?' Brother Gébennach sighed. 'I have read the work of
Theodotus of Byzantium in our *scriptorium*. Most of the early
followers of Jesus – who Paul's Greeks called Christos, the anointed
one – believed the title referred to merely an ordinary man. He was
a wise and just man but he criticised the Sanhedrin, the temple of
the Hebrew faith, for accepting the Roman occupation of their lands.
By doing so he aroused the support of the Zealots, those Hebrews
fighting against their Roman masters. For this he was executed in
the traditional Roman manner, on a wooden cross, slowly suffocating
to death.

'During the early years, Yeshua's brother Ya'akov became leader
of his philosophy in Jerusalem. It was accepted that he too was a
righteous man who taught the word of the one God. It was Ya'akov,
who was called James in Greek, whose writings were destroyed,
suppressed or distorted after he was also killed by the Romans.
There arose many branches of the Faith, each with differing views
which are now called heresies by those in Rome, who seem to have
invented their own faith.'

Eadulf, who had been following the discourse, was shocked by the idea. 'But the whole basis of the Faith is that Jesus is the Son of God, otherwise what renders Him superior to all the other divinities that are being rejected through the many nations of the world? It is surely that divinity which has caused the New Faith to spread to all the lands?'

The young keeper of books was cynical. 'You think the empire of Rome and its culture had nothing to do with it? The first council of the church to declare the divinity as something all the Faith should follow was the council of Nicaea held under Hosius, Bishop of Carduba, with the patronage of the Roman Emperor Constantine who was the first emperor to convert to the New Faith and declare it the Faith of the Empire. It was the imperial order alone which changed those small persecuted groups who believed in Otherworld salvation to relieve their suffering and assured them of some salvation in this world. That was the incendiary that caused the New Faith to spread like fire across the empire.'

'Your library must contain many interesting books and texts on this matter,' Fidelma remarked innocently. 'Has the library many items that come directly from Rome – texts that the Bishop of Rome would not like people to read; that he would want to be kept secret? For example, books that would support your view of Constantine and the earlier teachings of the Faith?'

The librarian looked at her suspiciously 'Why do you ask?'

'Out of interest. Did the Roman emperor convert only for reasons of political opportunism?'

'Constantine undoubtedly converted to the Faith because he saw a political chance to keep the empire intact, especially against the growth of the cults in Byzantium,' the young man answered immediately. 'He used the Faith as a weapon to control the empire and he used the elevation of the man that the empire had executed to a god-man to replace the other divine beings. He renamed the great city of Byzantium after himself and established a new ruling class who favoured the New Faith. Constantine ordered the council of Nicaea to approve certain concepts of the New Faith that he supported.'

The young librarian was speaking with passion, his voice rising in volume and his right hand hitting the air in emphasis.

It was Aidan who interrupted his flow with a harsh voice.

'Lady, Spelán's cabin is on fire.'

CHAPTER ELEVEN

They had paused on the rise looking down the rocky hillside to the small copse where Spelán the shepherd had his cabin. Through these trees they could see the rising column of black swirling smoke and knew there was no other source for such a density of smoke than the cabin itself.

The track was too precipitous for a canter, let alone a gallop, but Fidelma nudged her pony, Aonbharr, into a trot. She was joined by Aidan, leaving Eadulf and Brother Gébennach to bring up the rear at a more sedate pace. It was not long before Fidelma and Aidan had halted their horses on the edge of the small clearing in which the cabin stood. They left their horses here, out of the path of the billowing smoke.

One end of the building was being quickly devoured in a crackle and snap of flames, which ate hungrily at the dry wood. Even the stones did not impede the ravenous tongues of fire as they demolished the mixture of dry mud, reinforced by horse hair, that bound the stone walls together. The thatch had long gone, and the heavy timber roof beams were now in such a dangerous condition that there was imminent danger of the roof collapsing. The heat was too intense to venture nearer.

'I must have left the fire alight when we left here,' Aidan groaned. 'A spark or something must have caught . . .'

'I don't think so,' cut in Fidelma. 'Look at the way the fire is burning.'

Aidan was puzzled but it was Eadulf, who had just arrived, who saw the significance of her remark.

'The fire is at the opposite end of the cabin to where the hearth was,' he pointed out.

Fidelma glanced at him appreciatively. 'So you see, Aidan, no spark could have traversed the length of the cabin and set fire to the far end to create the conflagration as it burns now.'

The relief on Aidan's features was palpable. Then he saw the significance of this.

'Do you mean that the fire was set deliberately?'

The young librarian had now joined them and was staring in dismay at the sight before them. 'Abbot Síoda is not going to like this. He had planned to place a new shepherd in this cabin.'

Eadulf was examining the fire. 'It is too well alight to douse the flames with just ourselves trying to gather water from that stream,' he concluded. Then he added in a low voice to Fidelma: 'Do you think we missed anything in the cabin which has been the reason for this deliberate act of destruction?'

'Let us hope we did not miss anything,' she replied grimly.

Brother Gébennach had tethered his ass with their horses and was starting to walk around the perimeter of the burning cabin.

'Have a care,' Fidelma called. 'Don't get too near the flames. There are many sparks about.'

The librarian grimaced. 'I don't intend to, lady. I am just going to inspect the grave, as the abbot requested.'

Fidelma had nearly forgotten the second purpose of the librarian's coming. She made sure the horses were tethered well away from the searing heat. While the concentration of the flames had been at the back end of the cabin, they were now licking hungrily towards the other end: the entire construction would soon be consumed. Shielding her face from the heat, she followed Brother Gébennach as he clambered across the rocky mounds at the back of the cabin, making for a small hillock behind it. She could see patches of earth that had been disturbed, as if people had been digging holes here and there.

The librarian had halted, looking bewildered.

'Animals?' Fidelma suggested half-heartedly. 'I am afraid that anything buried can be sniffed out by wolves, foxes . . .'

'So tell me what animal can remove large stones?' the young man replied. 'When Spelán showed me the grave, he had placed several large stones on it. Now they are scattered – and not by wolves or foxes.' He pointed to a mound of earth by a deep hole. 'That was the spot where Spelán said that he had buried the body of his wife.'

Fidelma followed in the direction of his outstretched hand towards the mound of freshly turned earth. She shivered. On it were perched three or four carrion crows pecking away at the disturbed earthworms and grubs. In disgust, she bent and picked up a few small stones and threw them at the glossy black-feathered creatures. With almost disdainful looks in her direction, they hopped across the earth and then, one after another, each took wing, soaring upwards.

The librarian moved across to the deserted heaps of earth. Fidelma followed and gazed down into a large, newly excavated hole.

'So someone has been busy,' she said, almost to herself.

Whether Brother Gébennach heard her or not was uncertain. Instead of responding he said hollowly: 'Whatever was buried here has been removed.'

'Not everything,' Fidelma corrected, having spotted something white in the earth at the bottom of the grave. She jumped down over the loose earth bank to the bottom and picked at the object, coming up triumphantly with a bone. She held it up towards the librarian.

'Then at least we have some part of Caoimhe to re-bury,' he said unctuously. 'It is important to follow ritual.'

To his astonishment Fidelma, after examining the bone, simply tossed it aside as she stared around the hole.

'I am afraid that was the bone of a sheep and now I see several smaller bones belonging to the same species.'

She noticed a piece of torn sacking, picking it up and peering carefully at the edge of the tear. Then she looked at some of the smaller rocks, A couple seemed to intrigue her. She picked them up – small, heavy, metallic objects – and placed them in her *marsupium* together with the torn sacking.

'What is it?' Brother Gébennach demanded. 'What have you found?'

Before she could reply, they heard Eadulf calling and a moment later he came hurrying from the end of the cabin towards them. There was some alarm on his face.

'What is it?' she demanded.

'Horsemen are approaching from the south. Three of them.' He paused, looked at her standing in the hole and added: 'What are you doing down there?'

She did not reply but held up a hand. 'Help me out of here.' As she scrambled out of the hole with his aid, she asked, 'What sort of horsemen? Are they warriors? What?'

'Not warriors,' he replied. 'At least, so Aidan says. He thinks they are led by that woodsman, Torcán.'

Aidan was right. There were three riders, two young men and the tall woodsman who dismounted first and seemed astonished as he recognised them.

'What has happened here, lady? We saw the smoke of the burning cabin and came straight away to see if there was anything we could save.'

'Good day to you, Torcán. I don't suppose you saw anyone on the path here or leaving the area before you spotted the fire?' Fidelma asked.

Torcán's eyes widened. 'Then it was not you who set fire to the cabin?'

Fidelma shook her head. 'A *dálaigh* has better things to do than go around setting fires and destroying important evidence. We have only just arrived here. So when did you notice this fire?'

'One of my sons,' he indicated one of the young men with him, 'saw the pall of smoke rising. Since you came yesterday, and we knew that Spelán was dead, we thought to come and save what we could.'

'Well, there is nothing much to save now.' Eadulf gestured disgustedly at the cabin, where the flames, having almost exhausted the fuel, were now dying down.

Torcán was turning away when Brother Gébennach, who had remained to examine the empty grave further, appeared round the corner. It was clear that the keeper of books and the woodsman recognised one another.

'For someone who has newly joined the abbey, you seem to be well known locally, my friend,' Fidelma observed quietly.

The young fellow shrugged. 'When I first arrived in this territory, I came to the cabin of the woodsman there. He and his wife were kind enough to give me directions to the abbey.'

'Did you inform the woodsman that Caoimhe had been buried behind this cabin?'

Torcán let out a whistle. 'Is that so? No one among our *tuath* knew that.'

'The abbot, who is your chieftain, knew it,' Brother Gébennach replied.

'Well, where *is* Caoimhe's grave?' Torcán wanted to know. 'We need to show our respect. We are all members of the same clan here.'

'The grave is no longer there,' Fidelma informed him quietly. 'In fact, I think the body, or whatever was buried in the grave, was removed within the last few days.'

Torcán looked shocked. 'What witchcraft is this?' he breathed.

'I hardly think it witchcraft,' Fidelma replied. She removed the piece of sackcloth from her *marsupium*. 'You will see that the tears on this are recent. The sackcloth was recovered from the grave but the tears show the material has not been lying in the grave more than a few days.'

'What else would this be but witchcraft?' demanded Torcán. 'Have you forgotten what this evening is? And did you not tell us that Spelán's body was found hidden in the Samhain fire that would have been ignited tonight to guard Cashel against the vengeful spirits of the Otherworld?'

It was pure coincidence but there was a sudden roar of flames from the cabin and the weakened timbers crashed into the centre of the building, spitting huge sparks of fire in all directions. For a moment, in the darkening cloudy sky, the burst of flames lit the horrified faces of the woodsman and his two sons. There were similar expressions on the faces of Eadulf and Aidan.

Only Fidelma and Brother Gébennach remained apparently unperturbed.

It was the young librarian who finally broke the spell. Glancing up at the sky, he said, 'Friends, I must continue my journey to Ara's Well across the great river. When I return, I shall inform the abbot about the happenings here. Farewell.'

They watched him in silence as he climbed onto his ass and began to amble away across the hillside in the direction of the river.

'If Caoimhe was buried here,' Eadulf said, turning to Fidelma, 'what gain would there be in removing her body?'

Torcán was gazing at the smouldering embers. 'I don't think there'll be another shepherd living here now, not once this story is spoken of. At least the roof falling in has made the flames die down. Even if we have no more rain today, the fire will soon be extinguished. Let us return home, boys.' The last words were addressed to his two sons, who had remained silent from the moment they had arrived. As they all mounted up, Torcán paused to gaze down at Fidelma.

'There is evil in this place, lady. I would advise you to hurry back to Cashel before darkness comes, for remember what tonight is.'

Without waiting for a response, he turned his horse and trotted away back down the hillside towards the woods, followed by his sons.

'I think he is right,' Aidan muttered, anxiously gazing up at the sky. 'It is pointless remaining here now. Let's get back to Cashel before dusk descends.'

Fidelma hesitated a few moments before saying to Eadulf, 'Just now you asked me a question: what gain was there, in removing Caoimhe's body from the grave.'

Eadulf nodded. 'Is there an answer?'

Fidelma reached into her *marsupium* and drew out the two small pebbles. Eadulf took them and stared closely at them.

'They are a bit like the little piece of metal Aidan found in the cabin,' he said, rubbing one against the other and seeing the sparkle of metal.

'Exactly so. In silver there is the profit.'

It was still daylight when they passed Della's homestead on the outskirts of the township but Fidelma decided not to stop for a chat as was her usual habit. Instead, they rode straight for the central square, heading along with a few other individuals towards the focal point of the great Samhain bonfire. Fidelma noticed that Aidan was keeping a careful eye on the people they passed.

'What's up?' she asked.

'Many of these folk are from the outlying homesteads and communities, not from the township.'

'Well, it's early yet,' offered Eadulf. 'Most of the locals probably won't emerge until after dark to see the bonfire.'

'That's not the way it is done,' Aidan told him. 'Most people gather while it is still light and start the feasting and games around

the bonfire before it is ritually lit. There just seems a lack of enthusiasm about attending this year's feasting.'

They came into the square by the corner of Rumann's tavern.
The unlit bonfire still towered in the centre. The woodsman Curnan
and his helpers had repaired the damage and done their work well.
It was a truly spectacular construction and once ignited, it would
be visible right across the great Plain of Femen to the southern
mountains. But there were far fewer people than usual in the square
and those that were there seemed far from in a festive mood. Small
groups huddled here and there, and the few traders stood waiting,
by their carts, bemused by the lack of custom. Where were the large
crowds on whom their livelihoods depended?

The three riders reined in their horses and examined the scene.

'Lady!' It was Rumann. He came hurrying out of his inn towards
them. Fidelma dismounted and secured her horse to the wooden
railing by the tavern. The others did the same.

'Greetings, Rumann. I wanted a word with you about that woman
called Brancheó.'

'That is exactly who I wanted to speak with you about,' he replied
fiercely, not seeming to be intimidated by her angry tone. He made
a motion with his hand as if to ward off her next question.

'It was a bad day that ever I spoke about her,' he admitted, turning
to the square and the isolated groups of people gathered there. 'Now
look!'

Eadulf smiled thinly. 'The people hereabouts have doubtless heard
the story of curses and murdered bodies, and are afraid to attend
the celebration this evening.'

'It is disastrous. I have never seen the Samhain festival so poorly
attended.'

But Fidelma was in no mood to be sympathetic.

'Did you expect otherwise, after you ignored my request to stay
silent and instead spread the stories of murder and her curse?'

'I thought it would give the evening an added attraction,' he blustered feebly. 'People are often fascinated by the bizarre and weird.'

'It did not work, did it?' Eadulf pointed out.

'That is true,' Rumann accepted. 'The majority of people here have come because they have not heard the story. Those who have, are too scared to venture forth.'

'All because of this woman's silly reminder that tonight is the one night when the Otherworld becomes visible to us and the forces of evil will threaten us.' Fidelma snorted. 'We have lived and celebrated that old belief for countless years. So why have we suddenly taken fright? It is ridiculous.'

'It is the way she has been pronouncing the curse, lady.' It was a new voice which made the explanation. They turned round and found Curnan the woodsman.

'In what manner had she been saying this curse?' Fidelma asked.

Curnan shuffled his large feet in the dust. 'There is a strange intensity about the woman,' he mumbled, looking sheepish.

'Who – Brancheó? Anyone can look intense, especially when dressed up in a raven-feather cloak, with accompanying all-black clothing so that they look the very image of how we imagine an evil entity to appear.'

'But it is the expression, the conviction in her voice . . .'

'Where is the woman now?' Eadulf wanted to know. 'I thought she had left yesterday. Has she returned to Cashel?'

'She has been going about the town since midday, calling forth curses,' confirmed Curnan.

'Stoking up the fears of people in order to prevent them from enjoying the end-of-summer celebration,' Rumann said resentfully.

'Succeeding, so it appears,' Eadulf said. 'And with some help from the tavern-keeper.'

'There is something else, lady,' Rumann said, ignoring the barb.

'What do you mean?'

The innkeeper cleared his throat nervously. 'She has been telling people that the curse that is about to come on this township is the fault of your brother, the King – and all the Eóghanacht. She blames all even on your ancestors right back to Óengus, the first Christian King to rule from Cashel. She says the old gods are angry and will extort vengeance before this very night is out.'

Fidelma was smiling. 'So I have heard before. Are you telling me that the townsfolk actually believe this nonsense?'

Rumann did not answer and so Fidelma gave an exasperated sigh, glancing from the tavern-keeper to the woodsman.

'Where is this so-called "raven-caller" now?'

'What she was saying was reported to the King, your brother, lady. He sent men of his bodyguard and they took her prisoner to the fortress,' replied Curnan.

'She is a prisoner in the fortress on my brother's orders?' Fidelma was startled.

'Yes,' confirmed the woodsman. 'Better there than flitting around like a shadow cursing the town and spreading panic.'

'*Shadow*, Curnan? I think you almost believe that she truly is of the Otherworld. But no – she is flesh and blood just as I am. And I can assure you that her prognostications of Otherworldly doom will be a matter of laughter by tomorrow.'

'But we have tonight to survive, lady,' muttered the woodsman.

Fidelma suddenly looked at him closely. 'One question before I leave, Curnan. Yesterday you were keen to visit Spelán's cabin. Have you been anywhere near it recently?'

'Not I,' he responded immediately, his expression guileless.

Fidelma hesitated a moment before turning to Eadulf and Aidan and saying briskly, 'Come, let us get to the fortress for we have much to do this evening. I wish we could have resolved things before my brother's celebratory feast. Perhaps he acted wisely in having Brancheó imprisoned for this night.'

As they entered the gates, dusk was beginning to settle. The stable boys came running forward to take their horses. Gormán was crossing the courtyard and she beckoned the warrior over.

'Good to see your safe return, lady,' he greeted her. 'Your brother has been fretting that you might not get back here in time for the feasting. The guests have all arrived. The princes of Muscraige Mittine, the Uí Liathán, the Déisi Mumana, Muscraige Breogáin . . .'

She held up her hand to stay his recitation of the local princes.

'I hear that my brother has imprisoned the woman, Brancheó,' she said, interrupting him.

'Indeed, lady. I was ordered to take some of the guard and search the town for her as reports reached your brother that she was uttering a prophecy bringing down the wrath of the old gods on Cashel and the Eóghanacht. She is in the cells of the Hall of Heroes, waiting the King's pleasure.'

Fidelma exchanged a frowning glance with Eadulf before saying, 'It may be that she is involved with the murder of Spelán. I shall want to question her.'

'But the hour grows late for the King's feast, lady,' Gormán protested. 'If you need to question her, 'twould be better you wait until later. I see that you and friend Eadulf are both in need of a bath and change . . . if I do not offend you by mentioning it. Aidan, too, appears in need of a good wash.'

Fidelma realised that the dirt and smoke from the cabin fire as well as their journey must have left their mark on all of them. She relaxed and smiled.

'You are right to remind us of protocol, Gormán. Off you go, Aidan, while Eadulf and I prepare for the feast. I hope my brother is in better spirits than when we left him?' she added as an after-thought to Gormán.

The guard commander was sombre. 'I too had hoped that he would be in a better frame of mind after spending time in the company of the Princess of Éile. Unfortunately, however, his mood has worsened as the day continues. I fear your brother has taken the evil prophecies to heart – but I shall say no more, lady. You may observe so tonight.'

Fidelma and Eadulf went first to reassure little Alchú of their safe return and to pay their son some attention before ordering Muirgen to prepare their evening baths. Then, having bathed and put on clean clothing as befitted the evening's feasting, they made their way to Colgú's great hall, where the King was due to receive his distinguished visitors and their partners. It was Dego who had been chosen to be in charge of the warriors on duty at the feast that evening. He was standing outside the main doors as they approached: his task was to ensure that no guest entered the feasting hall carrying a weapon. It was an old tradition and established by law. Before opening the doors to allow them to pass inside, he whispered to Fidelma: 'Forgive me, lady, a quick word.'

'What is it?' Fidelma asked in surprise.

Dego gave a conspiratorial glance around as if anxious not to be overheard.

'The King is in an ill humour. I think he has imbibed a little too much *corma*.'

'What?' Fidelma remembered that Gormán had warned her about her brother's low spirits.

'After you left this morning, the King began to grow morbid. He kept asking when you were returning, and had there been any word to say that you had resolved the death of the shepherd. His mood grew worse when he heard about this strange woman, the raven-caller, who has been uttering curses and prophesying the end of Cashel during the festival tonight. I have never seen him so distraught, lady, or less able to hold his liquor.'

'I thought the Princess of Éile was going to be his companion throughout the day. Were they not due to go riding?'

'There was some problem,' replied Dego. 'I think they had a disagreement of some kind and the King shut himself in his chambers for most of the afternoon. The Princess Gélgeis went riding with her ladies and one of her guards this afternoon.'

Fidelma compressed her lips for a moment. 'Thank you for alerting us, Dego. Stay close, this night. You may be needed before it is over.'

'I shall, lady,' the warrior assured her quietly as he opened the doors into the feasting hall.

The great hall was a long, narrow room. The tables stretched on either side but with the seats placed so that each guest and his or her consorts sat only on one side of the table, with their backs to the walls as tradition ordained. On the walls behind them were hooks for shields or pennants, placed depending on the rank of the guests. Behind each chair of a noble was room for the shield-bearer to stand. Shield-bearers stood only as a symbolic act, for no one but the commander of the King's bodyguard was allowed to bear arms in a feasting hall. At the far end of the room was a dais on which a table was placed broadside on. The King and his personal retinue sat at this table. As Fidelma passed down the hall to the places allotted to Eadulf and herself, she did not need to consult the shields and pennants to recognise the princes, lords of territories, and their wives.

There were several important guests missing that night. Finguine, the young heir apparent to the kingdom, cousin to Colgú and Fidelma; the Chief Brehon Fíthel, and, of course, the Abbot of Imleach, as Chief Bishop of the kingdom, who usually attended special functions. At the foot of the long tables, closest to the doors, sat Brother Mac Raith, as steward of Imleach. With him were his three religious colleagues. They seemed ill at ease in the company. However, Brother Conchobhar sat with them and by his side, they also saw Febal. The young poet of the Uí Briúin of Connacht had not been assigned a shield-bearer or pennant. While all courtesy was extended in accordance with the law of hospitality, the fact remained that he was a suspect in Fidelma's investigations. However, the young man seemed completely relaxed, even a trifle debonair, for he inclined his head pleasantly to Fidelma and Eadulf as they passed, pausing in his conversation with his neighbour, the old apothecary. Fidelma and Eadulf overheard some light-hearted banter on the subject of poetry in Latin. It seemed to amuse both men.

In the absence of members of the King's personal household, only Fidelma and Eadulf were conducted to the left of the central chair of the King on the dais. They acknowledged the greetings from the group of guests, of which there were only thirty or more in the hall. This was unusual for an official feast but the story of the curse had spread swiftly and many found excuses not to attend.

As they sat down, Eadulf whispered, 'I have never known your brother to drink more than was good for him.'

'I fear this curse upon the family and Cashel has touched something in him,' she replied quietly. 'He always believed in ancient prophesies when he was younger. I wonder . . .'

In a corner, near the King's chair, stood a *fear-stuic*, a trumpeter, who suddenly raised his instrument to his lips and gave three short blasts.

The curtain behind the King's chair was drawn aside and Gormán entered. As commander of the King's bodyguard, his role that night was to stand in as steward to the King. But for the running of the palace, Colgú relied on the plump female *ainbertach* or housekeeper, Dar Luga. Fidelma was still unused to the fact that her brother had declined to appoint a new *rechtaire* or steward of the palace who, with a staff of office, would usually preside over the protocol of the feast. Instead of the traditional banging of the staff on the floor, Gormán simply called for silence.

Colgú then entered and, on his arm, was the attractive young Princess of Éile, Gelgéis, who immediately smiled at Fidelma and Eadulf and mouthed a silent greeting towards them. However, her face showed she was strained and unhappy.

Gelgéis was of average height, slim, with corn-coloured hair drawn tightly back and fastened behind her head. Her skin was delicate and fair and she had azure-blue eyes and a quality of innocence. Yet she ruled her little border kingdom with a rod of iron, paying allegiance to Cashel but not allowing her kingdom to be overwhelmed by either Muman to the west nor Laighin to the east. In spite of her sweet appearance, there was a steely determination in the girl. That quality had attracted Fidelma. She hoped that Gelgéis and her brother might marry one day because she knew that Colgú needed a steady companion with the princess' strong attributes.

Gormán stood dithering, unused to the service he was performing, and then bent to whisper in Colgú's ear: 'Lord, should I make some sort of announcement? Protocol, you understand.'

Colgú gave a roar of laughter and playfully pushed the warrior aside. Fidelma and Eadulf silently acknowledged that Dego was right; it was clear that Colgú had already been imbibing.

Colgú called out: 'Friends, tonight is without formality. Wasn't it old tradition that tonight, the end of the summer and the first of our new year, always started in chaos? So let chaos reign during this feast. There is no protocol here tonight. We are here to cast off the old and pay homage to the new . . . whatever it has in store for us. Whether we will welcome in the creatures from the dark plains of the Otherworld or the wraiths of those we have done wrong to . . . or whether we pass this night in drunken revelry, we welcome all to our ancient feast of Samhain.'

He slid into his chair, more with the help of Gormán and Gelgéis on either side.

The guests, having recovered from their surprise at the strange lack of protocol, immediately settled ready for the meal as the side doors opened and attendants came hurrying in. Dar Luga, Colgu's housekeeper, had done her work well. Firstly came the *deoghbhaire*, the cupbearers, who strove to keep the guests supplied with their choice of beverages. Then came *dáilemain*, carvers, who brought in freshly cooked dishes of roasted boar, venison and even mutton. While they helped guests to their choice of cuts, other attendants carried dishes ranging from goose eggs and sausages to various cabbages spiced with wild garlic, to leeks and onions cooked in butter.

Fidelma leaned towards her brother as the cupbearer poured his wine. 'You have surely drunk enough already, brother,' she whispered primly. 'Remember you have a special guest with you.' She indicated the Princess of Éile.

Colgú turned to her, his eyes a little unfocused. 'Enough mothering, little sister. If you were concerned about me, you would have solved the ritual killing that has plagued us, and stopped the curses of the spirit of death. Now the Samhain feast is upon us and we will be lucky to survive the night.'

Fidelma was disconcerted by her brother's petulant tone. She had never seen him drunk either in private or in public. What was going on?

Princess Gelgéis leaned across to Fidelma in order to speak.

'I can cope, lady,' she assured her in a discreet murmur. 'The governance of Éile is not always an easy task, for our menfolk are no abstemious and pious religious. On nights like these it is not unusual for them to do away with constraints. Responsibility is sometimes in need of irresponsibility.'

'Within limitations,' Fidelma corrected firmly.

The noise in the great hall had developed into an uproar as the feast got underway. Fidelma realised that, even with Gélgeis and herself on either side of him, her brother seemed isolated, as if his thoughts were somewhere else. Suddenly one of the diners – Eadulf thought it was the Prince of the Muscraige – called to Colgú: 'Tonight is Samhain. Is it not usual to have musicians to entertain us at the celebration?'

The remark seemed to register with Colgú. He stirred and then gave forth a drunken chuckle before he banged on the table with the pommel of his knife.

'I stand rebuked. My friends, you shall have entertainment. But not merely music. This night is special, as you know. So I have reserved an equally special entertainment for you. I want you all to hear your fate from a soothsayer.'

Fidelma froze. 'If you are about to do what I think you are, then I must protest,' she hissed. 'Brancheó is in this fortress as a suspect waiting to be questioned by me. She is not to be made sport of. She has rights.'

Colgú gave his sister a disapproving look, exaggerated by the fact that the drink was in control of his speech and actions.

'You are in no position to criticise your King, even though you are my sister. Our family and this palace have been threatened by this madwoman. So she will be brought forth so that my good friends and guests will hear all her nonsense about the Samhain curse on the Eóghanacht.'

Ignoring her protests, he turned to where Gormán was waiting.

'As I have ordered, so let it be done.'

Gormán glanced uncomfortably towards Fidelma. He was clearly unhappy with the order. When Colgú saw the gesture, he roared at his bodyguard commander: 'Do you hesitate to obey me? Do I have to ask someone else to carry out your King's orders?'

Gormán stiffened, never having been rebuked by Colgú in public before. He hesitated a moment, but seeing the warning glance from Fidelma, he marched off to fulfil his orders. She breathed out a sigh of relief, for a slight to a warrior's honour, especially in front of such guests as these, could easily lead to disaster.

It was a while before Gormán returned with the tall, dark woman walking before him. Gormán guided her firmly but gently to the table where Colgú sat. Fidelma was clearly upset, for despite her pleas, her brother now stood in breach of the law. However, there was little she could now do to protect the woman's rights under the law without directly challenging her brother before his guests.

'So, raven-caller,' Colgú greeted her in a supercilious tone. 'I have summoned you to this company so that you can repeat your attempts to curse your King and his family. I wish all our friends to share a knowledge of what you claim is about to visit this palace before this night passes.'

Brancheó was not cowed but regarded him almost with pity on her face. She looked from him to Fidelma and addressed her.

'I realise that it was not you who has summoned me in this illegal fashion, *dálaigh*. You would know better. But you should have taught your brother something of your knowledge of law. For he clearly is ignorant of legal protocol.'

Before Fidelma could answer her there was a call from one of the guests. Brother Giolla Rua had leaned forward and now shouted loudly and indignantly, '*Rex non potest peccare!*'

Brancheó's smile broadened into a sneer. 'So speaks the language of the New Faith. And if, as you say, the King can do no wrong, this scion of the Eóghanacht is guiltless. But doesn't the ancient law say: who is higher in power, the King or his people?' She turned back to Fidelma. 'Answer me that, *dálaigh*, and answer it loudly so your brother may hear and learn.'

Fidelma's mouth compressed. She knew well the answer.

'I will tell you, if you don't wish to speak,' declared Brancheó, breaking the silence. 'The people are higher in power than a King for it is they who appoint the King. The King does not appoint the people.'

'What double-talk is this?' demanded Colgú, blinking uncertainly. 'Silence, woman, or I'll . . . I'll . . .'

'Let her speak, Colgú,' Princess Gelgéis advised gently. She had been fairly silent throughout the meal, trying to reason a little with the King. 'Let's hear what she has to say. For it is true that this is what the law texts say. It is this woman's right to speak. This is not a court of the Brehons where there are rights – but here there should also be courtesy.'

Colgú stared at her for a moment or two and then muttered, 'I am the King. Let her incriminate herself and then we shall judge her,' and he reached for his wine.

'You know there is nothing that you can threaten me with, Colgú son of Failbe Flann,' Brancheó declared. 'You, who boast of your ancestors who ruled here in the New Faith. The New Faith – but what is that? Some foreign mysticism that arose from the east and which those who claim to represent it can barely understand.'

There were gasps of outrage from Brother Mac Raith and his companions. But she ignored them.

'The years that have passed since Óengus mac Nad Froich rejected the ways of his ancestors and embraced this eastern Faith have been but the blink of an eye compared to the generations of your ancestors who stood firm in the Old Religion. Some fifteen Kings of the Eòghanacht have presided over the Rock of Cashel since Óengus. What is that, compared to fifty-nine generations of great kings who ruled this kingdom since the time of Eibhear Fionn, son of Golamh, who brought the children of the Gael to this land? Fifty-nine great kings, all who ruled wisely and well in the Old Faith from the time beyond time.'

'I am afraid, lady, times change and we must change with them,' Fidelma intervened softly, feeling she should say something to dilute the tension.

Brancheó turned to regard her, still with her expression of pity.

'Little change in us, lady. We are bound up on the great wheel of life that, turn it as swiftly as you dare, will always return to the same point.'

'You speak a pagan treason,' Brother Sionnach cried out.

'You talk of treason?' Brancheó did not even turn towards him but stood continuing to face the King. 'I know you, Sionnach of

Corcach Mór. You will bring no light to destroy the Abbey of Ráth Cuáin for it is already marked for destruction.'

'Have a care, woman,' Brother Sionnach called back. 'You do not know of what you speak.'

For the first time, Brancheó turned to face him. She said coldly, 'I speak of what I know: that you have come here to seek what will never be yours. You cannot steal an idea and bury it in earth or encase it in stone. It will escape into the air no matter how you hide it. Even the greatest of your Brehons will tell you – truth is great and it will prevail.'

Brother Sionnach had paled slightly. 'I don't understand you, lady,' he said, but his voice lacked his previous confidence.

'You have made a long journey across land and sea, my friend. But even you will find that your light will be eliminated. A man has been murdered and an attempt made to disguise the murder by a false ritual. That will not work, for as I said, the truth will prevail and there is nowhere people can hide, to protect themselves from the truth. Truth is the one thing that never dies. It can be hidden for a while – but it will always re-emerge to claim its own.'

'Stop speaking in riddles,' Colgú slurred, trying to understand the exchanges. 'If you can't speak plainly, perhaps we have finished with our entertainment.'

'You should never have started such so-called entertainment,' Fidelma admonished quietly. She was about to suggest to Gormán that he remove the prisoner, but Brancheó was not to be silenced.

'Scion of the Eóghanacht,' she called loudly. 'I have spoken plainly to those who have the ears to understand the words they hear. Eibhear Fion and his brother Eremon came to this island with their new truth and thought to fight the Eternal Ones. But the Eternal Ones were strong and it was Eibhear Fionn and Eremon who had to accept them and promise them allegiance until Time itself had ceased. Your ancestors, Eóghanacht, promised they would keep faith with the Eternal Ones and, in token, continue to accept the names of the three goddesses of sovereignty as the names for this island. Do their names not still resound in our ears in spite of our rejection of them? Éire, Banba and Fodhla – the names of our goddesses are still ours to call upon. But be warned, scion of the Eóghanacht, they grow impatient that we do not call upon them for protection of the Five Kingdoms from a foreign deity.'

'Are you warning me?' Colgú was frowning, befuddled, unable to follow what she was saying.

'I am warning all who thought they could reject the True Faith, the Faith of the time beyond time,' replied Branchéo, unperturbed by the drunken anger in his face. 'I am warning those who think they can kill to prevent the truth being heard. A man has gone to his death in order that his tongue may be stilled – and in such a way that I may be blamed for it. But I say again: the truth will emerge.

'It has been revealed to me that there is restlessness in the Otherworld. The gods and goddesses are stirred in anger towards those who would deny them. Tonight is the Samhain festival, the time when the vengeful souls of the Otherworld come to seek their revenge on those who have wronged them. Tonight, the gods themselves will come to seek retribution on those who have desecrated this very spot which was once a passage to the Otherworld. Remember – a passage can lead both ways and they will come . . . they will come. That is all I have to say. I make no threat. I demand nothing in return, but I simply say the Donn waits to transport souls to the House of Death.'

Eadulf spoke up then. 'For someone who claims not to be issuing warnings, that does sound remarkably like a threat.'

'No threat. This palace of Cashel was once called "the ridge of the Otherworld people" – Sidh-druimm. Why was it called that?'

Fidelma felt she should intervene. 'Do you claim to be teaching the Eóghanacht their history?' She forced a smile.

'I am only reminding them of what has apparently been forgotten,' the woman replied with equanimity. 'What brought the Eóghanacht here in the first place; what made them establish their capital here?'

'That's easy enough. Conall son of Lugaidh, when he was King, decided to set up his capital here.'

'Not so easy. For you should remember that he was only the son of a Prince of Muscraige. The gods sent him a vision through his swineherd who drew him to this spot and promised, if he set up his capital here, he would become King and be supported by the gods and goddesses at this, their portal between the two worlds.'

'The story of the finding of Cashel is well known.' Fidelma spoke coldly. 'Cuiríran, the swineherd, and his friend, Duirdriu, were herding their pigs here. The legend goes that the gods caused a great tiredness to fall on them. They were supposed to have slept for three days and nights and dreamed that Conall would be hailed as the true descendant of Eibhear Fionn and King of Muman if he set up his capital here. It is all a legend.'

'No! The story is true. The pact was made with the gods and thus Conall came and put his foot on the sacred inauguration stone while his chief bard sang the ancient *forsundud*, the praise poem about the ancestors of the Eóghanacht from the time they first came from across the seas to take this island.'

'We have had enough entertainment for tonight,' Colgú suddenly announced. 'I grow tired of these tales. Tales to scare young children, not . . . not . . . Go!'

'I will go, Colgú, son of Failbhe Flann. Have no fear of my going but have a fear of what is coming.'

'That is definitely a threat,' Fidelma snapped.

'Seeing what the future portends is no threat, Fidelma of Cashel. You would be wise to remember the ancestor whose name you bear.'

'My name?' Fidelma asked uncertainly.

'Are you sure that you do not know who Conall mac Luagaidh's foster-mother was?'

If Fidelma had known, her memory was now lacking and she said so.

'Why does the name Fidelma appear among all the generations

of the Eóghanacht?' asked Brancheó. 'I will tell you – Conall's foster-mother was a great Druidess who bore that very name – Fidelma. She was his protector when the evil Mongfind tried to destroy him, to prevent him from becoming King. How was he given the name "Corc" – for it is as Conall Corc he is known. That is because Mongfind tried to burn him to death, but Fidelma deflected the fire so that only his ear was singed. Fidelma consigned the evil one to the utmost reaches of the Otherworld. That was on the eve of Samhain, which you celebrate this very night. That you bear a name so respected among those who have now rejected the Old Faith is something that you should not treat lightly. I see, even now, you try to fulfil the role of Fidelma the Druidess by seeking to protect your King.'

'Enough!' Colgú almost groaned. 'Gormán, remove this woman from our presence. I grow tired of her prattling. Tell her to be gone. This is not the entertainment I want. Send for more wine and the musicians.'

Gormán touched Brancheó lightly on the arm and indicated the door of the great hall with a slight nod of his head.

'It would be wise to go voluntarily,' was all he said in a quiet tone.

She cast a disdainful look around the assembly. 'Enjoy this last night, Eóghanachtaí,' she said, using the plural form.

Fidelma turned to her brother in disgust as they left. 'What purpose did that serve?' she accused him. 'She did nothing but repeat the old legends and it got her so worked up that I will be unable to question her about the death of the shepherd until tomorrow.'

Colgú turned a bleary-eyed gaze on his sister. 'You should have resolved that matter before this night came upon us. Don't you chide me, little sister. I have had more than enough of ghosts and portents and other warnings. The Samhain festival is a time to celebrate the coming year, not for dwelling on the darkness and the Otherworld.'

Fidelma would have liked to follow Brancheó immediately, just to see if she could question her. But etiquette dictated that she could not leave an official feast before the King left or gave her permission. And to do so before the guests started to leave was unthinkable. The musicians had entered the feasting hall by now and had begun to prepare themselves. Fidelma was shocked that some guests, on seeing the King's condition, were not obeying protocol. Brother Mac Raith's party, for instance, were having some trouble leaving because the young poet of the Uí Briúin Seóla also seemed to be in a hurry to pass through the door before them, forcing them to stand aside. It crossed her mind that Febal might have left in pursuit of Gormán and the prisoner.

Colgú now lay slumped with his head on the table. Princess Gelgéis smiled sadly at Fidelma.

'Your brother has had enough entertainment for the evening,' she said. 'I know that he has been under some strain, for he seems to take this curse more seriously than I would have expected. I will get Dar Luga to find attendants to assist him to his chamber.'

Fidelma returned the girl's smile with sympathy. 'I can only say that this behaviour is not my brother's usual way of dealing with such matters. I apologise.'

However, it was now the appropriate opportunity to leave the feasting hall for a while. She asked Eadulf to remain, saying that she would return shortly. As Fidema left the hall, she noted that Brother Mac Raith and two of his companions were still talking animatedly in the passage outside. With a nod to them she reached the line of cloaks hanging in the corridor and took her own woollen one, draping it around her shoulders. Then she hurried out into the chilly courtyard and peered round with the help of burning brand torches which lit the paved area with a flickering light. She could see no sign of Gormán or of Brancheó, although she spotted the figure of a religieux vanishing towards the chapel and presumed it was the third scholar in Brother Mac Raith's group.

'Your brother organises a good feast, lady,' a voice said close by. She turned and found Febal leaning against the wall. She had the impression he was regarding her in amusement. 'But it was too liquid in form for my taste. I must also say that music is fine and the contention of the poets is better entertainment than the one he provided.'

'I apologise for the shortcomings of the feast, Febal,' she replied quietly. 'It is not often my brother takes more wine than is good for him. He, as are we all, is worried about recent events. You will forgive our lack of etiquette.'

Leaving him with dignity, she went across the courtyard. There was still no sign of Gormán or the woman as she hurried to the gates. Enda was on duty and he looked surprised when she asked him if Gormán had taken Brancheó to the cells set aside for prisoners.

'Gormán has already left the fortress,' Enda replied. 'He did so only moments ago.'

'He's left?' Fidelma was taken aback.

'I think he was upset by something the King said to him. He told me that he felt the King no longer needed him. Dego is now in charge. So he has gone to be with his mother and wife at the big fire in the town square.'

Fidelma groaned inwardly. It was clear that Gormán had felt Colgú's insult keenly.

'And the woman he was escorting – she is back in the cells?'

'Why, no, lady. Gormán released her at the gate.'

'Released the woman?' Fidelma tried to keep her amazement in check. 'Wasn't she taken to the guard room?'

Enda was bewildered. 'Why should she be?'

'Because I wanted to question her, that's why.' Fidelma felt her dismay give way to anger.

'But Gormán thought she was to be released,' Enda protested. 'The King himself told the woman to go. Gormán took her to the gate and told her to be on her way. So she left first. Then he spoke to me to tell me that Dego had been left in charge. After that, he left.'

Fidelma groaned loudly.

'What is it, lady?'

Fidelma realised that she could not blame Gormán. Her brother's order was not specific, and due to his drunken state it was easy to mistake his meaning. This Gormán had done. *'Tell the woman to be gone.'* He had simply been following orders.

'It's all right, Enda,' she said, calming her thoughts. 'It was just a misunderstanding, that's all.'

She walked slowly to the centre of the gates, with a puzzled Enda escorting her, and stood looking out across the township. She could see, across the darkness that separated the elevated limestone rock on which the fortress was built, the township silhouetted against the smoky orange glow which was arising from the great fire on the square. For a moment or two she was in half a mind to go down into the darkness herself, towards the fire in pursuit of the woman known as the raven-caller. Then the thought occurred to her that if anything were to happen to fulfil the woman's prophecy, she should not go off alone and unprotected, that night of all nights. If any Otherworld vengeance was going to overtake her family, she should not put herself in harm's way. She could not help the sudden violent shiver that ran through her.

'It's a cold night, lady,' Enda observed sympathetically, misinterpreting the cause of the motion.

Fidelma smiled in the darkness, realising that she was almost as bad as her brother; making herself believe in this mysticism. 'The great fire is dying now,' she indicated the township with a nod of her head. 'The moon will soon be descending and people will be going homeward.'

Enda chuckled. 'Those that are capable of finding their way, lady. I'm sure that Rumann will make a good profit from his brewery this night.'

Fidelma agreed. 'I suppose there is some escape from the shadows of the Otherworld in alcohol,' she muttered. She glanced around the tall walls and towers of her brother's palace and drew her cloak more protectively around her. It was suddenly very cold.

ChAPTER TWELVE

T here was a distant sound of a voice calling and a muffled
banging noise. Fidelma stirred in the warmth of the bed and
opened her eyes. She became aware that it was daylight. Beside
her, Eadulf was yawning in protest, still unwilling to wake. It took
several moments for her to realise that it was well past dawn. It
was the first day of the New Year. The Samhain festival had passed.
It had passed and she had not been visited by any vengeful beings
from the Otherworld! She breathed out in a long sigh of relief and
began to smile.

But someone was still hammering on the door of their chamber.

'What is it?' she managed to mumble.

The door opened and Muirgen the nurse came in, looking anxious.

'Forgive me, lady. That young warrior, Aidan, is outside. He
demands to speak to you immediately.'

Fidelma blinked a moment. Eadulf was still half awake.

Muirgen repeated herself. 'It is beyond first light and the warrior
Aidan wants to speak with you both – urgently.'

Fidelma now came to her full senses and reached out to clutch
her robe, swinging out of bed to draw it on. 'All right, Muirgen;
let him come in.' Saying this, she went to a water jug and poured
herself a drink. As she swallowed, Eadulf sat up and was massaging
his forehead, groaning quietly now and then.

'Why is it that we are continually pestered by people wanting to speak with us before we can finish a decent night's sleep?' he grumbled, in between attempts to massage away his discomfort.

'Too much *corma*?' reproved Fidelma, without sympathy. She returned to a little jug, removed its cork and poured some of the liquid into another cup before handing it to Eadulf. 'Better take that to get rid of your headache. It's Brother Conchobhar's remedy; a distillation from willow leaves.'

'It would have been insulting to refuse to drink the many toasts that your kindred kept proposing last night,' Eadulf grunted between swallows of the liquid and screwing up his face as he did so at the taste. 'Intoxicating liquor is always part of these wretched celebrations but I had to follow custom.'

'You did not have to try to follow the example of my brother,' she said. 'His behaviour was unseemly for a leader of his people.'

'I have never seen him in such a mood as last night,' Eadulf admitted. 'I almost think that he really believed in that woman with her prophecies and was expecting the worst and so drank to shut out the spiritual visitations.'

Fidelma gave a snort. 'And I suppose your rendition of that pagan Saxon song was also to keep evil spirits at bay?'

Eadulf frowned. He seemed to recall singing something. 'It would have been a song of the East Angles,' he protested automatically, trying to remember what it had been.

'It was a song about some goddess of your people called Eostre,' sniffed Fidelma, 'and something about fertility and the New Year.'

'The New Year?' Eadulf stared at the light coming through the window. Then his mind jolted wide awake. 'It's morning!' he exclaimed unnecessarily. 'Samhain has come. Has anything happened? The first day is here and—'

'And Donn, the god of death, has claimed his victim as it was predicted he would.' Aidan's hollow voice sounded from the doorway.

They swung round to the young warrior as he made his dramatic entrance.

'I am sorry to disturb you thus, lady, and you, friend Eadulf,' he went on apologetically. 'I have just come from the town square below. A body has been found in front of the dead embers of the Samhain bonfire. From what I saw, it is another of those threefold deaths. The wounds were inflicted in the very same manner in which Spelán met his end. The body was laid out ready for burial and placed there for all to see this morning.'

Eadulf gave a sharp intake of breath but Fidelma controlled her reaction. 'Has this body been identified?' she asked quietly.

'It has, lady.'

The pause was tantalising and more than Eadulf could bear. 'Then for God's sake, tell us. The curse was on the Eóghanacht! Whose body is it?' he demanded.

'It is that of the woman who called herself Brancheó.'

The town square was eerily silent. Apart from the two warriors standing guard by the burnt-out remains of the great bonfire, and the object that lay on the ground before it, there were just a few people gathered nervously before the tavern door, the figure of Rumann among them. They stood watching as Fidelma and Eadulf, accompanied by Aidan, came into the square and made towards the warriors.

No words were spoken as Fidelma bent down to the figure on the ground. A warrior's cloak had been thrown across it. She drew it back.

'Has anything been disturbed?' she asked.

'Nothing, lady,' replied one of the warriors. 'You see the body as we found it. I placed my cloak over it for decency's sake.'

The body lay on its back, arms and legs straight, the face in repose with eyes closed. There was no mistaking the features of the woman who called herself Brancheó, the raven-caller.

'Eadulf?'

Eadulf bent in obedience at the side of the corpse and started to make a quick observation.

'A wound over the heart, the throat cut and . . .' he raised the head slightly and turned it. 'Yes, there has been a powerful blow to the back of the head.'

'Just like Spelán?' Aidan asked, standing behind them. There was some emotion in his voice.

'Just like Spelán,' echoed Eadulf softly.

'Except for one thing.'

Eadulf frowned at Fidelma. 'Which is?' he asked, casting his eyes over the corpse.

'There is no odour from the body.'

Eadulf sniffed. 'Ah, true – the smell of lavender is lacking. Is that important?'

Fidelma rose to her feet without replying and looked at the warriors.

'Who found the body?'

One of the men looked awkwardly at his companion and then decided he should be spokesman.

'I believe it was the tavern-keeper, Rumann. He said that he discovered it at first light, lady. I am told that he did not move anything until he sent for us.'

'I will question him in a moment. Presumably that body was put here after the Samhain celebration ceased. When would that have been – do you know?'

'I know the festivities went on until late, lady,' the warrior replied. 'It is usual to wait until the Queen of the Night is waning in the sky before people return home on the Samhain feast. It is the hours of deep darkness when the dangers of the Otherworld are at their greatest . . .'

Fidelma stopped him with a motion of her hand. 'I am well aware of it. So you are saying that people were here almost until first light?'

'The tavern-keeper will know. All we know is that he sent his boy to fetch us, then we in turn sent for Aidan. He left us here while he went to alert you.'

'Were either of you part of the celebrations here during the night?'

The warrior shook his head. 'We were both on duty at the palace at first light so we were early to bed.'

'Did you see this woman at the palace last night?'

'We heard that she was a prisoner there. She was taken by Gormán to the King's feasting hall and released soon after.'

The second warrior added: 'As my comrade said, we retired early so we didn't see her, but we were told she had been allowed to leave the palace and came down into the township at about midnight.'

Eadulf had been examining the ground. 'I think she was slain elsewhere and the body dragged here and laid out in this fashion. The killer would have had ample time between the waning of the moon and first light to lay the corpse out as if for burial, just like Spelán who was also killed elsewhere.'

'Except there is a notable difference. Brancheó's body was laid out with the feet pointing west.'

'Is that significant?'

'The New Faith wishes corpses to be laid out with their feet towards the east, towards the risen Christ. The Old Faith points the feet on the path to Otherworld, which is west.'

'So indications are that the perpetrator is one of the Old Faith?'

'Or someone wants us to believe so. Very well – you may remove the body to Brother Conchobhar's apothecary. Ask him to check for the Tau-Rho mark and we will talk to him later.'

The warriors looked puzzled and she had to repeat the words 'Tau-Rho' distinctly.

'What now?' Aidan asked.

'We will talk to Rumann first and then we will find Gormán and see what he can tell us of what happened after he escorted Brancheó from the feasting hall last night.'

Rumann watched them anxiously as they approached him. The few onlookers who were with him slowly faded into the background. The tavern-keeper's eyes were darting hither and thither as if seeking something to focus on other than Fidelma.

'A bad business, lady,' he muttered in greeting. 'A very bad business.'

'When did you find the body, Rumann?' Fidelma began without preamble.

The innkeeper made a slight motion of his shoulder. 'I don't know if it could be described as finding, exactly,' he prevaricated.

'Then describe it in your own words. But first, tell me when you did so.'

'It was before first light.'

'While it was still dark?' she enquired. 'Why were you astir so early? Or was it that you had not gone to bed? I would have imagined the celebrations carried on here most of the night.'

'This year the feasting was more subdued on account of the death of the shepherd and the threats about the destruction of Cashel by the old gods.'

'So when did it end?'

'The moon was in the last *cadar* of her journey, pale and low. I had several guests who stayed on, of course. They are still asleep even now – the ale had circulated well. However, animals do not tend to themselves and neither do the duties of an innkeeper. So I started my chores early. It was not first light; the darkness was still with us. I came out of the door and glanced across to the remains of the bonfire.'

'You could still see in the darkness?' Eadulf queried. 'Was the bonfire still alight?'

'It had reduced to a glowing pile and it was by that glimmering light that I saw the dark outline of a figure stretched on the ground before it. At first I thought it was merely someone who had taken a little more drink than was good for them and had fallen asleep there. I was about to attend to my own business when I suddenly remembered the laws on drunkenness and the harm that could come to one so incapable, especially so close to the embers of our fire. I knew my responsibilities under the law as a tavern-keeper and while it might be argued that the person had not collapsed and fallen asleep in my tavern, the figure was near enough to it. I did not want to get into trouble with the law.'

'So you went to examine the figure?'

'I did so, lady. I took my lantern and went over. It was then I realised that it was the pagan witch; the woman Branchéo who had been cursing Cashel.'

'How was she lying?' Fidelma asked.

'Exactly as she is now; stretched out as if ready to be placed on the *fuat*, the funeral bier, and taken to her grave.' He shivered.

'Nothing was touched?' enquired Eadulf. 'You did not move anything?'

'Nothing at all. I bent over her with the lantern and when I saw the blood glistening at her throat, I realised that she was dead.'

Eadulf looked at him sharply. 'The blood was glistening, you say?'

'I saw that her throat had been cut,' the innkeeper confirmed, and swallowed noisily.

Eadulf addressed Fidelma. 'If the blood was glistening, it means that it was still moist – not dry. That would indicate that she had been killed only a short time before Rumann found her.'

Fidelma acknowledged the point before turning again to Rumann. 'So, what did you do next?'

'I went back to the inn, roused my son and sent him up to the palace to inform the guard. Two warriors came and then Aidan arrived. He went to fetch you and Eadulf. It is a bad, bad business. Maybe there is something to this curse on Cashel? I have an inn to run, lady, and what if it was known that these deaths occurred right outside my door? I would lose my livelihood!'

'You do not seem unduly concerned with the woman's loss of her life, but only by the loss of your customers,' Fidelma observed. 'Last night you were only too keen to publicise her curse in order to attract the morbid curiosity of people.'

'I am a good adherent of the New Faith, lady,' Rumann replied spiritedly. 'She was probably responsible for the death of Spelán and brought fear and devastation to the annual Samhain festival. I suspect she brought death on herself. I was amazed that she had been allowed to wander free after the things she said. Why, last night, there were many who would gladly have . . .' He suddenly halted, realising what he was saying.

Fidelma regarded him grimly. 'Many who would have wanted her dead? For example, you felt she should be punished?'

Rumann looked unhappy. 'You know I am not capable of such a thing. I have run this inn in the shadow of your family's fortress for long enough that you know me well, lady. The woman put fear into many in this township and, I am willing to admit, the fear was in me as well. However, the solution to such evil is not murder.'

'But you said that many in the inn last night expressed that very thought,' Eadulf pointed out.

'So they did. Curnan the woodsman, for instance. He was all for gathering a group and running her out of the township after we heard that she was released from the palace last night.'

Fidelma immediately asked: 'So when did you hear that she had been released?'

'Gormán came to join his mother, Della, and his wife, Aibell, at the bonfire later on. He told us that she had been questioned by the King himself and that he had been told to release her. We did not want her coming to curse the fire and our festivities again so we kept a watch on those attending the fire ceremony.'

'Did she come to the festival fire?' Eadulf asked.

'Not so far as I am aware. No one else saw her except . . .' He paused thoughtfully.

'Except?'

Rumann put his head to one side. 'I think it was Curnan. He was bitter about her because, as I mentioned before, he had been in charge of building the festival fire this year and he wanted to be remembered by it. Now it will be remembered for all the wrong reasons. He felt it an affront to his honour.'

'We should speak again with Curnan,' Eadulf advised. 'Is he still here, sleeping off the effects of the night?'

Rumann shook his head. 'He left not long before I started to attend to the morning chores and took himself off to his home. He was not affected by drink.'

'Was he not?' Fidelma said reflectively. 'And he left before the body was discovered or afterwards? I thought his duties would be to see that the fire had been safely extinguished and to clear away the debris.'

'Oh, it was before I saw the body. He said he would return later to accomplish that before this day is out.'

'So he did not see the body?'

'Obviously not, lady.'

'Who else was in your inn when it was mentioned that Brancheó had been released from my brother's fortress? I mean those who agreed with Curnan that the woman should be chased out of this township?'

'The place was crowded as befits the occasion. I don't think I could recall the names of them all.'

'We will discuss it later after you have had time to remember,' Fidelma told him, aware that it was not going to be a profitable line of inquiry. 'If you see Curnan before I do, tell him that I shall want a word with him.'

They left Rumann, still nervous and worried looking, and made their way through the drowsing township towards Della's homestead. Aibell, Gormán's wife, was already busy grooming the horses in the paddock when they arrived. She waved gaily to them as they entered the gate and made their way to Della's porch. Gormán had heard their approach for he came out to greet them with a smile of welcome.

'You have timed your arrival well,' he said. 'My mother is in the kitchen preparing a meal to break our fast with, lady. You are very welcome to join us. But why are you so early abroad? You, too, Aidan. I would have thought that you would all be resting after the festivities of last night.'

Fidelma's expression was serious. 'I am afraid it was not for breakfast we came here,' she told him. 'Nor shall we disturb Della in her cooking.'

Gormán raised an eyebrow in query. 'You sound solemn, lady. What is it?'

'When my brother asked you to escort Brancheó from the feasting hall last night, what did you do?'

'Do?' Gormán echoed, puzzled. 'I obeyed his order. He told me to take her and tell her to go.' He confided, 'I will admit to you, lady, that I had no liking for the King's behaviour last night. He was not himself.'

Fidelma was impatient. 'I want the details, Gormán.'

Gormán had seen her in such a mood before and was not offended. 'In response to your brother's order, I escorted her from the hall to the main gate and told her to go. That is all.'

'So she left without a word?'

'Far from it. Brancheó was as malicious in speech as when you saw her at the feast. She continued to curse the entire race of the Eòghanacht, the Rock and all who served there and dwelled in Cashel. Her curses were quite colourful and she repeated that, by the end of the Samhain festival, Cashel would be destroyed. With that parting shot she vanished into the darkness.'

'At what time was that?'

'I did not delay, lady. I took her from the feasting hall directly to the gates. I would say that the moon was not yet at its zenith.

So it was before midnight. The bonfire in the town below was still blazing and you could hear the celebrations continuing. I had left Dego in charge of security in the feasting hall and, frankly, by the look of the amount of the beer and wine being consumed, there was little point in me staying. I had promised my mother and Aibell that I would join them at the bonfire as soon as I could.'

'You must have followed close behind Brancheó after she left the palace?'

'Not that close. Before I left I had a few words with Enda and by that time, the woman had vanished into the night. I didn't see her at the bonfire either when I reached it and found my mother and Aibell.' He paused. 'There was one curious thing, now that I come to think of it.'

'Which is?' Fidelma prompted, trying to curb her impatience.

'As I was taking the woman across the courtyard to the gates, one of those religious scholars came after us. Well, I am not sure that he came after us or was merely on his way to the chapel. It was a dark area but I think that I would know him when I saw him again.'

'You mean it was one of the scholars who arrived for the council with Brother Mac Raith? They were at the feast.'

'One of those,' agreed Gormán.

'What happened?'

'Well, the religieux seemed to follow us from the feasting hall. It was as if he were observing us and Brancheó noticed, for at one point she halted and looked back at him. The fellow had also stopped, and was standing in the shadows with one of the brand torches behind him. She looked at him and gave a strange laugh.'

'Were any words exchanged?'

'Yes – but I had no understanding of what they were talking about.'

'Do you mean that they were conversing in a language that you did not know?'

'No – they were speaking in our language.'

'Can you not remember anything that was said?'

Gormán thought carefully. 'She said – "I have been warned about you." Then the figure in the religious garb said something like: "Have a care, raven-caller, for you associate too closely with the evil ones." To which she replied: "I am told your name means 'lightbringer' but I know that in this matter you bring neither light nor illumination." Then the religieux replied: "If you think that you know so much, raven-caller, I guarantee that it will be returned and its words hidden from those who would use them to create chaos in this world. That must be, even if you conjure legions of wraiths from the Otherworld." Something along those lines, anyway.'

There was a silence as Fidelma and Eadulf considered this curious exchange. 'It? What was "it" a reference to?'

'As I said, lady,' replied Gormán with a shrug, 'I had no understanding of that exchange other than the thought that the religieux was contesting the power of her Samhain curse. I did, in fact, ask the woman what was meant. I also asked how she knew the man. She merely laughed and said that she had been told about him and that it was not for a mere warrior to know the hidden truths of the world. That was when she started to curse the Eóghanacht again.'

'Are you sure that you would know the religieux again, Gormán? You are positive that he was one of the newly arrived brethren?'

'I am certain of it. Why?'

Fidelma was thoughtful. 'You say that Brancheó said his name meant "lightbringer"? As you know, I like to understand the meaning of names. But none of the religieux of the council bear any name that has that meaning.'

'Lightbringer? Isn't that the name of the Morning Star?' Gormán queried.

Eadulf was frowning. 'It is also the name of the Devil, who is depicted as the fallen Morning Star in the New Faith. That is certainly a suitable name in these circumstances.'

'What do you mean?' Fidelma asked.

'The Hebrews called the fallen one Heylel, the Greeks called him Hesopharos, and when Eusebius translated the texts into Latin, he was known as Lucifer.'

Fidelma gave a dismissive sniff. 'Well, none of the scholars in Brother Mac Raith's group have a name like any of those.'

'I could certainly recognise the man,' Gormán stated once more. 'It was dark but there was light enough from the brand torch.'

'Then it will be your task to identify which of the religieux it was. We will need to question him.'

'Wouldn't it be simpler if we could find Brancheó and ask her who he was?' Gormán suggested.

Fidelma pursed her lips. 'That will be impossible, Gormán. It is why I am questioning you. Brancheó was found dead this morning by the Samhain fire.'

The warrior stared at her in silent shock.

Eadulf nodded confirmation. 'We have just come from viewing her body. She was killed in the same manner as was Spelán.'

'Do you mean she was a victim of the threefold death?' The warrior was clearly shaken.

'That is, indeed, the manner in which she was despatched.' Fidelma changed the subject. 'Were you planning to come to the fortress today?'

Gormán's head came up as if in defiance. 'Yes, lady. I was coming to offer the resignation of my command to your brother.'

'You feel your honour was affronted by the way he spoke to you in front of the guests last night,' Fidelma said softly. 'Do we not have an old saying, my friend, that when the wine is in, the sense is out. Sometimes it is better to forget the mistakes of a drunken tongue.'

'But, lady . . .'

'I am sure the law is right to assert that a decision made when one is drunk must be reconsidered when one is sober. Come to the fortress and identify the religieux. Identify the man who had the exchange with Branche 6. Forget my brother's foolishness as he will have probably forgotten what was said. You are needed at his side, Gormán, especially now.'

There was a slight hesitation again and then Gormán sighed and inclined his head in agreement.

'Be sure you do it in a surreptitious manner,' Fidelma added as she turned to leave. 'We do not want to forewarn the man that you are seeking him out. Just let me know which of the three scholars it is.'

'It shall be done, lady.'

'My regards to your mother, Della, and regrets that we are unable to stay for breakfast.'

On the way back to the fortress, Fidelma was strangely thoughtful. Once or twice Aidan and Eadulf opened their mouths to speak but decided not to break the contemplative silence.

Colgú had no such compunction as he greeted them when they entered the courtyard. He looked the worse for wear and almost a little ashamed.

'Is it true that the witch has been killed?' he demanded without preamble.

Fidelma gave him a withering glance. 'You look terrible, brother. And your behaviour last night was not seemly.'

Colgú was in no mood to be reproved. 'I asked a question, sister!'

'The answer to that is – Branche 6 is dead. And in the same manner as the shepherd was killed, apart from two discrepancies.'

'A revenge killing?' he asked, surprised. 'Maybe friends of Spelán killed her in the same manner to make a point?'

'Except that I do not think he had any friends.'

'Well, she was blamed by some for his death because she spouted all the ancient curses and so on. Others might have taken exception to that.' He smiled in grim satisfaction. 'Yet here we are still. The Eóghanacht have not been transported to the Otherworld. Cashel has not yet fallen and we are not destroyed.'

'Only your reputation is damaged, brother,' Fidelma said curtly. 'I trust you have made appropriate apologies to Gelgéis?'

Colgú flushed. After a moment he added in a sober tone: 'You do not have to advise me in that matter, sister. I will make my apologies just as I now apologise to you and Eadulf there.'

'I think you owe more of an apology to Gormán for your temper.'

He frowned. 'Things are hazy. If I have offended him I will apologise. He is a good man, one of the best commanders of the Golden Collar.' He raised a hand as if to silence what else she was going to add. 'I will apologise,' he repeated. 'And now I want to know how your investigation of these murders is progressing.'

'Nothing is ruled out at this time,' Fidelma told him. 'It seems unlikely that Christians would revenge themselves on Branchéo by using the ritual killing associated with the Druids and of which she claimed to be one. It seems too obvious.'

At that moment, the elderly apothecary, Brother Conchobhar, came hobbling across the courtyard towards them.

'Aidan's warriors brought me the woman's body as you instructed, Fidelma,' the old man said immediately. 'You are right that it is exactly the same method in which Spelan was killed. I would go further and say it is so precisely similar that it looks as if the execution was done by the same hand. There are two differences, however.'

'Which are?' pressed Fidelma.

'There was no engraving of the Tau-Rho on the body,' he revealed, 'and no smell of the aroma of lavender.' The latter fact they had already noted.

Fidelma looked troubled. 'But you really think it is the same killer? What do we know about this ritual? What does it mean? If Branchéo was a self-professed member of the ancient faith that used it, why would she have perished in this manner?'

'There is something that is not right here,' Eadulf declared. 'Is someone seeking to mislead us into believing this is connected with the ancient faith of this land?'

'That I don't know,' Brother Conchobhar replied. 'Nor would it aid anyone if I made a guess.'

Fidelma was silent and thought lines creased her brow. 'I wish I knew more about the ancient rituals.'

Colgú was irritated. 'I thought your knowledge on such matters was complete?' If he meant it as sarcasm, Fidelma did not take it as such.

'Not in this matter, brother.'

'I know little or nothing,' Brother Conchobhar confessed. 'But from what you told me that you have discovered, there do appear to be factors that are at odds with the stories I have known of the ancient ways; especially when someone who professes to be of the Old Faith is killed in this manner. It is curious.'

'So: are we dealing with people carrying out ancient rituals or people who are merely copying them?' Fidelma asked the question of herself.

'I believe you should seek advice, lady,' the old man said. 'What you need is some expert on the ancient faith. I agree that we have all heard stories of ritual killings such as this threefold death, but it is essential to know the circumstances in which it is usually enacted.'

'Where could I find such an expert?' she demanded in exasperation. 'I should imagine that adherents of the Old Faith are reticent about revealing themselves these days.'

'There are plenty of folk who still cling to the old rituals,' observed Colgú. 'The woman Brancheó was not reticent.'

'And look what good it did her,' Eadulf noted sardonically.

Fidelma was thinking hard. 'I know of no one who has such knowledge of the old ways,' she finally said. 'At least not in this part of the kingdom.'

Colgú smiled thinly. 'A shame on your memory, sister. You once had an encounter with such a person, albeit some years ago . . .'

'You don't mean the fanatics we encountered when the High

King Sechnussach was murdered and we were summoned to Cashel to investigate?' Eadulf asked. 'They were all wiped out, so I thought.'

'I do not mean those,' Colgú answered. 'It happened before you met with my sister.'

'I have it!' Fidelma exclaimed. 'You mean the hermit . . . the hermit Erca who lives on the Blue Mountain.'

'The same,' conceded her brother. 'If anyone has the old knowledge it is the hermit of Cnocgorm.'

'Cnocgorm?' Aidan screwed up his features as if to help his memory. 'That is only a short ride to the east.'

'We can be there and back by this evening,' Fidelma agreed enthusiastically. 'Go, get the horses saddled, Aidan.'

Eadulf stifled a long-suffering sigh. He had been hoping for at least one day free of riding long distances.

Meanwhile Fidelma had turned to Brother Conchobhar.

'I would be happy,' she said, 'if you could advise my brother, old friend.'

'Advise? Advise me about what?' Colgú asked before the elderly apothecary could frame the same question.

'About being cautious with regard to his drink consumption; he put no constraints on it last night. It did not impress the Princess Gelgéis of the Eile. Does my brother think that he is ever going to get a wife if he behaves in such a fashion?'

As Colgú's face began to crimson in anger, she set off towards the stable with Eadulf moving quickly after her. There came a verbal burst of outrage from the King behind them. To Eadulf it was almost inarticulate and if Fidelma understood the words, she paid no heed.

In the stables, she paused to watch Aidan finish saddling his horse.

'What's on your mind, Eadulf?' she asked him suddenly. 'I noticed that ever since we left Gormán, you have been thinking about something. Best express it than brood over it.'

Eadulf pulled a face. 'I thought you were too preoccupied with your own thoughts to notice. You were certainly quiet enough on the return.'

'Not so quiet that I cannot see your mind working,' smiled Fidelma.

'I have been thinking about what Gormán said,' Eadulf admitted.

'As have I,' she responded. 'Let's share our thoughts.'

'You said that you liked to know the meaning of names. Gormán told us that Branche6 had said that the name of the man she spoke to in the courtyard last night meant "lightbringer".'

'We have already discussed this. The three religieux are called Sionnach, Duibhinn and Gíolla Rua . . . none of these names could be construed in such a fashion. It doesn't help.'

'Not unless one of them was using a false name and Branche6 recognised their real one,' Eadulf observed.

'It is a good point, except it does not allow us to go further, does it?'

'It might. What does the Latin name Lucidus mean?'

'But they are not called . . .' Fidelma started to object, but then her eyes widened as she stared at Eadulf. Finally, she let out a long, low breath. 'I had forgotten all about that message from the Venerable Gelasius. A Brother Lucidus would contact me about some important matter. Is he a member of this council, here under a disguised name? Is he the Brother Lucidus that Gelasius has referred to? Then, if so, why has he not contacted me? Why is he in disguise? What can it all mean?'

chapter thirteen

Cnocgorm was not a high mountain; it was more a large sprawling hill rising little more than some 240 metres and lying almost due east of Cashel. The name had arisen as a compromise by local people in an argument with members of the New Faith. The latter wanted to claim it was called Hill of Churches – Cnoc na Cille. But there were no churches there and the locals maintained the name was, and always had been, Cnoc na Coille – Hill of the Woods. This was more appropriate, for in spring and summer it was covered in the native rowan or mountain ash with its dusky green-blue leaves. So it was now called Cnocgorm, the Blue Mountain.

Summer was over, however, and as they approached the hill, they could see that the rowans had succumbed to their autumnal colours of yellow with their bright scarlet berries, and already Eadulf could hear the curious chirping of the *smólach mór*, the mistle thrush, who would make a fierce defence of its chosen berry patch against all comers.

When Fidelma and Eadulf arrived at the small deserted cabin at the foot of the hill, Fidelma decided that Aidan should remain to look after the horses while she and Eadulf would climb the hill to where she knew the old hermit's cave was. Although it had been many years since Fidelma had visited the hill and the old hermit, she seemed to have a sure and certain memory of the path through the trees and rocks. Eadulf was surprised at how rocky the hill was under its canopy of rowan but then he remembered that rowan loved stony soil, so he should not expect the terrain to be any different.

'Why couldn't this man live in a more accessible place?' he puffed as he stumbled after Fidelma, who was ascending the steep mountain path swiftly.

Fidelma paused to allow him to catch up with her and stood shaking her head in mock admonition.

'Erca is a hermit,' she replied with feigned patience. 'Where would you expect him to live? In the middle of a township?'

She turned back to survey the path in front of her. A wave of nostalgia washed over her as she recalled the last time she was here on the slopes of Cnocgorm. She had not long left Brehon Morann's law school when she received a commission to defend Brother Fergal, who had been charged with the murder of a local woman called Barrdub. The defence of Brother Fergal had been handed her by his abbey, not because of her ability in law but for the reason that everyone thought he was guilty. The loss of such a case might have harmed the reputation of the abbey's more senior advocate. The abbot had thought it was an open and shut case. Brother Fergal had been found in a cabin on the slopes of this very mountain. He was asleep. By his side was the body of the girl, Barrdub. She had been stabbed to death. There was blood on Fergal's hands and on his robes. When he was awakened, he claimed that he had no knowledge of anything. He had no defence at all.

At that time in her life, Fidelma had not been so cynical about the religious and so she did her utmost in the belief that no one who professed the Faith could be guilty of such an act as murder. In the instance of Brother Fergal, she had been right. She was able to demonstrate that he was innocent – but her naive notions of the religious were quickly dispelled by her subsequent career, leading her to quit her abbey and eventually leave the religious altogether. But Brother Fergal's case was many years before that time, and

Fidelma had afterwards referred to the case as the 'Murder in Repose'.

It was, however, at that time she discovered there were still many who lived in the mountains or in remote fastnesses who continued to practise the old ways; many who had not been won over by the teachings from the east; many areas where the ancient gods and goddesses of the Five Kingdoms still reigned supreme. Cnocgorm was one such place and her brother had been right to remind her that if Brancheó was known anywhere, it would be the hermit Erca who might provide some clues. His arcane knowledge had helped Fidelma resolve the mystery of who had really killed Barrdub and to prove Fergal innocent.

'How much further?' complained Eadulf as he scrambled after her.

'Not far,' she replied cheerfully. 'His cave is just around those rocks on the ridge up there.'

Eadulf stifled a groan. If Fidelma heard him, she did not answer but continued to ascend towards the ridge that she had indicated.

Erca was a thin, dirty-looking individual; he had wild, matted hair and staring eyes. His garments were torn and ragged and he wore a single threadbare woollen cloak around his bent shoulders. When they found him, he was seated before a smoking fire at the entrance to a large cave. An iron tripod had been erected over the smouldering wood from which a small iron pot hung with a fragrant aroma emanating from its bubbling water. He had obviously not heard their approach, so intent had he been in mixing his herbal brew. He glanced up, startled, as they emerged into his line of vision. He sprang up with surprising agility.

'Peace, peace, Erca. Do you not remember me?' Fidelma greeted the man in a calming tone.

The little man looked at her and then at Eadulf. His face was a mask of hatred and his voice cracked as he spoke.

'All I see is a man clad in the robes of a servant of the foreign god and wearing the tonsure of the foreigners. May the gods and goddesses of the Sidhe rise up and drive them all from the land.'

'Eadulf is my husband.' Fidelma tried to pacify the irate old man in a soothing tone. 'We mean you no harm.'

'He's one of those arrogant foreigners who grovels to Rome,' Erca returned angrily. 'In that alone there is much harm.'

'I don't grovel to anyone,' Eadulf replied, resentment rising in him.

The old man was not to be silenced. 'The crow's curse on you, foreigner. May you leave without returning.'

Fidelma shot a warning glance to Eadulf, hoping that he would ignore the ancient insults because she needed information from Erca and arguing with the hermit would not be the way to get it. So she continued to smile at the old man. 'Come, Erca, we will not trouble you for long. You do not recall me?'

'I remember you well enough,' Erca replied grumpily. 'You came to seek my advice on the herbs that grew around here. It was a knowledge that even a child could learn before your religion restricted what they should and should not know. Oh yes, I remember you well enough.' He frowned as his memory stirred. 'Yet you are no longer wearing the robes of your New Faith. Before, you called yourself Sister something or other.'

'I am Fidelma of Cashel.'

The old man gave a bark of sarcastic laughter. 'An Eóghanacht? I should have known. Betrayers of the Old Faith. Why have you come to pollute my hill, descendant of Óengus son of Nad Fríoch, the Great Betrayer of the Old Faith?'

Fidelma regarded him with disapproval but she knew that she had to persevere in order to gain the old man's confidence.

'Seeing that you set such great store by the old religion, the old ways and culture, I would have thought you might have retained the same respect for the old customs.'

Erca hesitated with one eyebrow slightly raised in query.

'The custom of hospitality was not invented by the New Faith,' Fidelma said. 'Or do you approve of old customs being discarded?'

Spots of red appeared on Erca's pale, shrunken cheeks. He pointed to a few nearby boulders.

'I have no use for chairs, so you may be seated there. There is a jug of cider here and I will offer a small mug apiece.'

'You are most hospitable, Erca,' Fidelma replied gravely. Only Eadulf heard the sarcasm in her voice.

Once the ritual of seating and accepting drinks had been made, Fidelma asked: 'Have you heard of a woman called Brancheó?'

The old man's eyes narrowed, showing that the name had immediately registered.

'The raven-caller? Why do you wish to speak of her?'

There was a note in his voice which made Fidelma ask a further question. 'Do you know her?'

Erca made a gesture with a skinny arm. Almost a half-wave. 'Who does not know of her among the followers of the old ways?'

'Then indulge me, Erca, for I had never heard of her and would know something more of her.'

'Why would a daughter of the Eóghanacht be interested in Brancheó?' he countered suspiciously.

'Perhaps it is because this daughter of the Eóghanacht is a *dálaigh* as well as being sister to the King of Muman,' Eadulf intervened with a heavy tone.

Erca did not even glance at him but continued to look curiously at Fidelma.

'On this mountain I do not concern myself with things of this world but I suppose that a *dálaigh* is deserving of some respect. Were not those who were immersed in knowledge, those called Druids, the original speakers of the law? Did they not stand at the Dál and give their judgements? Even before the children of the Gael came to this land, did not Partholon bring the first Druids to the Five Kingdoms? Aye, I remember their names well. Fios, whose name was "intelligence"; Eólas, whose name was "knowledge" and Fochmarc, whose name was "inquiry". By their names, they were the three foundations of our Faith, our law and society.'

Eadulf was looking a little helpless as the old man delivered his words with vehemence. Even after all the years that he had spent in this land, there was much about this country that he did not know. Fidelma took pity on Eadulf and she turned to explain.

'Partholon was, according to the ancient chronicle, the leader of the second settlement in this land. He and his people were survivors of a great flood, the Churning of the Waters. He had murdered his mother and father out of envy and greed to be a king. People rose up and he lost his left eye and thereby the kingship. That was the evil curse on him and, although he had been hailed as "chief of all the crafts", he was forced to wander seven years before he came to this island where he and his people settled and, as Erca says, brought the first Druids and lawgivers to the land.'

The old man was nodding slightly, his eyes unfocused as if he were dreaming of ancient times; 'the time before time' as people referred to them. 'Aye, I remember their names well,' he echoed. 'Partholon's years were not long, for he did not elude the curse entirely.'

'It is an ancient legend,' Fidelma said.

'If the curse followed him, what happened?' Eadulf wanted to know.

'He perished, of course,' Fidelma replied shortly. 'And his people also perished of a great plague. They were all buried at a place called Tamhlacht in the kingdom of Laighin, which is why it bears its name.'

'That means the plague burial place?' translated Eadulf.

Erca smiled thinly. 'You have a good knowledge of our language, stranger.'

'We are deviating from the purpose of my coming,' Fidelma said sharply. 'I was asking about Branche6.'

Erca stared reflectively into the fire. 'Ah, yes. Branchéo.'

He stared for so long that Fidelma began to think that he was merely ignoring the question. She was about to chide him when he sighed and said, 'You were going to tell me why a *dálaigh* would be interested in the raven-caller. There is no law of the Brehons that forbids the practice.'

Fidelma decided that the only way to progress her inquiry was to be open.

'There is no law about being a raven-caller, certainly, but there *is* a law about killing one.'

Erca's head jerked up so suddenly that he nearly fell off his seat.

'Who has been killed?' Erca's voice caught with a curious emotion.

'The woman Branchéo was killed in Cashel.'

A long, low sigh escaped the old man's mouth, like the whispering sound of a wind. Then Erca seemed to grow suddenly older and thinner. There was a long silence before he licked his dry lips and coughed a moment. 'She was killed? By whom? Was it . . .?' He suddenly caught himself.

'We are trying to find out who killed her, Erca. That is why we need to know more about her. The poor woman was a victim of the threefold death.'

For a long while Erca sat immobile, staring into the fire.

Fidelma broke the silence: 'Erca, you were about to ask, was it . . . what name did you intend to say?'

'No one,' the old man replied immediately. 'But Branchéo was my daughter.' His voice was hollow.

Once again there was a silence as they digested this news. For some moments the old man continued to gaze into the flickering flames of his fire.

'How did you say that she died?' he asked eventually. 'Did you say that she was killed . . .' he passed a hand over his face . . . 'by the ritual of the threefold death?'

'It was by the ritual that is described in the old stories as the threefold death,' confirmed Fidelma.

The old man nodded slowly. 'So that is the way of it,' he said enigmatically. 'Those who do not know, betray themselves with a lack of knowledge.'

'What do you mean?' Fidelma was puzzled. 'I have heard of this tripalism from the ancient texts, but have no understanding of its mysticism and significance.'

'You must know that three is the perfect number of our philosophy. Do not the ancient gods always come in threes – the three goddesses of sovereignty, the three gods of arts and crafts . . . yes, even the three goddesses of death. All are triune deities.'

'I don't follow,' Eadulf said.

Erca looked at him sadly. 'Even in your distorted belief you have to admit there is a beginning, a middle and an ending to life; there is a past, a present and a future; there is a before, a behind, and there is a here and now. In the time beyond time, the belief was that the perfect death came in the ritual form known as the threefold death. The philosophy was perverted by the non-believers so that murder was conceived as having to be done in three ways in order to escape the vengeance of the gods.'

'Are you saying that genuine followers of the Old Faith would not use the threefold death?' queried Fidelma. 'That it is, in fact, a perversion?'

Erca's bloodless lips formed a grimace. 'That is precisely what I am saying.'

Eadulf was now following the argument. 'Was the perpetrator's intent that we should think this was a pagan ritual when it is not?'

'The death that you have described is a perversion of our ancient philosophy. Therefore, whoever killed my daughter was not one of the true keepers of the Old Faith.'

'As this method was employed,' Eadulf went on, considering the matter, 'someone intended us to believe that she was being executed by her own Faith. But could it not also be that they might have shared the Faith but had a different interpretation of it?'

'In the very same way that many Christians do?' Erca sneered. 'I have heard so many different accounts of your own Faith that you never will agree on one interpretation.'

It was a point Eadulf felt he had to concede, especially in view of the recent discussions on heresy.

'Tell me,' he asked, trying a different aspect, 'does the perfume of lavender play a part in your beliefs?'

Erca was bewildered by the question. 'Lavender? No, it plays no part in any of our rituals, although I have heard it is used by the Greeks and Romans who trade it for enormous sums. Why, Roman merchants at Port Lairge expect the equivalent of a month's labour in return for a single bag of the dried flowers.'

'But it does grow here?'

Erca shrugged. 'Some have tried to grow it. It has little use although I have heard herbalists say it prevents the bite of midges. Others maintain it is a stimulant. But it has no ritual significance for us. It is grown in Gaul and the southern lands inhabited by the Romans.'

'Let us return to your daughter, Erca,' Fidelma said gently. 'I presume she dwelled here with you?'

'No, she dwelled up by the icy lakes in Na Comeraigh.'

Eadulf knew these were the twelve tall peaks that lay to the south across the great Plain of Femen. The name seemed to have an effect on Fidelma.

'When did you last see her? How long ago?' she pressed.

Erca considered for a moment. 'It was at the feast of Lughnasa.'

The pre-Christian feast had continued, being accepted by the New Faith as the occasion to mark the harvest festival, the ripening of the grain and the weaning of calves and lambs. All four of the calendar feasts of pagan tradition had, in fact, been incorporated into the New Faith.

Fidelma was disappointed. 'So you did not see her more recently and she never mentioned her intention to pronounce a curse on Cashel at the time of Samhain?'

Erca's eyes widened a fraction and then his gaze returned to his fire.

'She did not, nor would I have thought Cashel stood in need of a curse. It is cursed already in my eyes, being the place where the ancient kingdom of Muman was betrayed by the Eóghanacht. The new religion will do your family little good. It is already written. There will come a time when the enemies of the Eóghanacht will take over and not just this kingdom of Muman; your enemies will assume power in all Five Kingdoms – but their years will be short. They, in their turn, will succumb when strangers come from across the water. Then Banba, Fodhla and Éire – the three goddesses who gave this island to the children of the Gael for as long as they kept faith – will truly be abandoned and many will forget their very names.'

Fidelma had heard this type of prophecy many times before from soothsayers that she had met along the way. Most of the time, their utterances were delivered in such an exaggerated style that it made them almost comical. Yet there was something chilling in the way Erca delivered it. He had hardly raised his voice, seated staring at some hidden images in the dancing flames of his fire, speaking as if he were commenting on the weather or some other mundane subject. The very fact of his monotone delivery made it almost mesmerising.

'Her curse was not exactly the same as your one,' Eadulf interrupted the spell in his down-to-earth way. 'She merely believed that Cashel was a portal to the Otherworld, and because of King Óengus' conversion to Christianity the ancient gods would emerge through this portal to wreak vengeance at the Samhain festival.'

'And was she murdered because of that?' Erca's voice was bitter.

'That is what we are trying to discover,' Fidelma told him.

Erca raised his arms and let them fall to his sides again. 'Maybe someone feared her and her curse.'

'Cashel still stands and the Eóghanacht remain,' Eadulf pointed out.

'But she was killed by someone trying to implicate one of the Old Faith.'

'Perhaps,' Fidelma agreed. 'Did you know the shepherd named Spelán?'

Erca looked up in astonishment. 'Where did you get that name from?'

'So you knew him?'

Erca's brows were drawn together. It seemed for a moment that he would not answer and then he sighed. 'When my daughter was here in the summer she told me that she had met a man at or near Cashel and would marry him. She said that his name was Spelán.'

It was then Eadulf placed the name of the mountains: Comeraigh. It was Nessan who had told them that Spelán had been planning to move there; he must have been planning to live there with his new woman, Brancheó.

'How long had she known this man? Are you sure that his name was Spelán?'

'She had recently met him on a journey to Ara's Well, because some sought her healing knowledge there. She said Spelán – that was the name he gave – paid her to curse a nearby abbey that had wronged him. He claimed to remain faithful to the old ways. Are you saying that he was the murderer of my daughter, that *he* killed her?' The old man looked anguished.

Fidelma shook her head. 'The night before Brancheó uttered her curse on Cashel, Spelán's body was discovered in the unlit Samhain bonfire. He, too, had been despatched with the threefold death.'

'I knew little of the man, except she wanted to marry him,' Erca reflected sadly. 'She told me that he would garner considerable wealth and then they would set up home in the southern mountains where she had her cabin.'

'Wealth?' queried Eadulf. 'He was an itinerant who had already lost claim to his dead wife's flock of sheep.'

'My daughter said something about him working in the mines.'

Fidelma shrugged. 'There are no mines near the Hill of the Bullock.'

'I can only repeat what she told me. I am not a *dálaigh* as you are, daughter of the Eóghanacht, but I would begin to turn my mind to those extremists of the New Faith who would contrive to lay blame on those of the old beliefs rather than pursue those who maintain loyalty with our ancestors. Someone killed the man my daughter wanted to marry – and perhaps that was the provocation for her curse on those she thought responsible.'

'You may well be right,' Fidelma sighed after a short pause. 'Then one more question: have you ever heard of Abbot Síoda of Ráth Cuáin which is on the Hill of the Bullock?'

To her surprise the old man nodded. 'I have heard stories of Ráth Cuáin but not of Abbot Síoda of whom you speak. Ráth Cuáin is a cursed place. It will be consumed in the fires of vengeance.'

'Why do you say that?'

'Because the abbey on that Ráth was built on blood. It was erected centuries ago, on a limestone hill that is riddled with caves. Time was, in the days of Tigernmas, son of Follach, the Lord of Death, that he rejected the old gods and set up a great idol of gold on Magh Slécht, the Plain of Adoration, and this idol was called Cromm Cróich, known as the Crescent One of Blood. People were sacrificed to it at the feast of Samhain. It is said that in those days, before Tigernmas met his own death in the frenzied blood worship of Cromm, many were slaughtered in those limestone caves.'

'May the martyrs rest in peace,' Eadulf added reverentially.

'Not even in your Faith will there be peace, Saxon!' exclaimed Erca bitterly. 'It became the fortress of a great seer and scribe called

Brogán. When Brogán refused to convert to the New Faith, Abbot Nathí sent warriors to seize the Ráth and in the mêlée Brogan was slaughtered. His progeny declared a blood feud and vowed that it would not end until the seventh generation had been wiped out.'

Eadulf heard him out then said pragmatically, 'Well, Spelán was no relation of Nathí or any other local man. So his death has yet to be accounted for, as indeed does the death of your daughter.'

Erca did not appear to take notice. 'Blood will be its fall,' he repeated as he gazed into the fire. 'Blood will be the fall of Ráth Cuáin.'

'In the meantime, Erca, your daughter's body must be buried tonight as is custom,' Fidelma reminded him gently. 'You have the right to be there and to have a say, and to claim her personal property. Spelán's body is also to be buried tonight as no burial could be made on Samhain.'

Erca shrugged. 'The only thing I ask is that there will be no mumblings of the New Faith over her body. It would be an insult to her and the gods of our fathers, and such insult would only rebound on the living of this world. Her soul is already on the way to the House of Donn to be reborn in the Land of the Ever Young.'

'The Land of the Ever Young?' Eadulf asked disbelievingly.

'Tír na Óg, the Plain of Happiness, Hy-Breasal, the Otherworld, call it what you will. Her soul will be reborn there. For us, death is merely a changing of place, and life goes on with all its forms and goods in the Otherworld. When a soul dies in this world, it is reborn in the Otherworld, so that there is a constant exchange of souls always taking place between the two worlds. So death has no dominion for us. Brancheó is in the Otherworld now.'

'But we are still in this world, Erca,' Fidelma declared. 'My task is to find out who murdered her and Spelán and bring that person to justice.'

'It matters not. For soon the vengeful shadows of the Otherworld will find the killer one way or another. They will soon be despatched, the murderous soul, to the Perilous Plain of wild devouring beasts. Now you have intruded enough. Leave me to my meditations.'

So saying, he rose and walked into the cave mouth without another word.

Eadulf glanced at Fidelma who was rising from her seat and so he followed her example.

'More confusing information,' he muttered as they set off from the hermit's abode. 'I do not think that we have made much progress in finding a resolution to this matter.'

'On the contrary, I think it has helped a lot,' she contradicted him.

He was about to query her statement when they heard Erca's voice rising in thin, reed-like tones from deep within the cave, then changing into a wailing, solemn chant. Fidelma paused with a slight shudder.

'What's that about?' asked Eadulf.

'A curse,' she replied shortly. 'Perhaps I should say it is more an exhortation for the gods and goddesses to intervene to discover the person who killed his daughter and exact their vengeance.'

'So much for his statement that he would leave it to the Otherworld to punish in their own time,' said Eadulf. 'Much good will cursing do him if he feels his gods need a little prompting.'

Fidelma was still listening. 'This is a powerful cry to the deities of the Old Faith, Eadulf.' Her voice was solemn. 'There are certain names that the Old Faith prohibited using, names for the sun and moon for example. He calls on the Fair Mare to gallop forth and shine her brightness on the killer so that he or she cannot escape her radiance.'

'The Fair Mare?'

'An Láir Bán,' Fidelma confirmed, 'one of the euphemisms we use for the moon, for her real name must never be spoken of. And Erca is calling on the gods by their forbidden names.' She shuddered. 'The day is growing colder. Let's get back down to where we left Aidan and the horses.'

Eadulf glanced up at the sky. It was true that it was darkening, for the days were getting shorter. 'It seems there is a mist developing on the upper slopes.'

He was surprised at the speed with which Fidelma led the way down the hill towards the place where they had left their horses under the care of Aidán. The young warrior was relieved to see them.

'I was getting worried,' he said, jerking a thumb towards the summit of the hill, which could no longer be seen. 'It seems as though a *droidechta* is developing.'

'A what?' asked Eadulf.

'What we call an enchanted mist – a Druid's mist,' Aidan replied. 'It's a dark, heavy type of fog coming down across the hillside.'

'It's just an ordinary mist,' snapped Fidelma. 'But come, let's get back to Cashel as soon as possible.'

Eadulf glanced at her. For a moment or two he wondered if she was taking the business of Druids' curses and the Old Faith as seriously as her brother had. Then he realised that it was a projection of his own fears, for he had been brought up fearing the great pagan deities of his own people and their powers of vengeance before he had encountered and converted to the New Faith. They were still a strong force in his imagination.

They rode back to Cashel in silence, arriving as dusk was beginning to settle with its rolling mists as the rising chill of the night met the unusual warmth of the day.

Gormán was waiting for them in the courtyard when they arrived. He appeared unsettled.

'Well, did you identify your strange religieux?' Fidelma greeted him as she swung off her horse. 'The lightbringer?'

'By default only, lady,' Gormán replied obtusely.

She frowned. 'Explain.'

'I saw the scholars with Brother Mac Raith. Two of them were not the one I recognised that night.'

'So what about the third one?'

'The third one, Brother Sionnach, is missing so I could not make a positive identification.'

'So we must find this Brother Sionnach!'

Gormán shook his head. 'I am afraid that is just the problem, lady.'

Fidelma looked at him closely. '*What* is the problem?' she asked impatiently.

'Brother Sionnach has been missing from the palace since last night. No one has seen him nor knows where he is.'

chapter fourteen

Brother Mac Raith greeted them with a glum expression as Fidelma and Eadulf entered the chapel where he and his colleagues, Brother Duibhinn and Brother Giolla Rua, had gathered on her instructions. Gormán accompanied them.

'I am told that there is some connection with these Samhain killings and the disappearance of Brother Sionnach, lady,' began the steward of the Abbey of Imleach before she could speak. 'What is it? Everyone is talking about it.'

Fidelma regarded him with disapproval. 'Doesn't Virgil say in the *Aeneid fama volat* – rumour travels fast? So already people are speculating. I myself prefer to wait and set more store by facts rather than rumour.'

'Are you saying that it is not so?' Brother Giolla Rua demanded belligerently. 'Everyone seems to think there is little question about the connection and these happenings.'

'I am not saying anything at the moment because I would want to obtain information before I did so,' Fidelma replied curtly. 'Now, let us be seated.' She waved to some chairs where the members of the small scholastic council had been holding their meetings. They obediently sat in a circle and waited for Fidelma to begin.

'Let us start with the facts that are known,' she began. 'The fact is that Brother Sionnach disappeared last night. Is that correct?'

'Just after the King's feast,' Brother Giolla Rua confirmed. 'On the night of spiritual danger from the forces of darkness.'

'That is just pagan tradition,' Brother Mac Raith rebuked his colleague. 'We, of the Faith, merely accept that it is just the start of our New Year.'

'Nevertheless, it was a feast of the dead,' asserted Brother Giolla Rua. 'Doesn't everyone have their own feast of the dead? Fifty years ago Pope Boniface reclaimed the ancient Pantheon in Rome as a church dedicated to the New Faith and to the faithful dead. He ordered that every first day of May, in the Roman calendar, would be a feast day for the dead.'

'In my language we call a saint *halig*,' Eadulf added. 'So in our calendar we call it All Hallows' Day.'

'But who keeps it?' Brother Brother Duibhinn of Ard Mór asked.

Fidelma examined him carefully as he had barely made any impression on her so far. He was a tall man with straggly ginger hair and a wispy beard which disguised the fact that he was still quite young. His eyes were glistening blue, and unusually prominent, giving the impression of someone who was permanently surprised and innocent.

'Spring is a time of light and optimism that has nothing to do with the dead,' he said. 'Our New Year begins with a time of rest and darkness. Throughout our land, and elsewhere where the Old Faith used to prevail, that was and still remains the right time for the dead to be commemorated by bonfires and feasting. No one takes notice of the new Roman feast days.'

Fidelma held up her hand in exasperation. 'I did not come here to join another scholastic debate on aspects of the New Faith,' she declared irritably. 'I have come here to ask questions about the disappearance of one of your number.'

Brother Mac Ráith cast a look of annoyance at Brother Giolla Rua.

'You are right to rebuke us, lady. Ask your questions.'

Fidelma settled herself back in the chair. 'Can we agree on when Brother Sionnach was last seen?'

'He was at the King's feast,' offered Brother Giolla Rua.

'But after that he attended the mass here in the chapel at midnight,' said Brother Duibhinn. 'That was held shortly after your brother's feast. We all attended, as you are aware.'

'And after the service?'

'We each of us went to our respective beds in the guest chambers attached to this chapel,' Brother Mac Raith said.

'Do you share a single chamber?'

'We do.'

'So Brother Sionnach retired to bed after the midnight service?'

'He did not,' Brother Giolla Rua replied this time.

'Are you saying that you all went to bed after the service but Brother Sionnach did not?' Fidelma turned to him.

'We went to the chamber and then, at the chamber door, Brother Sionnach turned aside. He said: "I will go for a walk around the fortress walls to clear my head. I will try not to disturb you when I return." My colleagues will confirm as much.'

Brother Mac Raith made a gesture of agreement. 'That's the truth as I recall.'

'And did he disturb anyone on his return?'

'That's just it, lady, we all slept soundly until first light when the bell went for morning prayers. His bed had not been slept in. I am sure that he did not return during the night.'

'When I awoke I noticed that his bed was undisturbed,' stated Brother Duibhinn. 'I drew this to the attention of Brother Mac Raith.'

Eadulf frowned. 'Could he not have risen earlier, made his bed and left?'

'Brother Sionnach was fastidious but I think we could have noticed if he had slept in his bed that night,' Brother Mac Raith said.

'Perhaps we can progress to some more specific facts,' Fidelma suggested. 'It seems that Brother Sionnach left his colleagues at the door of the bedchamber and went for a walk around the walls of the fortress. He did not return. Is that correct?'

She looked towards Gormán who immediately pre-empted her next question.

'I have already asked those of my warriors who were on guard duty last night if they recall seeing him. However, if he had walked around the walls then he must have worn the Druid's mantle of invisibility.'

The three religieux looked at him with slightly shocked expressions.

'I think the commander of the King's bodyguard is being sardonic,' Eadulf explained in a dry tone.

'Given that the warriors patrol the walls of the royal fortress night and day,' went on Gormán, in that same, slightly mocking tone, 'I think you may rest assured that Brother Sionnach did *not* go for his walk around the walls.'

'Which means,' intervened Eadulf, 'that if he left here for the purpose of going to one of the flights of steps to the walls, he was distracted from climbing it and ascending to the walkway. As the nearest stair to the walls is only a short distance from the back of this chapel, across the small courtyard before Brother Conchobhar's apothecary, then we can accept that he did not make it. On that wall there are three guard points, manned by guards whose views of the entire walkway are uninterrupted. He would have been noticed if he had reached the top of the steps to the walkway.'

Gormán nodded in appreciation. 'You have a good eye, friend Eadulf. That is exactly the way it is. None of my guards saw him.'

'Not even in darkness?' Brother Giolla Rua sounded sceptical.

'Not even then, for the steps are lit by brand torches,' Gormán replied firmly.

'This means one of two things,' Fidelma concluded. 'Either

Brother Sionnach did not go in that direction or he was waylaid by something or someone before ascending the steps.'

There was a silence before Eadulf turned to Gormán. 'I presume that we have checked with the guards at the main gates?'

'Of course.' Gormán was visibly aggrieved at the suggestion that he had overlooked so simple a matter.

'I had to check,' Eadulf apologised. 'Have you also instituted a thorough search of everywhere in the palace?'

The commander of the bodyguard shuffled his feet for a second, glancing at Fidelma. 'Everywhere? I have to have special authority to do that.'

'Then you have the authority from a *dálaigh* and sister to the King,' she told him. 'Use as many men as you can. It should not be beyond the ability of the guards that such a search could be accomplished in a short time.'

'It shall be done at once, lady,' acknowledged Gormán contritely.

Once he had left the chamber Fidelma sat back again and looked at the three religieux. 'Having gathered what facts we can, let us see what we know of Brother Sionnach's background. Often such details point somewhere from which we can make progress. Brother Mac Raith, I understand that Abbot Cuán of Imleach called this gathering to discuss the beliefs of the small Abbey of Ráth Cuáin. What was the reason Brother Sionnach was chosen to be a member of this council?'

Brother Mac Raith looked uncertain. 'The reason?'

'What qualifications did Brother Sionnach possess for this task? You were all here to discuss the deviation in interpretation that Ráth Cuáin held as opposed to what we regard as the teachings of the Faith. How was the choice of Sionnach made?'

'It was the Abbot of Imleach who made the choice,' replied Brother Mac Raith. 'As the steward of Imleach, I was appointed to be interlocutor of the council and speak on behalf of Abbot Cuán.'

Brother Duibhinn added: 'As you see, lady, we represent four of the largest teaching abbeys in the kingdom. Imleach, Ard Mór, Ros Ailithir and—'

'I know the abbeys,' Fidelma intervened patiently. 'But what of your qualifications for this task?'

'Brothers Giolla Rua, Sionnach and Duibhinn are considered the kingdom's leading experts on the Holy Scriptures,' the steward of Imleach replied. 'They are scholars who have long contemplated the works that comprise the great texts of the New Faith.'

'Especially for our knowledge of the Holy Scriptures as written in Latin by the Blessed Eusebius Sophronius Hieronymus,' added Brother Duibhinn quickly. 'That task was commissioned by the Holy Father himself. Eusebius revised the Vetus Latina translation into a new form, comparing it with the original Greek and Hebrew texts. These were then approved by various councils of the faithful and are the cornerstone of the Faith.'

Brother Giolla Rua sniffed. 'Except that Eusebius' translation, in spite of the subsequent approval, was heavily criticised, even by the Blessed Augustus of Hippo, as I have pointed out several times.'

'But it is now accepted and approved?' queried Eadulf.

'That is not so . . .' began Brother Giolla Rua.

Fidelma heaved another exasperated sigh. 'I want simple answers to my questions and not some pedantic debate on scholastic difference. I take it that the answer to my question was that you were all chosen because of your scholarship on the texts of the New Faith?'

'That is so,' agreed Brother Mac Raith.

'We can now accept that Brother Sionnach was here because he was such a scholar?'

'That much is obvious,' Brother Mac Raith agreed with a quick look of annoyance at Brother Giolla Rua.

'What brought him to the Abbot of Imleach's attention?'

Brother Mac Raith made an encompassing motion with his hand. 'His commentaries on the Septuagint, the early Greek translation of the Old Testament, are considered essential. It is said that Ptolemy the Second Philadelphus ordered the translation to be made so that he could understand the Hebrew faith. Brother Sionnach has a vast knowledge of Kione Greek, the ancient form as it is called. His commentaries point out that it was this version, the Septuagint, which Paul of Tarsus quoted in his epistles to the early members of the Faith.'

'You have lost me,' Fidelma confessed. 'I am no scholar of the New Faith but have been merely tutored in matters of the text as they are taught to us, being the Latin translation of the Bible by Eusebius. I will readily accept that Brother Sionnach is a scholar in this field.'

Brother Mac Raith inclined his head. 'Yes. The scholarship of my colleagues is why they were chosen to attend here. Abbot Síoda of Ráth Cuáin and his followers have long argued their differences of interpreting the sacred texts. Successive Abbots of Imleach from the time of the Blessed Ailbe, who brought the New Faith to this kingdom, have claimed them to be heretical. Our meetings were to present a case that either Abbot Síoda must abide by our interpretations or that he and his acolytes shall be expelled from the Faith for this heresy.'

Fidelma looked carefully at the others.

'Do you all speak with one voice on this?' she asked cautiously. 'From what I heard of your previous argument with Brother Sionnach, and with your recent comments just now, I gather there are several points that you are not completely agreed upon.'

Brother Giolla Rua smiled broadly. 'You are perceptive, lady. In any argument there are areas of disagreement and interpretation to be explored.'

'But none of you agree with the faction called Psilanthropism?' Eadulf asked unexpectedly.

The question caused some sharp intakes of breath while Brother Giolla Rua looked at Eadulf with narrowed eyes.

'I understand why you ask the question, Eadulf of Seaxmund's

Ham, but you base your logic on little knowledge of the subject. That is dangerous. I am, in fact, of the sect called Manichaeists, taught by Manichaeus the Persian. He was criticised for his belief by the Bishop of Rome, Theodosius, two centuries ago. Why? Because we teach that good and evil are equally powerful, and that evil must be confronted. All material things are evil. Why does Rome condemn us? Because we say that once the Emperor Constantine became a Christian, the Church of Rome has pursued material power in this world; its bishops have become replacements for temporal princes and lords, and have set up their fiefdoms and exert material power over the faithful.'

'This is not the belief of all of us,' Brother Duibhinn declared hotly.

'Nor of the Abbey of Imleach,' Brother Mac Raith added.

'It was certainly not the belief of Brother Sionnach.' Brother Giolla Rua's smile was malicious.

'I am not interested in the claims of your various sects,' declared Fidelma. 'My head is spinning with all your vaunted scholarship. I am merely here to discover why Brother Sionnach has vanished from your midst. I have already seen evidence of the way you enforce your disagreements. Can this have been why he is no longer with you?'

Brother Giolla Rua laughed outright. 'I see where you may be heading, lady. In spite of differences and the resulting loss of a tooth, there is no disagreement which would cause me to wish Brother Sionnach to disappear.'

'But there are some points where you would engage in a physical fight?' Eadulf observed quickly.

'I admit, tempers can be brought to boiling point. But that is just in the heat of argument. It is not the same as a slow coldness that leads to wishing extreme harm to your antagonist.'

'I presume that you have all known and debated with Brother Sionnach for many years?' Fidelma asked.

She and Eadulf were amazed when Brother Mac Raith replied, 'No. I met him for the first time here. Neither Abbot Cuán nor I had met him before but only heard of his reputation as a scholar of the ancient texts of the New Faith.'

She turned to the others and found Brother Duibhinn shaking his head in a negative gesture while Brother Giolla Rua shrugged.

'We knew him by reputation only,' he confirmed. 'I too met him in person for the first time when he arrived here. To be frank, I hope I will not have to encounter that narrow-minded, egocentric fellow again.'

'So Sionnach was really a stranger to you all?' Eadulf sought their final confirmation with some astonishment.

'Not completely a stranger,' corrected Brother Mac Raith. 'His work at the Abbey of Corcach Mór was well known to us.'

'It does not matter when scholars meet,' put in Brother Duibhinn. 'They know each other by their works.'

'So what is known personally about Brother Sionnach other than his scholarship?'

'What do you mean? Where he was born?' Brother Mac Raith replied. 'His accent marked him as being of the Cenél nÁeda, who live so close by the Abbey of Finnbarr.'

'He mentioned that he had recently been on a pilgrimage to Rome in order to view some of the early texts from which Eusebius worked,' offered Brother Giolla Rua with a look of disdain. 'That was no surprise, as he thought Rome to be the centre of all things and not just the New Faith.'

'Did he ever use the name of Lucidus?' Eadulf asked.

They all regarded him with curiosity.

'Why would he do that?' Brother Mac Raith frowned. 'That's a Latin name. His name was Sionnach.'

Their bewilderment prompted Fidelma to make some explanation.

'Several of the religious of the New Faith have taken Latin names, as they believe this associates them more closely with it. Benen the son of Sesenen took the name of Benignus after he was converted. There are other examples. Sechnail became known as Secundus, Cathal was Cataldus and so on.'

'Brother Sionnach was besotted with Rome, judging by the things he said,' admitted Brother Giolla Rua. 'However, at least he was proud enough of his own name to keep it and maintain some reality.'

'Indeed, since his name, Brother Sionnach, has always brought him the respect due to a reverered scholar, why would he change it? He is well respected at the Abbey of Corcach Mór. It is why he was chosen, because of his reputation as being loyal to the teachings of Rome.' This was Brother Mac Raith talking.

Fidelma frowned thoughtfully. 'Loyal to the teachings of Rome?' she mused. 'Yet the scholars of our churches in the Five Kingdoms are always in conflict with Rome on many basic principles. I, myself, have attended several rather stormy councils between scholars who were loyal to the teachings of Rome and those who were loyal to the practices and laws of the Five Kingdoms.'

Brother Mac Raith shifted his weight in his chair uncomfortably for he knew well the conflict of which Fidelma spoke, between the native laws and the Roman concepts which were called 'Penitentials'.

'It was essential that we had a diversity of scholastic opinion,' he said. 'The texts that Abbot Síoda and his followers quote are false and heretical. Those following these texts claim the originals are known to the Bishop of Rome but safely hidden away from prying eyes. They accuse Rome of being heretical while they claim to follow the truth of the original texts.'

'Very well,' Fidelma sighed. 'This does not help us discover where Brother Sionnach has vanished to, nor why.' She rose from her seat. 'What is the intention of this council now?'

Brother Mac Raith told her, 'I suppose we must finish our deliberations and discuss the matter with Abbot Síoda at Ráth Cuáin before dispersing. I will take a full report to the Abbot at Imleach and it will be up to him to decide if there is to be any action taken against Síoda and Ráth Cuáin.'

Leaving the chapel, Fidelma and Eadulf made their way across the courtyard to the King's quarters. Luan, a warrior they knew well, was on guard outside the main building which housed the King's feasting hall and chambers, and which led to the chambers reserved for the distinguished and personal guests of the King. Nobles and bishops often stayed there.

Luan greeted them with a rueful smile. 'I was in charge of the guard after midnight,' he explained when Eadulf asked him why he looked so downcast. 'Now we have that strange woman getting killed and then this scholar going missing. Gormán is acting as if I am at fault.'

'I am sure he doesn't believe that,' Fidelma assured the young warrior. 'You have nothing to fear so long as you have done what is expected of you.'

They passed into the building and found Colgú in his private chambers. He was sprawled in a chair before the log fire, a flagon of *corma* on the table before him. Even in the soft light of the lamps, lit to illuminate the autumnal evening, they noticed that his face almost reflected the colour of his red hair. It was a worrying sign.

'Didn't you drink enough at the Samhain feast last night, brother?' she said. 'Yet now you are indulging yourself further while there are important matters to attend to.'

Colgú looked up with a groan. 'Don't you start again. Since you like throwing Latin sayings at me, here is one for you, sister: *similia similibus curantur!*'

Fidelma eyed him grimly. She knew the saying well that something is cured by the same thing that created it. Seeing the angry spark in her eye, her brother added as if to gain her sympathy: 'The Princess Gelgéis and her entourage left for Durlus Éile at midday.'

Fidelma was unsympathetic. 'I don't blame her. I expect that she was not best pleased at your excesses last night. Gelgéis was the perfect match for you, and now you seem to have spoiled that.'

'I don't need your match-making,' her brother snapped. 'I have enough problems to attend to.'

She nodded to the flagon. 'So I can see. And once you have attended to that, all your problems will be solved? I think not.'

'What are *you* doing to solve the problems of two ritual murders below the walls of my own fortress?' Colgú challenged her. 'And now, in addition, Gormán tells me that we have the disappearance of one of the religious scholars to cope with! Will that turn into another murder? What am I to tell the Abbot of Corcach Mór – that his leading scholar has vanished while under my protection as a guest in my palace? Then there is the matter of keeping this so-called noble of the Uí Briúin Seóla under restraint here. What is being done about that? Do we want another war with Connacht? After Muirchertach Nár died a few years ago I thought we could rest easy along our northern border. But his cousin, the new King of Connacht, is as ambitious as Muirchertach and his own father Guaire Aidne was. Connacht would welcome an excuse to test our watchfulness along the border.'

Fidelma spared a moment of compassion for her brother. It was true that the new King of Connacht, Dúnchadh Muirisci of the Uí Fiachrach, was making various bellicose noises. He had begun his kingship with a swift consolidation of his power by putting down his own rebellious chieftains along the entire stretch of the Muaide, the river rising in the high peaks of Sliabh Gamh with its rich lead and copper mines and running 110 kilometres to the great western ocean. Control over this area had made him very rich and powerful. She could understand why her brother did not want to provoke him.

She sat down opposite Colgú but her severe expression did not soften. 'Wine in the bottle does not quench thirst,' she said, using another of the Latin proverbs of which she was so fond. 'You would do better with a clear head to concentrate on these problems.'

Colgú opened his mouth to retaliate and then his shoulders suddenly slumped.

'Sometimes I wish I were a simple *céile*, a clansman who has nothing more strenuous to worry about than cultivating the land,' he muttered.

'If you think farming is a less strenuous task than your own, then you are in for a sad awakening if you ever attempt it, brother,' Fidelma replied.

Colgú glanced up at Eadulf, who was still standing, and he waved a hand towards a chair.

'I would offer you a drink, friend Eadulf, but I fear I would be reproached for doing so.'

Eadulf smiled and took the seat. 'It will soon be time for *prainn*,' he said, referring to the principal meal of the day, for it had been dark for some time now. 'No one will be reproached for taking a drink with their dinner.'

Colgú smiled thinly. 'Always the diplomat, Eadulf. And has your diplomacy managed to secure answers to the mysteries that assail us?'

Eadulf made a negative gesture with his hand. 'Personally, I found no answers – only further questions.'

Colgú turned to his sister. 'Did you see the old hermit Erca and was he able to give you information?'

'He was,' asserted Fidelma. 'In fact, he said that Branche\u00f3 was his daughter.'

The King's eyes widened a little. 'I suppose he was full of curses and cries for the destruction of Cashel then?'

'He cursed those who murdered his daughter; that is so. Colgú, I am coming to the conclusion that this business of the old religion has been deliberately created as a smokescreen to distract us from some other reality.'

Colgú waited impatiently for a further explanation and then had to prompt her.

'What I mean,' Fidelma was forced to explain, 'is that I think that the way Spelán and Branched were killed has nothing to do with Samhain or curses or the ancient pagan religion. I sense that we must look more closely at this debate about the New Faith.'

'Do you also mean that the disappearance of Brother Sionnach and the debate of this so-called heretical abbey are all connected?' Eadulf asked.

'The resolution to all this will be found in Ráth Cuáin,' Fidelma admitted. 'I feel it.'

Colgú stared at her blankly. 'I've never heard you resolve anything by merely feeling the answer,' he commented.

'Nor do I mean to now, but . . .'

There came a respectful knock on the chamber door. Gormán entered and after saluting the King, he inclined his head towards Fidelma and Eadulf.

'I was told that you would be here, lady,' he said. 'I need to report that we have searched everywhere for the missing scholar. The stables to the chapel, the food storage, the guards' barracks and—'

'There is no sign of him?' cut in Colgú.

'None, lord,' Gormán confirmed.

'You are sure that absolutely everywhere has been searched?' Fidelma pressed.

'Everywhere, lady, except the personal guest chambers of the King. I have asked your housekeeper, Dar Luga, to accompany two of my warriors and go through the chambers. There is only one in occupation at the moment and that is occupied by Febal, the poet of the Uí Briúin Seóla.'

'But everywhere else has been thoroughly checked?' The King was not satisfied.

'Every place my warriors could conceive of and more. I trust my men with my life and can assure you that all places have been examined.'

'The mystery deepens.' Eadulf gave a sigh. 'Brother Sionnach must, indeed, be possessed of your famous *feidh fiadh*, your cloak of invisibility . . . or else . . .'

'Or else?' demanded Colgú.

'Well, I do not believe in the powers of sorcerers, so I would leave it with the "or else" reason.' Eadulf was serious.

Gormán regarded him with narrowed eyes. 'And what is your reason?'

'That the man left the fortress during the night and somehow managed to elude your guards in the darkness. No magic but simply they failed to see him leave.'

Gormán's jaw tightened. They could almost hear the crunch of his teeth. Colgú was nodding his head.

'It is a logical conclusion – but if a man can elude your guards, Gormán, then there must be consequences.'

'I'll take responsibility for my men. I cannot believe it was possible that this Brother Sionnach could have left the chapel in the middle of the night and walked out of this fortress without someone seeing him.'

'Whether it is possible or not, it appears to be the only explanation,' Colgú said.

'Luan was guard commander last night,' Gormán said. 'You all know Luan and he is not one to shirk his duties.'

'No one is blaming Luan,' Fidelma assured him. 'But Luan cannot be everywhere. Anyway, is it not an axiom that however strong a man may build a prison to keep people in, they will always find a way to escape. Cashel is not even a prison, nor was Brother Sionnach a prisoner. So blame does not come into it.'

There was a sudden commotion outside the door; the voice of Luan was raised, together with that of a woman. Then the door was thrown open without the usual formality of a knock. Colgú sprang to his feet as Gormán swung round, already removing his sword from its scabbard in defence.

The plump figure of Dar Luga, the *ainbertach*, the housekeeper of the palace, pushed herself forward. Her hair was awry and her features were working in shocked distress. She halted for a moment, staring wild eyed at them. Behind her Luan stood uncertainly. Dar Luga seemed to have trouble trying to speak.

'It's . . . it's . . .'

Fidelma rose and moved forward, laying a hand on the woman's arm.

'Calm yourself, Dar Luga. Calm . . . yourself. Take a deep breath . . . and then tell us slowly what has happened.'

The housekeeper did as she was advised, then spoke on a sob. 'Oh, lady. It is the young man Febal. He has been found in the guest chamber . . . dead.'

'What?' cried Colgú in the silence that followed. 'How can that be?'

Dar Luga took a few more moments to gather herself. Then she turned to Gormán and said: 'I went with your warriors to search the guests' rooms. The only chamber in current occupation was the one where Febal was placed.'

'There was supposed to be a warrior permanently on duty outside his door,' said Colgú. 'Although a guest, he was a guest under duress.'

'There was usually someone there,' Dar Luga agreed. 'Anyway, I went with the two warriors and we searched the empty rooms first before going to the one in which Febal was installed. I knocked. There was no answer. I thought it strange for I have not seen him all day, not since the feast last night. But then, there are many who have been . . . have been resting today,' she glanced automatically at Colgú, 'after the extent of the feasting last night.'

Colgú grimaced impatiently. 'So, you received no answer.'

'I tried the door. It was unlocked. So I called his name. There was no answer. We entered and found him on the floor, face downwards. There was blood. So much blood.'

She ended with a sob. It was left to Fidelma to comfort her.

'Where are my men now?' demanded Gormán.

'They are with the body in the room. They sent me to inform you.'

'I will go up to them,' Gormán said with a swift glance at them, as if seeking permission, before leaving them in the King's chamber.

Colgú had slumped back in his chair, holding his head. 'I knew something like this would happen,' he muttered.

'You knew the poet of the Uí Briúin Seóla would be killed?' Fidelma asked her brother.

'Of course I did not mean that,' Colgú snapped. 'Did I not say that I feared the new King of Connacht might use Febal's presence here as some pretext to stir up animosity between the kingdoms? With the death of this young man, there is the perfect excuse.'

'Dar Luga,' Fidelma told the tearful housekeeper, 'you had best go to the kitchens and get something for your shock.'

When she had gone, Fidelma turned with a serious look to her brother.

'I think it probably wise that you send a messenger to find the Chief Brehon,' she said quietly. 'Where did you say Fíthel was?'

'He is still at the fortress of Prince Gilcach making inquiries about the thefts from his boats along the great river.' Colgú was troubled. 'You think things will develop badly?'

She did not reply directly but said, 'Perhaps Finguine, as heir apparent, should also be here as well? Did I hear he was completing the new treaty with Donennach of the Uí Fidgente? Well, if the clans of Connacht are going to use this as an excuse to start raiding into our territory, the territories that they will be crossing into will be those of the Déisi Tuaiscirt and the Uí Fidgente. We need to make sure that they are on our side.'

Colgú ran a hand through his red hair distractedly.

'Connacht warriors could easily cross north of Loch Oirsean and into the Muscraige Tír, which would leave Éile without protection.'

'True enough, but there will be time for war councils after Finguine and Fíthel return,' said Fidelma. 'We must keep matters quiet until I can discover what is behind Febal's death and Sionnach's disappearance. And indeed, whether they are connected with the other murders.'

'So you do believe they are connected?' Colgú was glum.

'There is such a thing as synchronicity but it so rarely happens. So yes, I am sure there is some connection, even though at the moment there seems no obvious link.'

Just then, they heard the agitated voice of a warrior calling for Gormán.

'Now what is it?' groaned Colgú.

Gormán hurried up the stairway and was gone but a few moments before he was calling for Fidelma.

'Lady,' came Gormán's voice, 'you'd best come immediately.'

Fidelma exchanged a puzzled look with her brother and then made for the door, Eadulf at her heels.

'I am coming, Gormán. What is amiss?' she called as they ran up the stairs to the chambers that were reserved for special guests.

Gormán was standing at the top of the stairs. Surprisingly, he did not answer her but merely beckoned her and Eadulf forward. Two of his warriors, with fixed expressions, stood outside a door and Gormán led the way inside.

There was nothing exceptional about the chamber into which he showed them. It was well furnished and appointed as each of the King's guest chambers were. There were few personal belongings in it except those which courtesy offered to guests if they had arrived without baggage as Febal had. The only unusual item in the room, which they saw immediately, was the corpse itself. It lay on its back on the floor by the bed with a pool of blood around its head.

Fidelma frowned. 'Have you moved the body?' she asked. Dar Luga had told them that the body had been found face down.

'I did so in order to identify it, lady. You will see there is some discrepancy about what Dar Luga told us.'

Fidelma had already noticed that the corpse was clad in religieux robes. That was curious. She moved forward to make a closer examination. Drying blood was everywhere. She was silent for a few moments while Eadulf was equally astonished.

'Why,' she said, after a moment or two, 'that is not Febal.'

Eadulf was staring down at the dead face. 'Indeed,' he agreed. 'That is not Febal, but his features do seem familiar.'

'This is the body of the man who had the verbal exchange with the woman Brancheó last night,' Gormán announced heavily.

'That is the body of the missing Brother Sionnach,' Fidelma said quietly.

CHAPTER FIFTEEN

'So now that we have found the missing Brother Sionnach we have yet another mystery to contend with.' Eadulf broke the silence that had followed the identification of the corpse. He went down on one knee beside the body and made a cursory examination.

'The good news,' he announced after a few moments, 'if there is good news, is that Brother Sionnach was not the victim of the threefold death.'

'Black humour does not become this situation, Eadulf,' Fidelma rebuked him. 'How did Brother Sionnach die?'

'A knife into the heart – one upwards stab. Inflicted with either luck or knowledge, as it appears to be a single blow. There is no sign of struggle, no sign that the man made any attempt to defend himself. He was obviously standing very close to his killer and I would say that he must have known him and could not have been anticipating any such attack.'

'Isn't that going too far, to suggest that Brother Sionnach knew Febal?' Gormán asked.

'Perhaps,' admitted Eadulf. 'But the way Brother Sionnach was killed showed that he did not perceive Febal as an enemy to be wary of. He was not dragged to his chamber but appears to have come here of his own volition.'

'Eadulf is right,' Fidelma agreed. 'Brother Sionnach must have known Febal, otherwise why did he come here in the middle of the night? But what was he doing in the guest quarters – and why did no one see him enter? Did he have some business with Febal? And should we assume that Febal killed him simply because it is he who is missing? Where *is* Febal?'

Gormán was looking troubled. 'It seems that we have been searching for the wrong missing person.'

'Having searched the palace for Brother Sionnach, I don't think your warriors would have neglected to mention it if they had found Febal,' Eadulf reassured him. 'After all, he was a guest here but under constraint while Fidelma was conducting her investigation. The logical presumption is that Brother Sionnach came to see Febal for some purpose, they quarrelled, Febal killed the religieux and fled.'

'Again the question: he fled, but how and where to?' Gormán asked, baffled. 'It is as difficult to flee from these guest chambers as it would have been from the chapel. If Brother Sionnach had a purpose in meeting with Febal, what was it? What was the link?'

'The link is Ráth Cuáin,' Eadulf said immediately.

Fidelma was smiling at Eadulf's change of mind about the abbey's connection.

'Explain your reason,' she invited.

'Brother Sionnach is one of the scholars come here to debate whether Ráth Cuáin stands in heresy. Febal arrives here when the religious scholars are meeting. He says he is on his way to Ráth Cuáin in search of a Brother Fursaintid and, in justification, tells us a rather romantic and intricate tale, worthy, no doubt, of the poet he claimed to be. He told us that this man, Fursaintid, had seduced and then betrayed his sister and that he was heading to Ráth Cuáin in pursuit of blood vengeance.'

Fidelma was nodding slowly in approval as he spoke. 'It is feasible,' she said. Moreover, Ráth Cuáin would be the perfect place to hide, for although it lies only a relatively short distance from here, I had never been there and did not, in all honesty, even know of its existence.'

'Yet exist it did and still does,' Gormán pointed out. 'It remains isolated because that area does not lie on the trade routes from Cashel. No major tracks or roads lead to it.'

'Yet, from what Brother Mac Raith has told us,' Eadulf added, 'the abbey has been of growing concern to the Abbot of Imleach as Chief Bishop of Muman, for many years. Why was this not more widely known?'

'Let us suppose that Ráth Cuáin *is* the connection with all these matters,' Fidelma said. 'But what would be the real connection? That Febal was going there to search for this Brother Fursaintid? That Brother Sionnach was here discussing what might be the future of the abbey? That Brancheó thought he was someone who might have been the mysterious Brother Lucidus? So many options. I think we should explore that connection more carefully.'

She paused. 'And as for this Brother Fursaintid . . .'

'Yes?'

'Did you know that the name Fursaintid means "one who illuminates"? In other words – a lightgiver.'

Eadulf was silent as he took this in. Then Fidelma turned to Gormán. 'Gormán, ask your warriors if anyone can remember seeing Febal after the feasting last night or during the course of this day. Perhaps they might come up with some idea of how he could have left the palace, though I doubt it.'

Gormán agreed somewhat morosely. 'If they couldn't do so with regard to Brother Sionnach, I doubt if they will with this man Febal.' Seeing her eyes glinting, he held up his hand to stay her displeasure. 'But it is better to explore all the angles, I know. I am going. I shall ask, have no fear.'

'And what task falls to us?' Eadulf asked when Gormán had departed.

'The first task is to make a search of this chamber to ensure that Febal has left nothing of interest behind, and after that, to search the corpse.'

In both cases there was nothing. Brother Sionnach's corpse revealed no hidden clues or treasures.

'Now we must have a word with Dar Luga and the household members. Someone might have seen something.'

'Didn't Brother Conchobhar say that he had heard of Febal as a poet?' Eadulf reminded her. 'We should also have a word with him.'

Fidelma acknowledged the point with a quick motion of her head. Eadulf had never seen her looking so frustrated. He remained convinced that the answer to the problem lay in the Abbey at Ráth Cuáin, but had no clear idea of how or why.

Certainly Dar Luga and those working in the King's private chambers were no help in uncovering any connection between Febal and Brother Sionnach. Febal had been courteous to those attending him during the brief time he was in the guest chambers but had offered little information about himself. No one ever saw Brother Sionnach visiting the guest chamber, least of all during the previous night. How Brother Sionnach had been able to enter the King's quarters and how Febal had left them was a complete mystery to everyone. Gormán had returned to mournfully report that on re-questioning his guards, none had been able to shed a light on this.

It was when Fidelma and Eadulf were crossing the courtyard on their way to Brother Conchobhar's apothecary that Fidelma suddenly came to a halt and declared that she had thought of a possible explanation.

'Do you recall that back at the time of the feast of Brigit, my brother was having some work done on rebuilding the south-west corner wall?'

'I do,' agreed Eadulf. 'We spent some time finding out how someone had left the palace and we made our way down through the scaffolding erected by the workmen. But the repair work ended during the summer and there is no scaffolding there now.'

'That is true. It went out of my mind as no cleric such as Brother Sionnach would have the ability to scale down the wall . . . but a warrior? Now that is different.'

'A warrior?'

'Have you forgotten? Febal admitted that he was once a member of the Gamanride, the élite warriors of the Kings of Connacht. A single, trained warrior could easily scale down the wall to the ground at that corner. Come on, let us see what Brother Conchobhar can add to our knowledge about this strange young poet.'

The information that Brother Conchobhar was able to give them was of little help, even though he had been seated next to Febal during the Samhain festival feast the night before and had conversed at length with him.

'I had vaguely heard of Febal of the Uí Briúin Seóla as I mentioned before,' the elderly apothecary reflected. 'Visiting poets spoke of him as a growing talent, not only in our language but in Latin also.'

'In Latin? Of course, I heard you conversing with him in Latin during the feast last night.'

'I was told,' Brother Conchobhar was almost reverential, 'that he had a talent for writing in the new Latin metre.'

'Which is?' asked a puzzled Eadulf.

'Quatrains of seven-syllable lines with rhyme and alliteration.'

'A former warrior of the Gamanride of Connacht writing poems in Latin? How did he become adept at that?' Fidelma asked. 'Did he tell you when you were in conversation at the feast last night.'

Brother Conchobhar rubbed his chin reflectively. 'I think he said that he had studied for a time in Rome,' he offered. 'I must admit that I have never read any of his poems, so do not know the quality of the verse. However, I can say that he had a great fluency in speaking, which surprised me.'

'Were you able to find out anything else about him?'

'Only that he said he had trained at Cluain Fois, which you already knew. That is the abbey that was founded by the disciple of Patrick – Iarlaithe son of Loga. I suppose on his return from Rome he was employed there as he admitted that he taught poetry there.'

'Do you place any credence in the story he told us about his sister? I suppose you heard about it – that he came here to pursue blood vengeance because a Brother Fursaintid had dishonoured his sister?'

The old apothecary shrugged. 'Stranger things have happened, lady. Although it seems curious that he would arrive here to announce he is engaged in a blood feud. Why did he not go directly to Ráth Cuáin where he suspected his quarry to be? Why come here at all?'

His questions gave Fidelma and Eadulf more food for thought. They left Brother Conchobhar and decided to go back to their chambers to refresh themselves. Muirgen, the nurse, brought them clean water and a change of clothing.

'Let us try considering the mystery from another angle,' Fidelma suggested when they were changing.

Eadulf looked at her expectantly. She began to tick off points on her fingers.

'A shepherd of dubious reputation is found half concealed in a Samhain bonfire. It was arranged so that the body could be seen. He had been killed in a ritualistic way associated with the old religion. Yet carved on him was the emblem of the nearby abbey which is also an emblem of a group that believes in a heresy. Why? He has come to this area, married a local woman, Caoimhe, and taken care of her flock, though he is not a shepherd by all accounts. She dies and he buries her but, appealing to the abbey, he is told that he has no rights and must leave his cabin, which he lets fall into disrepair. At this time he is reported to be poor and desperate. He meets up with Brancheó, who claims to be a Druidess, and asks her to perform an ancient pagan curse for him. Then, suddenly, he comes into some form of wealth and makes plans to live with her in the southern mountains.'

She paused, and Eadulf nodded. 'That much is known. But where does this lead us?'

'Why were we meant to find his body? Was it a warning of some sort, and if so, by whom? We are told Brancheó wanted to marry him. That would appear to let her out. We are also told that no member of the Old Faith would perform such a ritual as the threefold murder. It is confusing.'

'If was as if the ritual killing was meant for our eyes. Was it a warning or a distraction? If so, from what?'

'If we believe Erca, the father of Brancheó, the ritual was not genuine. He says that when his daughter was visiting the area, she met Spelán and fell in love with him. A questionable taste, true, but if we accept that, she had no reason to be involved in his death. And, of course, she, too, met her end by the same bizarre ritual, although without the symbol of the abbey or heresy carved on her as it had been with Spelán. Her body too was clearly meant to be found and displayed in a very public fashion.'

Eadulf thought for a moment or two and then said: 'There is only one answer I can think of.'

'Which is?' prompted Fidelma.

'If we were meant to find the first ritual killing, then the second one was intended to disguise the significance of the first.'

Fidelma was smiling broadly. 'Exactly! The second ritual killing was the distraction, not the first. But distraction for what purpose? We have leaped to the obvious conclusion that the killings were something to do with pagan rituals. Then we have the conflict concerning the heresy of the abbey to consider. There is the mysterious note from our friend Venerable Gelasius saying we might be contacted by a Brother Lucidus. We became confused by the complication of the various meanings of names central to lightbringing.'

Eadulf sighed deeply. 'We are back with more questions than answers.'

'So you think that, in spite of everything, Brother Sionnach was really someone called Lucidus? It overlooks the fact that Brother Sionnach seems to be well known to the religious brethren, to scholars who respect what he has written. Therefore, he could not hide away from the public view of scholars under any other name but his own.'

'Agreed, Eadulf. We don't even know what the mission was that Venerable Gelasius mentioned. Why would this Brother Lucidus want to seek my help – and for what purpose? What was the mysterious missing book that he needed help to find, and why did he not make contact? In fact, we know nothing of Brother Lucidus: who he is, where he is, what was his question.'

'So in which direction should our footsteps turn? To Ráth Cuáin?'

'Before that we must return to Brother Mac Raith and his quarrelsome colleagues. Now we know Brother Sionnach is dead and Febal has disappeared, they might be more forthcoming with information.'

However, Brother Mac Raith, Brother Giolla Rua or Brother Duibhinn could volunteer no further information that associated their murdered colleague with Febal. One by one they repeated that they had only seen Febal once at the Samhain feast the previous night. They had been separated by the width of the feasting hall. Only Brother Duibhinn remarked, as an afterthought, that he felt that Brother Sionnach had behaved curiously later on. When pressed to explain, he said it had happened when the King had become tired of trying to make entertainment out of the pagan woman Brancheó. As soon as Gormán had left, escorting the woman, Brother Sionnach had risen, almost with indecent haste and ignoring etiquette, saying that he had much to do and left the hall. At the same time, Brother Duibhinn recalled, Febal of the Uí Briúin Seóla had also left the hall.

Fidelma already knew that Brother Sionnach had followed Gormán and Brancheó and that an exchange of curious words had taken place in the courtyard. After the midnight mass, it appeared that Sionnach had made his way to Febal's chamber – but why? What made Febal kill him and flee? Was it something to do with the 'lightbringer' connection?

Fidelma concluded the interview by asking Brother Mac Raith to show her and Eadulf where Brother Sionnach slept. It was in a corner of the small chamber-like room that was really part of the chapel but set aside for visiting religious dignitaries of lower ranks. All four members of the council had chosen to use it so that they could extend their deliberations into the night if they so wanted. Brother Sionnach had a wooden cot in a corner. By it stood a stout wooden staff, carved from oak, leaning against the wall. Hanging on a peg was a large satchel, a spare robe and a new pair of leather sandals. It seemed that Brother Sionnach was fastidious about his appearance and always travelled with extra clothing.

On examination, the satchel was found to contain one unusual object – a *graib*, a pointed metal stylus used for writing on a waxed tablet. The tablet was usually a small frame made of wood with raised borders so that wax could be poured into it when hot. The wax then cooled and by the use of the *graib,* notes could be written. The wax could be softened into a smooth surface when needed again, often by simply the heat of the hand rubbing on it.

'Curious that he carried a stylus and nothing to write on,' Fidelma commented, having exhausted a search of the dead man's belongings, even turning the straw mattress on the wooden cot in case something had been hidden there.

Eadulf, meanwhile, was putting down the folds of the hanging robe. He let out an exclamation as his hand closed over a hidden object. He had to rummage a bit before carefully removing a small wooden tablet from a linen *sacculus*, a pouch-like pocket that had been sewn into the interior of the robe. Fidelma looked at him questioningly.

Eadulf grinned triumphantly. 'I remembered when we first worked together on the murders during the council at Streonshalh. Do you recall that the murdered religieux Seaxwulf followed the new fashion of keeping a hidden pocket inside his robe? It is now being adopted by many instead of a bag hanging from the belt. People think it keeps their personal items safer from thieves. The idea came from Frankia, as I recall. Anyway, that was where Brother Sionnach was keeping his wax tablet. It appears to have writing still on it,' he added, glancing at it.

Fidelma took the small rectangular frame of beechwood and went to the window to hold it up to illuminate the dark wax surface.

'Latin,' she said, examining the text that had been inscribed there. Then she breathed out sharply before reading it aloud.

'"Look for Tau-Rho. Secret book there. It must be returned. Danger in wrong hands. Perhaps 'Lightbringer' not to be trusted".'

Fidelma stood leaning against the sill of the window, her brows knitted in a frown of concentration.

'I think, we may have finally found the thread that will lead us to resolve these mysteries,' she whispered.

'The thread?' echoed Eadulf. 'Brother Sionnach mentions that Lightbringer might not be trusted. That tells us that we must discount any notion that Sionnach was this Brother Lucidus or Lightbringer. Why did Brancheó think he was?'

'That was your interpretation of what she said,' Fidelma gently reminded him. 'She simply referred to him as a "lightbringer".'

'Anyway, Gelasius tells you to trust a Brother Lucidus if he contacts you about some matter of a book. Now this note from Sionnach says Lucidus is not to be trusted.' Eadulf looked perplexed. 'I don't understand it. The only thing I recognise from his note is the reference to the Tau-Rho sign because it is the sign of this group at the Abbey of Ráth Cuáin, where I have always felt the mystery has its source.'

'It seems that you are right,' Fidelma agreed. 'However, now I know what the main clue is, some things appear to be coming together.'

'The main clue?' Eadulf was bewildered.

'The secret book. More to the point, I have seen it on Abbot Síoda's desk. So now we shall definitely go to Ráth Cuáin.'

The day had turned out to be surprisingly warm and pleasant as they rode once more into the lands of the Sítae, the clan lands around the Abbey of Ráth Cuáin. Even the coarse hills circling the central Hill of the Bullock looked serene and peaceful under the soft autumnal sun. Fidelma could not think of the young and handsome Abbot Síoda without remembering that he also held secular power over the small group of people who dwelled there as far the great river, the Siúr. She disapproved of any person holding both religious and secular power, but many Brehons argued that churchmen had to obey the ancient laws as much as the temporal princes and chieftains, and that any abuse of power would be opposed. She personally did not think this a sufficient safeguard, having seen several abuses by churchmen abandoning the law to accept the new Roman ideas of the Penitentials – which gave them unprecedented power.

Aidan, as usual, was riding in front, with Fidelma following on her white-grey pony, Aonbharr. Eadulf brought up the rear on his steady roan cob. There had not been much to talk about since they left the outskirts of the township and Fidelma never believed in talking when it was not necessary. It was relaxing to sit at ease on their horses, almost giving the beasts their heads, as the faint afternoon sun in a cloudless sky warmed them whenever the soft breeze allowed. Now and again rabbits would pop up alongside their path and then bound away unafraid by their passing, as they continued off on some mysterious search of their own. In the distance a fox, in its bright russet colours, would be seen trotting across the hillside; it would halt suddenly as their scent reached its sensitive nostrils, stare in their direction, sitting to examine them calmly, before rising again and trotting off about its business. Once again, as before, there was little sign of livestock on the gently sloping hillside.

To their left, the ground rose steeply in a series of craggy rocks. Their approach startled a small flock of starlings which fluttered into the sky, rising with glossy iridescent plumage and yellow bills in a twirling mess, arguing with each other in aggressive cries as they sought some morsel of food to assuage their voracious appetites. Now and then Eadulf thought he heard the call of other birds among them. Then he realised that the starlings were expert mimics and were making calls to intimidate their fellows from what they considered their prey. All of a sudden silence fell; the wheeling swarm vanished behind the rocky outcrop. Eadulf glanced up and saw the dull brown flash of a female merlin, with pointed wings, ascending, ready to drop on its prey below. No wonder the starlings had fled. A moment later, a cacophony of bird calls came to his ears and other birds began to rise up and fly away from the rocks above.

Alerted by the sound, Aidan had halted his horse and was glancing upwards.

'It's only starlings and a merlin in search of prey,' Eadulf called to him.

But Aidan paid him no heed.

'You remember the sense of danger I felt, the first time we rode along this trail?' he asked Eadulf, keeping his voice low.

'When you suspected that we were being followed? Yes – and it turned out to be Branched on a path above us.'

'I have the same sense now,' Aidan confessed quietly. Then: 'Don't glance up,' he added urgently.

Fidelma reached forward to take a water bottle from her saddle bow and drank.

'Do you know who it is?' she asked, under cover of her actions. 'Is it one person or several?'

'I am not sure on either account, lady,' he said. 'I had an uneasy feeling for some time . . . then the birds alerted me and I saw the flash of the sun reflecting on what might be a sword or shield. Up ahead is the place where the track turns sharply and where Brancheó was waiting for us. That is an ideal spot for an ambush.'

'Why would anyone intend to ambush us?' Eadulf asked.

'Who knows? There are many things that have occurred these last few days that seem beyond logic to me.'

Fidelma glanced to the left-hand side of the path. 'The hill slopes quite gently here. We could leave the track and ride down towards the forest below. That would provide cover, and then we could approach Ráth Cuáin from the south by a more circuitous route. Would you be able to ride down this hill, if we need to hurry, Eadulf?'

Eadulf, no great horseman, viewed the terrain bleakly. 'I could try, but don't ask me to canter or I will end up breaking my neck.'

Fidelma put back her water bottle. She smiled encouragingly at Eadulf. 'Then follow me. I'll make it as easy as I can.'

She turned her pony, Aonbharr, and nudged him forward. He snorted and then without further protest began to trot rapidly down the incline. If Fidelma had meant it to be easy, her horse thought otherwise, for the animal broke into a quick pace, although not moving directly downwards but at an angle to the slope. Even so, Fidelma had to stretch back in the saddle to maintain her balance.

'Go, friend Eadulf,' Aidan hissed, as Eadulf seemed to hesitate.

He was aware of Aidan suddenly unhooking his shield and swinging it around behind him just as something hit it with a clang on the metal. It wasn't until he felt the wind of a missile speed by the side of his face – a sound like a passing wasp – and saw an arrow embed itself in the ground nearby, that he realised what was happening. The three of them were under attack – and the aim was to kill them.

ChAPTER SIXTEEN

A s Eadulf urged his usually placid cob forward, he closed his
eyes and trusted in his animal's instinct as it moved rapidly
down at the same angle to the slope as Aonbharr. It would have
been too dangerous to move straight downwards, but Eadulf's cob
was intelligent. They were moving quickly down and away from
the brow of the hill. Somewhere in the dim recess of his mind,
Eadulf realised it would be difficult for bowmen to hit a target from
where they were shooting. He clung on for dear life, hearing the
raucous breath of Aidan's mount close behind but not daring to
look.

The ride seemed to take a long time down the bare open hillside
until Eadulf felt they had reached a level area. Opening his eyes,
he saw that they were already on the edge of the woodland that
spread across the valley. Only when they entered the cover of the
trees did Fidelma draw rein as Eadulf managed to pull his sweating
cob to a halt beside her.

'Are you hurt, Aidan?' she asked as the warrior pulled up next
to them.

The young man grinned. 'I swung my shield behind me just in
time,' he replied. 'One arrow hit the shield boss. A second one, as
you can see . . .'

It was then that Eadulf saw an arrow protruding from the warrior's saddlebag. He felt a cold shiver on the nape of his neck and glanced back up the hill. There was no sign of pursuit. All was quiet.

Fidelma reached forward from her horse and pulled the arrow free, examining it carefully.

'This is no hunter's arrow,' she commented. 'What do you make of it, Aidan?'

The warrior took it from her, turning it over between the thumb and fingers of his right hand.

'A war arrow,' he confirmed. 'But not one from this kingdom.'

Fidelma pursed her lips. 'Uí Briúin Seóla?' she queried.

'Certainly it is of the type used in Connacht. I have seen similar when I was a young shield-bearer during the wars against King Guaire Aidne.'

Eadulf knew arrows usually had special markings to identify their origins; therefore he was not surprised by the question and answer.

'Are you saying that it was Febal who tried to ambush us up there?' he asked.

'Febal – or possibly his confederates. Someone who uses the arrows of Connacht,' Aidan said. 'As I turned, I saw the heads of at least two bowmen emerge on the ridge. They clearly meant to ambush us had we ridden on. Don't forget that Febal might claim to be a poet but he was once a member of the Gamanride.'

'Are we in danger here, do you think?' Fidelma asked.

'There is no sign of them following us down the hill. Nevertheless, if they mean us harm, it might be wise not to tarry here, lady. What shall we do – return to Cashel?'

'Why would Febal want to prevent us reaching Ráth Cuáin?' interrupted Eadulf. 'Because he killed Brother Sionnach? Surely, this attack is as good as a confession; it indicates that there is some murderous conspiracy afoot. Do we conclude that he is involved in some plot from Connacht?'

'Eadulf has a point, lady,' said Aidan. 'Perhaps we should alert your brother, the King.'

'We do not have enough information,' Fidelma disagreed. 'I think it was just a warning, intended to dissuade us from reaching the abbey.'

'A warning?' Aidan was surprised. 'It seemed pretty murderous to me, lady.'

'We must carry on.' Her tone became determined. 'We shall make our way to the cabin of Éimhin and Torcán and stay there until nightfall. Then we can ride on to Ráth Cuáin in darkness so that they are not expecting us.'

'In the darkness?' Eadulf was astounded.

'In the darkness.'

'How will we gain admission to the abbey? I doubt if Brother Tadhg will admit us.'

Fidelma smiled reprovingly. 'As Seneca said – *aut inveniam viam aut faciam.*'

Eadulf groaned while Aidan looked puzzled. Eadulf took pity on him as Fidelma turned her horse to find a path through the trees.

'She is fond of quoting from Latin sages,' he apologised. 'It means she'll either find a way or make one.'

Aidan shrugged. 'I suppose if anyone can, she can,' he replied stoically, following her lead.

'That is true,' Eadulf sighed to himself, as he nudged his cob to follow the others.

After a while, as the track through the forest broadened and Aidan had eased himself in front, Eadulf brought his horse alongside Fidelma.

'I think you should share your plan with me before we reach Torcán's cabin. You mean to stay there until nightfall? What if the woodsman and his wife are not as against Abbot Síoda as they have claimed?'

Fidelma cast him a thoughtful glance. 'You always come out with a quiet wisdom, Eadulf, whereas I am too impatient to get on with matters. You are right.' Pulling rein, she called: 'Aidan! Just here is a good stream. We'll refresh the horses and rest a while.'

Soon they had made themselves comfortable on some fallen logs by the stream while their horses drank from its sparkling waters.

'As you both know, my first plan was to go directly to Ráth Cuáin and just confront Abbot Síoda about certain matters. The ambush has given me pause to rethink that idea.'

'Agreed,' Eadulf replied. 'But if you aim to go to the abbey after nightfall, how can we gain entrance? Is it worth taking such a risk?'

'I think so. I have found only a few pieces of thread to start unravelling this mystery. I confess none of them led the way to any conclusion until we found Brother Sionnach's *ceraculum*.'

'His what?' Aidan queried.

'A tablet of wax on which he had written a note,' Eadulf explained.

'He had written some interesting things,' Fidelma said. 'One was that Lucidus was, perhaps, not to be trusted. Why was he not to be trusted – and by whom?'

'Who is Lucidus then?' Aidan demanded.

'That is just the point. We don't know. If he was not Brother Sionnach, who was he?' Eadulf said. 'The questions multiply.'

'Look for the Tau-Rho, the note said. So which abbey bears the symbol Tau-Rho on its walls – the very symbol carved on the corpse of Spelán?'

'I still don't understand,' Aidan sighed.

'That is why we need more information before alerting Cashel,' replied Fidelma. 'We have a connection between Brother Sionnach to Lucidus and the Tau-Rho, linking it to Ráth Cuáin. But that is not the most important part.'

'Then what is?' Eadulf frowned. 'Febal? I fail to see how he fits in, apart from killing Brother Sionnach and, perhaps, the ambush sprung on us just now.'

'The book,' Fidelma answered promptly. 'That is central and the reason why I plan to enter the Abbey of Ráth Cuáin tonight. The Venerable Gelasius asked for my help. Brother Sionnach wrote about the secret book that must be returned. He says it is dangerous in the wrong hands. I believe that this matter revolves around that fact.'

'What secret book – and returned to whom?' Aidan asked. 'And why would a book be dangerous in the wrong hands?'

'That is where my visit to Abbot Síoda comes in. He received me in the library and on his desk was a book in Latin. An ancient book, leatherbound, but it was impressed with the seal of Vitalian, the Bishop of Rome and there were Latin words scored into the dark leather.'

She paused tantalisingly, a habit that irritated Eadulf for he had seen her do it so often for dramatic effect in the presentation of her cases in court. Aidan was not so used to it. He simply breathed: 'Go on, go on. What were the words?'

She smiled in satisfaction at his response. '*Non videbunt: habere occultum.*'

Aidan was no Latin scholar, so Eadulf explained: 'It means "None shall see this. Keep it secret".'

'I did not consider it before I saw those words written by Brother Sionnach,' Fidelma admitted. 'Then I remembered how Abbot Síoda tried to cover the book on his desk. Then there was the message from the Venerable Gelasius and then the note made by Sionnach.'

'So you think this is the secret book that Venerable Gelasius and Brother Sionnach believe is dangerous in the wrong hands and should be returned – returned to the Bishop of Rome by this Brother Lucidus?'

'I am sure it is. Whoever Brother Lucidus is, Gelasius had charged him with recovering a book that was stolen from the Lateran Palace, the palace of the Bishop of Rome.'

Aidan whistled softly.

'And because Brother Sionnach was involved in a critique against the theology of Ráth Cuáin, it would seem that this book might provide evidence in support of their philosophy – and hence therein lies the danger,' summed up Eadulf. 'It was evidence in support of . . . of psil . . . psil . . .'

'Psilanthropism, it is called,' finished Fidelma. 'But Gelasius asked me to help Lucidus while Brother Sionnach says that he is not to be trusted. So we are back to the same question: who is Lucidus and why isn't he to be trusted? However, the first thing we must do is to ascertain whether this book is still at Ráth Cuáin. We can deal with the other questions later.'

'Questions that are difficult to answer,' Eadulf said gloomily.

'Questions that might still be answered by diligence,' Fidelma responded.

'So your plan is to simply to enter the abbey after nightfall, find the book and discover who Lucidus is or was – all at the same time?' Aidan was astonished.

'I don't mean to do anything simply. Nothing is simple. But I am sure the book is in their *scriptorium* and possibly on or in the desk of the abbot. The possession of the book will give us a catalyst which should make the worms hereabouts come out of the woodwork.'

'I am not sure of the analogy,' Eadulf said ruefully. 'The worms hereabouts seem to have sharp stings.'

'True enough,' Aidan agreed. 'Earlier the plan was to ride up to the abbey in broad daylight and demand to see Abbot Síoda. Now you appear to think we can gain entrance to the abbey after nightfall – but how? Asking that miserable wretch of a gatekeeper politely is not going to work, is it?'

'Sarcasm doesn't become you, Aidan.' Fidelma felt irritated because she recognised the fault of having an acerbic tongue herself.

Undeterred, Aidan went on: 'I mean, if the abbey is protected by warriors from Connacht, that gives us a problem. And if the gatekeeper won't let us in during daylight hours then we must assume that he definitely won't allow us to enter during the night.'

'My plan is to enter the abbey by myself,' Fidelma told them quietly.

After a moment of stunned silence, Eadulf and Aidan both began to object.

'You two will wait outside while I get inside,' she told them, ignoring their protests. 'One person may accomplish things where two or three may not.'

They continued to argue, but Fidelma was adamant. 'I have the right to enter under law as a *dálaigh*. That should be my protection if anything goes wrong. But I do not intend things to go wrong. I have a plan.'

'Tell us the plan and I'll carry it out!' exclaimed Eadulf immediately. 'If you can enter the abbey, then I can.'

Fidelma shook her head. 'You will not know what you are looking for, nor where. You two were confined to the stables while I was taken to the library, so I know the layout of the buildings and where the library is. I can also identify the book.'

'That still does not tell us how you will gain entrance,' Aidan pointed out. 'That surly gatekeeper will not let you in, and the walls are high enough to defend the place from a military attack.'

'Ah, but I intend to enter by other means.'

'Such as?' Eadulf questioned, refusing to let her get away with being mysterious – another one of her faults.

'Remember the conversation we had with Brother Gébennach, the librarian? We were talking about Sister Fioniúr.'

'The herbalist? That was because of the lavender, the smell of which was so prominent when we examined Spelán,' Eadulf recalled.

'Indeed. In passing, he told us that there was a herb garden at the back of Ráth Cuáin with a gate where traders came and did business with the herbalist. Remember that we rode around the walls of the Ráth and saw it? The herb garden led to the kitchens of the community. I could, from memory, easily gain access to the herb garden.'

'There will be a door into the abbey that is obviously barred and bolted at night,' Eadulf objected. 'So what then?'

'And the walls of the building are just as high there as anywhere else around the Ráth,' Aidan put in.

'Indeed they are, but there are some windows.'

'Windows that are so high that six tall men standing on each other's shoulders would not be able to reach them. Probably higher.'

'The ivy,' she said quietly. 'Have you never climbed ivy when you were a child, Eadulf?'

Looking bemused, he shook his head.

'Brother Tadhg mentioned that he had often told Sister Fioniúr that she should have the ivy removed. Thankfully, she has not. If the door be locked, then my route will be to climb up the ivy to one of the windows above.'

'That is a dangerous climb,' Aidan said.

'Even so, that is my route. You will wait outside until I return, hopefully with the book. Then we will ride back to Cashel, having left a message for Abbot Síoda to the effect that he can come and discuss matters with Brother Mac Raith and his colleagues.'

'Will Abbot Síoda respond?'

'Perhaps not. My intention, however, is to stir up matters so that out of the murkiness the culprits may start to emerge into the open – and the mystery will be cleared away.'

'It seems an extreme course,' Eadulf commented doubtfully.

'It is the only course that we are faced with, so far as I can see.' Fidelma's tone was resolute. Then she glanced around. 'We have waited here long enough. Remember, while we are in the company of Torcán and Éimhin, as pleasant as they seem, we must mislead them for the time being. We shall say that we are passing to the Ford of the Ass to meet someone. We do not mention the abbey. Hopefully, they will offer us the hospitality of a meal while we are waiting for nightfall.'

Éimhín was sitting before a blazing fire outside the log cabin when they rode into the clearing. Startled, she looked up from her task of preparing vegetables. Delicious aromas filled the air as Torcán stood turning a spit on which a joint of mutton was roasting. His features broadened into a grin of welcome as the newcomers dismounted.

'I suppose it was the smell of my roast that drew you here?' he joked in greeting.

Éimhín had risen and was clearly pleased to see them.

'Take no notice of him, lady,' she said to Fidelma. 'You and your companions are always welcome to share what we have.' She went to a pitcher and began to pour cider into wooden mugs without asking.

'We would welcome your hospitality and company for a time for we need to rest a while,' Fidelma replied, taking a seat as did the others. 'We are making our way to the Ford of the Ass.'

'It will be dark soon,' Torcán observed. 'A strange time to be heading for the great river crossing.'

'Unfortunately, it is not a time of our choosing. But I can say no more. It is a duty that I must carry out as a *dálaigh*.'

'Then some advice, lady,' Torcán said. 'Whatever your task is, if it means that you are loitering on the banks of the great river in darkness, have a care.'

'Why so, Torcán?' She asked. 'What is it?'

'The river brings little good these days except violence.'

'Violence?'

'There have been attacks on cargo boats coming along the river. Several attacks have taken place near the very spot you are heading for – around the Ford of the Ass. That is because the boats have to slow down when crossing over the ford and they become vulnerable.'

'How do you know this?'

'Last night, at dusk, one of my sons was riding back from Aona's place at Ara's Well. He was heading along the riverbank when he saw something that made him nervous. There was a boat coming down the great river.'

'What was so strange about this boat?' Fidelma asked.

'There were many men in it. As I said, it was dusk but our lad could see well enough. The men all wore the robes of religious.'

'The religious do often travel in groups, especially down the river there,' Fidelma returned.

'True enough. But although they wore the robes of religious, our son felt they looked and acted more like warriors. He even saw some weapons.'

'I don't suppose your son noticed anything else? Where is he tonight?'

'After spending the Samhain observances with us, this morning he went to stay with his Uncle Curnan. As I told you, he is helping him clear some of the overgrowth on the main road from Cashel to Ara's Well. To be honest, I was hoping he would be here tonight as I have to take a cartload of logs up to the abbey tomorrow and could do with the help.' He gave a disgruntled sound.

'So what do you make of these river attacks, Torcán?' Eadulf asked.

'It is not my place to make anything of it,' the woodsman said cautiously. 'I just thought you should be warned.'

Fidelma smiled tightly. 'Then we shall be warned. You don't think the boat had anything to do with Ráth Cuáin?'

Torcán immediately shook his head. 'Ráth Cuáin is atop a rocky hill. The river swings widely around it. Abbot Síoda's warriors do not hide themselves when they ride out to collect tributes.'

'His warriors?' Eadulf frowned.

'I have told you that it is the right of Abbot Síoda to use his authority as chieftain of the Sítae to maintain a company of warriors,' Torcán reminded them.

'So you did,' agreed Fidelma. 'Brother Gébennach, the librarian, was on his way to Ara's Well yesterday. Do you know if he has returned?'

'My son saw him there earlier today and understood that he was waiting to meet the librarian from the Abbey of Mungairit, or so he told my son. Something about exchanging books. Brother Gébennach had a book to give the Brother from Mungairit and likewise the Brother from Mungairit had a book to exchange with him. So he has not returned to the abbey yet.'

Fidelma ignored Eadulf's sharp intake of breath, saying quickly: 'Well, I doubt whether Ráth Cuáin would have anything to do with mysterious religious on the river. Now, let us have some more of your delicious cider, if you will, and then we shall be delighted to join you in helping in the disappearance of that succulent roast you have prepared.'

The moon had risen in a cloudless sky. The mildness of the night was unusual for the time of year and there was no frost on the ground. In fact, if anything, Fidelma felt that the moon was a little too bright for comfort. However, ideal conditions were never readily available just because one wished for them.

Éimhin and Torcán were already drowsing when the three visitors quietly arose and led their horses from the clearing. In this matter, Fidelma had been grateful to Aidan for ensuring that their hosts had imbibed more than their fair share of the cider, which was homemade and strong, while they themselves had sipped but sparingly. They had walked their horses along the forest track to the bottom of the hill which led up towards Ráth Cuáin. Then they had mounted and trotted up its southern slope until they came to the tall, dark shadows of the abbey buildings.

The moonlight helped them to ascend safely, making use of the cover of boulders and clumps of trees until they reached the point where a tall wooden fence marked the area which they had previously identified as the herb garden. About fifty metres away from it was a cluster of boulders and great thrusts of granite, and a few trees that clung tenaciously to the rocky soil. These made an ideal shelter for their horses. It was here that they left them while making their way to the wooden wall. There was certainly a gate in it but it was strongly secured from within.

Fidelma spent some time examining the walls in the moonlight before she turned to the others and whispered, 'This is where I shall leave you. This is a good enough place to climb over into the herb garden. If I have not rejoined you by first light, then you and Aidan must accept that I have been detained. Ride back to Cashel and inform my brother and Gormán.'

'Wouldn't it be better if one or both of us accompanied you now?'

'And get caught alongside me?' She was stern without raising her voice. 'Think, Eadulf. If I am caught with you and Aidan, who will be there to effect a rescue? Now leave this part to me. I have seen the layout of the buildings and think I can get to where the book will be. So no more arguments. I shall go alone.'

Eadulf was still reluctant. 'I do not like it.'

'Nor I, lady,' whispered Aidan.

'Sometimes we have to do what we do not like,' she countered.

'Very well.' Eadulf admitted defeat as he had always known he would have to. 'Aidan and I will wait in the cover of the rocks. If you are not out by first light then we shall come and find you.'

'No! Don't try anything on your own,' she insisted. 'Ride for Cashel and get help.'

'We hear you,' Eadulf acknowledged.

'First light – not before,' she emphasised.

In the darkness she gave Eadulf a quick embrace and turned for the wooden fence that enclosed the herb garden. Eadulf linked his hands to form a stirrup to propel her over it. Then he and Aidan went to take up their positions in the shelter of the rocks beyond the abbey walls.

Fidelma had always had pride in her agility. At least several times a week she would practise the exercises that went through the ancient defensive techniques – the art of *troidsciathagid* that the missionaries were taught before they were sent to take the Word of the New Faith into foreign lands. It was said that it was used by the ancient adepts before the coming of Christianity and, as such, was frowned upon until it was realised that it was unwise to send people into unknown lands among potential thieves and robbers who might attack and even kill them when they had no defence. Didn't the New Faith exhort people not to kill? What better defence could they have than to adopt the ancient 'defence through battle'; the unarmed combat of their pagan forbears. Several times this knowledge had saved Fidelma from the attentions of would-be antagonists. It gave her a suppleness and strength that usually went with a younger person, along with quick reflexes.

It took her but little time to scale the wooden walls of the abbey's herb garden and she dropped down onto the soft, freshly turned earth of some plant beds. Their fragrances rose into the air and seemed familiar, but were not immediately known to her.

It was lucky that the night was cloudless, so the moon and stars actually provided a shadowy light for, as she looked up at the walls of the abbey, no faint glow of a lamp or candle showed from the black interior. In a way, that was a welcome thing for the conditions she needed. A path led through the garden and she was able to follow it easily to the door that gave access into the abbey buildings. As she had expected, it was locked. Nevertheless, she was smiling confidently to herself.

The abbots of Ráth Cuáin, even in their role as chieftains of the clan area, appeared to possess an imperfect knowledge of defence. The front of the abbey was certainly well protected by high walls, an impregnable gate with a suspicious gatekeeper, along with those high walls which encircled the community. Here, however, at the rear, they had relied on the rocky – almost cliff-like in places – slopes as a barrier. True, the back door was strong, but they had allowed ivy to make its way up the walls. The dark green growth ascended almost ten metres to the roof of the buildings. Fidelma knew how tenaciously it clung and this she was counting on as she approached the faint honeyed scent where some of its leaves had been crushed. It had just ceased its flowering period but little patches of yellow flowers showed light against the foliage. Inconsequentially, the fact that it was claimed by the ancients that ivy was a symbol of fidelity came into her mind, although the berries were slightly poisonous. It led to the thought that this was not so in Eadulf's country: she ought to remind him to treat the ivy with respect because of the differences in the species. She blinked to clear her mind of such random thoughts and peered upwards.

She saw what she was looking for some five or six metres above her. It was a darkened window that appeared to have no glass to obstruct an entrance through it. She reached into her *marsupium*, hanging as usual from her *criss* or belt, and took the *lámann*, the strong leather gloves that she usually wore when riding, and put them on. She knew the ivy had many fibrous, adhesive-covered roots that enabled it to climb so vigorously over the walls, and she would need to protect her hands.

Taking a deep breath, she seized the growth and pulled experimentally. It clung fiercely to the grey stone wall beneath it. Using her full weight, she hung on for a moment. It continued to hold. Slowly she began to climb, hand over hand, up towards the inviting aperture. Surprisingly, it did not take her long. Almost before she felt an ache in her arm muscles, she was beside the open window and scrambling in undignified manner over the sill before tumbling onto the stone-flagged floor of a corridor beyond.

She sat huddled for a few moments to regain her breath and to rub her painful upper arms. The corridor was darker than the exterior, for the pale orb of the moon did not really penetrate into the building. She became aware that there were several doors along this passageway; she presumed they were part of the living quarters. Setting off quietly, she tiptoed along the corridor to the end where a spiral staircase of stone steps descended to the lower floors of the building. She went down carefully, for there was nothing to hold onto, keeping to the broader end of the steps with her back against the wall for balance.

She had actually descended into the kitchen area and there was warmth from the fireplace where the coals had only recently been extinguished for the nighttime. Obviously the cooks here were careful, for she had heard several stories of how even mighty abbeys had been burned to the ground because of carelessness when fires had not been thoroughly doused. Now she saw the outline of the door that had blocked her entrance, forcing her to climb the ivy. It took but a few moments to cross to it and feel how it was fastened. There were two great iron bolts and a lock. An instinct caused her to feel on the wall at the side of the door and she was almost immediately rewarded by finding a key hanging on a hook. She decided to take the chance of inserting the key in the lock and releasing it before putting the key back in place. Then she gently withdrew each bolt.

She stood still for a moment in the gloom. At least if she had to depart by this door in a hurry there would now be nothing to impede her progress.

With a little more confidence, she turned and felt her way through the kitchen and into the next large chamber. Even in the gloom she could see that this was the refectory, with long tables and benches. It seemed to house a substantial community for what she had initially reckoned was only a small abbey. She had passed through the *praintech* or feasting hall and eased through the main door at the end to find herself in the main courtyard of the abbey complex. Here she had to halt and take care, for there were several brand torches flickering around this inner courtyard. She moved quickly back into the shadows as she caught the slap of leather soles on the stone flags.

The dark outline of a tall figure crossed the far end of the court-yard and disappeared.

She looked swiftly around. She would, indeed, have to be watchful, for it seemed that not all the community was asleep. If the memory of her previous visit served, the library building that she was seeking was through an archway to her right, across a smaller courtyard and then she would have to ascend some stone stairs to a second level to access the library. But to get to that archway would be risky; the building on the corner was well lit and it was into this building that the tall figure had entered.

The fact that she had heard the slap of leather on the stone flags caused her to bend and remove her own stout *brogan*, the shoes she usually wore when out in the countryside. Then, walking swiftly and silently, like a cat, she moved along the courtyard, keeping among the shadows of the walls. Reaching the corner building, the one that was lit, she paused, listening carefully.

She could now hear some low conversation – but to her astonishment it was of a kind that she did not associate with a clerical establishment. There was suppressed mirth and several lewd words and expressions that she felt were more in keeping with warriors' encampments than a religious community. She strained forward to see if she could make out something intelligible from the ribaldry but could not. So, with a mental shrug, she moved forward again. She reached the corner without mishap, then something made her pause. It was as well she did so, for a door suddenly opened nearby, and a voice spoke from just a metre or two away.

'Your men were stupid to shoot before they were certain of their target. And if they had done so, what then? To kill a *dálaigh*, an Eóghanacht of Cashel at that, would bring the entire army of the King down on us. That would be disastrous now that I have arranged the transport back to the coast. We should leave here tomorrow or the next day.'

The voice was familiar, but speaking so softly, she could not place it. She was sure she had heard it before – and recently.

'My apologies,' answered another voice and she recognised immediately that it was Febal who was speaking. It was impossible to mistake his clear, well-modulated tones. 'I told them not to shoot at the woman but thought that if they hit the warrior or the foreigner who accompanies her, it would be a good way of warning them off.'

'Warning?' The first speaker was clearly displeased. 'Things have gone beyond giving warnings! In fact, they were entirely out of hand before I arrived. Killing the traitor was one thing, but the silly bizarre manner of the ritual was insane.'

'Well, you know whose idea that was, and it wasn't mine. The aim was to frighten people. Had I been in charge I would have simply killed and buried the fellow. I have no time for the perverse sense of humour your relative displays at times.'

'Instead, that humour as you call it, immediately caused the *dálaigh* to start investigating,' sneered the other. 'And were you instructed to go to Cashel and pretend to be looking for someone who had wronged your sister?'

Febal chuckled. 'Personally, I thought it was a pretty good notion, especially as the story was based on truth – except that I was the rogue who seduced the sister of my chieftain. That's why I had to leave Connacht.'

'I was told you claimed to be looking for a man called Fursaintid. What made you come up with that name?'

'It's something Spelán said before he died. He found out that a man making inquiries about our activities was called the "light kindler" or some such name. Obviously, there was only one matter this "light kindler" could be investigating and it fell to me to protect what we were doing.'

'But "light kindler"?'

'Spelán must have told his woman about this before he died because she identified Sionnach as that person. So I dealt with them both.'

'But "Sionnach" does not have that meaning. Are you sure he was the man?'

'Brancheó identified him as such and it was clear to me that Sionnach was investigating our activities.'

'What I don't understand was why you killed the woman in a similar way to Spelán?'

'It was meant to distract the *dálaigh* from the real cause of Spelán's death. Make her think that it was some ancient cult group of which they had fallen foul. Anyway, there was no other way but to kill her as well. The fool was about to reveal everything.'

'One stupidity leads to another,' replied the other voice in suppressed anger. 'I tell you, this *dálaigh* is clever. The more she is unable to explain things, the more determined she becomes to resolve matters. She is tenacious.'

'Had your relative not decided to try to extract information from Spelán and become a little over-zealous in her efforts, we would not have had to attempt to disguise things with the threefold death rite and—'

'Stupidity! All of it! Now we must be prepared to move everything down to the coast as soon as possible and halt any further attacks because that *dálaigh* will come back soon. I know it. You must leave well alone for a while. This affair has engendered too much interest in this place.'

'The men will not like it. There is no reason; there is still much profit to be made,' grumbled Febal.

'I will tell you whether there is reason or not,' the other said curtly. The door was slammed shut.

Fidelma stepped back into the darkness as she heard the man moving away. If he came by the corner of the building where she stood, there was nowhere in the courtyard to hide now. One man she might be able to deal with, but he would call out, the scuffle would be noisy and there were obviously several warriors inside the building.

But the man did not appear. He had gone in another direction. Her heart sank, for it was surely the same direction in which she had intended to go. She chanced a cautious look around the corner of the building and saw the back of the tall figure going through the arch that she had identified as leading to the small courtyard before the library in which Abbot Síoda had greeted her. It was Febal. She moved silently after him, pausing when she reached the arch.

There was only one brand torch lit and that was on the far side by the steps that led up to the library. She peered round to try to discern where the man had gone. Febal could not possibly have reached the steps and gone into the library before she got to the archway. Then she heard a lewd chuckle almost next to her. It was so close that she flinched before reasoning in a split moment that the column of the arch was between Febal and herself, shielding her in the darkness. Then a woman's answering chuckle came.

'I have been fretting for you,' came her lascivious tone.

'I had to speak with your brother first. He seems displeased at what we have done.'

'He is always worried. Forget him,' she replied.

'I understand he has all the arrangements in hand. Then there will soon be no need for secrecy.'

'I said forget him. There are other things to think of now.'

There came a seductive murmur. 'Indeed – and the whole night is ahead of us . . .'

There came the sounds of an intimate embrace and Fidelma was aware of a distinctive scent wafting through the air before a door was shut quietly.

Fidelma was left leaning against the wall of the arch, trying to still her pounding heart and breathe naturally again. At least she had heard from Febal's own mouth that he admitted killing Spelán, Sionnach and Brancheó. Proving why he had done so was another matter.

Two narrow escapes were two too many, she told herself. However, since all was quiet now, she decided to continue with her task. She moved swiftly across the small courtyard to the flight of stone stairs and, without pausing, she ascended them quickly. Luck continued to be with her, for the door of the library was unlocked. She slid quickly inside.

She stopped for a moment and inhaled the scent of lavender, as she had before when she had entered the library. It was then the thought struck her: it was this same aroma that had predominated when she had examined the corpse of Spelán.

She pushed herself away from the door and squinted around the room. Now that she was here, she had to find the book with the seal of Vitalian, the Bishop of Rome.

In the gloom of the library, however, she was beginning to regret her confidence. But she was convinced that the book marked *Non videbunt: habere occultum* was central to unravelling this mystery: it undoubtedly was the missing book that the Venerable Gelasius had mentioned. After all, it had the Bishop of Rome's seal on it and he would hardly be sending a book that he wished no one to see to an heretical sect. She felt her way to the desk and found a candle in its holder. She would have to try to light it in order to search for the book. And how on earth was she going to locate it among so many in the library? She rebuked herself for not having thought this matter through.

She reached into her *marsupium* in search of her *tenlach-teined*, the flint and tinder, and then changed her mind. It would take an age to ignite the candle and, moreover, the light could be seen and bring people to investigate before she had found the book and escaped. She turned back to the desk, reaching out with her hands to feel among the objects and hoping for the best luck of all. But she knew it was a forlorn hope even before she started. The abbot would not have left such an important item lying around.

It was then she felt the prick of cold metal just below her left ear and a harsh voice said: 'Remain very still, woman, if you want to live.'

The voice held no emotion, and she sensed that if she so much as twitched, the metal would bite deeply into her neck.

Fidelma stood in frozen immobility. The point was still at her throat, which meant that someone else must be gripping her wrists and binding them none too gently behind her with a rough cord. Before she could react in any way, a blindfold was put on her eyes and secured at the back of her head. She made an attempt to speak . . . and then something hard and painful smashed against her skull. She felt a curious unreal moment of consciously knowing that she had received a blow and then . . . then she was falling into a dark space, twisting and turning in a neverending abyss.

Chapter Seventeen

It seemed that only a moment or two had passed when Fidelma became aware of a throbbing in her head and soreness at the back of the skull. She blinked several times but it was black and she realised that she still had the blindfold secured over her eyes. It was cold; the chill cut through her very fibre and she was shivering violently. She attempted to move but her hands were tied fast behind her, the cord cutting into her wrists. Her mouth was not obstructed by a gag of any kind so she tried to coax some saliva around its gritty interior with her tongue. Eventually her voice came out like a crow's croak. She swallowed and made another try at speaking.

'I'd like to sit up.'

There was no reply but a strange scuttling sound.

'I'd like some water,' she said again in a stronger tone, and this time she noticed that her voice had a curious echo to it. There was no response. She listened carefully. The silence felt oppressive and the chill and dampness surely meant she was no longer in the library. Things slowly began to make sense again. She had been knocked out and taken somewhere else. But where?

She also realised that she was lying on her back on cold stone flags. She reached out with her tied hands behind her and almost immediately encountered a wall. Gradually, she eased herself into a semi-sitting position and then pushed back so that she could rest her shoulders and head against the wall.

She wondered how much time had passed since she had been knocked unconscious. Had Eadulf and Aidan realised something had gone wrong? She hoped they were already on their way back to Cashel to raise help. Then her thoughts turned to those who had attacked her in the library. She had no idea who they were – but they must have known who she was; even if they had not known at the time they made the assault, they would have realised soon afterwards – and that was why they had brought her to this place.

Where was she?

The smoothness of the stone flags on which she was sitting made her think that it was not an ordinary cave; she must be in some underground room or cellar – a *tech talman*. The coldness and stone made her decide that it was too large to be a *fotholl*, usually a wood-lined cavity or room for storing food. This was a fair-size souterrain probably used for the same purpose. Ráth Cuáin would certainly have one. Someone had told her once that the fortress or abbey was built on caves. Who was that? Ah, it was something the hermit Erca had said. She shivered suddenly, for she realised that it could also have another purpose: it could be an underground burial chamber. She had encountered such places in abbeys in the past.

She remembered vividly when she had been visiting Abbot Colmán at Tara that a member of the palace guard, Tressach, had declared that he had heard a scream from a sepulchre among the great memorials of the High Kings buried there. It came from the long-sealed tomb of Tigernmas who had forsaken the old gods to worship a bloodthirsty idol dedicated to vengeance and slaughter. The tomb was opened and the body of a man, Fiacc, had been found. He had been sealed in while still alive and it was his last despairing cries that Tressach had heard. It was not a case that she wished to remember; certainly not at this time and in this place.

Fidelma knew that she was wasting time, sitting here and letting her mind dwell on her fears. She must find out where she was and how she could escape. That meant freeing her wrists and getting the blindfold off her eyes. Her wrists were tightly secured behind her and she was certainly no contortionist. Her feet were free, that was true, but she was somewhat reluctant to try to stand up as she did not know how high the ceiling was and had no wish to bang her head again after receiving the painful blow that had knocked her senseless.

She sat forward a little and let her fingertips explore the wall behind her. The blocks of stone seemed smooth enough but they were placed one on top of another – and blocks had edges to them: stone edges. There was only one way to loosen her constraints. She twisted round and, using her fingertips again, sought for an edge that was sharp enough to commence what she had in mind. Raising her bound wrists, she slowly began to rub the cord against the edge of the stone. As she grew in confidence, she began to work more swiftly. Up and down, with her arms and wrists aching. Even so, she realised it was going to take time; a long time before she would be able to sever even one of the cords that bound her.

Eadulf felt a nudge against his shoulder. He had been dozing. He stared guiltily at the figure kneeling by his side.

'I didn't mean to drop off,' he protested before his companion had a chance to remonstrate with him.

'No matter,' Aidan replied quietly. 'It only needed one of us to keep a watch. Nothing has stirred so far. All is quiet.'

'The night feels different,' Eadulf said, shaking himself and peering around. 'It is colder.'

'The Lightbringer has risen,' Aidan said solemnly.

'The what?' Eadulf was startled for the moment, his mind flooding with the references to 'The Lightbringer' that he had discussed with Fidelma.

Aidan pointed into the pale sky. 'The morning star,' he explained.

Eadulf glanced up to see the spangled radiance of Venus, the brightest object in the sky after the sun and moon. Its appearance in the sky heralded the dawn; hence it was referred to as 'The Lightbringer'.

He sat up, wide awake now, realising what it meant. 'It will be fully light shortly,' he said. 'There is no sign of her?'

Aidan shook his head. 'None, friend Eadulf.'

'Then something has happened to her.' He rose to his feet abruptly.

Aidan pulled at his sleeve. 'Have a care. I heard some horses go by a short while ago. Warriors, I fear, for I heard the clink of their shields and weapons. I like it not.'

Eadulf crouched back against the rocks. 'Well, we must do something to get Fidelma out of the abbey. Who knows what has happened to her by this time.'

'She told us to ride to Cashel and bring help.'

'By which time it will definitely be too late to effect a rescue. No – we must do something now.'

'But what? There is just the two of us. It is too light now to attempt to enter the abbey in the way she did. Do we just knock on their gates and say – say what? "The lady Fidelma broke into your abbey in the dead of night and has not been seen since. Something is wrong; may we come in and search the abbey for her?" How would they respond to that?'

Eadulf stopped and stared at his companion.

'That is not a bad idea,' he said firmly.

'What?' Aidan stared at him as if he were mad.

'That is precisely what we will do. We will go to the gates and demand entry. But we will make a slight variation to what we say.' He explained, but Aidan shook his head dubiously.

'I doubt that will work.'

'Perhaps not, but it gives them the benefit of the doubt. It also alerts them to the fact that it is known she is in the abbey. The odds are that she is a prisoner. If they realise that this is known, they may think twice about holding her. They can then release her, declaring some mistake, for they will be aware that it is illegal to make a *dálaigh* captive and that it incurs heavier punishment when the *dálaigh* in question is the King's sister.'

Aidan looked uncertain. 'But if they don't release her, what do we do then? Do we ride for Cashel?'

'I don't want to leave here before I have attempted a rescue.' Eadulf was adamant.

'I can't say I like it.'

'Better to do things by talking than by an all-out assault with people being killed or injured. That is what will happen if we bring Gormán and your comrades to attack the fortress.'

Aidan sighed. 'But that is what she told us to do.'

'Fidelma is not infallible,' Eadulf replied irritably.

Aidan hesitated only a moment and then acceded. 'We'll let the day brighten a little more and then ride round to the main gate and demand to see the abbot. Then we will ascertain whether he holds Fidelma a prisoner in the abbey and is willing to release her.'

A short time later, on horseback and leading Fidelma's riderless mount, they made their way up to the gates of Ráth Cuáin, with its imposing Tau-Rho symbol carved on the oak gates, and pulled vigorously on the bell-rope. The bell emitted its clanging, unmusical peal.

It took some time before the thin, disapproving figure of the gatekeeper appeared, looking down from the parapet above the gate. Aidan nudged his horse back a little to look up to the man.

'What is it?' the gatekeeper cried sharply.

'Do you recognise me, Brother Tadhg?' called Aidan. 'I am Aidan of the Nasc Niadh, the warriors of the Golden Collar, bodyguards to Colgú, King of Cashel.'

'I do not doubt it,' came the unfriendly response. 'What business have you here, warrior?'

'My companion, Brother Eadulf, and I seek entry and a word with your abbot, Abbot Síoda.'

'The Abbey of Ráth Cuáin does not welcome strangers. Depart in peace!'

Aidan frowned angrily. 'We believe that Fidelma, sister of the King, and a *dálaigh* under protection of the law, is currently in the abbey and illegally detained against her will. We *demand* to see Abbot Síoda to discuss the matter.'

'Demand to see the abbot?' the gatekeeper sneered. 'You have no right to demand anything of this abbey, warrior, nor does your foreign companion.'

'Are you denying that Fidelma is in your abbey?'

'Anyone entering the abbey does so of their own free will. They could not enter otherwise.'

'Then they can depart of their own free will,' Aidan pointed out. 'So Fidelma of Cashel is able to depart. Tell her that her companions are here to see that she does so. Where is she?'

The gatekeeper gave a bark of laughter.

'You speak in contradictory terms, warrior. Are you claiming that we have made her a prisoner here? If she has entered this abbey, she could only have done so of her own volition for it is not our custom to abduct people. Neither do we freely admit people and then stop their leaving. Only if a person forces entry against the law would that person have to answer according to the law. Have I made myself clear enough? Now begone!'

Brother Tadhg turned and vanished behind the wall.

'I warned you that it would not work, friend Eadulf,' Aidan said with a worried look. 'What can we do?'

Eadulf gestured for them to ride a little distance from the gates of the abbey so that he was sure they were out of earshot.

'You realise that was double-talk,' he declared. 'Fidelma is definitely a prisoner and I am sure that the gatekeeper knows that fact full well. So now we know she is held there, we must attempt a rescue.'

'So now do we ride back to Cashel?'

'I am loath to leave here.'

'Then I should ride back to Cashel and return with a company of warriors to force entry, if you prefer to remain.'

'We'll decide in a moment. Before that, let's ride down to the copse where Spelán's cabin is. If we are watched from Ráth Cuáin they might think they have got rid of us. We can discuss matters there out of sight of prying eyes.'

They had hardly reached the shelter of the copse with its burnt-out ruins that had once been the shepherd's cabin when Aidan called a warning.

'A rider on horseback is approaching up the hill . . . no, not on horseback but on an ass.'

A moment or two passed before the rider drew closer.

'Why, it is Brother Gébennach, the librarian,' Eadulf said, recognising the man. 'Do you remember that he was on his way to Ara's Well on the great river to exchange a book with another religious brother from the Abbey of Mungarit? He must be on his way back to the abbey now. We might be in luck.'

'In luck?' Aidan was puzzled.

'We might be able to persuade him to help us get into the abbey. We could argue that the alternative to refusing would be to face the wrath of the King – and not only the King but the entire legal system. Fidelma is a *dálaigh* whose influence and reputation is felt even in Tara.'

Aidan's lips twisted cynically. 'That didn't have much influence on the gatekeeper, Brother Tadhg.'

'If that is not of influence on Brother Gébennach, I shall rely on you to show him that he has little choice in the matter.'

'I still believe that I should ride to Cashel, as Fidelma wished.'

'It might be the very thing that they – I mean those who tried to ambush us yesterday – are expecting us to do,' Eadulf pointed out. 'Fidelma would take that into account and do the unexpected, even though she originally told us to do this. I am fearful that any delay increases her chances of coming to harm.'

'They shall face the justice of the King if that has happened,' replied Aidan grimly.

'Better to pre-empt it in the first place.'

They both looked down at the approaching figure on the back of the ass.

'I suppose we had better put ourselves in a position to ensure that he makes no attempt to escape,' Aidan said. 'Let's conceal ourselves behind the ruined cabin so that we can surprise him. I'll go to stop his forward path and you go around the rear.'

Eadulf gave way to the warrior's authority in such matters. They eased back behind the cover of the burnt-out cabin. Aidan signalled for Eadulf to dismount and, following his example, secured the horses behind the cabin. Thus hidden, they listened to the sounds of the ass; its heavy breathing was discernible as it plodded its way up the hillside, bearing Brother Gébennach.

It seemed to Fidelma that several *cadar* of the day had passed since she had commenced rubbing her bonds against the sharp edge of the stonework. She felt tired and her arms, stretched out and bound behind her, were painful and aching. Yet she refused to give in. She would *not* give in! She only wished there was some light in this strange, dark vault. She had no means of measuring time and no idea how long it had been since she had been knocked unconscious and brought to this place. That thought immediately set her off wondering what Eadulf and Aidan would be doing now. Had they made it safely to Cashel and alerted her brother and Gormán?

It was while she was reflecting on this that she suddenly felt one of the cords give slightly. With renewed vigour she increased the motion of rubbing against the stone and then, within a moment, she felt the strands of a cord loosen and snap. She set to work with a will now, and it was not long before she felt the other strands begin to give. Soon she could wriggle one of her wrists free and then she could draw her arms and wrists in front of her, still with some of the cord dangling from one wrist.

Her first thought was to relax her aching limbs, feeling the blood flowing through them after being confined in an awkward position. It was almost as painful for the first few minutes as the constriction had been. Then she raised her hands and tore off the blindfold, blinking to adjust her sight. Her fears were immediately confirmed. She was confined in some underground chamber, the dimensions of which she had no way of knowing, for it was almost pitch-black. She needed to explore, but before she could do that, she began to massage the aching muscles of her upper arms and then her shoulders. She could feel the soreness of her wrists and wished there was some water nearby in which she could bathe them. However, her next concern was to remove the remains of the cords from her numb wrists. Using her nimble fingers, she was able to accomplish this with the minimum of effort.

By the time she had restored movement and confidence in her physical shape her eyes had grown used to her surroundings. Instead of being in total blackness now the chamber had become outlined in dark greys. While there was no window in the room, there was a small aperture in what must be the door. A grey glimmer did filter through this hole. It was then that Fidelma realised that her captors had removed her *marsupium*, which contained a few items that might have helped her in her plight.

Moving carefully, raising a hand above her head in case the ceiling was low, she moved towards this source of light. Had she been holding out any hopes of exit, she would have been disappointed for the door was obviously barred from the outside and it was made of thick wood. She could tell that by feeling the width of the door. Unfortunately the aperture was also just above her head level, so she had no way of peering through to see outside the room.

Judging from the light, it was also underground, perhaps a corridor. She guessed that she was in the cave complex under the abbey of which Erca had spoken. But this was of no help to her at the moment. She might have escaped her bonds but she had not escaped her confinement.

She turned with her back to the door so that the light filtered in from behind her. Now she could vaguely see that she was in a place that was more of a natural cave than a *talman*. The cave had been blocked off by stone flags and the door. The roof was uneven but there was still a good clearance for her to move so she need not have troubled herself about her head hitting it. She tried to estimate its dimensions. It was not very big; two men of average height could lie prone across the width and the same number for the depth. The place was cold but the dampness lay in the natural stones in which the cave had been formed.

The place was entirely empty. There was no bench to sit upon nor bunk to lie down on. She made a circuit of the walls to make sure that her eyes were not missing anything in the grey light. But having done so, she realised that her first assessment was the correct one. There was no way she could get through the door, no other means of exit. She could not be released until someone came to the door to draw back the bolts or turn the lock. She gave a deep sigh. What was it that old Brehon Morann, her tutor, would say? 'When there is nothing to be done, do nothing.'

She moved back to the wall and sank down onto the stone slabs again; sitting in the most comfortable position she could manage, she folded her hands before her and closed her eyes. The old art of meditation had long been handed down by the ancients, and the language had many words to describe the practice. She was grateful that she was well acquainted with the art of *imradud*: the art of clearing the mind and relaxing in a deep, meditative state. There was nothing else to do but wait.

*　　*　　*

'Now!' signalled Aidan, suddenly launching himself around one end of the ruined cabin, while Eadulf hastened in the other direction.

'Greetings, Brother Gébennach!' Aidan called as he sprang onto the path in front of the beast, causing its rider to start nervously. Eadulf had moved quickly to get behind the rider and once again he saw the man's tell-tale gesture of his hand as if to go for a sword which was not there.

The young librarian of Ráth Cuáin glanced behind him as if he knew by some uncanny distinct that Eadulf was there.

'What are you still doing here?' he asked in surprise. It was at this very spot that he had left them to continue his journey yesterday to Ara's Well.

Aidan smiled thinly. 'Rather than being still here, we have been away and returned. Many things have happened since we last saw you.'

'So where is Fidelma of Cashel?' asked Brother Gébennach. 'Is she also hiding behind those boulders?'

'She is not,' replied Aidan. 'We have reason to believe that the sister to the King has been made a prisoner in Ráth Cuáin.'

Brother Gébennach was clearly startled. 'A prisoner? Why? How?'

Aidan moved forward to catch the reins of Brother Gébennach's ass. 'We ask you to alight, keeper of books, and bide with us awhile so that we can explain and tell you how you may help us.'

The young man looked uncertain for a moment and then shrugged. He swung from the ass and secured the animal to a nearby bush. Then the three men took seats provided by some of the nearby fallen trees.

Aidan left it to Eadulf to explain as much or as little as he felt the librarian should know. In fact, Eadulf was well aware of the limits of what he should tell the man, for here was the librarian of the abbey – and it was because of a book that Fidelma had entered the abbey, in order to find and remove it. He was not sure exactly why Fidelma had made the connection between this and the killing of Spelán or Branchéo but he knew that it would be best to avoid the subject in case the librarian was involved.

'Last night, Fidelma entered the abbey,' he began.

Brother Gébennach raised a quizzical eyebrow. 'The abbot agreed to speak with her again, did he?'

'Not exactly. Fidelma was convinced that the murder of Spelán, the shepherd, was connected with the abbey.'

The librarian frowned. 'I thought she had spoken to Abbot Síoda about that and he had dismissed the matter?'

'But not to her satisfaction. A woman called Branchéo was murdered also. Then a man from Connacht came to Cashel, saying he was looking for a fellow called Fursaintid, who was thought to be at the abbey. He disappeared from Cashel and a Brother Sionnach was found murdered there . . .'

Brother Gébennach's expression was one of genuine shock. 'Febal was at Cashel?' he said.

'You know him?'

Brother Gébennach was still staring at him. 'And you say Sionnach is dead?'

'You know Sionnach too?' pressed Eadulf.

There was no disguising the look of horror on the librarian's face.

'Sionnach dead, you say,' he repeated softly.

'We think Febal has fled to Ráth Cuáin. What do you know of him?'

For a few moments Brother Gébennach remained mute, his eyes focusing on some unseen, distant object.

'Brother Sionnach of Corcach was a good friend of mine,' he said eventually, his voice flat. 'He was a great scholar. Febal is a mercenary warrior who is paid by Abbot Síoda.'

'Are you saying that Febal is not a poet from Connacht?' Eadulf pressed.

'He is a warrior hired by Abbot Síoda,' the young librarian repeated. 'He might come from Connacht but he hires his sword to whoever will best pay him.'

'Will you help us?' Eadulf took advantage of the situation presented by Brother Gébennach's shock.

'It depends what you want to do.' The librarian seemed uncertain.

'We want to get into the abbey unobserved so that we can rescue Fidelma.'

'What exactly are you and Fidelma investigating in the abbey?'

Eadulf decided to give him the barest of explanations.

'We believe that the same person who killed Spelán the shepherd also killed Brancheó and your friend Brother Sionnach. Fidelma entered the abbey last night because she thought she could find a clue to unlock the killer's identity. Now she has not emerged and the gatekeeper refuses us entry.'

Brother Gébennach thought for a while. Then he said: 'There is a complex of caves under the abbey.'

Eadulf suddenly recalled what the hermit, Erca, had said.

'Do those caves lead into the abbey itself?' he asked.

'Abbot Síoda showed me the way into the caves from the main courtyards of the abbey when he asked me to accompany him to fetch some materials that were stored there. Several of the caves are used for extra storage space for food, wine and other items.'

'But is there a way into them from outside the abbey?'

'There is. I discovered it when I took a wrong passage, saw light ahead and found that it was an exit onto the hillside behind the abbey. Brother Tadhg found me as I was coming out into the fresh air. He was furious at my mistake, as if he didn't want me to know there was another exit or entrance. Anyway, he raged that I could have wandered the caves, been lost and no one would have ever found me. I found that curious as I was perfectly all right; his concern was unreasonable. Anyway, the cave system didn't appear to me to be that large or complicated. I think I remember where it would lead out to.'

'So will you take us there – take us to this place on the hillside where you think this entrance to the caves would be?' Aidan asked.

The young librarian looked questioningly at Eadulf. 'There is one thing I want to understand. I had heard that Fidelma was Sister Fidelma and yet she does not seem connected with any religious house. Why is this?'

Eadulf was surprised by this sudden change of topic.

'Why do you ask?'

'Because I need to know why I am helping you.'

'The facts are widely known. Fidelma left the religious some time ago. She is now legal adviser to her brother, King Colgú, and no longer a religieuse.'

'Ah, they did not know that in Rome,' Brother Gébennach reflected, almost speaking to himself.

'It is some time since we were both in Rome,' Eadulf told him. 'She would hardly be known there.'

'Why did she leave the religious?' the young librarian queried again, almost brusquely this time.

Eadulf shrugged. 'Quite simply, she was not destined to be a religieuse. When she qualified in law, her brother was not even the heir apparent at Cashel, even though her father had been King. I know little of the intricacies of your ways of royal succession. However, the cousin of Fidelma and Colgú was King at the time and not well disposed to them. Fidelma was in need of security. The Abbot of Darú, some distant relative, advised her to join the religious and, as it happened, the Abbess of Cill Dara needed a legal adviser, so Fidelma joined the abbey for a while. Then she left. It is as simple as that.'

'I see,' the librarian said thoughtfully. 'She does not hold any strong views about the Faith?'

'Strong views?'

'She did not follow any particular philosophy or sect that would make her oppose any which disagreed with her?'

Eadulf was puzzled for a moment and then he shrugged. 'Oh, you mean the conflict between the church practices of the Five Kingdoms as opposed to Rome? She disagreed with the ideas that Rome was putting forward at the counsels at Streonshalh and at Autun. But you must know, most of the churches of the Five Kingdoms and even beyond in Britain and in Gaul, do not fully accept dictates of the councils of Rome even while accepting the main tenets of the New Faith.'

Aidan made an impatient sound. He had been silent during most of the exchange. 'We are losing time,' he said. 'Let us not waste it, debating religion.'

Brother Gébennach nodded. 'I apologise. I was just interested in whether the lady Fidelma had any special opinions about the Faith and why she left it. Please forgive me. It is the librarian in me who reads omnivorously about religious matters.'

'We are purely interested in gaining access to the abbey,' Aidan replied shortly, 'because we believe that Fidelma is being held there against her will and her life may be in danger.'

'What makes you think this?' replied Brother Gébennach. 'You said that she entered the abbey last night. How? Who let her in?'

'No one let her in. She . . . she gained entry through the herb garden and climbed in by a window.' Eadulf felt it time to admit some of the truth.

Brother Gébennach put his lips together in a soundless whistle. 'And this was during the night?'

'Yes. We waited for her and by dawn she had not returned or communicated with us. So, we decided to confront the gatekeeper by riding up to the main gate and demanding to see her.'

'What happened?'

'Brother Tadhg came to the wall, not to the gate. He gave us a lot of nonsense but basically denied that she was being held a prisoner, saying that those who entered of their own free will could leave of their own free will. That makes me think that she was caught and made prisoner. Her life hangs in the balance.' Eadulf swallowed hard.

'So that is why you want me to guide you through the cave system and into the abbey?'

'If you are certain that is an alternative way into the abbey.'

The young librarian hesitated. 'Do you believe that Febal killed Brother Sionnach?'

'Exactly so,' Eadulf agreed.

'In that case, I will take you to where the entrance is. However, it is best we leave the animals here and climb to that point. On foot we have less chance of being spotted by Febal's warriors.'

Eadulf looked to Aidan for advice and the warrior agreed. They left the cabin, having ensured the horses and ass were near water and something edible to keep them going. They were about to leave the sheltering copse when Aidan motioned them back. Not far across the slopes of the hill where a gentler incline carried a track, they saw a wagon piled high with logs being pulled by a couple of sturdy mules. The figure of the man who sat guiding them was familiar. Aidan identified him first. It was Torcán the woodsman.

'He seems to be taking wood to the abbey,' muttered the young warrior.

'He mentioned something about having to take logs to the abbey this morning,' Eadulf remembered. 'Best let him pass. We'll stick to our plan not to involve him.'

'He will continue on that track to the main gate,' Brother Gébennach said. 'We ourselves will swing round to the back of the abbey – but from lower down the hill. That is where the cave entrance is.'

The grey stone buildings of Ráth Cuáin rose menacingly from the hilltop as they ventured around the lower slopes. They reached a spot where the ground began to rise upwards with a steeper elevation. The southern slopes of the Hill of Bullock were more precipitous than on its northern side. The land was mostly rocky and bare. However, in one or two places there were stony breaks in the ground that formed small, cliff-like falls.

Eadulf could see why the local chieftains had built their fortress on such a hilltop. It would not be so easy to attack from this direction and could be well defended on the less precipitous slopes.

'Let us hope no one sees our approach, for now we are in open countryside with only the boulders and dips in the hill to cover us,' Eadulf fretted.

'I don't recall that Febal and his mercenaries bother to watch this side of the hill. It is too difficult to approach,' answered Brother Gébennach cheerfully. He peered around and then pointed. 'You see that clump of trees there?'

A little way ahead, an isolated group of grey willows that were more shrubs than trees provided one of the few areas of cover on the hillside.

'I believe the entrance to the caves is not far above those trees as I think I recall seeing them when I was looking out of the cave mouth.'

'Hopefully, not far above,' muttered Aidan. 'If we need to get to our horses in a hurry, it is now a long way to the burnt-out cabin.'

Brother Gébennach showed slight irritation for the first time. 'If you had brought them any closer, warrior, the horses would be seen.'

They paused among the boulders and the curious copse of willow trees to examine the terrain. Brother Gébennach suddenly let out an exclamation and pointed up the stony hillside to a flat patch in front of what appeared to be a natural wall of grey limestone rock. Fronds of ivy and other similar growth obscured most of this wall. It took the men but a short while to ascend onto this natural shelf. Brother Gébennach walked to the ivy-clad wall, turned his back to it and stared out over the hillside. Then he smiled broadly.

'That is the view I saw, that I told you about. So the entrance of the cave must be . . .' He turned and pulled at the growth which hung like a curtain over a small natural opening.

Brother Gébennach chuckled. 'Behold, my friends, your entrance into the caverns beneath the abbey.'

Eadulf stood back and gazed upwards. 'We are still quite a way below the foot of the abbey walls,' he reflected. 'That must mean the caves or vaults are considerably deep underground.'

'You have a good eye, my friend,' agreed the young librarian. 'It is true. I recall now that we descended many rock-hewn steps. But the tunnel you are about to enter here rises on an incline and there are several side caves leading off it. Then there is also a series of steps cut into the rock that take you further up until you reach the main caves which are used as the abbey storage rooms.'

'Presumably the passages will be in darkness,' said Aidan, thinking of the practicalities of the situation.

'If I remember rightly, they keep brand torches not far inside the entrance,' Brother Gébennach said. 'We can use those. Wait here, I'll fetch them.'

With that he disappeared behind the plant growths obscuring the entrance. Eadulf immediately cast a worried glance at Aidan.

'All of a sudden, this is getting too easy,' he whispered. 'The news of Brother Sionnach's death seemed to shock Gébennach. He clearly knew him – and not just by reputation. Be on your guard. I no longer trust our helpful librarian entirely.'

Aidan snorted. 'I never did.'

Just then, Brother Gébennach reappeared. In his hand he held an oil lamp.

'This is even better than a brand torch, for they would probably have been damp and hard to light,' he said, holding it out. 'However, I trust you can supply the *teine creasa*, warrior?'

Every warrior carried a flint, steel and tinder as the means of lighting a fire. Some warriors were proud of the quickness with which they could produce what was also known as *tene lám* or handfire. Aidan immediately took the materials from a leather pouch on his belt and set to work. The lamp was soon alight.

'Excellent,' the librarian said, turning to the tunnel entrance. 'I saw a second lamp with this one, so we can light that as well.'

True enough, a short distance in was a rock shelf on which there was certainly another lamp and the remains of stubs of candles, some burnt out. Brother Gébennach lit the second lamp and handed it to Eadulf.

'I'll lead the way,' the librarian announced.

The tunnel quickly ascended, twisting a little this way and that. Eadulf noticed there were several small areas, no bigger than alcoves, that led off from the tunnel and he glanced into each in passing. But there was little of interest in them, just empty spaces. It was only when the incline became less noticeable that Eadulf saw smaller passages leading off the main one.

'Have these ever been used?' he called.

The librarian turned back with a frown. 'I don't know. We are only a short distance from the main cave in which the storage areas are situated, along with the steps leading into the abbey kitchens.'

Eadulf had raised his lantern high. On a jagged rock a little way inside the entrance of one of the small passages, a torn piece of sacking was hanging as if it had been ripped off as someone passed by and had not noticed its loss.

'Something tells me that I should take a look,' he declared, turning into the tunnel. Aidan followed behind.

This smaller tunnel had a few natural cavities. While the main tunnel that they had been following had been hewn and expanded for many generations so that it was no longer a natural cave entrance, this was definitely formed by nature. Here, the area was cold, damp and neglected. There were even curious pointed rocky growths hanging from the roof and some even ascending from the floor, and Eadulf was aware of the constant sound of dripping from hidden water deposits. Within a short distance the roof began to lower and now and then he had to duck to avoid banging his head. He was about to turn back when a dark aperture caught his eye. He moved forward, lamp before him, then he let out a sharp breath. The niche contained a number of sacks, piled one upon another.

Aware that Aidan, who had been following dutifully, was standing behind him, Eadulf turned and handed him the lamp.

'Hold this and let me have your knife.'

The warrior obeyed without a word. Eadulf leaned forward and cut at one sack. Then he put his hand in and took out a hard metal lump. It shone silver in the flickering light of the lamp.

Aidan gave a soft whistle. 'I think we have found Prince Gilcach's stolen silver.'

CHAPTER EIGHTEEN

Aidan lifted the flickering lamp as high as he could in the confined space. 'Look at these sacks,' he breathed. 'There must be nearly a dozen – and all filled with silver ore. Most of it seems smelted already.'

Eadulf did not want to confess that he was more amazed than Aidan at the find. Then he gave way to a little smugness. His instincts had been right: the mystery *was* all connected with the attacks on Prince Gilcach's boats taking silver from his mines to the sea port of Port Lairge. Here was the proof. It was not the mysterious book that Fidelma had thought lay at the centre of things. Spelán had simply been involved in the theft of the silver, and the caves of the abbey were being used to store it.

'There is more than a fortune here,' he whispered.

'I had heard from Gormán that Brehon Fíthel had gone north to start an investigation into the thefts – and all the time the silver was stored here,' declared Aidan, sharing Eadulf's satisfaction.

'You have done well, Brother Gébennach, in bringing us here,' Eadulf began, turning to address him.

Brother Gébennach was not behind him.

'I can't remember him following us in this cave,' Aidan admitted, looking round in consternation. 'Sorry, I was too busy following you.'

'He's probably waiting for us in the main tunnel,' Eadulf said. 'I'll take a piece of this silver as proof and we'll rejoin him.' He took a small pebble of the metal and held it to the flame of the lamp. 'It looks similar to the piece you found in Spelán's cabin. He was obviously involved.'

Back in the main tunnel, there was no sign of the librarian nor any glow from his lamp to indicate he was waiting for them.

Aidan swore softly. 'I thought he was right behind us. I fear he has gone to warn them. I think we have been betrayed. We should have kept a better watch on him.'

'It's too late now to speak of blame. I am going to move on and see if I can find Fidelma. You don't have to come.'

'Come I will,' Aidan asserted. 'Our first task is to rescue Fidelma, not to report this stolen silver. She is the one who is most in danger.'

'Then let us move before Brother Gébennach alerts his comrades,' Eadulf instructed, turning and leading the way along the passage that they had been following originally.

It was only a short distance before the passage opened out into a central cave that was already lit with brand torches. There were many signs of continual use. Boxes and barrels were stored here and there.

'Look!' whispered Aidan, pointing across the cave. 'Some of the side caves have been blocked off as separate units and wooden doors have been made. There are three doors over there. This must be the main storage cave.'

In one corner there were artificially cut steps, leading upwards. Presumably these would bring them into the courtyard of the abbey itself.

'We'd best check those smaller sealed caves first before we go up into the abbey. If Fidelma is a prisoner, she could well be kept there,' advised Aidan.

With a nod, Eadulf moved quickly across the cave and checked the first of the three doors – stout wooden affairs with iron handles and bolts. He tried each in turn but, peering inside with the use of his torch, he saw they were mainly storerooms for food, and one was clearly used for keeping strong liquor. None of the three caves revealed anything more. He then noticed another small side tunnel. It was barely visible, but a greying light at the end of it revealed it was a means to an exit. He drew Aidan's attention to it.

The young warrior looked, then whispered: 'I think it is another exit onto the hillside, but the entrance seems to be completely overgrown. Doubtless it is covered by the all-pervasive ivy on this side of the abbey walls.'

'Well, at least we know that we have a choice of two exits,' Eadulf murmured cheerfully. 'That could come in useful when Gébennach returns with his friends.'

'In that case, we'd better check it out to make sure we can escape in that direction,' Aidan said.

'We are losing time,' Eadulf objected. 'It's curious, though – I would have expected a hue and cry to have erupted before now.'

'It will take but a moment.' Aidan set off down the narrow corridor. He had not gone far when Eadulf saw him halt. 'There are a couple of doors here, blocked-off side caves, and . . .'

Suddenly there was a muffled cry.

'Lady!' Aidan cried, bending forward to a door. Then Eadulf was racing down the passage to join him.

'Fidelma, is it you?'

'More a ghost of me. I am cold and hungry!' she called. 'Can you see the cave I am imprisoned in?'

'We are outside the door,' Aidan assured her. He was examining it with the light of Eadulf's brand torch held high behind him. 'I think we are in luck. I can see only two bolts.'

He bent to draw them back. They slid free easily and, using the metal ring handle, he swung back the door. A dishevelled Fidelma staggered out into Eadulf's arms. After a moment or two she pushed away.

'What took you so long?' she demanded, although there was humour in her tone.

Eadulf said ruefully, 'That is an even longer story.'

'Have you brought Gormán and the others from Cashel?' was her next question.

Eadulf looked guilty and shook his head. 'I thought the more imperative task was to rescue you.'

'We'd best be on our way to somewhere safer to discuss it,' Aidan cautioned them, glancing nervously over his shoulder. 'Our luck can't last for ever.'

'I think it has already run its course,' Eadulf muttered.

They followed his gaze. There were flickering lights at the far end of the tunnel. Eadulf had the wit to extinguish his lantern but a shout indicated that the light had already been seen.

'Quick!' Aidan urged. 'We'll try this exit. It's the only way out now.' He rushed forward, drawing his sword in order to cut a path through the thick curtain of creepers. He had managed to push the canopy of growth aside when he teetered and seemed to be trying to regain his balance, almost dropping his sword in the process. He managed to pull himself backwards with difficulty.

As they joined him they saw that the entrance beyond the growth emerged onto a rocky part of the hillside which, in effect, was a cliff face with a sheer drop of at least fifteen metres. There was no other way down.

'I might be able to make it,' Aidan observed, glancing quickly to the sides of the opening. 'If I can get over to those creepers at the left side there, I should be able to climb down. It needs just a good swing.'

'We couldn't all make it in time,' Fidelma said.

The light behind them had come closer and there was a deep rasping laugh.

'Well, well. Were you leaving us so soon, lady?'

They turned to find themselves facing three men, two of them armed with crossbows, the bolts aimed so that they could not miss. The third man, who held high a lantern, was unmistakable – it was Brother Giolla Rua of Corcach Mór.

'Well,' Fidelma smiled thinly, 'I wondered what your real connection with this place was.' Then she suddenly snapped: 'Aidan!'

The young warrior knew immediately what she wanted him to do. Before anyone could react he was through the curtain of fronds and the cave entrance. With a shout, one of the bowmen, instead of releasing his bolt, rushed forward but Eadulf, dropping the lantern from his hand, blocked his passage, struggling with the man who was forced to release his grip on the bow.

'Lady,' Brother Giolla Rua yelled, 'tell your Saxon friend to stop, otherwise you will be dead.'

In the light of Brother Giolla Rua's lantern, the second bowman had raised his weapon and was aiming at Fidelma. Eadulf immediately released his hold and stood aside. As the man he had been struggling with pushed forward to see where Aidan had gone, Eadulf's foot came out and the man went flying through the curtain of fronds. They heard his cry of fear and the sickening sound of his body falling the fifteen metres to the rocks below. Eadulf stood back, turning a bland expression to Brother Giolla Rua.

'Your man seems to have tripped,' he said, without any emotion.

The second bowman had swung his weapon round to Eadulf and was about to release the bolt when Brother Giolla Rua told him to hold.

'Just cover them both. You will both now be moved back along the tunnel. The first one who does not obey will be dead. Of that, I can assure you.'

Threatened by the bowman who, with Brother Giolla Rua, backed slowly along the tunnel before them, they soon came abreast of the cave they had just quit, the one Fidelma had been in.

'Now, get inside . . . both of you!' ordered Brother Giolla Rua.

Reluctantly, Fidelma marched into her former prison followed by Eadulf, still covered by the unwavering crossbow.

Brother Giolla Rua smiled grimly in the flickering light. 'At least this time you will have a companion, lady – until I have completed my transactions.'

'Your transactions?' Fidelma tried to make the question sound innocent.

'As if you did not know, lady.'

'I suppose Brother Gébennach alerted you?' Eadulf's tone was bitter.

For a split second a look of puzzlement crossed the features of Brother Giolla Rua. 'You mean the librarian of this place?' he said in surprise. When Eadulf did not bother to answer, Brother Giolla Rua simply shrugged. Then the door was slammed shut. Darkness descended as the lantern was taken away and they heard the sounds of Brother Giolla Rua and his companion moving back down the corridor.

'What now?' Eadulf demanded, hoping that his eyes would soon grow used to the half light to be able to see a little better.

'Now?' Fidelma's response was resigned. 'Let us hope that Aidan was successful in his attempt to grab those creepers and scale down the rockface. Thanks to your fancy footwork, he seems to have managed to get to the creeper without harm or we should have heard it.'

'Unlike Brother Giolla Rua's companion.' Eadulf added dryly. He had only meant to impede the murderous bowman, not kill him. He had no illusion that to fall head first down that height was certain death. '*Requiescat in pace*,' he murmured unctuously.

'If Aidan makes it safely, I trust he will go straight to Cashel as I originally wanted you to do and bring back Gormán and his warriors. A *catha* of the warriors of the Golden Collar would soon overcome this place.'

There was no rancour in her voice but Eadulf felt guilty that he had not followed her instructions; this detracted from his satisfaction that he had resolved the mystery of the abbey's connection with the attacks on Prince Gilcach's silver cargoes.

'It is going to be difficult,' he replied glumly. 'We left the horses at Spelán's cabin. It was Gébennach, the librarian, who brought us into the cave complex and betrayed us. He will have probably ensured that the horses are no longer there. It is a long way to Cashel if you are walking these hills without a horse.'

'Gébennach brought you into the cave complex? Well, since we have nothing else to do, I suggest that you tell me all about it and how he betrayed you. Anyway, Aidan is good in difficult situations. He will manage one way or the other.' Fidelma hoped her voice did not carry the lack of confidence she felt.

Aidan was not on his way to Cashel. He was lying at the foot of the rocky plunge, unconscious.

When Fidelma had shouted to him, he had known instinctively what she wanted him to do for there was no other choice. He pushed through the curtain of fronds and creepers and, glancing to his left, he examined the hanging ivy in a split second to search for a suitable spot before launching himself across the short space. He had no option but to let his sword fall, as he stretched out both hands to grab for the vines. He caught and clasped them. They gave immediately under his weight but after dropping him a metre or so, they held. He clung on, praying they would take his weight.

It was in that same moment he heard a scream and saw a body tumbling by him. For a cold moment of panic he thought it was either Fidelma or Eadulf but then he saw it was a man, an abandoned crossbow falling with him. As he heard the sickening thud of the body on the rocks below, he realised it must have been one of the bowmen who had rushed to follow him, and somehow missed his footing and fallen. But there was no time to dwell on this. Gritting his teeth, he sought to lower himself down the small cliff as quickly as possible, for the ivy was not as strongly attached to the cliff face as he would have preferred. Every so often it gave and he dropped short distances, scrambling for a new hold.

It was only in the last three metres that he lost the battle. The ivy snapped and came away from its precarious hold, sending Aidan plummeting backwards. He waved his arms wildly, hoping to land in a less awkward position. But a moment later he experienced a terrible pain in his right leg; the scream he heard was his but it was silent. He had no time to utter it aloud for at that moment he sank into merciful unconsciousness.

Torcán the woodsman had left the Abbey of Ráth Cuáin, having deposited his weekly load of logs, and swung his mule cart through the great gates, around the northern slope of the Hill of the Bullock and across to the south-west towards the sloping path that led into the forest and home. Brother Tadhg, the gatekeeper, had been as abrasive as ever but the price for the exchange of logs had been fixed by the abbot, so there could be no argument on that score. As Torcán guided his ass team along the track, he wondered if the folk from Cashel had been successful in their curious rendezvous at the Ford of the Ass, the previous night. He rather liked the lady Fidelma and her companions. She was not what he expected a princess of Cashel would be, far less a *dálaigh*. She was not haughty at all, but able to sit down with a woodsman and his wife and exchange gossip without the arrogance that he had usually associated with such folk. He even found himself liking the quiet, thoughtful Saxon . . . why did the man keep correcting him, to say 'Angle'? He had known some Saxon travellers passing along the great river and they certainly spoke the same language.

He had not gone far down the track when he suddenly saw a horse standing in the middle of the way, chewing at a bush growing along the side. Drawing rein on the mules, he halted his cart and stared at the beast for a while before recognising it as the grey-white pony that the lady Fidelma had been riding. He dismounted from his wagon and saw the reins were loose but with a small piece of broken branch and some leaves caught up in them. To a woodsman of Torcán's experience, he saw that the reins had been tied to a bush or branch to secure the animal. Some motion of the horse must have snapped this makeshift tether and the animal had wandered freely. It was then he realised that he was near the copse where the ruined cottage of Spelán stood. Could it be that the lady Fidelma had gone back to the cabin and lost her horse? It would not take him long to check.

Torcán walked up to the pony, took the reins and led him to the back of his wagon, where he fastened him to it before climbing back onto the seat and urging his team forward, manoeuvring the wagon away from the main path and down towards the copse. Once there, he immediately saw two other horses and an ass. These were securely tethered. He called several times and examined the nooks and crannies of the ruins. There was no sign of anyone.

He stood for a few moments wondering what he should do. Should he take all the horses and ass back to his cabin or should he leave them here in case Fidelma and her companions returned? It was a difficult choice. It was while he was contemplating this that a sound impinged on his mind. It was high pitched, a dark 'crouk-crouk' cry, almost a cracking sound – and it was not one cry but several. Torcán shivered, for he knew what the rising cries indicated. He made his way to the edge of the trees and stared up into the sky. He was right. Soaring high over the hill were at least a dozen dark shapes with diamond-shaped tails, black shiny birds, circling and calling triumphantly. The harbingers of death, the birds of ill-omen . . . ravens.

Torcán knew enough about the scavenging habits of these birds to be aware that it was something substantial which made them behave so; it was not their usual fare of small mammals, birds or insects. This was the behaviour of ravens gathering to feast on the dead after a battle. Someone further up the hill was dead or help-lessly injured. The thought came to him immediately – and here were abandoned horses. The woodsman had no second thoughts now. Seizing his stout staff, he swiftly and athletically began to ascend the hill, keeping his eyes on the central point of the circling birds of prey.

Guided by these black harbingers of death, he came to the rocky ledge under the tall walls of Ráth Cuáin, and was shocked to find two bodies there. He averted his eyes from one, which was clearly beyond help: the ravens had already started to feast on it. The head was twisted at a curious angle and it was apparent that the man had died before the ravens had descended. A snapped crossbow, the type that was rarely used by warriors in the area, and a spilled quiver of bolts, as he knew these short arrows to be called, lay nearby.

In disgust Torcán twirled his staff around his head to clear off the hovering birds and then moved on to the second body, which was half covered by fallen ivy. Pulling it away, he recognised the man immediately. It was the warrior who had accompanied the lady Fidelma. There was no mistaking him, even if he had not been wearing the golden circlet at his neck which denoted he was a warrior of the Nasc Niadh, the Golden Collar, and bodyguards to the King of Cashel. Nearby lay the young warrior's abandoned sword. He stooped down to pick it up, for such a sword was valu-able. Then he stood wondering what to do next. At that moment there came a soft moan from the warrior and Torcán realised that the young man was still breathing. He saw that one leg was bent under the body and it was covered in blood. Should he alert the abbey? Should he try to carry him there and seek help?

Something prompted him to hold back. Perhaps it was the ques-tions that the lady Fidelma had asked during her visits that made him think that it might not be the right course. But he had to get help – and quickly too. Someone would be coming to search here soon – he was sure of it. Torcán bent down and replaced the young man's sword in its scabbard. Then he knelt and tried as best he could to straighten the young warrior's body into a position where he could lift him on his shoulder. Years as a woodsman in the forest had given Torcán tremendous strength, enough to hoist a great log across his shoulders and move at a trot for a hundred metres or more without fatigue. Now he hefted Aidan's body across his broad shoulders and moved sure footedly down the hill and back in the direction of the ruined cabin.

Fidelma peered into the gloom of their cell and sighed long and deeply. 'I can't see you clearly, Eadulf,' she muttered.

A shadow stirred at the side of her. 'I'm here, wherever here is.'

She reached out a hand and found his, and their hands entwined. 'As the man said, at least we are together. I'm not sure how long we've been here though,' she added. 'I just hope Aidan has made it.'

'There must be something that we can do,' Eadulf said.

'Nothing. Except . . .'

'Except . . . what? Don't tell me to go in for meditation stuff. There is no way I can calm my thoughts.'

Fidelma smiled in the darkness. 'I won't. It takes many years of practice to do so. I was thinking that instead of wasting this time we might go over the facts of this mystery and see what resolution we can arrive at.'

'Ah, the resolution is simple. It is all to do with the cargoes of silver that have been robbed from the boats hired by Prince Gilcach. This abbey has been at the centre of the robberies, as I discovered.'

'How did you make your deduction?'

Eadulf hesitated a moment. 'Well, more by luck than deduction,' he admitted.

'Tell me.'

'When we came into the caves here . . .'

'How was that?'

'As I said, Brother Gébennach showed us the way. However, I began to suspect that he was in league with the thieves and brought us here so that we could be captured. Unfortunately, it did not strike me until we found the silver. He must have informed Brother Giolla Rua, who then came to stop our escape.'

'I don't quite follow that. You had better tell me the whole story.'

Eadulf outlined what had happened when he and Aidan had realised that Fidelma was a prisoner, the meeting with Gébennach and the passage into the caves where Eadulf had found the sacks of silver ore.

'So you think Brother Gébennach was part of the gang of thieves?'

'He certainly knew something about Febal and Sionnach.' Eadulf realised that he had no positive proof. It was just circumstantial. He wished he could see Fidelma's face in the greyness because he was uncertain of the tone in her voice.

'That much is obvious,' he went on, 'for, as I say, he disappeared and the next thing Brother Giolla Rua emerged and here we are.'

There was a silence. 'So you conclude that Brother Gébennach was working with Giolla Rua as part of this gang of silver thieves – but what of Brother Sionnach? Why was he killed? Are all the council scholars who met at Cashel part of this criminal organisation?'

'Of course not. Sionnach had uncovered the conspiracy of thieves. That's why Febal, who was obviously leading the gang attacking the boats on the river, killed him.'

'Why would Sionnach go to see Febal if he had known this? He would be too cautious. And if Febal knew that Sionnach was investigating the thefts, why would he wait for so long before killing him? What about the reference to the secret book – and why was Brother Lucidus not to be trusted? Moreover, who *is* Brother Lucidus? There are many pieces of your puzzle that don't quite fit together.'

'Well, Spelán was certainly one of the gang of thieves and we found a piece of silver in his cabin,' Eadulf replied defensively.

'Why was Spelán killed?'

'Perhaps he was betraying his comrades.'

'So why was it done in the ritual fashion?'

Eadulf was silent, for he could not think of an answer.

'And why was Brancheó killed?'

'If she and Spelán were lovers, the explanation is easy. He probably confided in her about the theft. Erca told us that she was expecting them to have enough wealth to set up home in the southern mountains. Maybe she knew too much.' Eadulf then lapsed into silence with a deep sigh.

Fidelma squeezed his hand. 'Oh, come on. You have picked up some parts of the puzzle, some very important parts, I'll not deny it. But there is something other than the theft of Gilcach's silver going on here, Eadulf. In fact, the more I consider the matter, the more I realise that you may have presented me with the key to the puzzle that now makes the pieces begin to fall into shape.'

Eadulf was disappointed. 'I'm glad you think so.' He was not happy at the way his deduction had been almost dismissed by Fidelma.

'All we have to do—' she began.

'All we have to do,' interrupted Eadulf in irritation, 'is escape from here, round up Brother Giolla Rua, Gébennach, Febal and whoever else is involved, and present the case to the Chief Brehon.'

Fidelma chuckled. 'Indeed, Eadulf, that's all. The problem is, I know we can't get out until someone comes and unbolts that door.'

'Then let us hope that Aidan is already bringing the warriors of the Golden Collar from Cashel.'

It had taken Torcán some time to carry Aidan's semi-conscious form down to the ruined cabin and place it on the back of his cart. He was puzzled to see that the horses that belonged to Fidelma and her companions were still there. Torcán tied the horses behind his cart and set off towards the forest and his home. The young warrior kept slipping in and out of consciousness, moaning at the pain in his leg, as the cart negotiated each bump and rut. Torcán drove slowly and carefully and it took a while before he reached the clearing.

Hearing his arrival, Éimhin emerged from the cabin and stared in surprise at the horses and at the dishevelled form lying in her husband's log cart.

'What's happened?' she demanded, as she scrutinised the features of the young man. 'Why, it's the young warrior with the Golden Collar!'

'Get a blanket and I'll lift him into the cabin,' Torcán instructed. 'I think his leg is broken.'

She hurried back to prepare their only bed, and by the time she had arranged it, her husband had managed to carry in the warrior and lie him, as gently as possible, on it.

'There, wife, you are adept at the natural cures – you must do what you can for him.'

Éimhin looked doubtful as she examined the warrior.

'He needs treatment,' Torcán said, looking on.

'He needs a physician,' answered his wife. 'The leg is broken and he has started a fever. He is beyond my help.'

'Come, you can set the leg of a sheep. Surely you can set the leg of a man? I will help you.'

'The break is in the lower leg,' Éimhín said. 'It is the larger of the two bones that has fractured; perhaps the smaller one as well. That usually happens when the larger bone is broken.' She thought for a moment. 'It might not be too complicated to reset it. However, even if I can do so, there is a chance of infection. It's probably started already because he has fever. Certainly there will be much pain, bruising and swelling.' She paused, listening to Aidan's moaning and taking note for the first time that the sounds were articulate words, not delirious ramblings. 'Why does he keep mumbling about going to Cashel to save lives? What does he mean?'

Torcán said unhappily, 'Those horses attached to the wagon belong to the lady Fidelma, the Saxon and this warrior – all abandoned. Perhaps Fidelma and the Saxon remain in danger. The warrior was lying injured and unconsciousness just below the abbey walls.'

'Well, he can't get to Cashel now. I will do my best for him, husband. I'll treat the fever with the bark of willow and I still have that mixture of elderflower blossoms distilled with apple-tree bark. It ought to bring down the fever. Anyway, let's get to work straightening the poor boy's leg.'

Torcán nodded. 'As soon as we've done that, I will take one of the horses and ride to Cashel. I'll tell them what's amiss and I'll try to bring back a physician. You will have to look after him until I return.'

Fidelma came awake in total darkness to hear Eadulf breathing deeply beside her. She felt comforted by the closeness and warmth of his body against her own. They must have dropped into an exhausted sleep together in the grey cold shadows of their prison. Then the thought struck her: they had dozed in the gloom of the cave when there were still shadows and dim silhouettes to be seen, the grey light travelling along the tunnel outside to filter through the small aperture in the stout wooden door. Now it was totally black, she could not see her hand in front of her. She blinked for a few moments as if the action might help her see better. It did not and the reason why became clear to her.

She reached out and nudged Eadulf.

'Wake up,' she whispered urgently. 'Eadulf, wake up!'

She felt the body beside her twitch a little and move as if stretching.

'Are you awake?' she asked.

'What . . . what is it?' yawned Eadulf.

'The light!'

There was a hesitation then a mumbled voice. 'There is no light.'

'Exactly. Night has fallen.'

'How long have I been asleep?'

'I've no idea because I slept as well. But it must be that an entire day has passed.'

'And we've been left here all that time? Do you think they mean to simply abandon us?'

'I have no way of knowing what is in Brother Giolla Rua's mind.'

Eadulf groaned. 'I wonder what has happened to Aidan? It was well before midday when we followed Brother Gébennach into the cave complex. That means, when he left here, once he found his way back to the horses, he would have been able to get to Cashel and raise the alarm not long after midday.'

Fidelma was silent. Eadulf prompted: 'Do you think he did not make it?'

'It's no use speculating, Eadulf. It's a waste of energy and thought.'

They both fell silent again as there seemed little else to say. They had to accept that they were helpless, knowing there was no way out unless their captors opened the door. So, in silence, time passed. Time passed . . . slow, excruciating, painful and unbearable. Time passed until Eadulf wanted to leap to his feet and give a shout of anger or despair, he did not know which. He envied Fidelma the ability to meditate, when she could sit and apparently do nothing.

Wait a moment! Was his mind playing tricks? But no – he saw a flicker, a flicker of light from the aperture in the door.

He moved and Fidelma's hand closed over his arm.

'Careful, Eadulf. Remain still,' she whispered quickly.

There were sounds along the tunnel and the flickering light grew brighter.

Hopes raised, Eadulf strained forward. 'Aidan!' he called, ignoring Fidelma's order.

In answer there came a malevolent chuckle and a familiar voice called: 'Stand away from the door. I have armed guards out here, so do not make any wrong moves.'

There came the scrape of bolts and the door swung open.

Brother Giolla Rua stood there and behind him, they could see he was not lying about being accompanied by armed guards. One of them carried a lantern which cast a light into their prison. Slowly Fidelma struggled to her feet and Eadulf moved to help her.

'I regret that it is uncomfortable, not being able to move or walk about.' Brother Giolla Rua sounded almost sympathetic to their plight.

'It is night-time,' observed Fidelma. 'How long through the night is it?'

The shadows on the man's face moved and they guessed his features had reformed into a smile.

'You are perceptive, *dálaigh*,' he replied. 'Indeed, night has fallen and dawn is a *cadar* away.'

They became aware that he was holding a small bag in one hand and a jug in the other.

'What do you intend to do with us?' Eadulf hoped he sounded more courageous than he felt.

'Me? I don't intend to do anything. However, I felt it my Christian duty to bring some food and drink to you.' He set down the bag and the jug on the stone flag of the floor and took a step back. 'Here is a meal to see you safely through the night.'

'How will we see it, if you leave us without light?' demanded Eadulf, the practical thought coming into his head almost at once.

Brother Giolla Rua smiled again. He half turned and motioned to one of the guards who took a candle and lit it from the lantern he carried and handed it to the religieux. The man turned to a small stone shelf near the door, dropped some grease from the melting fat of the candle on it and set the candle down.

'There you are – what more do you want than food and light to sustain you?' he asked ironically.

'Our freedom would not go amiss,' Fidelma replied.

The religieux chuckled. 'Alas, that is beyond my power. My compatriots are most insistent on that. However, I shall depart from here come dawn, my business concluded for the time being. But I fear I must leave you in some distress waiting for the dawn because my compatriots have decided that you should be . . . er, eliminated. You see, I am afraid that you know too much. Febal will come to do the honours. He has certain superstitions that hark back to olden times. It is thought that the coming of the Morning Star is a good time to depart to the Otherworld as the Lightbringer shines the way to the House of Donn, where Donn is waiting to collect the souls for transport to the . . . oh well, you know the old legends as well as I do.'

Brother Giolla Rua suddenly stepped back, still chuckling, through the door. It swung shut with a bang; the bolts rasped into place.

Fidelma and Eadulf were left alone once more in the cold cave now lit by a small, flickering candle. Their prison seemed more desolate and oppressive now.

chapter nineteen

In spite of the cold, the damp and, most of all, the threat of Brother Giolla Rua, Fidelma and Eadulf had been dozing. Eadulf was in that half-dreaming, half-waking state, as faint noises started to combine with images in his mind. The sounds were of people in chaos: shouts, screaming, rising and falling like the waves of an incoming tide. Then came a sudden bang of a heavy door and running footsteps.

He realised he was awake and Fidelma was also stirring at his side.

His heart started to pound when he saw the flicker of a lantern growing brighter in the passage outside.

He rose unsteadily to his feet and helped Fidelma up.

'I think the time has come.' His voice was thick and he swallowed a couple of times, hoping not to sound as fearful as he felt.

The footsteps had paused outside.

Fidelma squeezed his hand as the bolts rasped back from their sockets and the door swung open. Two men with swords in their hands entered the cavern.

'Come along!' one of them snapped. 'Don't give us any trouble otherwise you die here and now. Move ahead of us.'

Fidelma demanded, 'If you are going to kill us, why not do it here and now?'

The leading man glanced uneasily at his companion.

It was then that Eadulf understood that the noises he had heard in his dreams were real.

'The abbey is under attack!' he cried, then exclaimed in agony as the point of one of the men's swords dug into his upper arm.

'If you don't want those words to be your last, prisoner, obey us. March in front of us. *Now*!'

Eadulf raised his left hand to his bloodstained right arm. 'Very well,' he muttered, as Fidelma reached out to help him. 'I'm all right,' he grunted.

Menaced by the sword tips, the couple moved slowly ahead of the two armed men.

'Where do you want us to go?' Eadulf said as they exited from the cave.

One of the men indicated with his sword. 'Just go along this passage and out into the main cave.'

Here, they could clearly hear the uproar from the abbey buildings above. Eadulf was about to turn to the stone stairway that he had deduced would lead into the main abbey buildings when the gruff order of one of the swordsmen stayed him. From the chaos and shouting, it seemed that Aidan must have reached Cashel and that Gormán and his warriors were storming the abbey.

'This way,' instructed one of their captors.

To Eadulf's surprise they were pushed towards the very tunnel through which he and Aidan had first entered the complex.

'What do you intend to do?' he asked, feeling more secure now that the abbey was being invaded.

The man who had done all the threatening simply said: 'Shut up.'

'That's not very helpful,' Eadulf replied, only to receive another sharp prod from the man's sword.

'I said – shut up!' he growled.

Eadulf suddenly halted and turned, surprising both men. 'I think you would have killed us already if you did not need us alive,' he declared. 'So come on – what do you intend to do with us?'

There were some moments of silence; the four of them standing facing each other in the dimly lit cave passage.

'We are giving you a chance to save your lives and our lives as well.' The second man spoke for the first time.

Eadulf's mind was working quickly. 'You are trying to escape from the retribution of the warriors of the Golden Collar,' he said, articulating his thoughts. 'You are using us as shields?'

'So you see that we have nothing to lose,' sneered the second man.

'Every rat for himself, eh?' Eadulf observed.

'What's happened to Brother Giolla Rua?' Fidelma wanted to know.

'He left before dawn. Before the Cashel warriors arrived at the abbey.'

Eadulf smiled in satisfaction. 'Doubtless taking the silver with him and leaving you to fight his battles?'

'When the warriors broke through the gates, Febal was ordered to despatch you so that you would not stand witness against us,' the second man told them.

'Febal was ordered . . .' Fidelma said the phrase thoughtfully. 'Of course. That was after Giolla Rua had left?'

The two men exchanged a nervous glance.

'So you have seized your own chance to use us as hostages,' Eadulf said cynically. 'What do you plan?'

'Shut up!' the leader repeated. 'One hostage is as good as another. I can kill one of you and still use the other – I don't mind which. So make up your mind. Go quietly before us or take the consequences.'

Fidelma reached out and laid a hand on Eadulf's arm. She didn't say anything but her meaningful look told him not to do anything hasty or impetuous. They turned with the sword points behind them and made their way along the rest of the tunnel.

Soon Eadulf could see the light ahead coming through the growth that he recalled had covered the main cave entrance. He felt a momentary despair because this side of the hill was so precipitous that Gormán would not think it worth covering. He would not know that there was a means of escape from the abbey through the caves. He wondered what the two men had in mind, for it meant a scramble down the rocky incline towards the forests, and beyond was the great winding river of the Siúr. Did they expect to find a boat there, and use it as a means of escape? How long would it be before they deemed it safe to release their hostages? Indeed – would they release them? His mind worked feverishly: if Brother Giolla Rua had come with his sacks of silver along this way, he had to have transport to do so. How else could he move a dozen heavy sacks of silver? Who did he have to carry them? In which direction would he go?

There was another sharp jab at his shoulder. They were within a few metres of the fronds and ivy that covered the cave entrance.

'Halt!' grunted the first man. 'You, woman, move to the entrance and draw aside some of that growth. I want you to look out and tell me what you see. Make sure the way is clear. No tricks mind, – or your companion will die instantly.'

Fidelma moved to the growth and reached out a hand, drawing back the vegetation.

'What do you see?'

'A beautiful dawn,' Fidelma replied without humour.

'Don't play games, woman. Your man's life depends on it.'

'I see the hillside, rocky and steep, and beyond that the start of the forest – and beyond that the glint of sun on the river and the hills to the south-west. What else is there to see?'

'Warriors!' The man's voice was raised in anger. 'Do you see any of the men of Cashel?'

'I see nothing for you to be afraid of,' she replied.

'Then both of you move out first – and be careful. We are right behind you.'

Fidelma nodded. 'Ready, Eadulf?' There was something in her tone which alerted Eadulf. His body became tense. They pushed their way through the fronds, out of the cave entrance and onto the open hillside. They were but a step or so outside when she shouted: 'Drop!' Eadulf did not question the order but threw himself down.

There came a shout, a cry, the sound of something whistling over him and the next moment, a body fell sprawling upon him. He heard some metal on metal and then a familiar voice was speaking: 'Are you hurt, lady?'

Eadulf blinked rapidly and tried to raise his head. There were people moving around him and the weight on his legs was being pulled off as he heard Fidelma exclaiming that she was all right. The next moment it was Enda who was helping him to his feet.

'Are you all right, friend Eadulf?' asked the cheery warrior.

'He's hurt,' Fidelma said before he could reply. 'That man stabbed him in the upper arm.'

'Well,' Enda replied, 'he won't stab anyone any more.' Eadulf looked, and saw two arrows embedded in the man's body. 'He tried to take another stab at you even when we shouted at him to surrender. The other man had the good sense to throw down his sword.'

Eadulf turned, holding his shoulder, and saw the second man having his arms firmly bound behind him.

Fidelma had moved across and was now examining Eadulf's shoulder. 'Luckily, it's a superficial wound but it needs attention in case of any infection.'

Eadulf looked around appreciatively. There seemed an entire company of the warriors of the Golden Collar emerging from their hiding places on the hillside.

'It was good that Aidan told you about this cave, though I think you have missed the chief villain and his cargo of silver.'

Enda shook his head. 'Aidan? No, it was Torcán, the woodsman, who came to tell us that he thought you were prisoners here. He didn't know the full story, but had picked up some information from Aidan. To be honest, Aidan was in a bad way, with a broken leg and a fever. But Torcán knew enough to alert us.'

'How bad is Aidan?' Fidelma asked immediately.

'If the fever breaks, he will mend,' Enda assured her.

'So what happened?' Eadulf pressed. 'Tell us about the attack.'

'The King himself led the attack. I know no more of it, as I and my men were sent to cover this side of the hill and the caves. Now I think we should join your brother in the abbey, lady. Shall we go back through the caves? It would seem the easier way into the abbey now. As the lady said, friend Eadulf, the sooner you get your wound seen to, the better.'

They emerged, led by Enda, into one of the courtyards of the abbey complex. From the number of warriors of the Golden Collar who were present, Fidelma judged that her brother had called forth an entire *catha* or battalion of his guards. She had not seen so many since the fight against Crónan in Osraige and the prevention of the attempt to invade the petty kingdom of Éile.

Colgú was the first to make his way through the throng to greet her, an expression of relief on his face.

'Are you well, sister?' he said urgently, holding out his arms to embrace her.

'Well enough, brother,' she replied. 'But Eadulf has been wounded.'

'Where's our apothecary?' the King demanded of Gormán who now came pushing forward, grinning with joy at seeing them both safe and sound.

'Come, friend Eadulf. Let's get you attended to. The abbey's herbalist is helping us tend to the wounded over there.'

Fidelma gazed round and noticed a pile of bodies in a corner. 'Was it a costly attack?' she asked sadly.

Her brother grimaced. 'I've known worse. There were only a dozen men who could be described as warriors. They were relied on to hold the gates. Of course, they didn't count against Gormán and his men. But we lost three men – good men. And several are wounded. The defenders were armed with bows and some were good at their craft. But most of those who tried to defend this place died here. It was as if they were just trying to delay our entry into the abbey. They must have known they could not withstand my companies.'

Fidelma was surprised when he used the term *feadhna,* a company of a hundred men, instead of a *catha,* a battalion.

Colgú shrugged in answer to her query. 'When Torcán came and alerted me to what was going on, I turned out three *feadhna* from our first *catha*, and we had this place surrounded well before first light. Three companies were more than enough to handle these mercenaries. I called on the abbot to surrender. When the gates remained closed and defended, I ordered the warriors of the Golden Collar to show Febal's mercenaries what real warriors could do.'

'Was Febal in command?'

Colgú looked grim. 'That treacherous bastard? He was wounded but he lives, which is a good thing because he can stand trial. It was not much of a defence. As I said, they just seemed intent on delaying the inevitable rather than with any hope of holding out against me.'

Eadulf looked out across the steep slope towards the river. 'I think I know why they were trying to do that,' he said hollowly.

'Because?'

'It has given time for Brother Giolla Rua to flee with the silver loot taken from Prince Gilcach and get across country to the river.'

Enda, who had been standing by, began to smile broadly. 'I think you'll find that particular religieux with four pack mules waiting impatiently by the riverside under the guard of Dego and his men. Our men were in place long before the Lightbringer rose in the sky.'

'So it was Giolla Rua who was in league with Febal, robbing the silver from the boats of Prince Gilcach's mines.' Colgú formed his lips in a soundless whistle. 'And is that what has been happening here? Is this is the centre of the silver thieves?'

'That's not the entire story,' Fidelma corrected him. 'But it's a long story and better for the telling in a formal court as soon as we can arrange it.'

Colgú heaved a sigh. 'Well, certainly Abbot Síoda seems as bewildered as I now am. I have talked with him and he claims it was Febal who refused to open the gates and ordered his men to fight us. The abbot said that he did try to get the men to lay down their weapons. He defends himself by saying that he was acting lawfully in hiring mercenaries, since no clansmen of his came forward to fulfil their obligations to him. Febal was put in command of this motley force. Whether true or not, Abbot Síoda will have a lot to answer for.'

'What of the other members of the abbey – did any of them resist?'

'The gatekeeper maintains he kept the gates closed under threat of Febal. We might give him the benefit of the doubt.'

'And the others? For example, the librarian Brother Gébennach and the other religious?'

'They all seemed to be horrified by the action of the mercenary warriors. The herbalist . . .'

'Sister Fioniúr?'

'As I mentioned before, she and her assistant have been helping with the wounded.'

'Do you have further news of Aidan?' Eadulf interrupted at this point. 'Should I not go to Torcán's cabin and tend to him?'

'Brother Conchobhar went there as soon as we heard the news.

I am told Aidan will pull through. Torcán and his wife set the broken leg and the wife, who is a woman of the woods and knows cures, was treating the fever.'

Fidelma let out a long sigh as she gazed sadly around her.

Colgú followed her gaze. 'Greed,' he said. 'Risking death, injury and even the existence of this ancient abbey and its community for the sake of a few sacks of silver.'

Fidelma was reflective for a few moments. 'It is not as simple as that,' she replied at last.

'You mean there is something more to this matter?'

'We must hold a Dál, a court, here as soon as it is possible to arrange,' she said. 'I shall submit my case to the Chief Brehon Fríthel. Prince Gilcach and the Prince of the Uí Briúin Seóla and their legal advisers must be sent for. Meanwhile, I would request the presence of Abbot Cuán and his steward Brother Mac Raith and Brother Duibhinn. They have an interest in the proceedings involving this abbey.'

'They know something about the silver thefts?'

Fidelma grimaced wearily. 'Obviously, the entire abbey is to be placed under guard, all members of the community to be isolated and no one is allowed to leave under any circumstances.'

Colgú stared at her in surprise for a moment. 'What – all of them?'

'It would be better there are no exceptions. That means sending guards into the caves below so that no one sneaks out. I presume Brother Giolla Rua will be brought back with his sacks of silver? He and those with him can be accompanied back here under guard as well.'

'For how long?'

'For as long as it takes the Chief Brehon and the others to get here. I would say the legal period of nine days should pass before we hold the Dál.'

Colgú ran a hand through his red hair as he stared at his sister.

'It sounds as though this is more than a simple resolution about the theft of silver.'

'It is a very complicated matter involving the murder of the shepherd Spelán, the woman Brancheó and Brother Sionnach. However, it started with an incident in the Lateran Palace in Rome.'

Colgú was stunned. 'An incident in Rome and the deaths . . . Are you ascribing all three deaths to this abbey?' he gasped.

'More or less,' Fidelma said off-handedly. Then she suddenly became very serious. 'I have realised that with the matter of the silver thefts and the murders, there has been one evil mind behind it all. If what I suspect is right, then I hope to uncover the owner of that evil mind during the hearing.'

She glanced around again. Eadulf was rising from a chair in a corner of the courtyard, helped by Enda. Apparently Sister Fioniúr had just finished binding up his stab wound and he was thanking her.

'Now, brother,' Fidelma said, 'if you can let me take Enda, Eadulf and I will go down to Torcán's cabin to see poor Aidan. I presume he is still there?'

'I hear that, with a broken leg, it was thought better to allow him to recover there until he can walk more easily.'

'That is good. We might even stay and sample Éimhinn's hospitality again. I feel famished. I am sure Eadulf does also.'

She turned with a quick wave at her brother and went to join Eadulf and Enda. As they crossed into the main courtyard, making their way towards the now blackened gates of the abbey, they saw the young librarian, Brother Gébennach, standing under guard of one of the Cashel warriors. He smiled ruefully as they passed.

Fidelma suddenly paused and turned back. 'Spoken words can fly away but written words remain and words can become truth and truth can breed hatred,' she said.

Eadulf stared at her in total bewilderment but Brother Gébennach seemed to understand. His smile simply broadened.

'*Vero, cucullus non facit monachum,*' he replied gravely.

She turned back to join the others as they moved on out of the gates,

'What did he mean by that?' asked Eadulf, still puzzled.

'Just what he said,' replied Fidelma airily. 'The cowl doesn't make someone a religieux, any more than you should believe a book contains the truth merely because it says it is the truth.'

CHAPTER TWENTY

It was nine days since the warriors of the Golden Collar had stormed and occupied the abbey of Ráth Cuáin – a period called *nómad* which was the ancient calendrical week that had existed before the adoption of the New Faith and attempts to fit in with the Roman calendrical concepts. It was also considered the legal period to allow time to elapse before a hearing that necessitated the attendance of representatives of other kingdoms. The large *praintech,* or refectory, of Ráth Cuáin had been converted into a Dál or courtroom.

A slightly raised platform had been constructed at one end of the refectory and chairs had been brought for the King to take his seat alongside his Chief Brehon, Fíthel, to his right. Behind Colgú's chair stood Gormán. On the left side of the King sat Abbot Cuán of Imleach in his position as Chief Bishop of the kingdom. Next to him was Prince Gilcach of Béal Atha Gabhann who sat with his Brehon, and next to them the Prince of the Uí Briúin Seóla with his Brehon. But these two Brehons attended as legal observers only, for this was a court of law of Muman and it was Fíthel alone who would conduct this hearing; his voice only would be heard in final judgement.

To the right of the platform stood a table and two chairs for the use of Fidelma, who would be assisted by Eadulf.

A short distance behind them was a chair placed there for Aidan, his right leg in a splint and stiffly bound. He looked pale and determined. According to the law of the Brehons the period of *nómad*, the ancient week, was also one allowed for resting if one was injured. Aidan had insisted that he must attend the hearing to bear witness to the events, in spite of Brother Conchobhar's advice that he should rest even more than the customary legal period.

Numerous warriors of the Golden Collar were placed at strategic points around the hall because the entire abbey community was still under restraint.

Directly opposite to Fidelma, on the far side of the hall, sat a scowling Abbot Síoda with his thin, bleak-faced gatekeeper, Brother Tadhg, and other members of the community. Among them was the young librarian Brother Gébennach, who looked remarkably cheerful. Next to him stood the dark-haired, attractive-looking herbalist, Sister Fioniúr, whose features bore no expression at all.

On benches facing the Chief Brehon, in the centre of the hall, were four desolate-looking prisoners. A surly Brother Giolla Rua sat alongside the sullen and bitter-looking Febal, whose arm was in a sling, having been wounded in the fighting. Next to them were two members of the mercenary warriors, one of whom was the survivor of those who had tried to use Fidelma and Eadulf as hostages. Behind them were a few other men who had apparently been the muleteers who had been caught alongside Brother Giolla Rua when they had tried to escape with the silver to the coast. They were all closely guarded by Gormán's warriors.

Apart from the prisoners, at the end of the hall, sat Brother Mac Raith, the steward of Imleach, with Brother Duibhinn, Brother Conchobhar, the woodsman Torcán and his wife Éimhín and their two sons, and even Torcán's brother, Curnan.

The hall had become hot and stuffy. Many of those gathered had begun to talk among themselves, creating an almost deafening hubbub. Eadulf found it impossible to concentrate. Finally, Brehon

Fíthel, after an exchange with Colgú, signalled to Gormán as holder of the staff of office. The warrior brought the oak staff down sharply on the wooden floor. He had to perform this several times before the noise gradually began to die down. An uneasy quiet descended and finally all were looking expectantly at the Chief Brehon of the kingdom.

'There is much to be heard and considered this day, and this can only be done with your cooperation.' Fíthel rose and looked round at the assembly. 'I proclaim this Dál in session. I want no interruptions while the *dálaigh* explains her case. Only when the charges are made clear will those who are charged be called upon to answer. Is this understood?' He paused a moment or two and then smiled grimly. 'Since all have agreed by their silence that they understand, we shall proceed.'

Again he paused, looking around before turning towards Fidelma. 'Are you ready to proceed, Fidelma of Cashel?'

Fidelma rose and inclined her head in silent agreement. Brehon Fíthel resumed his seat and signalled her to begin.

'This matter started with the discovery of the body of a man hidden in the pile designated for the Samhain bonfire in the town square of Cashel. The man had been killed by what, in the legends of our people, was thought to be an ancient pagan ritual called the threefold death. His skull was smashed in, he was stabbed in the heart and his throat was cut. This was thought to be significant as we are all acquainted with the former symbolism of Samhain. Sharp eyes saw the body and it was removed before the fire could consume it. It was identified as a shepherd, the widower of Caoimhe of the clan Sítae from the Hill of the Bullock. His name was Spelán. Carved onto the buttocks of this man was a symbol – it is called the Tau-Rho . . .'

She was interrupted by gasps from the majority of the community who had not known this.

'The Tau-Rho,' she continued, 'is an early symbol of the New

Faith and one that is now used by those who follow certain beliefs that the Bishop of Rome would consider heretical. It is the symbol of this abbey.'

She paused and let her gaze wander over the silent hall.

'This was the starting point of a mystery – a mystery that was so deep and impenetrable that it was not until I realised that I was dealing with more than a single mystery that clarity began to emerge. In fact, there were two separate mysteries that conjoined within this abbey. Because they were overlaid, I could make no sense of this first murder and, indeed, the subsequent murders of the woman Brancheó and of Brother Sionnach. But then the mist began to clear. My problem today is how to explain the conjoined mysteries in simple terms; how to make their interweaving into one logical narrative.'

Again she paused dramatically, but her question was rhetorical and needed no intervention.

'To explain this, I will leave the murder of Spelán, and start with the place rather than the victims.' She looked across at Abbot Síoda. 'Ráth Cuáin is a special place in the order of abbeys of our kingdom. It was the fortress of a petty chieftain of the clan Sítae which occupies this area. It still is. The abbot exacts tributes from the local population both as chieftain and as abbot.'

'Nothing unusual in that,' interrupted Abbot Síoda loudly. 'It is my right under law.'

Fíthel turned to him with a warning frown. 'Remember what I said about procedure, Abbot Síoda of Ráth Cuáin,' he warned coldly before turning back to Fidelma. 'However, this is true. There are many abbots and bishops among the Five Kingdoms who are elected to their rôles because they are also princes or chieftains of their people. As such they are entitled to tribute, both secular and ecclesiastical.'

Fidelma bowed her head in acknowledgement. 'I did not mean to imply it was unusual. I merely wish to emphasise the status of

Síoda. Of course, under the same law, the chieftain has an obligation to his clan, so in return for tribute from them there is a duty of care and protection. Anyway, the transition from secular fortress to a centre of the New Faith took place over a hundred years ago. In those hundred years, the philosophies and outlook of those pursuing the New Faith have often changed. New ideas and new rules and attitudes have been adopted and discarded at the many councils throughout the lands that have adopted this New Faith, which we now call Christendom.

'In this abbey, some of the ideas once adopted at the birth of the New Faith still remain and are stoutly defended against the new decisions from Rome.'

Brehon Fíthel raised a hand; his expression was thoughtful. 'The same can be said for most of the abbeys of the Five Kingdoms. We have consistently rejected the new theories and philosophies from Rome – even to the dating of the Pascal festival, the rules of behaviour, and even to the cutting of the male tonsure to mark their status in the Faith. We have always argued against Rome's attempts to impose their rules at councils like Streonshalh and Autun in which you, Fidelma, went as an adviser to our delegations concerning our laws, especially how they clashed with those known as the Penitentials.'

'This is so,' she agreed. 'But let us look at the Faith as accepted by this abbey, for it is of especial concern in this matter. I admit, I stand here as a *dálaigh* not as a theologian. I do not interpret but only recite the facts. The Faith that is taught here at Ráth Cuáin is called Psilanthropism. It is a Greek word. What it means is that the Christ whose name we take from the Greek form of the Hebrew word *mashiack* or *messiah*, meaning "the anointed one", was merely a human being; never divine, but born of man and woman. This idea became popular for a time in the teachings of the sect called the Nazarenes and was later expounded by Theodotus of Byzantium.

'In the second century of the Faith, Victor, the Bishop of Rome, declared it to be wrong. But the Bishop of Antioch, Paul of Samosata, continued to teach it during the third century of the New Faith. It was condemned at the first council of Nicaea in the fourth century, which was called by the Roman Emperor Constantine. He was the first Roman emperor to convert to the New Faith and declared that all citizens of the Roman Empire should accept the rules laid down at Nicaea; he imposed those rules by use of the Roman army and government.

'However, this basic idea of Psilanthropism has continued here and there and in many derivations – Apollinism and Arianism, for example. But for Rome, the basic teaching of the Faith was that Jesus is divine; a god and son of the eastern God called Jehovah.'

Brother Mac Raith had risen in his seat and signalled that he wanted to speak.

Brehon Fíthel frowned for a moment as if debating with himself whether he should allow this. Then he said: 'Recognising that the learned *dálaigh*,' he nodded at Fidelma, 'by her own admission, does not speak as a theologian of the Faith, I am prepared to allow words of explanation from the steward of the Chief Bishop of this kingdom.'

'I have nothing to correct in terms of how the lady Fidelma has described this heresy,' Brother Mac Raith said, inclining his head towards Fidelma. 'Psilanthropism, as she says, is a Greek term for being merely human – indicating that Christ was an ordinary man. But the majority of Christendom recognise it as a heresy and this includes the Chief Bishop of this kingdom. We too maintain that it is so. We have been worried that for many years this abbey maintains this heresy. That is why, some days ago, Abbot Cuán of Imleach invited leading theologians from Corcach Mór, Ard Mór and Ros Ailithír to meet with me, representing the Chief Bishop, to discuss the merits or otherwise of this heresy before deciding how we should organise a council with Abbot Síoda in attendance so that we might bring this abbey into line with the fundamental teachings of the

Faith. As you know, one of our council was murdered in Cashel. Now we find,' he eyed Brother Giolla Rua, 'another of our number stands charged with criminal involvement with this abbey. We trust these matters will be resolved by the *dálaigh*.'

Fidelma looked confidently at Brother Mac Raith. 'They shall be so resolved – in due course,' she replied.

Abbot Síoda was now on his feet, wearing an angry expression.

'I protest at where this is leading. Is my abbey or am I myself being accused of the murder of this Brother Sionnach of Corcach Mór? As for Brother Giolla Rua, as far as I am aware, he has had no dealings with me. I demand to speak in defence of the theology of my Faith which is far older than the new rules and theology from Rome that comes to this kingdom via Imleach. It is they who are the heretics, not this abbey!'

Brehon Fíthel was stern. 'It is only because you have some justification for your outburst, Abbot Síoda, that you are not going to be fined for interrupting. I am well aware that any criminal accusation against you or your abbey may be defended with equal force. Do you make such criminal accusation against Abbot Síoda, Fidelma of Cashel?'

'I make no accusation at this stage,' Fidelma said calmly. This caused some surprise among those in the hall. She went on: 'Nor do I expect to make any accusation about the heresy of the theology here. I am not qualified on that – and only the Chief Bishop of the kingdom and his advisers can do so. I trust, however, that Abbot Síoda agrees with my description of the Faith as it is accepted in his abbey and which Brother Mac Raith from Imleach also accepts.'

Abbot Síoda made a dismissive motion of his hand which, when pressed by the Chief Brehon, he explained meant that he had no argument with Fidelma's description of his abbey's interpretations of the Faith.

'Good,' Fidelma acknowledged. 'Then we may now proceed.

Rome claims to be the centre of the New Faith and the Bishop of Rome is styled the Holy Father of the Universal Church. Of course, not everyone agrees even on that. Many churches exist which hold to many different interpretations of the Faith. But Rome has, from the early days of the Faith, maintained a vast number of manuscripts and documents that are stored in the Lateran Palace, the palace of the Bishop of Rome. It is called the Secret Archive. Some months ago, early in the summer, an ancient book was stolen from that Secret Archive.'

A curious tension had suddenly became manifest in Abbot Síoda and Brother Tadhg, the abbey gatekeeper.

'As some of you will recall, seven years ago Eadulf and I were in Rome. At that time, I became acquainted with the *Nomenclator* of the Lateran Palace, the Venerable Gelasius, whose task was generally to run the affairs of the Bishop of Rome's household. A few days ago, as Brother Mac Raith will confirm, I received a message from him. It said that a certain book was missing; perhaps I should say "stolen". The Venerable Gelasius said that in the wrong hands it could be a great danger to the very existence of Christendom. He further indicated that the suspects involved in the theft were from the Five Kingdoms. He had sent a Brother Lucidus to attempt to retrieve it. If Brother Lucidus needed help then he would contact me and the *Nomenclator* urged me to assist him.'

Brehon Fíthel was shaking his head. 'I am getting confused. What has this to do with the murders?'

'I confess, nothing directly,' replied Fidelma. 'I have explained about two mysteries coalescing. So let me continue. When I came to see Abbot Síoda about Spelán's murder he had a book on his desk. Before he had time to cover it up – which is what he tried to do – I was able to read the Latin titles and caveat. It was marked with the seal of the Bishop of Rome and the Secret Archives, along with the words *Non videbunt* – none shall see.'

'Are you saying that this is a book worth killing for?'

'In this case some people might think so. But only Brother Sionnach was a victim. He met his death at the hands of Febal in the mistaken belief that he was investigating the theft of the silver. He was not. He was helping Brother Lucidus in trying to retrieve the stolen book.'

'Now I am really confused,' complained Brehon Fíthel.

'It was acknowledged that both Abbot Síoda and Brother Tadhg had been on a pilgrimage to Rome during the summer.'

'So you are accusing them of the theft?' the Brehon asked sharply.

'I am now making that accusation.'

There were gasps around the great hall.

'And did this Brother Lucidus contact you?'

'He was actually not in need of my help for he had traced the book to this abbey with the help of his colleague Brother Sionnach. He had even managed to join the abbey and place himself in a position of trust so that, given the right moment, he could remove the book and return to Rome with it.'

'That is ridiculous!' Abbot Síoda called. 'We have no Brother Lucidus here and not in such a position. Anyway, a Roman among our company would stand out like an ass among a team of horses.'

'Thankfully, Brother Lucidus was not an ass nor was he a Roman.'

'But the name . . .?'

'Names can be changed. Anyway, he was no Roman. He was a son of the Gael who used the name Lucidus when in Rome. But here he would use his own name.' She turned to the cheerful young librarian. 'Is that not true, Brother Lucidus?'

The keeper of books simply smiled. 'My name is Brother Gébennach,' he asserted.

'And tell us, what does that name mean?' she prompted him.

'I am sure you know,' the young man countered.

'One who illuminates,' went on Fidelma. 'What better translation of Lucidus, than the bringer of light . . . one who illuminates? You corrected me on the meaning of your name, remember? You also mentioned that you had recently been in Rome. I was not completely sure if you were the emissary of the Venerable Gelasius until Eadulf and Aidan told me how you were willing to show them the secret passage into the cave systems under this abbey. You were only willing to help once you were told Eadulf was investigating a separate issue that did not endanger your search.'

'I wondered why you had disappeared as soon as you had shown us the way in,' declared Eadulf, unable to refrain from comment. 'I thought that you had done so to betray us to Brother Golla Rua. So where did you go off to?'

'He had just returned from meeting the librarian of the Abbey of Mungairit who had shown him some notes on the book in question which would have helped him identify it. He knew the book was in the abbey library and his priority was to go there and retrieve it. When he had done so, he could hide it until he was able to return it to Rome.'

'I am still confused, Fidelma,' Brehon Fíthel declared helplessly.

'The great library of Mungairit has many books, including the original textual reference to the one that was stolen. Brother Lucidus had found that out from Brother Sionnach. At one period Mungairit's scholars flirted with the philosophy of Psilanthropism. That is why Brother Mac Raith told us that no representative of that abbey was included on the council debating this matter. Moreover, that knowledge was also given to him by Brother Sionnach.'

'But if Lucidus was supporting us, why did Brother Sionnach say he was not to be trusted, or might not be trusted!' exclaimed Eadulf.

'We misread the sense of his note,' Fidelma assured him. 'Sionnach, having been accused of being the "Lightbringer", made a note that the password between Lucidus and himself – the word "lightbringer" – could no longer be trusted as it was known.'

'How did Brother Giolla Rua come upon us then?' Aidan asked.

'Like friend Eadulf, I thought he had been alerted by Brother Gébennach.'

Fidelma shook her head. 'This was where the other series of events that were taking place coincided.'

'May I ask a question?' It was Gormán standing behind the King's chair who spoke. Brehon Fíthel turned in annoyance. He had almost given up ruling on interruptions.

'It is unusual but put your question.'

'It was in my company that the woman Bran. Branlcheó appeared to claim that Brother Sionnach was Lucidus. At least, she referred to him as a "bringer of light". If Febal believed this was the code of someone investigating the theft of the silver, was that why he killed him?'

'It was. She made that mistake because Spelán had wrongly informed her that Brother Sionnach was heard using the term. "Lightbringer" was the code word which Brother Lucidus used with contacts during his search for the stolen book. Under the torture, Spelán had revealed this password to Febal. As Brother Lucidus will tell you, Sionnach was his friend and had been making inquiries for him; so this is where two mysteries joined.'

'Do you confirm this, Brother Gébennach, or whatever your name is?' demanded Brehon Fíthel.

The young librarian sighed. 'Brother Sionnach was, indeed, a good friend of mine. I consulted him as soon as I came home to this island because he, if anyone, would know which abbeys would be interested in this heresy and therefore in the stolen book. Sionnach, as you have said, was from Corcach Mór, and first made inquiries in his own abbey. Sionnach did meet me by the great river and that must have been where Spelán heard the code word of "lightbringer" pass between us.'

There was a silence before Fidelma continued.

'So we have, to an extent, cleared up the first mystery. Brother Lucidus, or rather Brother Gébennach, returned to this land in search of an ancient and important book. Through the inquiries of Brother Sionnach, he came to this abbey as librarian and was able to retrieve the book. He can now return it to Rome where it belongs. So far as his mission from the Venerable Gelasius was authorised, I would now submit that we do not hinder him further.'

From the far side of the room Brother Gébennach, with a slight smile on his lips, raised his hands and offered her silent applause.

'The lady Fidelma is correct in every way,' he addressed the Chief Brehon. 'The book, I am pleased to say, is already in my possession and once I hear your judgement I shall return with it to Rome. It will be up to the Chief Bishop to take any action thought necessary against Abbot Síoda and Brother Tadhg, who removed the book from its rightful place in the archives of the Lateran Palace. The one thing I hope that the lady Fidelma will now reveal is who is guilty of the murder of a great scholar and my good friend, Brother Sionnach of Corcach Mór.'

'Is Abbot Síoda accused of ordering the murder of Brother Sionnach as well as stealing this book from Rome?' Brehon Fíthel asked.

'Once more I remind the Dál that there is a second criminal matter concurrent with this one,' Fidelma said strongly. 'Spelán had wrongly identified Brother Sionnach as Lucidus. He had told this fact to his lover, Brancheó, before he revealed it under torture to Febal. He had told the leader of the gang of thieves he was involved with that he knew a religious who was making inquiries about the abbey. Mistakenly, he believed these inquiries were to do with the thefts of silver, and not that of the book from Rome. Febal was ordered to come to Cashel for the purpose of identifying whoever this religious was among the scholars gathered there. By misfortune, Brancheó, going on Spelán's erroneous information, identified Sionnach. Febal was a witness to that and duly killed him.

'Sionnach, unsuspecting, had been trying to get information for his colleague, Brother Lucidus. So he innocently entered Febal's room and was killed. Febal then easily escaped and returned here to the abbey. Febal, as the Brehon of the Uí Briúin Seóla, who sits here today, will confirm, was dismissed from the service of the Gamanride. He pursued a career of selling his sword to the highest bidder.'

'What alerted you to this?'

'As an excuse to stay in Cashel, Febal invented a story that he had come to find the man who had dishonoured his sister and to exact blood vengeance. It was a colourful story and parts did not ring true. You will hear that the part that *was* true was that Febal himself had dishonoured his own chieftain's sister. Yet that was not what alerted me. When he was pressed to name this person he sought, he used the name Brother Fursaintid. It confirmed to me that Febal was a man of whom to be suspicious.'

'But why? Fursaintid is an ordinary name.'

'Not exactly. It also means "a lightbringer".'

'I presume that the learned Brehon of the Uí Briúin Seóla will confirm that Febal is who Fidelma claims he is?' the Chief Brehon enquired dryly.

His fellow judge bowed his head. 'We have been looking for Febal for a long time as he has been accused of various killings, thefts and crimes. However, we of Connacht have no objection to him receiving his punishments here in your kingdom.'

'So now we must deal with the murders that started this tangled web,' Brehon Fithel urged. 'The slaying of Spelán and the woman Brancheó. I suppose that you are now in a position to reveal who murdered them?'

'Of course,' replied Fidelma solemnly.

'Then try not to make it as complicated as the previous matters.'

Fidelma smiled without humour. 'Sometimes events in life are complicated. I should not have to remind the Chief Brehon of that fact.'

'Just continue,' Brehon Fíthel said grumpily.

'It is now common knowledge that during this summer there was a series of thefts of silver shipments along the river. The silver came from the mines of Prince Gilcach in the Silver Mountain. The vessels carrying it sailed along the great river on their way to Port Lairge on the coast. Several boats were attacked, the silver taken. In the process some of the boatmen were injured and one was killed.

'It is also common knowledge that the silver has been recovered. We also know that the thefts were physically carried out by Febal and his mercenaries, and the booty stored in the caves below this abbey. Brother Giolla Rua, who played a crucial role in this business, was caught removing the crates of silver by mule, heading for the coast near Corcach Mór.'

The Chief Brehon's face grew dark. 'Are we saying that this abbey is not only responsible for stealing an ancient book from the Bishop of Rome's palace but were also engaged in stealing silver from Prince Gilcach?'

'That is a lie!' yelled Abbot Síoda, springing to his feet. One of Gormán's warriors had to step forward and push the abbot back. 'I admit that Brother Tadhg and I liberated the book from the Lateran archive, but we know nothing of this silver.'

'The thefts began this summer,' Prince Gilcach pointed out angrily. 'No one would take the risk of storing the goods in your cellars if you were not somehow connected with it. If the thieves were from elsewhere, why store the booty there? They would have simply sold the silver for ready cash and then have vanished.'

'Brother Tadhg and I were in Rome during the summer, so if the thefts started then, we were not here!' raged the abbot.

Fidelma had raised a hand to signal for quiet and smiled gently at the consternation that had been caused.

'The silver thefts were conducted by Febal and his mercenaries. The boxes were stored in the abbey, waiting for someone to arrive from the coast, collect them and transport them down the river to the ship of a merchant from Gaul,' she said. 'And, of course, the person in charge of this transaction was Brother Giolla Rua from the Abbey of Corcach Mór, which is next to one of the busiest ports of this kingdom.'

Brother Giolla Rua did not answer but merely sat looking at the floor.

'But Brother Giolla Rua is a respected scholar,' protested the steward of Imleach. 'That's why he was invited to join our council. Why would he be involved?'

'Even scholars can get greedy,' replied Fidelma. 'Of all the group of scholars, Giolla Rua could not hide his profound cynicism with regard to the Faith. One of the aspects of scholarship is that increasing knowledge of how things come about, the interaction of people and the arbitrary way certain men and women make rules for others to follow, does make one disillusioned. And from that can come self interest. Self interest leads to focusing on one's own earthly security in life – and that usually means the accumulation of wealth.'

'An interesting explanation,' sneered Abbot Síoda.

'One that I think you will find sits easily with the philosophies of your abbey,' replied Fidelma, unabashed.

'What you are asserting is that this abbey was involved in the stealing of Prince Gilcach's silver shipments, supported by Brother Giolla Rua.' The Chief Brehon seemed puzzled. 'How could this be?'

'The thieves and their leader in the abbey were waiting for Brother Giolla Rua to come with the news of the arrival of the Gaulish merchant to take the silver. When Giolla Rua received the invitation to come to Cashel to attend the council, it suited his plans exactly. His main purpose for coming was to arranging the shipment of silver to the coast. But events were happening too quickly.'

'Events?' questioned Fríthel. 'Yes; I suppose we are finally coming to Spelán's death?'

'Just so. As it happened, Spelán was a former miner who had

absconded from Prince Gilcach's silver mines to seek an easier way of life. He came here, married and herded his wife's sheep. The trouble was, she died after a few months. Under law, he now had nothing to sustain him because, being without kin, the chieftain of her tribe confiscated what wealth she had. Spelán, having observed the shipments of silver passing so easily along the river without let or hindrance, and without warriors to guard it, realised it was there for the taking. He went to the abbey where he knew there were some mercenaries who might be persuaded to join him. But he needed a go-between. So he spoke to someone at the abbey who took over his idea and employed the mercenaries to carry out the raids. For Febal and his men it was far more lucrative than collecting tribute for the abbot.'

'I was not involved in the thefts,' Abbot Síoda protested yet again.

Brehon Fíthel regarded him severely. 'Some of them have paid for that work with their lives, including Spelán.'

'Spelán resented the fact that he had not been given his due share of the loot. After all, it had been his idea. He was certainly given enough to make his life easier. But he wanted more. So he tried the age-old game of the greedy and ignorant. He thought he could blackmail the leader of the thieves into increasing his cut. His reward for that was death. He was murdered to keep him silent – but not before he had been tortured by the carving of the Tau-Rho on his living flesh. That was to make him reveal whether he had told anyone else. While he told of the investigation of Sionnach and the code "lightbringer", he thereby also implicated Branchéo.'

There was a tension now through the hall.

'What exactly was Branchéo's rôle?' demanded Brehon Fríthel.

'She was Spelán's lover. He promised her riches. They planned to marry and disappear into the southern mountains. But his death altered that. Now Branchéo was of the Old Faith. She believed in curses, as we all know. In fact, that was how she first met Spelán. He had paid her to curse the abbey – for Spelán too believed in the old curses. When it became known that he had confided his criminal activities to her, her reward was the same as that meted out to Spelán.'

'Febal, the leader of the thieves, also killed her to keep her silent?'

'Exactly so.'

'Then Febal is both murderer as well as thief?'

'Febal was certainly the person who struck the blows that killed Sionnach and also Branche6. He doubtless killed Spelán, but he was not the person who ordered his death, nor was he alone when Spelán was killed. Another person carried out the torture by carving the symbol of the Tau-Rho. There was only one person in this abbey who was responsible for organising the thefts *and* ordering the deaths.'

'And you will tell us who that is, will you?' Abbot Síoda mocked. 'For if you claim it was I . . .'

'Do I hear a threat in your words, Abbot Síoda?' Brehon Fíthel broke in sharply. 'May I remind you that the act of threatening a *dálaigh* when making their case during a hearing such as this constitutes the offence of *díguin* – a violation of the protection given to the *dálaigh*. The penalty for that is the payment of the honour price of the person protected. That is, in this case, the honour price of the lady Fidelma.'

'I meant no threat.' The abbot retreated reluctantly. 'But I am not guilty of inciting Febal to commit the thefts and the murders.'

'I think I have already come close to indicating who the organiser of these thefts was and thereafter responsible for the murders,' Fidelma declared coldly. 'Someone with a sadistic mind who was not above mocking the Tau-Rho symbol.'

There was a baffled silence. She waited a moment or two but no one seemed to make the connection.

'Very well,' she sighed. 'I'll reiterate. Spelán came from the northern part of the kingdom. He had worked in the silver mines of Arada Cliach, but he came to this territory, formed a relationship

PETER TREMAYNE

with Caoimhe and looked after her sheep. Perhaps he truly loved her, perhaps not. At any rate, he never made any friends in the vicinity and was regarded as no saint. When Caoimhe died of some fever last spring there came an end to his security.

'He went to the abbey to plead his case. Not able to approach the abbot, who was in Rome, he went to someone with whom his wife used to do business. We were told she used to sell herbs to the abbey. As I said, Spelán told them all about the silver mines and the shipments down the river. For a while the arrangement worked well. It had been noticed in Cashel, in Rumann's tavern, that Spelán seemed to have come into money. Someone saw that he had some silver. Indeed, we found a silver nugget hidden in his cabin wall. We later found another silver nugget concealed behind his cabin. Like all good thieves he was helping himself to the haul, unbeknownst to his fellows.

'When it was discovered that Spelán was a liability, he had to be got rid of. What better way to avert suspicion than have him killed by a means that would implicate the old religion? It was the right time of year and the threefold death would make everyone think the worst. The plot to kill the blackmailer in their midst was devised to lay the blame on Brancheó as a practitioner of the old religion.

'Spelán was therefore killed in his cabin and his body taken to be hidden in the bonfire. But not too well hidden – as that would have destroyed the purpose. The body was placed so that it could be seen.'

Brehon Fíthel interrupted: 'I can accept the threefold death, but would the incision of the Tau-Rho on the body endorse the idea of mocking the New Faith?'

'I have said it was part of a torture to make Spelán reveal what else he knew and who else he had told,' replied Fidelma patiently.

'Brancheó was not arrested and charged with the murder,' pointed out Brehon Fíthel.

'If she had been, she might still be alive. I am to blame for that. Because I did not arrest her, Febal felt he had to kill her also, especially when he realised she knew about the "lightbringer" and also thought it was a code for the investigators of the silver thefts. Stupidly, Febal thought that if he killed Brancheó in the same way as Spelán, it might add to the mystery and avert suspicion. For that he was rebuked by Giolla Rua. One mistake had followed another. I admit that I was misled until I discovered the reality of the three-fold death from Brancheó's own father, Erca.'

'You have talked about the leader of the thieves as if it were someone else other than Giolla Rua or Febal,' Brehon Fíthel said heavily.

'The clues are all there. There was one other person in the abbey who came from Corcach Mór. Indeed, this person was related to Giolla Rua. The same person, I was told, had some knowledge of the ancient religion. Brother Mac Raith told me this. It was the same person that Caoimhe,' Spelán's wife, used to sell her herbs to. The same person that Spelán went to see at the abbey and to whom he spoke about the silver shipments. The same person who then organised the band of thieves through her lover, Febal. For that was how she manipulated Febal. The same person who ordered the killing of Spelán as punishment for his threats and devised the threefold death to put the blame on Brancheó. The same, sadistic person who took a knife and carved the Tau-Rho symbol on Spelán to make him speak.'

During this recital, Fidelma had turned her gaze directly to Sister Fioniúr, who sat silently throughout but with a mask of hatred distorting her attractive features.

'The same person whose fondness for the distillation of lavender was the main factor that led to her downfall. That strong aroma impregnated the body of Spelán; it was noticeable throughout the abbey but especially on Febal. The same aroma hung on the air in Spelán's cabin where he had been tortured and killed. When I was in the abbey and hiding, I saw Febal meet his lover: I did not see her but the aroma of lavender was all-pervasive.

'Sister Fioniúr was the mastermind of the thefts and the person who ordered the murders, even if she did not participate in all of them.'

There was a scream as Fidelma sat down. It took two warriors of the Golden Collar to overpower and confine the hideous, screeching harridan that the usually quiet, attractive herbalist had become.

L'ENVOI

'A complicated matter, Fidelma,' Colgú said with a sigh as they relaxed in the King's private chambers in Cashel some days later. 'In fact, I am not sure that I have completely understood everything. However, I don't doubt that you will quote Publilius Syrus at me or something.'

Fidelma grinned in amusement. 'And what sort of something would I quote?'

'Something like *si finis bonus est, totum bonum erit.*'

'All is well that finishes well? Your Latin is improving, brother.'

'But my comprehension is still not as good as your own, for there is one question that still troubles me.'

'Which is?' prompted Fidelma.

'I presume it was Sister Fioniúr who splashed Spelán's body with her distillation of lavender. But why? As the herbalist who created it, it was surely as good as a confession of her guilt?'

'Fastidiousness can be a weakness in people; so it was with her. The smells in Spelán's cabin were quite revolting. Della mentioned that the man often smelled foul. Maybe, at some stage during the horrific scene in the cabin, when she and Febal tortured the man, she took out the bottle of perfume to distract her from the smell. She either splashed it or dropped it on the man.'

Colgú shook his head for a moment and then said: 'Well, I am told that Brother Lucidus and the stolen book are on their way back to Rome. The silver is returned to the safekeeping of Prince Gilcach. The surviving thieves and killers, Fioniúr, Febal, Giolla Rua and the others are all awaiting sentences from Brehon Fíthel. They will answer for the deaths. Of course, Abbot Cuáin is dealing with the former Abbot Síoda and his heretical supporters. I am told the abbey will be taken over by more orthodox hands.'

'What will happen to them? I mean Abbot Síoda and his supporters?' Fidelma asked.

'Probably exile to some remote place, one of the islands off the coast where their ideas cannot prosper. Thankfully, it's up to the Chief Bishop.'

Fidelma was thoughtful. 'I hope Brehon Fíthel will take into account my plea that the next Dál of the Brehons of the Five Kingdoms should consider amending the laws so that no chieftain nor prince nor even a king be allowed to have ecclesiastical rank at the same time as exercising secular power. The abuse of power by Síoda is a good example of why this should be.'

'Perhaps. But it is the way of bishops to aspire to be princes and the way of chieftains to aspire to be bishops. I sometimes struggle with the office of King.' Colgú looked suddenly awkward. 'In that role, there is an apology I must make to you and to others.'

'That is interesting, brother. For what do you wish to apologise?'

'For my behaviour at the feast of Samhain. I let the stress of the events destroy my good sense.'

'There is one, I think, that you should apologise to before all others,' Fidelma murmured.

Colgú nodded. 'Tomorrow I shall be riding for Durus Éile,' he said contritely.

Fidelma smiled. 'That is good to hear, brother. I hope the Princess Gelgéis finds herself able to see beyond the intoxicated state you presented. Also, some form of contrition should be made to the other guests that attended.'

Her brother coloured a little but said, 'It has been done.'

'Well, at least your assault on Ráth Cuáin has restored your reputation among the warriors of the Golden Collar,' she added. 'Especially Gormán.'

To her surprise Colgú suddenly chuckled.

'I think, as King and commander-in-chief of the warriors of the Golden Collar, I should demand compensation from you, sister.'

'Compensation?'

'So that I might pay my warriors extra for their services whenever they are asked to work with you.'

Fidelma noticed the amusement in his eyes despite the gravity of his voice and so responded with equal gravity: 'Why should that be, Colgú?'

'Have you realised that there is more chance of one of the warriors of the Golden Collar being killed or injured with you than in all the battles I have had to order them to take part in for the protection of the kingdom?'

Fidelma frowned. 'I am not sure what you mean.'

'Aidan comes back with a broken leg, which I am assured will mend; Dego had his right arm amputated because of a wound; Gormán was nearly executed; Cass, a great warrior of the company was, in fact, killed during that affair of the children at Ros Ailithir; then there was Capa and then Caol, who were forced to lose their honour and position as commanders of the Golden Collar. I wonder just how long my warriors can survive while trying to protect you.'

Fidelma joined in his black humour. 'Do not look forward to the ending. It is the journey that counts. I'll try not to lose too many of your warriors along the way.'

For a moment her brother tried to look shocked but burst out laughing.

'I can't guarantee my warriors will approve of such an outlook.'

'Sometimes, when facing death, humour is a means of escape,' she replied solemnly. 'They have survived many adventures. I have no doubt that they will encounter many more.'

Colgú rolled his eyes. 'Now of that, Fidelma, I am sure. But how many more of your adventures shall *I* survive?'